CW00864178

1

Written by Colby Bettley

ITS OKAY TO SAVE YOURSELF.

COLBY BOTTLEY

UGLY WORDS | Colby Bettley
First Edition | Publication Date: February 7, 2023

Cover design & Formatting by V. Domino @3Crows.Author.Services

Editing by Jessaca Willis @author_jessaca_willis

Novel & Noted by Colby Bettley @Colby_bettley

DISCLAIMER

Ugly Words features strong language, scenes of sexual nature, self-harm, disordered eating, and mental health conditions which may be considered triggering for some. Reader discretion is advised.

For those who feel alone.
You are worthy, you are loved, and you will find a way
out of the darkness.

PLAYLIST

You Broke Me First – Tate McRae
Before You Go – Lewis Capaldi
Villain – Arcana
Stronger – Kelly Clarkson
Anyone – Demi Lovato
A Little Bit Stronger – Sara Evans
Broken – Isak Danielson
Achilles Come Down – Gang of Youths
Dancing With Your Ghost – Sasha Alex Sloan
Lose You To Love Me – Selena Gomez
You Are The Reason – Calum Scott
As It Seems – Lily Kershaw
I Wanna Be Yours – Arctic Monkeys
Go Tell Her Now – Tom Odell

ONE

For a moment, the only noise in the room was the sound of my heart breaking. I stared out into the darkness, searching for something to hold onto, but finding only shadows and silence.

The familiar notes of *L'Air de la Poupée* started to play through the speakers around the gymnasium, signalling the start of my performance. My limbs moved on their own accord, an invisible force pulling me to-and-fro. It felt as though I had strings tied to my wrists and ankles, a puppeteer orchestrating this charade.

The numbers snapped the count in my head—which sounded way too close to my mother's voice for me to feel comfortable—as I repeated the step over and over.

"Practice makes perfect, Emmeline. You best get practicing."

Perfect, perfect, perfect. A simple word that had been transformed into a mantra. It haunted me every second of the day.

One... Two... Plié... One...Two...Plié...

Form was important in ballet, but I could never seem to perfect it, no matter how much I practiced. I closed my eyes now, shutting out one darkness for another, and listened for the quiet beat behind the music. It flowed through me, sending a current across my skin until my body moved on its own accord.

My limbs disconnected from my brain, becoming one with the sweet melody. As I advanced across the room, it was as though I was floating. I was no longer Emmeline Beaumont; I was the lost lover of a deity. My heartbreak, my sorrow, was exemplified in every gesture and movement of my body.

I felt weightless as I danced, though I ached to be free. The heartbreaking notes of the song continued to play, and I wanted to scream, but no sound came out. I bit down on my tongue in anger, the metallic taste of my blood filling my mouth.

The tips of my slippers touched the laminate floors as I stood, straightening my back, and extending my arms into a pirouette. I imagined that my love could see me dance for his return. He would make his way back to me, across oceans and land and planets, until his arms could slip around my waist and my heart would be returned to its rightful owner. Silent tears fell from my face as I danced the pattern of the finale, where I would be lost in my deity's arms for eternity.

But it wasn't real. He wasn't here.

My chest rose and fell in steady beats, and I came back to myself, opening my arms and finding I was once again in the dark. Slowly the lights began to flicker to life, illuminating the audience before me. Rows of benches were filled with people who featured in my every nightmare, both awake and asleep, causing me to startle. Worse was the fact that my mother was sitting front and centre, looking at me with disgust.

"Even when someone is pulling your strings, you can't do what you're supposed to." She stood, coming close enough for me to see the anger beneath her scowl. "A ballerina is grace and poise, and you are neither, Emmeline. How utterly disappointing."

Her words stung me, and I tried not to wince at the ice in her tone. Though I hated what she said, I also knew she was correct. Dance could be beautiful and moving and you could get lost in it, but I loathed it, nonetheless. It turned my mother into a monster, and I was nothing but an obstacle in its path.

Turning her back on me, my mother stormed through the doors and left me standing on aching feet, my tears forming a puddle at my toes. I squeezed my eyes together and willed for it all to stop, to disappear and leave me to my solitude. But my wishes were never granted.

"Little miss piggy thinks she can dance," a voice sneered from the crowd.

Someone cheered and added, "What a pathetic display!"

I tried to cover my ears, but my arms were pinned in place by my side, forcing me to hear every comment.

Too fat for tutus.

Too ugly for ballet.

I was too much of everything they hated, and too little of what they wanted. Never enough and never quite right — I was the muse for their mocking and the target of their hatred.

"Show us again," yelled someone from the crowd. "Let us see how an animal dances."

No amount of pleading or crying made them stop, my pain only fuelling their fun. The fat one; the ugly one; the boring one... the easy one to hate. I was a waste of a body, of life. They were right; my entire existence was pointless.

"Emmeline," said a voice, calling me from across the hall.

I pried my eyes open, the tears blurring my vision. The rows before me were still filled with people heckling me, but I could no longer hear them. A wall of silence was separating us, and I breathed a sigh of relief.

"Emmeline," the voice said again, louder now that the crowd was silenced.

A blinding light caught my eye from the edge of the gym. I tried to turn towards it, but my body remained stuck in place. My eyes burned from crying and prevented me from seeing who called to me, but the voice was gentler than those of the crowd.

"Petal, it's time to get up. Emmeline, let's go."

My throat closed up with emotion as I realised who the voice belonged to. It had been so long since I heard his voice, heard his pet names and soft tone for me, that I hadn't instantly recognised it. But I would know him anywhere.

"Daddy!" I cried out, fighting against the invisible bonds holding me in place. "Dad!"

The light from the open door shone brighter, beckoning me. "Emmie, love, come on. It's time."

As the door opened wider, I struggled against the grasp on me. Broken sobs tore free as I tried to escape, to run toward the person who had always made me feel loved and safe. But the more I struggled, the tighter the grips on me became.

"Petal, you need to hurry. I can't stay much longer," my dad called to me.

I could see the light slowly start to fade, the door closing as I fought for my freedom. My screams ricocheted around me, and I sobbed, broken-hearted, as the light finally flickered out. The moment the door clicked shut, the restraints on my limbs loosened and I was released, dropping to the cold floor soaked in my tears.

Pain erupted from every part of me, and I screamed at the top of my lungs, rage and grief and loathing laced in every decibel. I didn't notice when the silent wall dropped, and the heckling continued. Nor did I notice when the room fell silent, and I was enveloped in darkness once more. I didn't even notice when the music started again, and I was pulled into position.

I didn't notice anything but the numbness in my heart and the fact that my heart was now so broken that I couldn't hear it beat any longer. It was broken, and so was I.

—

The incessant beeping of my alarm stirred me from my sleep. I groaned, rolling over and patting my bedside table in search of my phone to make the screeching stop. I peered at the phone through my eyelashes and sighed. Seven forty-five, which meant I was going to be late for school.

The comfort of my king-size bed made it difficult to get up for the day. Not to mention, the nightmare still plagued my mind, making my bones weary. It had come again, the same torturous sequence playing in a loop. The dance. The clone. Our simultaneous deaths. My body was coated in perspiration from the fear I found rooted inside me every time I slept. After all, the scariest monsters were the ones inside our heads.

I needed to get moving. With a huff, I rolled myself over and planted my feet on the cold laminate flooring of my bedroom. A chill ran through me, my shoulders twitching in response before I padded out of my bedroom and into the bathroom to shower.

Once my monotonous morning routine was complete, I finally looked at my reflection in the mirror. I tilted my head to the side and stared at myself. It was a bizarre feeling to not quite recognise my own reflection, but recently I hardly recognised anything about myself. It's why I had gone to the salon the previous day. I wanted the mirror to reflect what I saw. Someone haunted by darkness and struggling to fit in with the world.

But as I stared at my reflection, I wasn't sure that I had made the right decision.

I attempted a smile as my fingers slipped through the soft curls. What was once long, blonde, and straight was now a crimped pixie cut, dyed a light shade of cocoa. I had chosen the colour in an attempt to be as opposite to my mum as possible, though the dark contrast made my shadows stand out in a way I wasn't sure I liked. The style, however, was a welcome change.

I offered my reflection a small smile in solidarity before making my way back to my bedroom to get dressed.

I pulled a pair of washed-out black jeans from my drawers and wrangled them over my thighs. I wished they were washed-out as an attempt at fashion, but they were really the only pair that still fit me. A plan, black, loose-fitting tee matched with a baggy jumper completed the outfit. Still a little out of breath from the feat of pulling on jeans, I perched on the edge of my bed and pulled on my favourite boots.

After unplugging my phone from the charger and grabbing my bag, I made my way downstairs, taking them two at a time.

I rounded the corner too fast and slid across the tiles as I entered the kitchen. Much to my dismay, my mum was already sitting at the island with a cup of coffee. Her bleach blonde hair was rightly clipped into rollers on top of her head, her face already covered in a thick layer of makeup. She looked beautiful, which only annoyed me more.

"Good morning, Mum."

"Morning, Em—" She cut herself off as she looked up from her phone, staring at my hair.

I smiled at her surprise. "You okay, Mum?"

"Emmie, what the hell have you done to your beautiful hair?" she cried, jumping off her stool. She rounded the island until she could stretch her arm out and brush her fingers across the strands hanging over my eyes. A small yelp escaped her lips. "Why?"

I rolled my eyes and stepped around her to grab a bottle of water from the fridge. "I just fancied a change."

"You had such pretty, long hair! Now you don't even look like my daughter."

I tried not to flinch, knowing she just wanted a reaction from me. I watched as she wiped a tear from the corner of her eye before taking her seat again to tap away on her phone. No doubt all of her friends would be getting the tale of her treacherous daughter who cut all her hair off in spite.

14

"It's my hair. I don't see what the big deal is," I said with a shrug.

She interrupted her texting to glare at me before returning her attention to her phone.

This had gone exactly as I had expected, so I wasn't overly bothered by her reaction.

I rummaged the cupboard for my Pop-Tarts, only to come up empty-handed. "Have you seen my Pop-Tarts?"

"Yes. I binned them." I twisted around on my heels and raised an eyebrow at her, waiting for an explanation. "They have so much sugar in them. I thought it would be best for you if we stopped keeping them in the house, darling."

Here we go.

"Mum, I paid for them myself. You can't just bin my own groceries."

She creased her brows and did her best to fake a look of compassion. "Look, Emmie, love. You've put on a few pounds over the summer. I really think you could do without the Pop-Tarts."

Did she really have to be so damn condescending? She always had to say something about my weight. She couldn't just let me be myself. But there was no point in calling her on it; I had tried that before and she always refused to listen to my feelings.

I grabbed my bag and rushed out of the house, doing my best to keep the tears from falling until I was well down the street and away from the prying eyes of our neighbours.

———

Knowing there was only one person I could trust to vent my feelings to, I decided to go to see my best friend. She was always the person to pick me up and validate my feelings of hurt whenever my mum made comments like that. The ten-minute walk was enough time to help me calm down and clear my head before I saw Kate.

Mum and I had a big house considering it was just the two of us, but it was nothing compared to the palace Kate lived in. She stayed in the posher part of town where the houses were actually mansions and the cars in the driveways were mostly for show.

By the time I had reached her, there was no sign that I had been crying, and I pushed my conversation with Mum to the back of my mind and locked it away to deal with later.

My best friend was waiting outside for me as usual, a book in her hand as she leaned against the wall of her garden. She was in her own world, so engrossed in what she was reading that she didn't hear me come up beside her.

I forced a cough to get her attention and tried not to laugh as she jumped from her skin.

"Hell, Emmie! That's not funny!" she cried, swatting my arm with her book as she tried to suppress her own laugh.

I grinned and took her bag from her while she smoothed out her striped pinafore. Her raven hair had been brushed into a tight bun and tied with a hot pink scrunchie. She always looked so funky and chic, her mismatched style somehow regarded as fashionable rather than weird.

If only I looked like her...

Kate snapped me out of my thoughts with a click of her fingers. She took her bag from me. "So, how did she react?"

I rolled my eyes, which made Kate bark out a laugh. "I don't even look like her daughter anymore, apparently."

Looping her arm through mine, Kate pulled me towards the school. She let her laughter die out and rested her head on my shoulder as we walked. "Urh, does she have to be so cruel? Well, I think you look incredible, and my opinion is the only one that actually matters anyway. Don't pay attention to her, Emmie."

16

I kissed the top of Kate's head and smiled, grateful to have her. Her intentions were kind, but it didn't matter what she said, my mum's words would always hurt. I could try and convince myself that it didn't bother me, but every time she said something horrible, it pierced my heart like a dagger, and I was left feeling smaller and more alone than before.

People who had normal families, people like Kate, just couldn't understand how dysfunctional mine really was.

We made it to school with ten minutes to spare, much to my surprise considering how late I had woken up. Apollo High School was a grand building situated in the dead centre of town. The sandstone exterior made it look dated and old, but the inside of the building was rather beautiful, with brightly coloured floors and murals painted on the walls by art students. As much as I hated school, even I couldn't deny that Apollo High School was pretty to the eye.

Kate kissed my cheek and ran off to the gymnasium, eager not to miss cheerleading practice and face the wrath of Penelope Williams—head cheerleader, head girl, and the head of the cruel clique of popular students. I often wondered why Kate would put herself in that position, having to hang around with a bunch of fakes. But they came from her world more than I did, and I didn't want to risk causing a rift between us by questioning her choices.

Shouting goodbye to my friend, I took a deep breath and stepped into the crowded hallway of Apollo. People were milling about in deep conversation, gossiping and swapping stories about what they had done over summer break. I could hear the chatter about family trips to the Maldives and attending concerts of bands I had never even heard of.

I wish my summer had been that normal.

Kate had gone to visit her grandmother in France for most of the six-week break, leaving me on my own. Without her, I had spent most of the summer locked in my room in order to avoid my mother and her pompous friends.

As I walked to my locker, I could feel the stares of everyone as they caught sight of my hair. Anxiety rose in me, my stomach beginning to churn as my classmates started to whisper.

I pulled my key out of my pocket and tried to insert it into my locker with trembling hands, missing the keyhole more than once. I breathed a sigh of relief when the key finally slid into the lock and opened for me.

Grabbing the textbooks required for my Spanish and History classes, I ran to class without making eye contact with anyone. I had almost reached my first class when I heard the clicking of heeled boots behind me. I could recognise that sound anywhere. I pulled my books close to my chest and tried to steady my breath, fearing the confrontation about to happen.

"Emmie, honey, did you borrow those clothes from my dad?"

Snickering echoed around me as I turned and came face to face with Rosie Fellows, one of Penelope's clones.

My cheeks burned as the gathering group closed ranks around us. I could feel my legs going weak under me. I backed up against the wall closest to me, Rosie following my every step. Her entourage flanked her, a girl gang ready to rip me apart.

"What do you want, Rosie?" I managed to squeak out, the sound of my voice suddenly foreign to my ears.

Rosie smiled, teeth bared and her hot pink lipstick making her look even more menacing. She reached out and I flinched despite myself, cursing inwardly as she took a strand of my hair between her fingers and tugged. "I don't want anything, silly. I just wanted to compliment you on your new hairstyle. It's very...chic."

I narrowed my eyes as she took a step back, smiling again. There was a glint in her eye that I couldn't quite decipher, making me feel more uneasy than I already was. Her friends all mimicked her, false smiles and fake eyelashes batting away.

I forced myself to stand up a little straighter and plastered on my own fake smile. "Thank you, I guess."

That was exactly what Rosie had been waiting for. The moment those words left my lips, the feral smile was back, and she winked at Amy, the girl beside her.

"I think I've seen it somewhere before. Let me think..." She tapped her finger against pursed lips. "I've got it! My little brother got that exact same haircut last week. I wonder if you went to the same hairdresser?"

The girl gang started laughing like a pack of hyenas while Rosie grinned, pleased with herself. She watched me steadily hoping for a reaction. Embarrassment rippled through my body, but I tried my best to keep my face straight, praying that I wouldn't cry in front of them and give them the satisfaction. I had made the mistake of breaking down before and they only used it as fuel for their vindictive games.

Time seemed to last forever as she surveyed me, a fire building in her eyes as she realised I wouldn't give her the reaction she wanted. She took a step towards me and leaned in close to my ear, her breath hot the side of my cheek. "Don't you dare think you can show me up in front of all these people. Remember your place."

Without warning, she smacked the books from my hands. Her lips curled into a cruel smile as they fell to the ground. Taking a small step back, she lifted her right foot up and dragged it across the top of my history book, leaving a chalky print on the cover.

"Oops. Clumsy Emmie. I think you dropped your books," she sang, pretending to act concerned as her pack giggled around her.

Blowing me a kiss, she spun on her heels and clicked her way down the corridor, leaving me to pick up the mess.

As soon as they were out of sight, I allowed myself to breathe again. A tear escaped as I bent down to gather my books, brushing the mess off with my sleeve.

I don't know why I thought a haircut would change anything in my life. It just made it worse.

Life *always* seemed to get worse.

I glanced at the time on my phone and saw that I only had two minutes to make it to class. During our commotion, the halls had emptied. Everyone had bustled to their classrooms, which meant I didn't need to worry about anyone seeing me cry as I walked the final few corridors to History. I wiped my tears away with a tissue from my bag and told myself to breathe.

"You can do this," I whispered to myself. But deep down, I knew it would only get worse.

What a wonderful start to the school year.

TWO

By the time the bell rang for lunch, I was exhausted beyond measure. My confrontation with Rosie had taken its toll on me. Afterward, I had sent a quick text to Kate, telling her about the situation. But upon checking my phone as I entered the cafeteria, she still hadn't replied despite a blue tick beside my messages.

I pocketed my phone with a solemn sigh and made my way to the far-too-long queue to get lunch.

Apollo High's cafeteria was much like every other school: clusters of round tables and uncomfortable plastic chairs, cliques loitering at every turn, and the wait for food that would take up most of the lunch hour. The plus side to eating from the school's limited selection was that it was mostly low-calorie meals in accordance with the new health board measures to combat obesity in children. It meant that I was able to eat my meal without hearing my mum's judgemental voice in my head, stomaching the fact that it may not look or taste all that appetising.

I could hear the young boys behind me sniggering and making comments about my weight. It wasn't like I was obese—I mean, sometimes it felt like that, but it didn't make it true. But I certainly didn't look like any of the girls around me. My thighs touched, my ass was prominent, and my hips were wide I was noticeable among the sea of my model-esque peers, even if I didn't want to be.

One of the boys whispered something vulgar, sending the rest of the group into an uproar. I turned around and flipped them off. This made them laugh even harder, so I swallowed the urge to shout and turned my back on them instead, taking my phone out of my pocket to check if Kate had messaged me back yet.

No new messages.

I sighed and tried my best to tune out the giggling while I focused on the shortening queue in front of me.

The menu said they were serving grilled chicken salad with a side of sweet chili sauce. It was my favourite out of the small salad options they usually served, and I wanted nothing more than to pour the sweet, sticky sauce over it and devour it. I was starving after having skipped breakfast, but my mum's voice drifted into my head again. I wrapped my arms around my stomach and tried to refocus. Every time I took a step forward, I could hear her telling me I could do with losing a few pounds.

When it was finally my turn at the head of the queue, I found myself saying, "Grilled chicken salad. No sauce, please"

I made my way to a table in the very back corner of the cafeteria, flopping down into a chair with my bag dumped on the floor beside me. It was far easier for me to watch people talk to each other than it was to actually get involved in the conversation.

Normally Kate would sit with me, and we would make up scenarios about what each group was talking about. The person who could create the most bizarre scenario would win, and the loser would have to buy the winner something from the vending machine as a prize. Kate's favourite was a peanut butter and chocolate breakfast bar; mine was the strawberry and cream chocolate bar that reminded me of being little and visiting my grandmother, who always seemed to have an endless supply of them.

Without Kate to keep me company, I felt extremely exposed sitting at a table in front of everyone. I opened the sealed container of salad and sunk my fork into it. Chewing on the leaves made me feel like a rabbit, but I munched down on the tasteless sustenance anyway.

I was about to take my second forkful when I was interrupted by the sound of a chair scraping across the floor. I turned my head to the left and saw Tate Harington.

If Penelope was queen of Apollo High, then Tate was king. With his chiselled jaw, piercing blue eyes, and a smile that could melt even the hardest of hearts, it wasn't surprising. His extremely good looks did not, however, mean he was a nice person. In fact, he was the most egotistical person I had ever had the misfortune of meeting.

And here he was, scooting his chair over to sit next to me: the outcast.

"Tate." I nodded, barely able to muster saying his name.

His merry band of idiots sat at the table a few feet away from us, each of them twisted in their chairs to watch as though a play was about to be performed. Knowing Tate, it probably would be.

"Hey, Emmie. Are you doing alright?" He flashed me one of his infamous golden-boy smiles that made girls weak at the knees. Not me though. For me it felt more like a lion preparing to sink its teeth into its prey.

I wasn't completely immune to his charms, of course—I was still human—and my stomach fluttered when his eyes met mine.

I forced myself to remember he was up to something, because there couldn't be any other possible reason for him being this close to me unless he had an ulterior motive, so I kept my guard up.

"I'm fine. Do you need something?"

Tate grinned. Turning his torso so he was blocking my view of his friends, he rested his elbows on the edge of the table. "When did you get a haircut?"

Remembering Rosie's fake pleasantness earlier was making me even more suspicious of the interest Tate was showing me now. And yet I couldn't quite bring myself to get up and leave.

Instead, I croaked out, "I went to the salon yesterday."

23

"It looks really good," he said with a smile that seemed so genuine I could've believed him.

He slowly brought his hand up and brushed one of the strands of hair away from my eyes, a tender action that I was not expecting. I held my breath, willing myself not to make a sound. His eyes searched mine and I had to stop myself from turning my head so his fingers would graze my skin.

I gave in, tilting my head into his touch, his hand travelling down my cheek in a soft caress. His fingertips brushed my neck, as soft as a breath. I closed my eyes, allowing myself to imagine for a second that social standards didn't exist and that in a parallel universe, Tate wouldn't be up to some boyish trick to humiliate me. Instead, he would be doing this for real, as though only him and I existed.

Before I knew it, his hand was travelling further down and roughly grabbed at my chest.

I gasped and leapt up, sending my chair flying backwards. "What the hell do you think you're doing?"

Laughter from nearby made my face flush with embarrassment. I looked around to see that half of the cafeteria was watching us, amused expressions on their faces. Tate's friends were watching intensely, too.

I turned my attention back to the boy in front of me, his angelic smile replaced with a cruel, crooked sneer.

"Oh honey, did you really think I was into you?" He threw his head back and barked out a bitter laugh. I curled my fists at my side, willing myself to stay calm. "Me and the guys had a bet going on. They said you were going through a sex change. But I said, nah, you were all girl somewhere underneath your hideous bargain-buy clothes. So, they told me to prove it."

I felt nauseous as he spoke. The room was spinning as I looked around at all the faces, each of them watching us and cackling at my public humiliation. I knew Tate could be a complete ass, but I didn't think he would do *this*. I cursed myself for being so stupidly naïve.

Tate turned to his audience, delighted with himself for putting on such a brilliant show. "What do you think? Did I prove my point?"

Bile was rising in my throat when I grabbed my bag and tried to push my way past Tate. He grabbed my wrist before I could get away though and pulled me onto his lap.

I squealed but he held me with one hand, using the other to grab one of my breasts so tight that it brought tears to my eyes.

His entourage whooped as I batted at his hands until I was finally able run from him once he let me go.

I pushed through the cackling spectators, no longer caring as the tears streamed down my face. As soon as I was out of the cafeteria, I stopped and allowed myself to hiccup fresh air into my lungs, making my way to the closest girls' bathroom. He had mortified me in front of half of the school and not a single person had seemed to care. I didn't understand why he had to do that—why did he have to do it to me? Wasn't the embarrassment Rosie had caused me enough?

Collapsing into the nearest empty stall, I sank to the floor and sobbed until my throat was raw.

I couldn't get the sound of their voices out of my head, telling me how much they hated me. I would never be as cool as them or look like them. Sitting on the dirty floor, snot and tears covering my face, I remained where I was even when the bell rang, signalling for the end of lunch break.

Closing my eyes, I lay my head on the wall behind me, praying for some higher power to tell me what I had done to deserve *that*. I just wanted it all to stop.

I pulled my legs to my chest and wrapped my arms around them, cupping my wrist in my hand.

The scene replayed over and over in my head, thinking of ways I could have stopped him. If I hadn't been so wrapped up in ridiculous fantasies, maybe I would have realised what he was planning sooner.

I tightened the grip on my wrist, my nails digging into the soft skin of my forearm. The pain grounded me. I rocked myself, allowing my mind to regain the smallest ounce of control. The stinging didn't come close to the agony of everything else I felt, but it came almost as a welcome relief.

I dug my nails in deeper and forced myself to breathe for counts of ten until it sounded almost regular. When I finally loosened my hold, tiny crescent moons were painted on my skin with blood.

Before leaving the stall, I wiped them with a piece of toilet paper and pulled my sleeve down to cover them. I grabbed a tissue from my bag and blew my nose, happy that there was nobody around to see me.

Once I managed to pull myself together, admittedly not that well, I grabbed my phone from my pocket to see I had a dozen of missed calls and texts from Kate.

Omg a bunch of first years just told me what happened.

Tate is such a dick!

Where r u? U ok?

Emmie? ARE YOU OKAY?

I have to go to class but pls call me after. xxxxx

I groaned and checked the time. I had missed Spanish with Mr. Robertson which meant I was in major trouble since I highly doubted anyone would be considerate enough to tell him about Tate.

Not that it mattered. I didn't have the energy for class now anyway. My body was numb and hollow. I wouldn't be able to concentrate on anything because I could barely stand up straight.

I picked up my bag and slipped it over my shoulder, deciding that it would be best just to go home. Mum would still be at work which meant I could go to bed without an argument about skipping class.

With my mind made up, I slipped out the fire exit and began to walk home. I decided to cut through the woods not far from the school to help me get home quicker. The serenity that the trees provided was a welcome comfort, the gentleness of the wind and the chittering of wild animals wrapping around me like a blanket and soothing my troubled mind. Normally I would have had to walk through the busy town centre with Kate to keep me company as she spent time abusing her parents' credit cards in some of the local boutiques. I usually found it therapeutic to watch the normalcy of her shopping and flashing around money as though it was endless—which I guess to Kate, it was—but I was thankful to have left school early and spend time on my own. After the day I had, spending time with other people was the last thing I wanted.

Once the pathway in the woods started to disappear, I crossed back into the main roads and continued the remainder of the short distance to my home. As I meandered past my neighbours' houses, I saw Mrs. Layton playing building blocks with her baby; Mr. Anderson standing behind the cooker, prepping dinner for his kids; Amelia and her little sister Olive playing with building blocks on the porch of their home. So many happy, normal households.

I daydreamed of what life would have been like if I was born to one of those families. Perhaps my mind would not be chaotic, and I would have had a different childhood. Perhaps I would have been spared the heartache that caused me so much pain.

My house was the last one on the street.

From the outside, our home would probably seem far grander than it actually was. The detached three-bedroom home was purchased when my mum found out she was pregnant and from what Dad told me when I was little, he spent hours fixing it up until it was absolutely perfect.

The long driveway leading to the front door was overgrown with weeds and I made a mental note to remind Mum to contact a gardener to trim back or replant some of the dead bushes. No doubt she would cause a fuss and ask me to do it myself, but if she could have all the luxuries she liked in life, then she could afford for someone to look after Dad's garden for him.

Brushing a spider's web away from the handle on the door, I unlocked it and stepped inside the hallway entrance. I was pleased to know that Mum was still at work as I had hoped. I dumped my bag on the bottom stair and walked down the hallway, taking my time to stare at the photos adorning the walls.

Each black frame held a picture of our family over the years; some of my parents before I came along, some after, each of them holding a sacred memory. I smiled as I came across one that I usually avoided looking at—a picture of my dad laughing at something my mum must have said while I sat on his shoulders, my tiny hands trying to cover his eyes. It broke my heart to see my dad and how happy we had been, only to remember that I would never take another photograph with him again.

I wiped away a tear and sighed as I caught the next image out of the corner of my eye. There was me, five years old, head to toe in a ballerina outfit as I danced in my first ballet class. I hadn't wanting to go—I never really saw the appeal of dancing if I was being honest—but Dad asked me to go to appease my mum. I hated every second of the recital and told my mum as much as she collected me from the class, but she was so insistent of me being a dancer like all of her friends' daughters that I never got to make my own choice. Dad died soon after and it meant I had to do what Mum wanted, even if it meant being shipped out every week to dance class. It was my idea of hell.

Pictures of me in various dance costumes lined the remainder of the wall until I reached the kitchen. Sadness crept over me. Without my dad around, I felt so alone and wondered when I would start to feel loved again. I had hoped and prayed so hard for a miracle to bring him back to me, to fix my life, to make things go back to how they used to be. And when that didn't happen, it broke my heart, and I learned that miracles didn't exist.

I had felt alone ever since.

Mum redecorated the place so many times that I could no longer remember what it looked like when I was small, but now it was *the height of elegance*, so she said. The walls were bright whites and creams, each room a different colour scheme to stand out. The only room that remained untouched by her very unique style was my bedroom; cream walls and black furniture, it still fit in with her theme but with a touch of blue and a hint of pink spread through it to claim it as my own.

Mum's makeup was scattered across the kitchen island despite her having a vanity in her bedroom.

Not bothering to remove my boots, I collapsed onto my bed and snuggled under the fluffy duvet. The feeling of safety I immediately felt brought tears to my eyes, making me burrow deeper below the covers as memories of my day flooded my brain. The tender touch of Tate's fingers on my face turned to rough grasping hands on my body. My gut grumbled and I retched, remembering how it felt as he claimed my body as though it were his property.

I threw my duvet off and ran to the bathroom, gripping onto the toilet bowl until my knuckles turned white as my body tried to vomit. With nothing but water and one measly bite of salad in my stomach, I continued to heave until my throat was raw.

I doubled over from the pain in my abdomen as my body continued to try and rid itself of the sickness Tate had caused.

When I was finally done, I wiped my mouth with a piece of toilet paper and sat on the cold bathroom floor, wishing for the pain to disappear.

But I heard keys turn in the front door and I knew my Mum was home. Picking myself up using whatever fraction of strength I had left, I made my way back into my bedroom and tucked myself under the covers once more.

The floorboards creaked as Mum climbed the stairs, the exasperated sighs loud enough to be heard from inside. I rolled my eyes and tidied up for her before grabbing a bottle of water and an apply and heading upstairs. "Emmie, are you in here?"

I peeked my head out from under the covers and saw her brows were furrowed and lips pursed together. With her hands on her hips, she stared at me from the end of my bed. "Would you like to tell me why you thought it was okay to ditch classes today?"

For a brief moment, I swear she looked almost concerned, as though she might actually have wondered why I skipped classes. But as I opened my mouth to speak, she cut me off and I knew I wouldn't even be allowed to explain.

"I don't even want to know what elaborate excuse you're about to come up with. It is absolutely unacceptable for you to skip classes without letting the school or myself know that you are leaving the premises! You have got to sort yourself out."

She let her face relax and dropped her hands to her side, letting go of the *I'm-The-Parent-And-I'll-Tell-You-Exactly-How-You-Should-Behave* façade. "Look, Emmie, I'll be straight with you. You've been acting like a brat all summer just because your little friend wasn't here. It doesn't give you an excuse to act out. Neither does grief,

30

now that it's been years since your father died. You need to get it together and grow up. He'd be ashamed of how you're acting."

She turned on her heels and stormed out of my room, leaving me alone with that unbearable, crippling thought.

My dad would be ashamed of me.

Mum didn't understand what my life was like. She didn't know or care about my problems at school. And she certainly couldn't see her own failures as a parent. And on top of all that, I had to spend every day of my life pretending like I didn't miss my dad because I didn't want to risk upsetting her. I was letting myself down. I was struggling and finding comfort in unhealthy things. I wanted to be mad at her for being cruel, but I knew she was right.

THREE

I must have cried myself to sleep because when I awoke, darkness had fallen outside.

A cold breeze blew through my room from the open window. I pushed my covers aside and groaned at the sticky feeling sweat on my lower back that was making my shirt cling to me. I closed the window and went back to bed, this time sitting on top of the covers with crossed legs.

I knew my first day back at school would be rough—it always was—but I hadn't anticipated so much happening.

I pulled my phone out of my bag and saw that I had a bunch of texts from Kate. They started out concerned when I wasn't replying. But then, over the hours of her beginning for me to call her and still hearing nothing in return, they'd grown angrier.

I had forgotten to call her in the midst of my exhaustion.

But my subconscious may have been partly responsible too because I was mad at her for ditching me at lunch. It's not like I expected her to be by my side twenty-four-seven—which I wasn't—but if she had other plans or couldn't make it, she could have told me before I got to the cafeteria and got manhandled by Mr. Popular in front of everyone.

I shook my head at myself. I knew I was being unfair.

Even if she had been there, Tate still might have acted the way he had. Perhaps it wouldn't have gone as far as it did—Kate did have some sway with the popular crowd because of her cheerleader status—but she couldn't have prevented it.

I sighed. It was unkind to ignore her. So, I fired off a quick text telling her I was okay and that I would see her tomorrow before slipping my phone back into my bag. I was still exhausted despite having slept for a few hours.

Putting on pyjamas and throwing myself back onto my bed, I closed my eyes and wished that I would forget about everything that had happened.

—

I woke up the next morning with the most intense headache of my life. It was worse than the time Kate had snuck a bottle of wine from her parent's cellar, and we had split it between us and drank until we puked.

The annoyingly insistent beeping of my alarm telling me to get up didn't help matters and I cursed myself for having deposited my phone in my bag rather than leaving it closer to hand.

I dressed myself as quickly as possible, noticing a few new stretch marks on my waist. My fingertips traced the zig-zag lines and my stomach twisted in knots I pulled a brush through my hair in a matter of seconds and decided my appearance would have to do because I didn't have the energy to even try.

What did it matter anyway? No matter how I looked, I would still be targeted.

Mum was standing by the sink when I entered the kitchen, a mug of freshly brewed coffee in hand. She took a sip from the steaming mug, the panda face printed on the side staring at me with the same judgement displayed in Mum's eyes.

She watched as I grabbed a bottle of water from the fridge and an apple from the shelf. She hid her smug smile behind the cup, but I knew it was there. The smugness of assuming she had won was evident without so much as a glance in my direction.

"Emmeline, I trust that you will be attending all of your classes today with zero exceptions?" She peered at me over the brim of her mug as she gulped down the last of her coffee, waiting for my reply despite the fact that we both knew it wasn't really a question.

"Yes, Mum."

She nodded, pleased with my response. Her blonde hair was tied tightly in a ponytail, her face makeup-free—which was odd.

Noticing me staring, she narrowed her eyes. "I don't need to be at work until later today. It means I'll be home late, so you can cook yourself something. There's plenty of stuff in the fridge for a salad or stir fry."

I matched her stare with my own narrowed eyes, her hints more than obvious. With a bitter smile painted on my face, I saluted to my drill sergeant and exited the kitchen.

As I passed by all the photos again, the chubby child in her ballerina outfit got me thinking about the extra stretch marks I had found earlier that morning. *Disgusting.*

As I walked past the entry table, I swapped my apple for my keys and made my way to Kate's house.

—

Kate was pacing the length of her driveway when I reached her home, her hair a mass of frizzy curls bouncing down her back as she moved.

When she caught sight of me trudged towards her, she came running and flung herself against me.

When she pulled away, she had smeared mascara lines down her cheeks from crying.

"Are you okay? I'm so sorry!" she shouted as she held me at arm's length. She inspected me for any exterior damage.

I nodded to pacify her, trying to force as close to a comforting smile as I could muster. She didn't need to know about the bruises shaped like fingerprints I noticed forming across my breasts as I put my bra on that morning.

"I'm okay," I lied, shrugging her hands off my shoulders as quickly as I could.

Even though I knew Kate would never hurt me, the very action of her gripping my arms made thoughts of Tate flash in my mind, and suddenly it made me extremely uncomfortable to have someone's—anyone's—hands on me.

Kate didn't seem to notice and let her hands fall. "Tate is such a jackass! Did he hurt you? I'm so sorry I wasn't there!"

I shook my head and started walking towards school, keeping my pace slow until she joined me. "I'm okay. You can stop apologising."

She looked like she was about to start crying again, so I bumped her shoulder with mine, watching as the corner of her lips tilted upwards.

"Penelope forced us into having an extra practice at lunch and I forgot to text," she explained. "I know it totally sucks, and I swear I wouldn't have let you down like that otherwise!"

I loved Kate with all my heart. We had been best friends since we were kids. But I wanted nothing more than for her to stop talking.

I didn't want to keep thinking about it. Keep reliving it. I just wanted to try and keep myself together and brace myself for walking into Apollo with the knowledge that the whole school would be talking about me. And considering everyone laughed in the cafeteria, I had serious doubts that anyone would take a side other than Tate's.

"Can we just drop it?" I asked, frustrated. "It's okay that you weren't there–really. You couldn't have stopped him from doing what he was planning anyway. Just have my back today, okay?"

She slipped her arm through mine as we walked through the school gates. "I'll always have your back, Emmie."

Just as I had suspected, the pointing and whispering started as soon as we walked into the hallway.

Kate flipped the first few people off, but the closer we got to the lockers, the more pointless it seemed to even react. I could feel myself shaking, but Kate remained by my side.

Guys proceeded to make crude gestures as we passed by, the girls giggling and talking behind my back.

It wasn't the first time people had acted like that—high school was a tough place to be the outcast—but the fact that it was all because of what Tate did made my heart sink farther than I thought possible. I had never done anything wrong to deserve the way people treated me, but I especially hadn't deserved to be groped by Tate Harington for the amusement of our classmates. I just wanted to get through my final year of school and get the hell out of town without any more trouble. Why couldn't people just let me get on with my life?

Kate accompanied me to my locker, trying to distract me by talking about the newest reality show she was watching.

I tried to tune in to what she was saying, but I was too distracted by everything going on around me. It seemed like the more I tried to listen to her, the louder everything else became. I watched her lips move but her voice didn't reach my ears. My surroundings began to blur, my eyes not quite focusing on anything.

I tried to tell Kate, but my voice wasn't working, and I felt the panic rise in me. My breathing sped up. I couldn't get a proper breath.

I grabbed Kate by the shoulder and pointed to the bathroom, running into the Girls' room as quickly as I could.

Once away from the stares of my peers, I entered a stall and sat with my head in my hands, practicing breathing techniques to help curb my panic attack.

A few seconds later, Kate came running in. She sat on her knees in front of me, coaching me through the worst of it until I was able to catch my breath properly.

I rubbed my hand across my chest and collarbone, something I had discovered was quite soothing after a panic attack.

After I was able to breathe steadily, my vision began to sharpen again, and I was able to focus on Kate. It took a few minutes for everything to look normal again, but it was a relief to be able to see clearly. I sagged against the cubicle wall, my eyes feeling heavy.

"Emmie, are you okay? Can you talk?" She placed her hands gently on my knees, but I pulled my legs away, pulling them up to my chest.

I tried to swallow; my throat was so dry that it felt as though I had shards of glass embedded at the back. I pulled my water bottle from my bag and took a few gulps, relieved as the coolness travelled down my throat.

"I'm okay. I'm just exhausted," I said as I sat up, forcing myself awake. "Attacks take a lot out of you. It feels like your body is drained of all your energy."

Kate frowned and sat back, letting out a sigh. "I'm sorry they happen to you. I knew you used to get them when we were younger, but I didn't know you still suffered from them." I shrugged and offered her a lazy smile, but she shook her head, still concerned. "Maybe you should go home and rest?"

My eyes widened and I shook my head profusely. "Absolutely not. Mum would go ballistic if I missed school again. She was fuming yesterday."

My best friend's brows furrowed. "Why was she fuming when you did nothing wrong?"

"You do remember my mum, right? She didn't even give me a chance to tell her. She just warned me not to miss school again. The *or there will be serious consequences* was heavily implied."

37

"What is wrong with that woman?" Kate shook her head angrily, pulling a face that made me laugh. "Well, if you insist on going to class then we should probably get moving so you're not late. I'll walk you."

My friend stood up and brushed herself down before holding her hands out to me. She smiled warmly, and I allowed her to pull me up and lead me out of the bathroom. True to her word, she deposited me outside my English classroom, pecking me on the cheek before running off to try and make her own class in time. I watched after her as she ran through the crowds, grateful that she would risk being late just to support me. I hoped she knew how much I had appreciated what she had just done to help me.

I took my seat at the back of the classroom, choosing to sit in the same spot as last year. My classmates filtered in, most of them sitting as far away from me as possible until there were barely any seats left. Some of them whispered to each other, and I heard my name uttered more than once. I folded my hands underneath my desk, my fingernails finding a patch of unbroken skin to pick as I waited impatiently on the teacher arriving.

"Did you hear that Emmie let Tate grab her boobs in the cafeteria yesterday?"

"Please tell me you saw Emmie totally embarrass herself yesterday!"

"Oh my God, did you see Emmie at lunch yesterday? She was all over Tate! As if he would ever go near her!"

I dug my nails deeper, dropping my head to give the pretence that I was looking over my books, and hoping that nobody would be able to see me wince as I drew blood. What happened at lunch yesterday had already been twisted into a hundred different tales and I knew there was no point in saying anything. Nothing I could say would be taken seriously anyway.

"Good morning, class!" My teacher, Mrs. Langford, announced herself as she entered the room, snapping me out of my own thoughts. I let go of my wrist and raised my head slightly so I could see her through the strands of hair covering my eyes.

Mrs. Langford was a middle-aged woman with a graduated bob, strands of grey hair filtering through the dyed brown locks. She wore black dress-trousers and a navy blouse, the pair of heels matching her top perfectly.

Mrs. Langford was a warm person and made classes fun, but she had strict rules, and everyone respected her enough not to break them.

As Mrs. Langford prepared the board for our lesson, there was a knock on the door.

A boy entered.

He was skinny and tall; he might've already been over six feet. His curly blonde hair bounced around his ears as he sauntered in, and a pair of statement black horn-rimmed glasses perfectly framed his blue eyes.

The whole class watched him in awe as he whispered back and forth with the teacher. I ran my eyes over his outfit, a small smile forming as I noticed he was wearing a bright blue checkered shirt tucked into skinny denim jeans.

He likes to stand out, I thought to myself as a blush formed on my cheeks.

Mrs. Langford nodded and finally gestured for him to take a seat.

He weaved his way through the desks, and I dropped my gaze down to my books as he took the seat beside me, despite there being three other options—including having a desk to himself.

I avoided meeting his gaze as he pulled his books from his bag and began to flip them open to the page we were working on. Once he had sorted himself out and Mrs. Langford started to explain the lesson, the boy stuck his hand out to me.

"Hey. I'm Benji."

His voice was deeper and sweeter than I had expected, a slight accent to it that I couldn't quite put my finger on but had an exotic melody to it. When he grinned, his cheeks nudged his glasses, making them sit lopsided.

A strange pull tugged on my stomach, and I shook his extended hand, despite the crippling thoughts of anxiety running through my brain. I didn't want to be touched, but to ignore his introduction would have been rude.

His grip was firm, but his hands were soft against my skin. "Nice to meet you. I'm Emmie."

He didn't recoil from my touch or take notice of everyone around us staring at him, whispering because he had sat with *the freak of Apollo High*. It was a bizarre feeling to speak to someone other than Kate. I returned his grin, trying to absorb his kindness before he could be warped by other people.

"Have you always lived in Apollo?" he asked.

I attempted a smile. "Unfortunately, haha. I want to go travelling or live somewhere other than this town."

Benji shrugged, the movement oddly adorable which caused my cheeks to heat. "I think it looks like a pretty cool place to be. We were in New Zealand for the first half of my life and *damn,* was it strange the first time we moved. Sometimes, the place we started is the best place to be."

By the end of class, I had learned that Benji was indeed the same age as me and had moved because his father had gotten a better job in Apollo. His dad was a lawyer and his mum stayed at home to look after his two-year-old little sister, Anya.

It was nice to have a normal conversation and pretend for an hour that I had made a new friend. Deep down, I knew that he would have moved seats by the next day, but I allowed myself a sliver of hope that he could be different.

As we exited the classroom, he tapped my arm, and I tried my best to hide the fact that it had made me jump. He swung his bag onto his shoulder and kept pace beside me. "What class are you in next?"

"Maths in the opposite end of the building," I complained with a smile, happy to take advantage of him still speaking to me. "What about you?"

He groaned as he checked his timetable, and I resisted the urge to laugh. "I've got Physics. How boring."

"Do you need help finding it?" I asked, shifting on my feet.

"That's kind of you to offer, but the office lady gave me a tour earlier, so I think I should be okay."

I nodded and tried to hide my disappointment. It would have been fun to show him around.

"Anyway, I suppose we both better go to class. It was awesome to meet you, Emmie!" he said with a wave, backing into a group of jocks and apologising profusely as they swore at him.

I walked to my next class, forgetting for a brief moment about all the issues on my mind. Instead, a smile continued to make an appearance on my face as I thought about the bizarre boy who clearly did not understand the social conventions that should've prevented him from sitting with a loser.

I liked him already.

—

When the hour for lunch came around, I texted Kate and told her that I absolutely would not be entering the cafeteria. So, we met at one of the benches in the grounds outside since I also didn't want to stay in the school hall.

She had tied her wild hair into a bun on top of her head, loose strands swaying in the wind. If she wasn't a cheerleader, she would be as much of an outcast as me, with her crazy sense of style.

She jumped up from the table as I neared her, pulling me into a tight hug and squeezing me until I wheezed.

"You survived the first half of the day! So proud of you!" she said with so much excitement that if I didn't know her, it would come across as sarcastic. Her golden retriever energy was a lot to get used to at first, but it was a comforting brightness in my life now.

"Yeah, surviving is the right term. Everyone is talking about me or giving me dodgy looks. I'm even more of a freak now, and I didn't think that was possible!"

I snorted before taking a gulp of my water. When Kate made a ridiculous face, I choked.

"We're all freaks here, darling!" She waved her hands around dramatically and pretended to tip her hat towards me, mimicking the Mad Hatter from *Alice in Wonderland*.

"You're messing up the quote. It's *we're all mad here*, you know?" I corrected with a pleased smirk.

She waved her hand, dismissing my correction and taking a bite of her cheese and pickle sandwich. "Well, I like my own version better. Anyway, did you hear about the new guy that just transferred in? Apparently, he's absolutely dreamy."

I screwed up my face as bits of Kate's sandwich flew from her mouth as she spoke. "Could you please pretend that you're civilised and not talk with your mouth full? And yes, I did hear that actually. He sat beside me in English today. His name is Benji."

"Did he now?" Kate's eyes were wide. "And? Is it true? Is he as dreamy as they say?"

When I suppressed my smile, one appeared on her face instead. Seeing right through my facade, she clapped her hands and giggled. "I knew it!"

I rolled my eyes and watched as she munched through the rest of her lunch. She opened a bag of vinegar crisps and the smell hit me, making my mouth water. My grumbling stomach caught Kate's attention. "You aren't eating?"

Shaking my head, I took another drink of water and tried to send signals to my stomach telling it to chill out. "Nah, I don't feel so good today."

Kate furrowed her brows and nodded. "It's probably the stress. You should have some soup or something for dinner to help ease the queasiness."

She crunched on another crisp from the bag and began to tell me about how her day was going. I tried to tune into her as she spoke, nodding at all the right things and pretending to be appalled by everything that annoyed her, but my thoughts were preoccupied by my hunger pains. I realised that I hadn't eaten a proper meal in a day or two. The stretch marks I found earlier that morning drifted into my head and I concluded that missing some meals every now and then couldn't hurt though. Maybe I could even lose some of the pounds Mum said I had gained over the summer.

FOUR

Picking a cheesy rom-com, I snuggled under some blankets and pressed play.

As I watched, I began to wonder how much different my life would be if it were like a rom-com. Would I get a miraculous makeover and the love of my life would suddenly fall for me? Would I get my dream job and buy a big house? Would I have a perfect relationship with my mother and visit her every Sunday for dinner with my family?

There were so many amazing ways my life could turn out, and yet I knew it would never happen. Life wasn't perfect. Amazing possibilities didn't just happen. The losers stayed losers, while people like Tate and Penelope would have everything they could ever want. Life was cruel and unfair like that, and it was designed to keep people like me down.

Realising that the light-hearted film was not improving my mood any, I sighed and finally turned the TV off. I made my way into the kitchen and inspected the fridge, hoping something would catch my eye. With my mum working late, maybe I could even make a feast.

Sadly, the same inedible food remained, and I cursed as my stomach rumbled again.

I pulled a piece of steak out along with some vegetables and decided to make myself a stir fry. It was simple, quick, and would ease the pains in my stomach. It would also be kind of healthy which would stop my mum from complaining if she came home and saw me eating it.

As I dropped the chopped pieces of meat into the pan, a loud sizzling broke the quietness of the house. The aroma of onions, peppers, and sauteed mushrooms filled the kitchen, making my mouth water, my body eager to have for sustenance.

When it looked as though everything was cooked through, the steak perfectly tender, I emptied the contents of the pan into a bowl and sat at the kitchen island. I almost drooled as I lifted the first forkful to my mouth, another aromatic wave filling my nostrils. I let out a small groan in delight as the savoury ingredients touched my tongue, the flavour more divine than I could have imagined. With my taste buds fully awoken, I began to devour my meal until the bowl was completely empty. It had been so long since I had been able to eat a meal without the guilt of my mum, and it was glorious to not hear her petty comments in my ear.

I thought of how quickly I had wolfed my meal down, making sure every morsel entered my system. A small pain in my stomach caused me to drop my dishes into the sink, my dinner churning around in my stomach. I felt disgusted with myself; I had shovelled it down like an animal. How could I have eaten that amount of food in such a short period of time? It was ridiculous.

Sharp pains continued to cause discomfort in my abdomen as I washed my dishes and put them into the cupboards. By the time I was done, I could hardly contain the vomit rising in my mouth and burning my throat like acid.

I gripped onto my stomach, gagging as I sprinted to the bathroom and heaved up my stir fry.

Sweat covered every orifice of my body by the time I had purged the contents of my stomach, and I leaned back against the bathroom wall. Closing my eyes, I tried to regulate my shallow breathing. If only sleep came as easy to me as hating myself did.

As much as my body hurt, a voice in my head was telling me that I had done the right thing. It had been too much food. I had piled on too much weight already, just as Mum had said. Losing a few pounds wouldn't be so bad.

I closed my eyes in an attempt to block out the voice, but a niggling feeling in the pit of my stomach told me there was some truth to what it was saying. Tears pricked at my eyes as I squeezed the fat on my stomach, examining just how much damage I had done by eating unhealthily.

I crawled over to the sink and turned on the cold tap, letting it run for a few seconds. Once it was cold enough, I cupped my hands together and gulped down some of the water, washing away some of the pain.

After such an eventful evening, I couldn't fathom trying to do anything else but hide under a pile of blankets in bed, so I made my way into my bedroom, albeit sluggishly. When I stripped off my sick-stained clothes, I caught sight of my lumpy, bumpy body in the full-length mirror in the corner of my room, and I wanted to sob all over again. Hatred towards myself had me clenching my fists, resisting the urge to shatter the mirror and my reflection with it.

I padded across the floor slowly, watching as my too-large hips swayed with every step. The stretch marks and scars littering my stomach and thighs stood out, reddened marks contrasting to the pale shade of my skin.

I sucked in a breath, and my stomach too, holding it for as long as possible as I ran my hand down my stomach, imagining what it would be like to be thin. It seemed a silly notion, to wish for something that would only make me more like my peers, and yet it was something I wondered about frequently. Would my life be different if I looked like the conventional young woman, like Penelope and her friends? As much as I wished otherwise, the world focused on appearances and revolved around the perception of perfection.

A sigh exited my lips, my hand falling away from my skin as reality set in. I wasn't made like the girls I knew.

Even if I tried my hardest, I doubted I could ever come close to how they looked.

I stared at my disgusting reflection, pondering how I managed to look the way I did when I had a mother who could have doubled as Penelope's twin in her youth. It seemed as though some higher power wanted me to suffer, forever standing on the edge of society.

I shook my head, running my fingertips through the soft curls around my ears. After my father died, I had decided to embrace my individuality, but it had only brought me more heartache. The bruises on my breasts seemed to stand out against my skin as prominently as my scars, another reminder of my place in the world. I tried to shake the feeling of his hands on me, but Tate's touch seemed to haunt me as much as my own demons.

The laughter of my classmates echoed in my mind, the scene replaying before me in the mirror. The reflection of my bedroom dissolved, and instead I was back in the cafeteria, being humiliated for sport.

I screamed at myself to do something—anything to get him to stop. But I was as useless then as I was now.

His hands accosted me, his friends watching him with pride. Tears burned in my eyes as I let it all happen, shame filling me to my core.

It was clear that I was unlovable. I deserved everything that was thrown at me, everything that was said and done. There was no amount of changing my appearance or personality that would make me who everyone wanted me to be.

Pushing myself out of my trance, I ripped open the drawer on my nightstand and pulled out my *special kit*. I placed each of the items on top of my duvet and studied them carefully: razor blade, cotton wool, antiseptic wash, plasters, and bandages.

Each product was placed in order of use. Each one was whispering for me to begin. I would punish myself and use it as a permanent reminder for how worthless I really was.

The razor was cool as it touched my skin, the blade marking a patch of territory on my thigh. A dull ache washed over me, and I gritted my teeth against the pain, finding a twisted sense of pleasure in the knowledge that I was back in control of myself, as a trickle of blood appeared where the razor had left, painting a solemn picture across my skin.

Once I felt stronger, I soaked the wool in antiseptic and prepared for the burn as I wiped it across the fresh wound.

I cursed under my breath, never quite prepared for the ache it caused.

Pinching my thighs together to hold the wool in place, I opened the plaster and carefully applied it to the cut, careful not to let the adhesive section disturb the wound.

The sound of the front door unlocking alerted me to my mother's return.

I quickly shoved the items back into the bag and crammed it into my nightstand. I ignored the throbbing pain in my leg, breathing through gritted teeth as I pulled on a pair of pyjamas and climbed into bed.

I heard the click-clack of Mum's heels as she walked into the kitchen and popped the cork off a wine bottle. It was her usual routine after a long shift: skipping dinner to drink a full bottle of chilled wine in front of the TV, taking a few painkillers to prevent a hangover the next day, and then going to bed for work the next day. I was surprised she was so opinionated about how I lived my life considering what I could choose to say about the way she lived hers, but she was still my mum and as much as I disagreed with her, I had to remember she was damaged by the same events that had so tragically damaged me.

Once she was settled and I was certain she wouldn't be coming up to check on me, I breathed a sigh of relief and relaxed into my pillows, tucking the duvet tight around me.

It was only nine o'clock which meant I could still browse on my phone without it affecting my sleep for school, but I sent a quick text to Kate first. I wanted to let her know I was feeling better, even if it was a lie. But it was a necessary evil to ensure she didn't keep worrying about me after everything that had happened.

Once I was sure she was convinced, I started to doom-scroll.

Being seventeen in a modern world was tough enough without the introduction of so many different social media platforms. I often wished I had been born in a time before technology was such a devastatingly huge part of our everyday lives. I didn't totally hate it—what teenager really wanted to live without their phone, after all—but every time I opened an app, I was reminded of just how much I didn't fit in with the rest of the world. The false hair; faces caked in makeup; photos edited with ten different filters — everyone looked the same, and I didn't look anything like them. I didn't like drinking, partying or social gatherings; I was boring in their eyes and, if I was honest, in my own eyes too.

It was cruel, really, for people to be subjected to such falseness.

As a child I would wish I was older and wiser but growing up really just meant looking at the world and seeing how broken everything and everyone is.

I sighed as images of Penelope and her posse scrolled into my timeline. All of them were picture-perfect with smooth skin, pretty hair, and enough makeup on that made me think they had bought out the entire store. I couldn't help but look through their pictures, seeing their poses change and their outfits become increasingly more revealing over the years.

I didn't want to be like them. Not really.

But I did want to experience what life was like for them. I never had the thin stomach, or the perfectly straight hair. I didn't know how to smile at boys and bat my eyelashes, how to enter a room like everyone inside should be kissing the ground I walked upon. I didn't know how to be worthy of love and affection from anyone, including my own mum.

Instead, I was always the outcast.

The nobody.

The freak.

Just once, I wanted to know what it felt like to be normal.

The cut on my leg throbbed as I shifted in my bed, my thighs rubbing against each other. I hissed and moved onto my back, spreading myself out across the mattress so that my limbs didn't touch. I should have learned by now; remembered the best way to lay to stop it from hurting.

Not that it ever really stopped hurting. Some wounds never healed.

As I continued to scroll through the endless images on my phone—double tapping the screen on the cute photos Kate had posted of her puppy, Baxter—a notification appeared in the banner at the top of my screen.

BenM29 followed you.

Clicking on his profile, I couldn't help the smile spreading across my lips. BenM29 was none other than Apollo New Boy, Benji Miller.

His feed was all family, friends, books, and scenery shots. A mixture of random and sentimental. Quirky and breath-taking.

There was a little girl in many of his pictures, and I could only assume it was his sister, Anya.

I stared at some of the selfies he had posted, admiring how carefree he was in all of them. He seemed so happy as he stared into the camera, his smile shining so bright it made my heart ache. I felt colour flush into my cheeks as I continued to scroll, feeling like an intruder as I viewed important moments of his life throughout the years, without him ever saying it was okay.

I looked through the hundreds of posts until my eyes drooped, my body weary and desperately in need of rest. I urged myself to power through, a crucial need to finish looking at the beautiful new boy who wasn't afraid to talk to me. But eventually, exhaustion won out.

As sleep started to take over, I made sure to tap the screen once more before I slipped into unconsciousness.

You followed BenM29 back.

FIVE

A burning sensation in my leg woke me from my sleep, causing me to hiss as my thighs touched together. I sat up quickly, cursing under my breath at the pain, guessing my wounds from the night before were irritated.

I rolled over and clambered out of bed to examine the damage I had done to myself.

I looked down and flinched as I saw the blood smeared across both of my thighs. The adhesive plaster from the night before had torn off in my sleep, and the wound on my thigh must have been disturbed. I ground my teeth together as blood trickled down my leg, a fresh coat over the dry blood which had already stained my skin.

I glanced at my bed and swore as I noticed red streaks across the previously white sheets. Mum would kill me, I thought to myself. I would have to strip my bed and shove everything into a wash before she could notice.

I grabbed my jeans and a vest and made my way into the bathroom to shower before getting dressed. Washing the blood without disturbing the wound was always difficult but I had it down to a fine art. Wincing only slightly as the unscented soap washed the remnants away, I felt relieved.

Pulling my jeans on gently so as not to cause myself too much pain, I figured I was ready to start my day.

Taking the duvet and sheet off my bed only took a few minutes, sneaking past my mum's room quietly and padding downstairs into the laundry room. I shoved the whites into the machine with a bunch of stain remover and set it to the right wash cycle, hoping the load would be finished by the time my mum got up for work so she didn't notice.

I glanced at the clock and saw that I had to leave, otherwise I was going to be super late.

Grabbing my bag off the stairs, I rushed out the front door, locking it behind me. So, I jogged down the street, praying that the plaster on my thigh wouldn't tear off, and grateful to know that if it did, at least my jeans were black.

By the time I arrived at Kate's house ten minutes late, my cheeks were the colour of beetroot. She was busy stuffing her mouth with chocolate and butter croissants which she nearly choked on when I told her about my new follower.

A squeal escaped her lips, neatly painted in ice blue lipstick to match the scrunchies in the space buns atop her head, as she jumped up and down. "No way! Emmie, the new guy totally likes you!"

She winked at me with those big doe eyes before taking another bite from her croissant again, careful not to let it go down the wrong way this time.

"Kate be serious. I've only spoken to him once!"

I rolled my eyes, hiding my own excitement. As much as I wanted to be rational about it, my stomach had fluttered when I had checked my phone again this morning and seen that he was still following my profile.

Kate let out a cackle and shook her head. "Emmie, Emmie, Emmie. Have I taught you nothing through our years of friendship? For starters, he must have been looking your profile up. Second—" she held up her hand and counted her points on her fingers "—he would not have randomly followed you unless he wanted to learn more about you. And third, didn't you notice that he hasn't followed anyone else from Apollo High yet?"

My cheeks turned a furious shade of red. It seemed absurd that Benji would like me. And yet, deep down, a part of me so desperately wanted it to be true.

"Well, it doesn't really matter in the long run, does it? You know what will happen when he meets Penelope. Or someone like Tate."

Kate frowned but didn't argue. She knew I was right.

It didn't matter who came across the popular kids, they immediately fell hook, line, and sinker. And there was no stopping it.

"Besides, I don't have the time for guys," I continued, bitterness edging my voice as old wounds that had never quite healed threatened to surface again. "I need to focus on my grades so I can get into university and get the hell away from my mum."

Kate's smile didn't quite reach her eyes, but she hooked her arm through mine. "That's right! Who needs boys? Sisterhood forever!"

"Sisterhood forever!" I mimicked, clenching her arm tighter.

"*But* if you so happen to decide to chase a certain handsome newcomer," she whispered conspiratorially, "the sisterhood pact can easily be broken."

We dissolved into a fit of giggles, and I wished terribly that I could have a lifetime of moments like that.

—

Classes seemed to pass by quicker than usual, probably due to my preoccupied mind. Whispers followed me at every turn, so I hid in my books, desperate to disappear and not to be noticed by anyone.

As the lunch bell neared, I retreated into myself further. Kate had already said we needed to eat in the lunch hall so that I wouldn't let Tate win, but she massively overestimated my strength. Even if Kate was coming from a good place, my head and heart were telling me not to make myself suffer like that.

I winced when the bell eventually sounded, and everyone rushed into the corridors. They barged into each other in a desperate attempt to beat the lunch queues, as if there wouldn't be enough food to go around.

People pushed past me, shoving me against the lockers as I continued to amble to the canteen.

Just as we agreed, Kate was waiting for me outside of the double doors, a proud grin across her face.

"There's my girl! Are you ready to do this?"

I let out a shuddering breath and lifted my shoulders into a noncommittal shrug. Kate's smile faltered slightly but she took my arm in hers and we stepped into the crowds.

Sniggering began almost immediately, and I stopped in my tracks, ready to flee. But Kate pulled me forward, tightening her comforting grip.

"You can do this," she whispered into my ear. "Don't let them win."

I often wondered where she got her strength from; I had never met someone so sure of themselves and eager to promote that in others. She was a beacon of light, a ray of hope, and a constant reminder to me that it wouldn't always be awful. One day, when school was nothing but a faded memory, it would be me and Kate sitting together on a porch somewhere, chatting and content.

I smirked at the thought and figured if Kate believed in me that much, then maybe I could believe in myself too.

Raising my head just a tiny bit higher, I pressed forward.

With Kate leading the way, we grabbed our lunches—I opted for a pasta salad with far too many carbs in it, while Kate chose a loaded plate of chili nachos that made my stomach rumble—and made our way towards our preferred table.

I sat my tray down and carefully slipped into my seat, acutely aware that they squeaked under pressure—and they *always* squeaked when I sat down on them. Kate took the seat directly across from me, probably in an attempt to keep my focus on her so I didn't start spiralling, but I still felt my skin tingle from the heat of everyone's gazes on me.

"Emmie, look at me," Kate commanded.

I blinked a few times and brought myself slowly back to the moment, finding Kate's face.

"I'm okay," I whispered. If I tried to speak at a normal level my voice would break, and I would be sitting in a pool of my own tears before I knew it.

"If it's too much, we can leave," she mumbled through a mouthful of chili, the scent of the spices making my mouth water.

I shook my head and tried to offer a reassuring smile as I stabbed my fork into my pasta. The strong tomato and basil sauce cause my stomach to both churn and grumble at the same time.

I eyed the calorie content on the side of the box and huffed. The box was highlighted red, making it not as healthy as I would have liked. But as my stomach continued to sound its grievances, I relented and took a bite.

A small moan escaped my lips as the pasta hit my tongue. I knew I shouldn't keep eating it—not if I wanted to take off a few pounds—but it tasted so good. I couldn't resist. Before I knew it, the tub was sitting empty before me, my stomach contentedly swollen.

Noticing my appetite, Kate grinned and shoved her tray of nachos towards me.

I declined politely and patted my stomach, pretending not to notice how repulsed I automatically felt when my hand touched the bloated fat.

"Girl, you basically eat like a rabbit. You can have some nachos." Kate rolled her eyes at me and mimed a rabbit munching on a carrot.

If I was telling the truth, I envied Kate. I wanted nothing more than to stuff my face with nachos and chili and everything else in the world that tasted so good. But I didn't have her figure and I couldn't eat like that without doubling in size.

"I couldn't possibly eat anything else, honestly! I'm so full," I protested. "And stop making fun of me!"

The sound of my laughter was loud in my ears, but Kate was cackling away, unbothered by the stares we were getting from people.

Reality suddenly hit me, reminding me that they weren't staring because we were laughing.

My laughter ceased. Kate's smile wiped from her face too, as though she knew exactly what I was thinking. She reached over and took my hand into hers, squeezing it gently. I tried to take comfort in her small act of reassurance, but my mind was already racing. It aggravated me so much that I had become the laughingstock of the school—more so than I had been before—over someone violating me.

I sighed at my own naivete. Of course, they were going to laugh at me. I wasn't part of their crowd, and I never would be.

I wasn't made for that.

Lost in thought, I hadn't noticed the person walking towards our table. An illuminous green shirt caught the corner of my eye, and I looked up to find Benji on his way to us. He had swapped his black glasses for a similarly shaped pair of turquoise frames, almost as vibrant as his attire. His mass of blonde curls was swept back and tucked behind both ears, one rogue strand falling over his eyes.

When he saw me notice him, a huge grin spread across his face, and he waved at me, almost dropping his tray of food in the process. I bit my lip to stop myself from laughing.

Noticing my sudden shift in mood, Kate spun around just as Benji reached us.

"Hey, Emmie! Is it cool if I sit with you?"

I blinked at him in surprise, suddenly finding myself unable to talk. I looked over at Kate, my eyes pleading for her to help me out.

She winked at me in secret before turning to him to say, "Take a seat if you don't mind being part of the loser club, friend."

"I've never been one for fitting in with the crowd."

Kate snorted as he sat down. Once he was settled, she extended her hand to him. "I'm Kate."

He politely shook it in return, seeming baffled by such a formal greeting. "I'm Benji."

I could have kissed her for saving the day.

My eyes browsed his face as he introduced himself to Kate and had to stop myself from staring at his perfectly angled features. He had a few freckles scattered across his cheeks, so pale that I didn't notice them at first. His glasses contrasted against a pair of spectacular midnight blue irises that I could see myself getting lost in. Not that I would ever have that chance. Not unless I looked like girls my age. Maybe then I would have a shot at being with someone as handsome as Benji.

"Welcome to the outcast table," I eventually managed to croak out. "We're happy to have you."

Benji appeared not to have noticed how many octaves my voice had changed and instead offered me another one of those dazzling smiles.

"Well, I'm mighty glad to be part of the crew!"

Me and Kate looked at each other simultaneously and burst out laughing. Benji looked between us with only slight bewilderment before he joined in, his deep chuckle sending shivers down my spine.

"So Benji, tell us how you're liking Apollo."

I smiled gratefully at Kate once again. She was always much better at small talk than me, probably because she was a people-person whereas I had crippling anxiety. It was so much easier to speak to people when she was around to act as a buffer.

Benji shrugged nonchalantly as he took a bite of his burger. "I mean, it's been okay so far. The town seems really nice, and the people seem friendlier than my last school."

Kate snorted.

I raised my eyebrows at him. "You think the people here are friendly?"

I shook my head at Benji, watching as a sad smile appeared on his lips. I had to agree with Kate on this. If only he knew what the people were really like.

"The people here aren't *really* nice, then?"

I opened my mouth to speak and closed it again. I didn't want to be responsible for ruining his perception of Apollo. If people were being kind to him, that could only be a good thing.

Guilt washed over me as I realized they would stop being so nice to him when they noticed him sitting with us. I wanted to be friends with him—so much more than I was ready to admit—but it would be social suicide for him. The only reason Kate got away unscathed was because she was a preppy cheerleader. Although I didn't want to make assumptions, Benji really didn't strike me as the preppy type.

Now what was I going to do?

I looked at Kate in hopes that she was thinking the same thing, but the look on her face meant she was ready to launch into a very lengthy speech about why the high schoolers of Apollo were directly descended from their own kind of Hell.

"Eh, some people are okay. I'm sure you'll get along with most people,".

Benji looked relieved. "That's good to know." Then his right eyebrow arched comically. "How come you guys are, as you said, outcasts?"

Kate glanced at me for my instruction. I shook my head subtly.

"It's a long and boring story that does not need to be shared over lunch. All you need to know is this: sitting with us could very well mean saying goodbye to your social standing. People may not be as nice to you if they see you with us. You could always change your mind and sit somewhere else."

I tried to hide the sadness in my voice as I warned him. I didn't really want him to leave but I also didn't want to make anyone else suffer on account of being my friend. He was new and kind and definitely did not need the stress of that.

The corners of his lips twitched upwards, and he winked at me. "I think I like the decision I've already made."

I blushed. I think I liked his decision too.

—

Eating lunch with Kate and Benji proved to be far more enjoyable and less awkward than I had expected. Conversation and laughter flowed easily between the three of us, and I found myself thinking that Benji seemed to fit into our group like the last piece of a puzzle; he completed our little club. That didn't stop me from cringing every time I opened my mouth, though.

By the time the bell rang to signal the end of our break, I was almost disappointed to have to go to class. Getting out of the cafeteria and being away from everyone's watchful eyes was a good thing but talking to Benji a bit longer could have been fun too.

"Let us sorrowfully part for now, so that we may be together soon," Kate announced with a bow.

I laughed and shook my head at her absurdness, questioning once again why she had elected to do cheerleading instead of drama.

Benji shouldered his bag on. "Could you translate that for me, Emmie?"

I snorted and threw my head back. Mentally, I made a note to find a less ugly way of laughing. "She means we should hurry to class and get through the rest of the day. That way it won't be long before we see each other again."

As he nodded, some of his combed curls loosened, falling in front of his eyes. Before I knew what I was doing, my hand was reaching up and smoothing the curls down.

Oh, hell.

My mouth gaped as I dropped my hand. Why had I done that?

I cringed with embarrassment as Benji caught my eye, blinking a few times before a slow—and totally disarming—smile spread across his face. My cheeks flamed which made him smirk.

"Thanks, beautiful."

I stared after him as he continued to class, pondering if I had just made it all up, or if he had really called me beautiful.

"Are you coming?" Benji called to me from over his shoulder and I was called back to reality. "We have English to get to, Emmie!"

I rushed to catch up to him, eager to have a class sitting beside him in the hopes that he might make a mistake and compliment me again.

The walk to the classroom was perhaps the longest walk of my life. Or at least, it felt that way. By the time we took our seats—and he had elected to sit next to me *again*—I was sweating more than was ladylike and almost wanted to disappear.

"Alright students, team up with the person sitting beside you. You can pick a play from the selection of books we have in class and choose a scene to practice. Some of you may decide to take part in the Apollo Play this year, and I would like to give you a chance not to fail."

I grimaced at the volume of Mrs. Langford's booming voice, and when she turned her back, chatter arose among the students.

Benji turned to me, beaming from ear to ear. He rested an arm on the back of the chair. "So, are you an actor?"

I rolled my eyes and placed my hands in my lap. "Absolutely not. Having that many people stare at me? I can't think of anything worse."

He furrowed his brows, tapping his fingers on the back of his chair. "I think people stare at you most of the time anyway, Emmie."

I flinched involuntarily and tried to ignore the shooting pain that knifed my stomach. It was inevitable that he would pick up how everyone looked at me eventually, but I wished it wouldn't have happened so quickly.

I tried feigning nonchalance. "Yeah, I guess they do. Everyone likes to have a front row seat to the freak show."

"That isn't what I meant, Emmie." Benji leaned forward, his face hovering in front of mine. "They stare at you because you're breathtaking."

Angling my face towards him ever so slightly, I felt the heat of his breath tickle my cheek. I expected to see him laughing, to discover that his kindness and friendship had just been part of some elaborate sick prank just like Tate's torture just days ago. But instead his eyes were on mine, his gaze so intense I feared I might burn up.

I opened my mouth to speak, but I couldn't find the words. Insecurity burned through me; the doubt of his sincerity still there at the back of my brain. Instead, I just watched him, and he watched me in return, the two of us examining each other. My palms were sweating from the attention, anxiety rising with my quickening pulse.

My head began to swirl, and I knew I couldn't handle this for much longer. How much time had even passed?

Seconds?

Minutes?

It felt like hours.

I cleared my throat. "We better get some work done."

Before another moment could pass, I turned back around to face the front of the classroom and busied myself with searching through the battered copy of *Othello* that was on my desk.

"How boring," he stated plainly, although I could hear the smile in his voice. "But I do suppose you're right,"

Why was this boy so taken with me? I had never been flirted with before in my life. I wasn't even sure he *was* flirting. But as much as I truly hoped he was, the voice in my head was still whispering to me, telling me that this was some joke.

But as I opened the book to the first scene, I found his gaze still on me, and I wondered if maybe one of my wishes had finally come true.

SIX

Benji had opted to sit with us during every break and I was not complaining about the extra company. My heart rate was sky high every time the bell rang to signal lunch beginning, but I was secretly pleased he hadn't yet been scared off. He hadn't complimented me again after calling me breath-taking in English class. He had, however, winked at me so many times that I felt as though my insides were now a puddle of mush. Sometimes I even allowed myself to play a game of what if…

What if…he liked me.

What if…he really was flirting.

What if…we kissed.

It was a dangerous game to play. It led me down a rabbit hole of inner thoughts, imagining the idea of actually opening myself up to someone. Perhaps I could try flirting and see where it led.

The weekend rolled around in what seemed like the blink of an eye, and I was left wondering what to do with myself. Kate had to attend a cheerleading course all weekend which meant I was on my own. As disheartened as I was to see her go, I wished her luck and hugged her tight the day she left. What After all, what was the point in having a best friend if you couldn't support them in doing what they loved?

I had struggled to sleep on Friday night, spending hours tossing and turning, casual conversations with Benji plaguing my thoughts as I overanalysed. My covers were ruffled, and my sheets had peeled from the bottom corners of my bed, which made me feel uneasy. I must have fallen asleep in the early hours of the morning, half-hanging over the edge of the bed like a sloth.

I woke up just before noon on Saturday, drool coating the side of my face, and tried to find the strength to get up out of bed.

I managed to force myself out of bed and stagger downstairs for a mug of coffee that I hoped would give me an energy boost. I didn't particularly like the taste, but caffeine was the answer to everyone's problems in movies, so I figured it wouldn't hurt.

The kitchen tiles were cold on the bare soles of my feet, sending shivers up my spine. I lifted the sugar jar and was about to add a few teaspoons to my cup before I re-evaluated the decision. Maybe I could do without sugar. Just this once.

I took a sip of the piping hot beverage and winced at the bitterness. I didn't understand the obsession people had with drinking coffee; the whole world seemed to worship it, and yet it tasted like dirt to me.

"Good afternoon, Emmeline." My mum had floated into the kitchen without me realising, and I almost dropped my mug on the counter.

"Morning, Mum," I said with as close to a smile as I could muster up.

I was surprised she was still at home and not already out lunching with her favourite girlfriends. The majority of them were pretentious and unbearably annoying but she seemed to think they were amazing. I, on the other hand, lost brain cells every time I was in the same room as them.

My mum floated into the kitchen in white jeans, a burgundy shirt, and stilettos for added flare. Her hair hung around her shoulders in tight curls, and just for a second, I missed when my own hair had looked like that.

"You got up late today," she said with a raised eyebrow. It was a statement, but she wanted an explanation, the demanding tone of her voice making it clear that she wasn't impressed.

I shrugged and took a long gulp of coffee before answering. "I was just tired, I guess."

If looks could kill, I would have been dead on the spot from the glare she sent my way. Apparently, my answer was not the one she was looking for.

"That's really not good enough, Emmie. You are only seventeen years old. You should have plenty of energy. You shouldn't be wasting half of the day away by lazing about in your bed."

There was no point in dignifying her with a response. She wouldn't be happy no matter what I did.

"What are you planning to do today?" she asked pointedly.

I considered her question carefully, but I didn't actually know what my plan was. What I wanted to do was to go back upstairs, curl up in bed, and watch movies or maybe even going back to sleep. But that wasn't what she wanted to hear.

"I figured I'd maybe just spend some time in the house today. I probably have a book I could read."

She tutted as she nudged me out of the way to make herself a cup of green tea. "You most certainly will not."

I didn't know what she wanted me to say or what she expected me to do. Most teenagers I knew were out getting drunk or high all weekend. I figured me staying home and reading a book would be something she'd approve of, but clearly, I was mistaken.

"I'm going out for lunch with Margaret and Rebecca-Ann," she said. "But I will be back in two hours. I expect you'll have left the house by then and will be off doing productive something with your day. Won't you?"

She turned around to face me and I saw from the look on her eyes that there was no point arguing.

"Yes, Mum."

Her stern expression washed away as she plastered on a smile, her teeth sparkling white against the contrast of her red lipstick. "Good girl!"

She blew me an air kiss and clicked out of the kitchen.

I groaned and gulped down the rest of my coffee, trying to think of what I could do for a day. Being without Kate for a whole weekend was really going to suck.

—

An hour and a half later, I was out of the house and aimlessly walking around the town centre. The heat from the sun was making me feel ill under my long-sleeved tee and black jeans. I fanned myself with my hands and wished that I was able to pull my sleeves up without fear of everyone seeing the scars lining my arms.

I made my way to the only boutique in our quaint, snobbish town that seemed to stock clothes in my size.

The shop was called Mystique and was one of my favourite places to visit. The shop owner was a bubbly Irish lady called Roisin. Her hair was a mass of orange curls that reminded me of bonfires. She was small and plump, her warm smile and cheery demeanour giving off a strong maternal vibe.

As I entered the shop, she rounded the counter to envelope me in a strong hug.

"Emmie, love! It's so good to see you!" I wrapped my arms around her and hugged her back, taking comfort in her embrace. I loved listening to her, jealous of her beautiful, rich accent.

Taking a step back, I smiled at the woman's freckled face. "It's good to see you too, Roisin. How is business?"

She waved a hand passively and shrugged. "It could be better, but it could also be worse. I like to thank my lucky stars that I have a roof over my head and a steady income. How are things with you, love?"

"They're alright, I guess," I said on a sigh. "But I am in desperate need of some new jeans. I've put on a little weight."

Saying those words out loud made me feel queasy. Despite knowing Roisin was someone I could trust – after all, I had been shopping at the store for years and had found her to be warm and comforting towards me every single time – I couldn't shake the disappointment I had in myself.

I began to peruse the new stock lining the shelves and hanging on the racks.

Roisin always did buy the best and most beautiful clothes. I picked up a pair of black jeans and held them up to my waist to measure them against my hips. Tears pricked my eyes when I realised I couldn't stretch the waistband enough to make them fit.

Disgusting.

Fat.

Ugly.

My lip began to tremble, and my hands shook, almost losing grasp of the clothing. I would have to jump a size—maybe even two—if I wanted them to fit me properly.

Unless…

Unless I could stop being so greedy with my meal portions. If I could do what my mum always counselled, and eat less, I could lose the weight and my clothes would fit again.

A pair of strong hands took the jeans away from me before folding me into another tight hug.

"A little meat on your bones will do you good, love." She held me at arm's length and emphasized every word. "You are a gorgeous young lady."

I sniffed and nodded my head, shaking myself out of my funk. As Roisin made her way back to the counter, I pondered the size of the jeans. Buying a larger size was just an excuse to put on more weight. I would just need to find a way to fit into my regular size.

Roisin regarded me with careful eyes. She checked the size and pursed her lips together but didn't say anything.

As she handed me my bag, she patted my hand kindly. "Just remember, Emmie, you don't need to change for anyone. Just be happy with yourself."

I smiled and thanked her, exiting the shop as quickly as I could. If I could be happy with myself, then it would be simple. But I wasn't happy. Not with how I looked. And I would need to change that.

The sun was still splitting the sky as I left Mystique, droplets of sweat already forming on my brow.

I looked around me at the shop fronts and people milling about, wondering where I could go to waste some time until I would be allowed to return home. Shopping would just depress me more, and I already had a stack of books I needed to get through. I didn't really want to do anything.

Deciding to allow myself to wallow like I would've been at home, I walked a few streets until I reached Apollo Gardens. It was a cute little garden, hidden behind some of the shops. It was tended to impeccably, never a dead flower or weed in sight, and there were eight little flower beds, each with colourful buds beginning to bloom.

I loved the gardens and was pleased when they added a few benches for the townspeople to sit and have a moment when they needed it. It was such a tranquil place; worries and woes melted away, leaving me staring at the beauty of nature.

It really was beautiful.

As I walked around a flower bed, I collided into the very firm chest of someone.

The guy swore and I staggered backwards, holding my nose which felt as though it had smashed into a wall.

I mentally slapped myself as Benji stood before me, looking at me like I was a broken doll. "God, Emmie. I am so sorry! I didn't see you."

"It's alright." Any attempt at a smile would've seemed like a grimace since my face was extremely sore, so I gave him a weak thumbs up instead, hoping it didn't make me look too much like a weirdo. Gesturing to the flower patches behind him, I added, "I'm surprised you even knew where this place was. It usually takes people a few weeks to find it once they've moved to town."

He shoved his hands into the pockets of his faded blue denim jeans, hunching his shoulders and causing the superhero tee he was wearing to crinkle on his torso. Studying him, I saw his demeanour change in discomfort. "I found this place by accident. I had an argument with my parents and stormed off."

Wincing, a moment of awkwardness passed between us. I reached my hand out and placed it softly onto his arm, squeezing gently. "I'm sorry, Benji. Is everything okay?"

He closed his eyes and took a deep breath before turning back to his usual cheerful self, as though a switch had flipped. The corners of his mouth twisted upward, and I was suddenly very aware that my hand was on his arm.

"What are you doing here?" The curiosity in his question made his eyes glint mischievously and I had to remind myself to breathe.

I chewed on my lip and let my hand fall, pressured by the playfulness of his gaze. "I just needed some fresh air, I guess. I found myself coming here."

He continued to stare at me, his smile never faltering. I shifted on my feet and tried to think of something to say, the silence between us becoming uncomfortable.

I was about to just walk around him when he finally said, "Want to get out of here? I'm sure we could think of something more fun to do."

The wink that followed caused a flush of colour in my skin.

My heart pounded against my chest, the rhythmic drumming echoing in my ears.

I didn't know what he was insinuating with those eyes and that smirk. What scared me most though was how excited I was to find out.

As though he could sense my confusion and panic—which was probably displayed on my face—he rolled his eyes and gave me a playful nudge. "Get your pretty little mind out of the gutter, Emmie. I was thinking we could go bowling."

My mouth gaped as he grabbed my hand and pulled me along the street. My feet dragged behind me as my brain tried to catch up with the situation.

Had Benji Miller just called me pretty? *Again*?

I looked down and panic seeped in again. He was holding my hand. Me, Emmie Beaumont.

Biting on the inside of my lip, I tried to stop myself from grinning. Benji was mumbling about how he had passed by the bowling alley on his walk, and he had thought it looked awesome.

But all I could think about was this amazing boy holding my hand, who not only didn't care that I was the town freak, but somehow thought I was pretty.

My stomach fluttered and I let the grin I'd been holding onto escape.

Was this a date? I didn't think it was. But I couldn't help feeling a little excited by the prospect of being out with Benji. Even if it was just as friends, I was happy to be doing something as normal as going out with a friend, someone other than Kate for once.

A sickly-sweet smell bombarded us as we entered the bowling alley. I hated how much the aroma of popcorn made my stomach grumble. It was tradition to get junk food when anyone went bowling; not being able to get any would be depressing, but I was determined to stick to my commitment. There was no way I would let myself look like a pig, stuffing my face with popcorn, in front of Benji.

A pretty blonde cashier with bright red lips and perfectly winged eyeliner was working the shoe desk. She glanced up as we got to the desk, looking as though she was ready to bare her teeth at any customer who came near her.

Her expression changed as soon as she saw Benji. Suddenly she was jumping up from her stool and eagerly awaiting us at the desk, her painted lips curling into a sultry smile.

"Welcome to Bobby's Bowling Alley. What can I do for you, handsome?"

She flicked her long hair over her shoulder and batted her eyelashes at Benji.

Wow, how subtle.

I felt an unfamiliar twinge as I imagined what she would do if he so much as winked at her.

Benji seemed unbothered by her flirtations though, and instead he threw his arm lazily over my shoulder. My whole body tingled as he did. He was the only person, with the exception of Kate, who ever wanted to be close to me; the idea that he wanted to *touch* me was almost too much for my mind to handle.

The cashier—Lyla, according to the silver badge that glinted on her uniform—glared at me as though it was my fault that he hadn't fallen for her two-second seduction technique.

"What size shoe are you, babe?" Benji whispered into my hair.

I tried my best not to tilt my head so that it was my neck being nuzzled by his lips rather than my hair.

"Size five," I said breathlessly, overly aware of how his arm was brushing against the skin on my shoulder.

Benji nodded. He turned his smile at Lyla the cashier. "Size five and ten shoes please."

Lyla huffed before disappearing to the shelves behind her and returning moments later to dump two ugly pairs of striped bowling shoes on the counter in front of us. She ran up a receipt and held her hand out for the money.

I rummaged in my bag, but Benji put his hand on mine and shook his head. He handed over money to Lyla before tugging me along to the lane where our names were displayed on a tiny screen.

I slipped my feet into the uncomfortable and unattractive shoes, with Benji perched on the bench opposite me as he did the same. I looked around the dimly lit alleys; a few families sat scattered around tables eating their burgers and chips, trophies taking centre stage as the kids boasted about their victories.

While Benji tied his shoelaces, I browsed the range of bowling balls waiting in the rack. It had been years since I had been here, and I forgot what one I normally used.

I hooked my fingers into a psychedelic green one and tried to lift it, nearly dropping it on my foot in the process.

Laughter echoed behind my shoulder, and I spun around to find Benji standing there.

"I don't think that's the one for you, Emmie." He cackled again. Reaching around me, his arm brushed mine as he lifted a marbled blue ball, holding it out for me. "This one is lighter, so it should be a better fit for you."

I harrumphed but took the ball from his outstretched hands.

"How are you so knowledgeable about bowling balls?" I asked, one eyebrow raised. "Is it like some hobby of yours?"

Benji rolled his eyes, but a smile edged at his lips. "I used to go bowling a lot with friends back home. The size and weight are pretty universal."

I was a little surprised that bowling was a hobby of his—to be honest, I didn't think many people even remembered that Bobby's existed in Apollo. But I was happy to be able to share his first experience of bowling in his new home.

Benji was up first and picked a rather intimidatingly large orange bowling ball as he stepped up to the line. He took a few seconds to arrange his stance so that his feet were placed perfectly before he pulled his arm back and sent the ball flying down the lane with a whoosh.

All of the pins scattered. The screen above us beeped with an animated video that said he had landed a strike.

Benji thrust his fists into the air and cheered himself.

When he spun around, he took a bow. "That's how it's done!"

I scoffed and brushed past him. "Don't get too cocky yet!"

Scuffing my feet off the laminate floor as though I was playing baseball, I mocked Benji as I shifted my footing a few times until I was ready. I pulled my arm back and threw the ball forward, flinching as it struck against the floor and promptly rolled into the gutter.

Groaning, I turned to face Benji, knowing he would be ready to gloat. But instead of finding his smirk aggravating, it just made me weak at the knees.

He tutted and shook his head at me. "What were you saying there, Emmie?"

Flipping him off, I waited for my ball to roll back onto the rack so I could take my second shot. My brows furrowed as I concentrated on where I wanted the ball to go. Sending it flying again, I whooped as it travelled down the lane, almost reaching the pins, before it veered off to the side and into the gutter again.

"God damn it!" I yelled playfully, shaking my head at my failure.

Benji's booming laughter filled my ears and I glared at him as he came up beside me, the smugness radiating from him. "Better luck next time, sweetheart."

He blew me a kiss and stepped up to take his shot.

I analysed his movements as he prepared himself, slowly pulling back and flicking his wrist as he released the ball. It sped down the centre of the lane and the video appeared again to announce another strike.

I groaned again, but still found myself smiling at his celebration. Seeing him happy, his mood having shifted from his earlier upset, made me happy too. He was having fun and it was satisfying to know that I was the one he was having fun with.

"I'm going to win, you know," I said with a wink, surprising myself by my own brashness. "I'm just getting warmed up."

Benji stared after me, the playfulness in his eyes turning into hunger.

I felt exposed when he looked at me like that, as though he was seeing something in me that even I wasn't aware of.

Distracted by my inner monologue, I carelessly took my shot. I watched helplessly as it rolled its way into the gutter once more, causing my cheeks to redden in embarrassment.

I was going to look like such a loser. It was such a simple thing, a game that even children were good at, and yet I was failing. There was no way of impressing Benji if I couldn't even get the ball to stay out of the gutter. I would have to do better – it was the only way to prove myself to him.

I didn't even look at Benji as I picked up my ball. Inhaling deeply, I made my way back up to the line again, praying that I would finally hit at least one pin. Lost in my own thoughts so deeply, I didn't hear the footsteps behind me until Benji put his hand lightly on my side.

I gasped and shrunk away from his touch, offended that someone would think it acceptable to put their hands on me without permission. My mind instantly flashed to the incident with Tate, the memories of him groping me flooding my mind.

"Relax. It's just me," Benji purred in my ear, once again putting his hand on my hip.

My mind began to race, panicking at the thought of his hand being so near to my scars. I worried that he would be able to feel the rough patches of skin through the layers of clothing, telling him how much of a freak I really was.

But as he rested his hand on me, I found myself losing track of any worries I might have had. I breathed slowly as the warmth of his breath tickled the hairs on the back of my neck.

"What are you doing?"

I felt him moving closer to me, my back pressed against his stomach. His free hand traced the length of my arm, his fingertips brushing my skin softly until he found my hand.

He wrapped his fingers over mine, a cool and welcome touch. "I'm going to show you how to bowl properly. Is that okay?"

I didn't trust myself to speak so I merely nodded, my curls brushing against his cheek.

His hands were firm on my body, ready to take the lead. Relaxing myself against him, I allowed him to control my movements. As he brought my arm back, I felt the faint touch of his lips skimming across my neck. I closed my eyes and inhaled his musky aroma as my body moved in time with his, sending the bowling ball clattering into the pins at the end of the lane.

I let out a gleeful scream as I realised we had hit a strike.

Jumping up and down, I spun around and pulled Benji into a tight hug. The comfort of his arms wrapping around me made me squeal and I thanked him over and over. "We did it!"

I pulled away slightly, sanity pulling me back and reminding me who I was. I bit awkwardly on my lip, hyper aware that I had just been wrapped in Benji's arms and it was amazing.

Benji watched me fidget, amusement on his face. He took a step towards me, and I held my breath, curious and apprehensive about what he was doing.

Since I didn't move or back away, he closed the space between us. He reached up and pushed a few strands of my hair away from my eyes, his fingers brushing mine ever so softly.

He traced my cheeks with his thumbs, cupping my face in his palms. "You are spectacular, Emmie."

I blinked at him in surprise and fumbled for the words to reply. Did I compliment him now? I racked my brain for the best way to tell him that I thought he was incredible too, but my thoughts were interrupted by the gentle pressure of lips on mine.

It appeared as though my brain had abandoned me, leaving me to be led astray by my eager heart as I tried to comprehend what had just happened.

I smiled sheepishly at Benji and closed my eyes as I found the bravery to return the kiss. My inexperience made me anxious, but I let myself be free of all anxiety instead, acting on impulse alone.

I had thought about my first kiss so many times – would it be filled with passion, shared with someone I was madly in love with – but I hadn't expected it to be with someone I barely knew, in a bowling alley, and over in seconds.

The second kiss was sweeter. Instead of being fearful, I allowed myself to enjoy the moment. My lips tingled at his touch, needing the kisses as though they were the air I needed to live.

Benji wrapped his arms around my waist and pulled me into him, holding me in place as he pried my lips open with his tongue.

I wanted to gasp at the strangeness of the sensation, but instead I let him guide me, my tongue mimicking his as we explored each other's mouths. He tasted of sweet honey and mint; my tastebuds set alight by him.

By the time we pulled away from each other, our lips were plump, and our cheeks flushed. Our eyes met and a giggle escaped from me. I was suddenly glad that I didn't wear makeup like Lyla the Cashier, otherwise our faces would have been covered in smeared lipstick.

"Well, that was certainly an interesting tutorial in bowling," I teased, feeling strange in myself. My voice was hoarse, and I wondered if it would always be like that.

Benji let out a low chuckle and I looked into his hungry eyes again, wondering if my expression matched his. It caught me off guard to realise that I wanted nothing more than to kiss him again, and perhaps live in the warmth of his touch forever.

SEVEN

After my impromptu date on Saturday, I was nervous to go to school Monday morning. I hadn't spoken to Benji since it happened, and I worried that it would be awkward at school.

Kate screeched when I told her, shaking my shoulders roughly for not calling to tell her about it as soon as it happened. Apparently, it was a better achievement than her team's win at the cheer competition.

Despite her reassurances that it would be fine, I still wondered if it had been a spur of the moment situation, and that Benji had been filled with regret after kissing me. I had barely slept since, my anxiety on high alert from the moment I said goodbye to him.

As we entered the school gates, dread was filling up like a pool in my stomach, and I feared I would drown in it. I made an excuse to Kate and rushed to the bathroom, sinking to the floor in the corner cubicle. I was spinning out of control as thoughts swarmed around in my head, clouding my judgement and stopping me from thinking straight.

My breathing became shallow, and I pinched the skin on my wrist, trying to feel something to ground me. I couldn't even feel that, no matter how hard I dug my nail into the thin layer of skin.

Panic seized me. I couldn't get a full breath.

I tried to run through the tips I had read online for how to combat panic attacks, but my mind drew a blank, consumed by hysteria. Sweat formed on my brow as I tried to think of the last time I had felt in control of myself, and my stomach churned at the memory, the toast I had eaten earlier that morning now unsettling.

My eyes shut softly, tears streaming down my cheeks as I realised what I would have to do.

Opening the lid of the toilet, I leaned over and shoved two fingers down the back of my throat.

Gagging, I pushed them further, heaving until my breakfast spilled into the bowl. I retched until my stomach was empty, the taste of vomit the only thing I could focus on.

I stood and made my way to the sink, running the tap so I could get a mouthful of water. Swirling it around in my mouth before spitting it into the toilet, I wiped my mouth with toilet paper and flushed away the remnants of my anxiety. I chewed on a piece of chewing gum to get rid of the bitter taste and allowed myself a moment to sob.

Getting into such a mess scared me. I couldn't fathom why I couldn't process things like other people, instead I had to hurt myself just to get through the day. I felt horrid, understanding why people found me so disgusting. Who wouldn't find someone like me repulsive?

I bit down on the inside of my cheek and tried to stop being so pathetic. Rising from the floor and brushing the dirt from my clothes, I took a deep breath and prepared myself for the possibility of running into Benji. Most people would have been thrilled to see the person they had kissed, but all I felt was an overwhelming amount of fear and anxiety.

The hallways were crowded and noisy as I passed by groups of other students, gossip and screeches pounding my ears from every direction. I hung my head and hid behind the wavy strands of hair shielding my eyes. Sweat soaked my underarms as my brain tried to filter through the hundreds of thoughts circling around it. I couldn't face seeing anyone, making eye contact with someone could result in me having to speak to someone.

Depositing my bag into my locker and grabbing a few books, I hoped that I wouldn't need anything more than what I could carry in my arms. I chewed nervously on the dead skin on my lip, wondering where Kate had disappeared to. I assumed she would just meet me at the lockers but maybe she had something to do.

Letting out a sigh, I slammed my locker shut, determined not to let myself break any further than I already had.

Barely two feet away, Tate Harington leaned against the lockers with his friends, his eyes burning into my skin. His sleazy smile curdled my stomach as he blew me a kiss, much to the amusement of his idiot friends. Their raucous laughter cut through all the other noise around me; all I could hear was them. Anger bubbled inside of me, and I wanted nothing more than to charge over to him and slap him across his face, marking him as he had so brutally marked me.

I thought of my father then, of the person he wanted me to be. When I was growing up, he had been so against violence that I had barely been allowed to watch TV. He thought that the best way to combat it was to rise above the cruelty of others, be the better person and walk away. He always said that I should remember to be kind, forgiving, and strong.

No matter how bad things got, I could never forget that.

So, as desperate as I was to hit Tate, I called on the strength my dad always thought I had and started to march past them without any sort of reaction. I held my head high and ignored them as their eyes followed my every movement.

Apparently, that wasn't good enough for Tate. He couldn't let anything go.

A vicious hunger flashed in his eyes. He pushed himself off the wall and matched my pace, walking as fast as he could until he could jump in front of me, stopping me in my tracks and blocking me from getting past him.

81

"Where do you think you're going?" He leered over me, his fists clenching at his sides impatiently as though he wanted to hurt me again. "We have unfinished business."

I growled at him through gritted teeth. "Get the hell out of my way, Tate!"

His expression quickly changed, and my heartbeat raced at the sight of his fury.

He grabbed my wrist, his nails digging into my skin. I whimpered, trying to pull away from his grasp. But he squeezed tighter and snarled in a blind rage that was directed solely at me for embarrassing him in front of his friends. I had never seen someone look at me like that before, and it terrified me more than I wanted to admit.

"Tate, please! Let me go," I pleaded through teary eyes.

But my begging only brought him more pleasure. His bottom lip curled, and I looked around me, begging for someone to step in to help. But everyone was either watching eagerly or pretending not to notice.

The message was clear: nobody should dare upset or annoy Tate Harington. Nobody wanted to face his wrath. People didn't want to find themselves in my place.

I tried to yank my wrist free, wincing as his nails pierced into my skin. I had to get away from him as quickly as I could. He looked feral, eyes widened, and pupils dilated with excitement.

"Get your bloody hands off her!"

A deep voice roared from behind me, footsteps thumping as the man ran towards us.

Shock registered in Tate's face, and he looked from me to his grip on my wrist, as though weighing his options. As the footsteps neared us, he made up his mind and let go of me.

I held my wrist in my other hand, wiping away the spots of blood with the sleeve of my jumper. Someone wrapped their arms around me, and I looked up to find Benji guarding me—protecting *me*—as he glowered at Tate.

I leaned against his chest and allowed myself to sob, taking solace in the safety of his arms. Nobody had ever defended me before or made me feel important enough to be fought for. It was almost unfathomable to me that Benji would; I hadn't done anything to deserve his support or be worthy of his protection.

"Ah, New Boy has arrived to save the day!" Tate declared. I pulled away slightly from Benji, watching as Tate spun around with his arms outstretched, reminding me of a circus ringmaster.

"How about you back up and stop being an asshole? If you would stop harassing and hurting innocent girls, nobody would need to save anyone."

"Who do you think you're talking to? Emmeline here isn't exactly a damsel in distress!"

Releasing me, Benji sprung forward and grabbed Tate by the collar of his shirt. His voice was low and venomous. "Maybe I didn't make myself clear. Touch her again and I'll end you."

Tate scoffed, rolling his eyes before turning on his heels and fleeing with his mates.

Benji relaxed his shoulders and pulled me back into his arms, caressing my head with his hand. "Are you okay, babe?"

I didn't think I'd ever be okay, but for once it was nice to know I wasn't alone in this.

"Yes," I whispered into his shirt.

I pulled away and looked at him, trying to think of the words to tell him how grateful I was for him saving me.

Benji just shook his head solemnly, a hint of pity in his eyes. I didn't have the energy to think straight and so I let myself fall into him again, wrapping my arms as tightly as I could around his waist.

"Let me walk you to class?"

I nodded and Benji slipped his hand into mine, leading me through the hallway. A few people moved out of the way as we passed, regarding Benji differently now that he'd had the confidence to stand up to Tate.

As I looked up at him, I was seeing him in a new light too. From being a new friend, he had turned into my protector. He had done something nobody else had done for me before and it made my heart swell.

He squeezed my hand, and I felt something stir inside me. He looked at me with a kindness that I had never witnessed before.

—

When lunch rolled around, I was pleased to find Benji waiting outside my classroom for me. He took my hand in his without hesitation and guided me into the lunch hall, pulling me up to our table where Kate was already waiting.

She glanced at our laced fingers and blinked rapidly but had the sense not to say anything when she noticed the worried look on my face. "Emmie, what happened?"

Benji grunted and shifted in his seat beside me, moving his arm so that it hung loosely over the back of my chair.

"Tate Harington happened," I said bitterly.

Confusion passed over Kate's face and she tilted her head at me. I blew a breath and started my explanation of what happened. By the end, I was surprised she wasn't breathing fire from the colour in her face.

"I'll kill him!"

"Kate, calm down."

"No, Emmie! He doesn't get to do that to you. Not after last time."

Benji perked up in his chair. "Last time?"

I huffed and shot Kate a look. She held up her hands in apology and I shook my head. "Forget about it. I'm sick to death of talking about Tate."

Benji watched me closely but eventually relaxed back into his chair, choosing not to press me. His hand traced my shoulder as I quickly finished an essay I had due, listening to Kate tell us about the exam she had just completed.

When Benji excused himself to go to the bathroom, Kate practically leaped from her chair to sit next to me. "So, I guess you and Benji are an item now? The dude is looking at you with serious puppy dog eyes."

I shrugged and hid my face in my hands so she couldn't see my blush. "I don't know. He defended me against Tate. That counts for something in my book."

Kate grinned and nudged my shoulder with hers. "Don't be so modest. Embrace that he likes you. Just make sure he doesn't hurt you, or I will have to rip out his heart."

She mimicked stabbing him using a plastic fork discarded on our table and we exploded into a fit of giggles. Benji found us doubled over when he returned, our cheeks red and tears streaming down our faces.

"What did I miss?"

The puzzled look on his face set us off again and he stared at us like we were crazy.

Kate leaned over and patted him on the shoulder, probably a little harder than necessary. "We were just discussing you, my friend. And I told Emmie that if you ever hurt her, I will personally hunt you down."

Benji started to chuckle and bowed his head in appreciation. "I would never dream of it."

He took his seat beside me and automatically linked his fingers with mine. I smiled at how easy it felt and kissed his cheek lightly. Kate pretended to retch across the table, and I threw a bit of paper at her.

I sat back in my chair and let Kate and Benji talk among themselves. I felt my smile falter as I came to the realisation that my happiness always seemed to be short-lived. Every time I felt the tiniest bit of anything other than sadness, something would come and knock me back down again.

Benji traced the back of my hand with his thumb, and I wondered if happiness with him would also be temporary.

The pessimistic part of my brain told me I would end up alone and heartbroken as I had always thought. But there was also a tiny part of me that believed I could have more than what I expected. I was curious—and admittedly apprehensive—to see which part would win.

When Kate left to go to her locker, Benji leaned in and pressed a light kiss to my cheek. "You doing okay there? It's been a tough day for you."

"I'm surviving," I said, offering him a small smile.

"I was thinking — what about if we go out for lunch tomorrow? Just you and me."

His hand reached up, feathering his fingers through the ends of my hair. I leaned into his touch, resisting the urge to close my eyes as I relaxed into him.

"What about Kate?"

He rolled his eyes and chuckled. "I'm sure your friend isn't going to mind you going out for lunch with your boyfriend. Come on—it'll be romantic."

"I don't know. I don't want Kate to be left on her own," I admitted.

"She can hang with her cheerleading friends for a day." Letting his hand drop from my hair, he caressed my neck, trailing his fingertips across my shoulders. "I just want to spend some time with you. It would be nice to be able to get you out of here, away from Tate and the others."

I sighed, shifting so I could rest my head on his shoulder. He made a good point; it would be nice to spend lunch together, even just for a day.

"Okay, let's do it."

EIGHT

Days passed by in a blur as we prepared for the winter exams. School seemed to drag on for hours and the weekends were packed full of fun dates with Benji. People had backed off a bit since his altercation with Tate and the most anybody did now was offer me a few glares. Tate had arrived at school the next day with a black eye and busted lip, but I questioned Benji, and he said it had nothing to do with him. Knowing Tate, he had probably argued with the wrong person.

Life seemed a bit calmer—for the most part.

Interactions with my mum were as strained as ever. Apparently getting a boyfriend was *not* what she had in mind when she told me to get out of the house more.

But I found myself not caring about her opinions as much when I had Benji to confide in. He was always there when I needed him, responding to my texts and calls as though I were the most important person in his life. I loved being able to spend so much time with someone who made me feel so good.

When November rolled around, Apollo High was fully immersed in the stressful holiday spirit, trying to organise everything in time for the Winter Wonderland dance.

I hated school dances with a passion. Having to find a date for them seemed like such an outdated notion and was obviously something I had never been able to do before. Apollo High's headmistress Mrs. Crayton had made the dances compulsory two years prior in an attempt to promote inclusivity and school spirit; I didn't particularly think it promoted either of these things. Instead, people were forced into doing something they didn't like doing, spending a full evening with people who made their lives hell and used the night to show off their status.

Since it was an event I couldn't ever seem to get out of, Kate had always been my saviour. We had made a pact to go to the dances together. I loved her for that. The whispers had started as soon as we walked into the gymnasium, but Kate had hooked her arm with mine and we danced until our feet hurt.

I hoped things would be different this year. Maybe I wouldn't need a saviour.

Benji squeezed my hand as we walked into school, pressing his lips to my ear. "So, the winter dance will be my first dance in Apollo."

I pressed into his shoulder and tucked my head under his chin, the scent of his spiced cologne tingling the hairs in my nose. "Oh yeah?"

His lips pulled in a devious smirk before he spun me around and pushed me gently against the wall. I huffed out a breath as he put his hands on either side of my head, leaning his face down to mine. He was looking at me like I was prey, and I felt my pulse quicken at the proximity of his lips to mine.

I bit my lip and looked at him with a matched hunger.

"I want you to go with me."

"I kind of have a deal with Kate. We go together every year."

Benji rolled his eyes and shook his head at me, blonde curls tickling my forehead. He leaned in slowly until his lips reached mine. Then all my thoughts were washed away by the sweet taste of his kiss, my senses consumed by Benji and Benji alone.

When he pulled away, I wanted to pull him back to me and beg him never to stop kissing me like that. The devious look in his eyes was all too familiar and he winked at me. "You're seriously going to ditch your boyfriend and miss out on an opportunity to get kissed like that for a full night?

Just because of something you and your friend decided before I was even around?"

He pursed his lips and frowned at me. He took a few steps back before turning and walking down the hall away from me, taking the heat and comfort of his body away in the process. "If that's what you want, it's fine by me."

Watching him leave made me feel like I was going through withdrawal, a pain tightening around my chest. I hated the thought that I could have hurt or offended him in some way, so I chased after him, placing my hand lightly on his bicep to stop him in his tracks.

"Stop. Please."

He spun around, and I saw his deep blue eyes glistening with tears.

I stood up on my tiptoes and pressed my lips to his, hoping he wouldn't pull away.

He shook his head slightly, putting distance between our lips. "Emmie…"

"Please don't be upset," I whispered as I took his hands in mine. "I'll go to the dance with you."

He didn't pull away, but he looked sadder than I had ever seen him. "I don't want you to feel like you have to go with me. I understand if you want to go with Kate."

I shook my head vigorously and cupped his cheeks, pulling his lips to mine. "No, of course I want to go with you! Why would I want to go with my friend when I have an amazing boyfriend I can go with?"

A triumphant glee appeared on Benji's face, and he picked me up by the waist, kissing me until my head felt fuzzy.

Once I arrived at class and was quietly studying for my exams, it registered with me that I would have to tell Kate I wasn't going with her. I turned to a blank page in my notebook and began writing a list of ways I could tell her, but each option resulted in the same thought: she was going to be pissed.

—

I texted Benji to tell him I was going to hang out with Kate after school so I could break the news to her about the dance.

He seemed disappointed that we weren't going to spend time together, but I explained how important it was that I tell Kate in person. He wished me luck—I was going to need it.

I waited at the edge of the football field for cheerleading practice to finish. The sky was a dull grey, and dark clouds blanketed whatever light was trying to peek through. A chill in the air made me grateful that had I worn so many layers, and I wondered how the athletes were able to stand being out in the cold for so long.

When Kate saw me waiting for her, she squealed and waved at me with her pom poms. I laughed and waved back at her, taking a seat on one of the rusting steel benches.

As their practice concluded, a group of peppy cheerleaders flounced past me with a grunt or a glare. I smiled kindly at each of them and ignored their muttered insults.

Following them, Penelope and Rosie cackled their way over to me.

"Hey, Emmie!" Penelope greeted me, her lips pouting together in an effort to smile.

Rosie stood just behind her right shoulder, one hand on her hip. Her face was so straight I would have thought she'd just been slapped.

I raised my eyebrows at them. "Hello."

Penelope grinned, though it looked more like she was baring her teeth at me. "We hear you're dating Benji! Is it true?"

I rolled my eyes at them and their incessant need for gossip. The sad part was that the most interesting thing in their lives was trying to confirm if I had a boyfriend.

"What was your first clue? When he threatened Tate— who was totally harassing me, by the way— or when you saw us snogging in the corridors?"

Rosie gasped over Penelope's shoulder, shocked by my audacity to speak so boldly. Penny shushed her and twirled a strand of hair around her finger.

"That's so awesome, Emmie!" Rosie stared at her with a gaping mouth before Penelope's smile turned cold. "Too bad he'll dump you as soon as he realises how pathetic you are. There are better options out there for someone like him. He really doesn't need to stoop to such low standards."

Rosie giggled as Penny flipped her ponytail and stalked off. Kate reached me just a moment later.

"What was that all about?" She took a swig from her water bottle and wiped the sweat from her reddened face.

I hugged her tight, even though she was a sweaty mess after cheer practice. "It's nothing. The important thing is food. Let's go and get something to eat?"

Kate grinned and put her hands to her chest. "Be still my beating heart. Maybe you're my soulmate, Emmie. Food sounds great!"

We made our way to a little café in the centre of town and managed to get a table next to the window. As we dumped our bags on the back of our seats, a pleasant middle-aged woman with a warm face handed us menus and told us just to wave her over when we wanted to order.

My anxiety was doubled as I waited for the perfect opportunity to discuss the dance with my best friend.

Kate rested her hands on the table and smiled. "So, it's kind of been a while since we've hung out."

I rubbed at my nose and fidgeted uncomfortably in my seat. "I know. I'm sorry. I've just been busy with Benji..."

She waved her hand with a flourish and grinned at me. "It's okay. I mean, I liked it better when we all hung out and I actually got to see you. But then you both stopped having lunch in the cafeteria."

"Benji found a little sandwich shop he really likes, so we started going there. I didn't think you'd want to tag along with us; I didn't want to make you feel like a third wheel."

"Well, it'd be nice to have been asked," she said, shrugging. "But it's fine, forget about it. At least we'll have Winter Wonderland to have a girl's night! Maybe you could stay at my place afterwards?"

She looked at me expectantly and I fumbled over the words. Just as I was about to break the news to her, the waitress brought our food over to the table. She set the plates in front of us, and I thanked her graciously.

I stabbed the pasta around the plate with a fork, hoping to avoid the conversation for as long as possible. Apparently, Kate did not feel the same.

"So, are you up for a sleepover?" She quipped as she bit into her wrap, sweet chili sauce dripping down her chin.

I shovelled pasta into my mouth and chewed as slowly as possible.

She impatiently tapped her foot on the leg of the table, and I knew I would just have to rip the plaster off.

"Please don't be mad at me. But I told Benji I'd go to the dance with him."

Kate winced and dropped her food back onto her plate. She leaned back against her chair and stared at me. "Are you kidding me?"

I swallowed hard. "No, I'm not."

I hated that she was looking at me as though I was doing something wrong. Benji was my boyfriend. He had stuck up for me against Tate when I was terrified, and he had never let me down. Plus, it's what boyfriends and girlfriends did. Why wouldn't I go to the dance with him?

"He's my boyfriend, Kate. It's not like you wouldn't do the same if you had a boyfriend."

"I can't believe you!" Kate scoffed and rubbed her hand across her face in disbelief. "You ditch me for weeks and make excuses every time I want to hang out with you so that you can go and hang out with Mr.-Bloody-Perfect instead. And now you're breaking our pact so you can hang out with him on the one night of the year that I actually need you?"

Anger flared in my veins, igniting a rage in me that I hadn't realised had been building.

"We made a silly schoolgirl pact! Honestly, Kate, grow up." I threw my fork down onto the plate with a clatter, causing some of the other customers to look over at us. "And don't start on my boyfriend! He hasn't done anything wrong."

Kate threw her hands up and barked out a sarcastic laugh. "He's distanced you from the one person who genuinely cares for you. I've always had your back!"

Shaking her head, she sat back in her chair and folded her arms. "I've never let you down, have I? I can see what he's doing, and you're so caught up in the idea of someone loving you despite all your craziness that you can't see it!"

Her words struck me like a slap across the face and I gasped.

She had never spoken to me like that before, and she had certainly never called me crazy. I looked at the person who used to be like my sister and wondered what had happened to make her change so much. The way she was speaking, it was as though she was a different person, and I didn't like it.

"Emmie, I didn't mean—"

I stood and pushed my chair back, grabbing my bag hastily. "Yeah, I think you did. And if you are the—what was it you said again? Ah, yes! If you're the only person who genuinely cares for me, then you wouldn't have said it. Thanks, Kate. I thought you were better than that."

I stormed out of the café, the wind wrapping around me like an icy blanket. My tears were washed away by the rain pouring from the ominous clouds hanging overhead.

Finding shelter in the storefront of a shop, I pulled out my phone and found the number for Benji. I bawled into the phone and slumped against the shop window, hoping the person I needed most would be there when I needed him.

NINE

By the time Benji came to collect me from my slump, my clothes were soaked through from the rain. My hair clung to my head and my shoes squeaked as I walked towards him. He had a huge umbrella with him and waterproof jacket on to keep him fully protected from the weather.

"What kept you?" I questioned, hiccupping over my tears.

"I don't drive. I got here as quickly as I could!" Benji snapped.

I shivered and wrapped my arms around myself, wishing he would hurry and put the umbrella over my head to prevent me from getting soaked further.

"I'm sorry, okay?" I started to sob again; my cries drowned out by the heavy pelt of rain.

Benji groaned and pulled me into him, a little roughly, so that I was sheltered under the cover of his umbrella.

"You know, it's not my fault that you're upset just because you had a argument with your friend. Maybe don't take it out on me, okay?"

I blinked at him. I hadn't realised my tone had been so blunt. How could I have been so stupid and selfish to take my anger out on him when he had travelled out in a storm just to come and get me, and make sure I was okay.

I stood on my tiptoes and kissed his cheek lightly. "I'm sorry, babe. I didn't mean to."

He smiled down at me and wrapped his arms around me. "I forgive you, gorgeous. Let's get you back to mine so you can dry off."

Benji had never taken me back to his house before. A torrent of thoughts began to spin around. What was he expecting us to do back at his? All we had done so far was kiss, and I wasn't ready for more than that. I hadn't even let him see underneath my jumpers, scared of the reaction I would get because of my scars.

I shifted uncomfortably in his arms, trying to loosen his grip a little. "I could go back to mine, you know. It isn't far."

Benji laughed and kissed the top of my head. "Don't be silly. Come back to mine." I tried to ignore how the mocking tone of his voice made my stomach churn – he wouldn't have meant anything by it.

Looking at him and his perfect smile, feeling foolish for thinking he would mock me. He just wanted to spend some time with his girlfriend, away from the prying eyes of the whole town.

Snuggling into him, I enjoyed taking comfort in the warmth of his body heat through my wet clothes. As we walked towards his house, I felt an unease in the pit of my stomach. The anxiety rolling through my body made me feel nauseous, but I couldn't use my methods of control if I wasn't at home.

I gulped down the horrible feeling and clung tighter to Benji, glad he was with me for support. I couldn't get over how Kate had acted. She was supposed to be my best friend, but the one time in my life when I felt happy, she seemed to want to ruin that.

We rounded a corner and Benji pulled me towards a large house at the end of the street. The original brickwork was still in place, discoloured and tainted with years of weather damage, but still beautiful.

As we entered his home, a strong smell of baby powder and tomatoes filled the air. I furrowed my brow, confused at the weird mixture of odours.

As though reading my mind, Benji whispered into my ear, "Anya's favourite food is tomato soup. She probably spilled it everywhere and my mum would have had to bathe her for mess limitation."

I giggled at the mental image and looked around the bare beige walls; the family must not have had time to put anything up yet.

Benji motioned for me to take my shoes off at the door and then took me by the hand and led me into the kitchen. Pots and pans were strewn around the countertops in various places, a small table cluttered with kiddie plates and cutlery. Tomato soup was indeed spilled across the table and left in a puddle on the laminated place mat.

Benji swore and kicked a chair as he made his way over to the fridge, pulling two bottles of water out and slamming the door behind him. I frowned at his anger. Surely, he wasn't embarrassed by a little mess.

I placed my hand lightly on his shoulder, but he shook it off and started down the hall, turning around when he heard I wasn't following. "Come on, then."

Pattering after him, I followed him upstairs, wondering why there were still loose boxes lying about all over the place. They were relatively new to town still, but they'd had months to unpack and living in so much clutter couldn't be a nice environment.

I shrugged my thoughts away and chastised myself for being so judgmental. Benji's mum probably didn't have time to unpack on her own considering she was raising a baby at the same time. It was commendable that she was able to do so much on her own, knowing that Benji's father worked a lot and Benji was always either at school or with me. If I was honest, I felt a little guilty for having taken up most of her son's time when he could have been at home helping her.

Benji opened the door to a small box-shaped bedroom and stepped inside.

The walls were freshly painted stark white, with the longest being wallpapered with a faux brick design. The room held a small single bed, a desk in front of the window, and a wardrobe for clothes.

It wasn't quite what I had expected Benji's room to look like, and the sight of his bed made me shiver.

I walked over to inspect the documents and books scattered on the desk, curious to see if he was reading anything other than the required school novels. As I picked up a battered copy of *Jane Eyre*, a small clicking noise made me look up. Benji had shut the door over and was watching me inspect his room.

"So, what do you think?"

I slashed him a sheepish smile and put the book back down on the desk. "It's cosy."

He crossed the room to me in a few strides and dumped the bottles of water on the bed, pulling me into his arms. I giggled and tried to back away, but he held on tight.

"Benji, your mum is home!" I whisper-shrieked and batted his chest, but he laughed and kissed along my jawline.

"Pfft, she's not going to care. Don't you like me anymore?" he feigned a stab to the heart and fell back onto the bed, pulling me down beside him.

Our laughter filled the room until my voice was hushed by his lips on mine.

I kissed him back softly at first, but the kiss became rushed and needier than he had kissed me before. He leaned over me, resting his arms at either side of my shoulders, pressing down against me as his deepened the kiss.

After a few minutes, I started to feel awkward at the idea of his mum walking in on us and I had to push him off me.

"Benji, stop. I really don't want your mum to come in and see your tongue down my throat."

Benji sighed and moved off me, sitting on the edge of the bed.

I shifted and sat up on the bed, my back pressed against the wall so I could see him. I noticed the wet patches on the bed from my clothes and tried to stifle my giggles.

"Look at the state of your bed now! See what you've done?"

He turned to glance down at the duvet and his expression went from moody to full of laughter, his booming voice giving me chills. "It's your fault for being so damn irresistible! I can't help myself when you're around."

My cheeks flushed with ferocity, but I rolled my eyes. His flattery was so ridiculous but a flutter in my stomach still filled me with pride at being able to say he was mine.

He took my hand in his, clasping it tight and kissing softly. "So, tell me what happened with Kate?"

I let out a shuddering breath and recounted my dinner date with my ex-best friend. When I finished, Benji had his lips pursed firmly together and was staring at the wall like he wanted to punch a hole in it.

"Are you okay?" I touched his cheek softly and he turned to look at me, a fire brewing in his eyes.

He growled, low and guttural, sending goosebumps down my body. "Of course, I'm not okay! Your friend has basically decided to start a hate campaign against me just because I want to take my girlfriend to a bloody dance!"

I flinched away from him, shocked to see him so upset. I cursed myself for opening my mouth, knowing I should have kept quiet and not told him anything.

"Well, she's not my friend anymore. Not after all that." I hooked my fingers under his chin and turned his head to face me. "Forget about her, baby."

But he stared through me as though I was a distraction to his thoughts.

He threw his head back and bounced off the bed to pace the room.

"How am I supposed to forget about it? She wants to break us up, you know? That's what this is about! Maybe…" he paused in the middle of the room to look at me with careful consideration, before starting to pace again. "Forget it."

"Maybe, what?"

"Do you think maybe she has a thing for me? I mean, she's clearly trying to get in between us for some reason. She could be jealous."

The idea struck me as absurd but the more I thought about how weird Kate had been acting, the more it seemed plausible.

"Do you want to break up with me?" His voice broke as he looked at me pleadingly, a vulnerability I hadn't heard from him before. Tears appeared in his eyes and threatened to spill down his cheeks, breaking my heart in two. "I know your friendship with Kate is important to you."

A tear fell from his eyes, and I felt myself well up just looking at him. The beautiful, kind, supportive boy who was willing to give up everything just for my happiness.

Kate was cruel for saying what she did considering she barely even knew Benji. Maybe she *was* jealous or fancied him, because if she knew him the way I did, she would see the amazing person I saw when I looked at him.

I reached out and grabbed his hands, pulling him over to the edge of the bed. I looked up at him and hoped he could see the love in my eyes, pouring from my hands into his.

"Breaking up with you is the last thing I want. Kate can go to hell for all I care, because she burned her bridges with me the moment she tried to turn me against you. You know how much you mean to me, right?"

A sob caught in his throat, and he dropped to his knees before me, crying into my shoulder.

I held him in my arms, whispering that it was okay. He had never been so open with me, showing such strong emotions, and I felt so honoured that he was letting me in.

After a few minutes, he pulled away from my shoulder and looked down at me, the corners of his eyes crinkled and stained with tears. "I'm so glad you said that. I don't know what I'd do if you left me."

He wiped at his tears, embarrassed for having been so emotional.

I cupped his face and pressed my lips to his forehead, my tears mixing with his. "I am not going anywhere, I promise you."

Benji lifted his head slowly, his lips brushing faintly across my lips. I hated how sad he seemed, and I wanted to fix it, to make him happy again. I wrapped my arms and legs around him and pulled him on top of me, my lips finding his in a passionate kiss.

He purred against my touch and moved his hands to my hips as he deepened the kiss, our faces crushed against each other in wanting. I bit on my lower lip as he moved away from my mouth and trailed soft kisses across my jawline, working down to my neck and collarbone. I ruffled his hair with my fingers as he planted kisses on any exposed skin he could find.

I brought his face back to mine and continued to explore his mouth, savouring each kiss and touch. He ran his hands slowly down my sides, my skin tingling through my clothes. A gasp escaped my lips as he traced his fingertips across my chest, pulling my top down slightly to explore my cleavage. I didn't know how to feel about his fingers on my skin; fear and excitement flooded my system.

I giggled as the lightness of his touch tickled me, my back arching and pressing me against him. I surprised myself when a small moan escaped my lips as he ran his hands down the small of my back, holding my body tight to his. I chewed on his lip, pulling it through my teeth and licking it over with my tongue, something which he apparently liked as he sucked in a sharp breath and pressed his lips and body harder against mine.

There was satisfaction in every intake of breath, every moan and gasp, every slight movement of pleasure that I caused for him. I had never made someone feel the way I was making Benji feel and the sense of pride and power it gave me was a welcome experience. I wanted to bask in his touch and never leave, staying forever entwined and content with each other.

I was lost to his touch, my mind void of anything but Benji. I was so consumed by how it felt to be with him that I almost forgot about the damaged parts of myself, the parts hidden beneath the layers of protection in the form of clothes, a design to stop anyone from seeing the scars of my darkness.

Benji started to lift my t-shirt up from my stomach, his hands sliding beneath the damp fabric to explore the areas of my body forbidden from even him.

I pushed his hands away and brought them up to my face instead, hoping he would understand the message I was trying to send him.

He buried his head into my shoulder and tried to distract me with kisses as his hands made their way back to my shirt, pushing the boundaries I was trying so hard to keep. I wished more than anything that I could let him see the scars of all my pain, but it was too much for even me to look at; how could I expect someone else to accept them if I couldn't accept them myself?

His hands slipped under my clothing, his fingertips a warm pressure on my stomach. I bit hard on my lower lip, a sign which he mistook for pleasure.

He let his hands wander more and I tried to pull at his arm, but he was stronger, his hands firm on my skin as his fingertips trailed closer to the marks on my skin.

"Benji, stop," I whispered, pleading as I tried to pull at his hand.

Benji's eyes flicked over mine, but it was a blank stare; he was lost to his own need.

His body was pressed against mine heavily as he touched areas that I was uncomfortable with.

It reminded me of Tate and how he had forced himself on me, gripping me without permission. My heart pounded in my chest, past and present blurring together and sending alarm through my body.

I called his name, but he didn't react, ignoring that I had spoken.

Tears pricked at my eyes as I shoved him as hard as I could, pushing him away from me and onto the floor. He blinked up at me, his mouth hanging open in shock as I pulled my legs up to myself and pulled at my clothes until they were covering as much of my skin as possible.

"What the hell is wrong with you, Benji?" I screamed at him, my voice breaking as hot tears burned at my eyes like acid.

Benji just sat on the floor, staring at me with bewilderment. I hugged my knees to my chest and buried my head in my arms, crying to myself. I couldn't believe he had acted in such a way, breaking my trust and being so cold.

I heard him shuffle around on the floor and the bed creaked as he sat next to me. He placed his hand on my arm, but I shook him off, hurt that he had pushed me when I wasn't ready.

"Emmie, please look at me."

I ignored him and kept my body wrapped up tight, my back turned to him so he couldn't see me cry. I couldn't fathom why he had continued to go against my wishes, trying to knock down my walls that I had built up so long ago.

"Emmie."

I glared at him and saw that he looked terrified, the vulnerability I had seen before had resurfaced. I softened but kept myself blocked from him, feeling exposed if I didn't physically hold myself together.

"I'm so sorry, Emmie. I thought we were just having some fun and, you know, like you were teasing me. I didn't know you were genuinely upset."

The tenderness and hurt in the look he was giving me made me reconsider how hastily I had reacted. It wasn't like he knew about my scars; if it weren't for them, I might've been fine with what he was trying to do. I bit on my lip and tried to calm myself down.

I couldn't exactly be mad at him just for being a guy. He was my boyfriend and that meant we would have to be intimate at some point. A dawning thought smacked me in the face as I comprehended what he was saying: I was teasing him! It wasn't his fault that I had freaked out at him trying to appreciate me. It's not like I was giving him much in the relationship.

Besides, he wasn't Tate. He wasn't trying to hurt me or take advantage; he was my boyfriend. He wouldn't do that. He had mistaken my panic for pleasure, which was understandable. Tate had set out to humiliate me. Benji was *different*.

My wrist began to hum with pain, and I looked down to see I had curled my nails into old scars without realising it, piercing the skin. I sniffed and pulled my sleeves down further to cover up the blood droplets, hoping Benji wouldn't notice the red taint underneath my fingernails.

Panic began to creep in again and I knew I had to get out of there. I was spiralling and my breath caught in my chest, an unfortunate sign I knew too well; my stomach heaved, and the contents of my stomach churned around. I needed to get home and control myself.

I jumped off the bed. "I need to go."

I shoved my jacket on, grabbing my bag from the desk chair where I had dumped it.

Benji strode over to the door and tried to block my exit. "Come on, Emmie. We were just fooling around, and you seemed to be enjoying yourself. Don't go…"

104

I brushed my lips across his cheek lightly and pushed past him. "It's not you, okay? I just need to go home. I'll speak to you later."

I sprinted from his room and down the stairs, shoving on my shoes as quickly as I could, ignoring the squelch as I stepped into them. A little girl was giggling somewhere and a woman who I assumed was Benji's mum peeked her head out of the kitchen. I waved sheepishly and tried to smile, feeling my face contort into more of a grimace. Her brow furrowed in concern—there was a random girl crying on her porch, after all—but waved back.

Stepping out onto the street, I was glad that the rain had finally decided to ease off and started to run back home. The comfort of my own home was what I needed most— and the possessions I desperately had to use to make me feel sane.

I wasn't sure at what point on my journey home that I started crying again, but by the time I reached my front door, my chest was sore from the racking sobs.

It was so ridiculous that I laughed at myself; what the hell was I even crying about? I hated myself for causing so much drama over nothing. Imagine reacting so over the top about something so silly!

But my stomach still felt uneasy, and I felt the urge to run upstairs and wash away the events of the night.

I was pleased that my mum wasn't home which meant I could go straight upstairs and to the bathroom, making a quick detour in my bedroom to get my supplies from my bedside table first.

Feeling clean and in control was the only thing on my mind. I just needed to get rid of the feeling of dread filling every part of my body.

TEN

"Mum?" I peeked my head into her bedroom, glad to see she was already awake and preoccupied with getting dressed for work.

She saw me in her mirror and nodded for me to come in. I took a step inside the pristine bedroom—unsure of how anyone could live in a room and have it sitting so perfectly all the time—but stayed close to the door.

"Good morning, Emmeline. What's wrong?"

I resisted the urge to laugh and ask what was right.

Benji had been calling me repeatedly all night even after I told him we were fine and that I just wasn't feeling well. I was exhausted and had sat up half the night speaking to him on the phone until he finally accepted that I wasn't mad at him. And worst of all, I wasn't speaking to my best friend, who was usually the one person I could talk through everything with.

"I really don't feel good. I'm running a temperature and I've been sick a few times." It wasn't totally a lie. I had stuffed my face with biscuits and crisps I had found in a cupboard, only to throw them up twenty minutes later. I struggled to admit that it made me feel proud because I could already feel that I had dropped a few pounds from the way my clothes fit on my body this morning.

"Emmie, this is exam season." She raised her brows at me in the mirror of her vanity table before going back to applying her lipstick.

I shifted from one foot to the other and tried to put on my best pleading face, even though I didn't have any hopes it would work. "Mum, please. You know I'm top of all my classes, and I can study at home. I just need today off."

She hummed and twitched her lips. I watched her carefully, surprised she was actually considering my request for once.

She spun around on her chair and regarded me with a surprising amount of concern.

"Well, you do look like garbage. So yes, you may have today off. But you've to do one hour of study for at least each subject. And you'll be in tomorrow. Am I clear?"

I thanked her, but she was already back to putting on her makeup in the mirror.

I let out a sigh of relief as I made my way back to bed, pleased that I wouldn't have to face school, let alone Kate or Benji. I didn't know what I was more nervous about, trying to avoid Kate all day, or having to apologise to Benji for being so weird last night.

It also brought up the thing I wanted to avoid most: I was going to have to tell Benji about my scars.

I shivered at the thought and crawled back under my duvet. School started soon which meant I would have to begin studying but my eyelids were drooping, and I stifled a yawn. I bargained that a small nap wouldn't interfere with the study time too much and I let sleep wash over me in a calming wave, the stress of life disappearing under the blanket of exhaustion.

When I next awoke, it was just after noon and the light was blinding as I rolled over. I fumbled for my phone and sighed when I saw the number of missed calls and texts I had received from Benji.

I hated that he was so concerned for me, but I just wanted a bit of time. It was rather annoying to have to listen to twenty voicemails just so I could get out of bed.

I quickly sent a text off to tell him I was okay, just sick like I had said before, and that he could call me after school, but I'd be studying with my phone off for the rest of the day. That would at least buy me a few hours to give myself room to think and breathe.

The coldness of the bathroom sent shivers down my spine as I entered. I took a seat on the edge of the bath and pulled my pyjama top up to expose the bandaged piece of skin on my stomach. I unwrapped the bandage slowly and gently peeled off the bloodstained piece of cotton.

I winced as the top layer of dried blood pulled away from my flesh and opened up the wound again.

Looking down at the roll on my stomach, I could see the gnarly cuts and blew out a breath. I had punished myself more than I had intended last night. The word carved into my skin was a stark reminder of my damage.

Freak.

It was scratched into the skin next to my belly button in jagged handwriting. It took centre stage, placed nicely between *Fat* and *Ugly*, the latter words now raised and scarred against my pale complexion.

I wondered if the people who had said those words to me so many times would ever think that they'd be with me forever. They had been held with me in everything I ever did and now they marked my skin as physical reminders that I was a lesser being than the people I aspired to be like.

I expected it would hurt more than it did, but I found myself becoming numb to the pain I subjected myself to. It was a justified measure to keep myself in check, a way of knowing my worth at all times. It allowed me to function, knowing I was in control rather than letting the events that were unfolding around me overpower me. I could pre-empt their cruelty and use it to stay sane.

I took a fresh piece of cotton wool and wiped the wound clean through gritted teeth, making sure any dirt was flushed out of the wound with antiseptic. Next, I had to reapply a plaster, leaving the bandage off this time, and added the blood-soaked ones into a bag, burying it in the bathroom bin beneath other rubbish so my mum wouldn't see.

It was uncomfortable to bend over as my pyjamas rubbed against the cut, so I held onto my stomach as I rose from my perch and made my way back to bed.

I grabbed my notebooks and spread all my schoolwork out on my duvet, trying to decide what to do first. I was mostly prepared for exams—Apollo High wasn't the type of school to let students fail. But I knew that I had been distracted in school enough that I had missed things when studying.

If I was being honest, it was refreshing to have some time to myself to look over everything. There was nothing I wanted more than to run from my past and everything that held me down, and in order to do that, I needed to ace my exams.

It was my only chance to escape, and I had to make sure I didn't waste it.

—

I decided that I could allocate forty minutes to each subject to allow me to study without completely frying my brain with information overload. Studying for so many hours the previous year had caused me to experience a panic attack every night when I tried to go to sleep, worrying that I hadn't covered all the required coursework to prepare myself. I really didn't want to get into that state again, so I would have to be careful about how long I allowed myself to invest in schoolwork today.

Switching my phone to silent, I opened my Mathematics textbook, hoping that my brain would be so occupied with equations that I wouldn't think about all the other problems I had. It was a good strategy in theory, I just hoped it would work.

—

I was scribbling out a timed essay when the doorbell rang. My legs cramped when I stood, and I groaned having to stretch out a bit before I was able to go downstairs.

The doorbell went again, and I rolled my eyes, wondering who was being so impatient that they couldn't wait a few minutes.

As I reached the bottom step, the unknown person rapped their knuckles off the glass.

"I'm on my way, for goodness' sake!" I shouted, yanking the door open a few moments later.

The annoyance drained from my face as Benji stood on my doorstep, looking extremely pissed.

"So, you're not dead? That's great to know!" he growled and barged past me, making his way into the living room.

I closed the door and followed sheepishly behind him, wondering why he was so annoyed. "I don't know what you mean?"

He flopped down on the sofa and crossed his arms, glaring at me. "I've been texting you all day! And you haven't replied to me once. I thought something had happened to you, but I couldn't get out of the stupid mock exams I had. I sprinted all the way here as soon as school finished."

I sucked in a breath and bit on my lower lip—I had completely forgotten that I had switched my phone on silent. Guilt clawed at my gut for making him worry.

I sat beside Benji and took his hands in mine, hoping he would forgive me, but he huffed and pulled his hands away from me.

"I'm *so* sorry," I tried anyway. "My mum said I had to study today if I was missing school because I wasn't feeling well. I put my phone on silent and just got lost in my textbooks."

"Well, maybe next time you'll think about the people who care about you before you disappear off the planet." His expression softened. "I was really worried."

"I promise. I'll be more considerate next time. I really am sorry," I whispered, tears brimming in the corners of my eyes.

He nodded and raised his brows at me, the corners of his lips still tugged into a half-frown. "Are you feeling better, then?"

I smiled at him and kissed his cheek. "Thank you for caring. Yes, I'm feeling much better."

He reached out and tucked a curl of my hair behind my ear, even though it was too short to stay there.

He peeked at me over the top of his glasses and twitched his lips. "Can we talk about last night? I'm not really sure what made you react the way you did…"

The smile wiped clean off my face and my stomach dropped. "I need to talk to you about something."

"Okay."

I scratched my arm through my t-shirt, an involuntary response that always followed me when I thought about my scars. I wasn't sure if there was a way to tell him that wouldn't result in him thinking I was a complete freak of nature, but I had to try.

"Last night, when you started to lift my shirt up, you got really close to an area that I feel really uncomfortable about."

"Emmie," he said sweetly, "we're all self-conscious about something. But if we're in a relationship then you're going to have to trust that I'll appreciate every part of your body.

"It's not that." I grimaced, knowing I wasn't saying what I meant to. Was there even a good way to tell someone your body was covered in scars from self-inflicted cuts? "Um, I don't really know how to say this. I have a lot of scars…"

I looked at him and pleaded that he would pick up on what I was inferring.

Sadly, he didn't.

"What do you mean, *scars*?"

I sighed and buried my head in my hands, pulling at my hair. "Please don't think I'm a complete psycho but...I had cut myself. Which is why I have a lot of scars."

Realisation finally struck him, and he made a face. "That's so dumb."

Benji was right. It was dumb... *I* was dumb.

His reaction confirmed everything I feared—he found me as disgusting and insane as I felt.

I cried into my hands, wishing I could be the person he deserved. Instead, he was stuck with this ugly abomination. He would leave me now and I would be back to the sad and lonely Emmie I was before I met Benji.

"I know you'll want to leave me, and I totally understand that. I get how screwed up it is, and I won't force you to deal with that," I choked out.

Benji stayed silent for a few minutes before he put his hand on my knee. "I'm sorry for saying what I said. Emmie, look at me please."

I slowly raised my head and wrapped my arms around my waist, looking at him through teary eyes. I was surprised he was still willing to touch me, knowing how broken I was.

His cheeks were reddened, and I was scared to hear what he was about to say. If I was him, I would have bolted straight away. It wasn't really fair of me to dump my issues on him; he deserved better.

"I don't care about your scars."

I blinked. Had I heard him correctly?

A half-smile curved his lips as he took my hands into his. "I don't care about your scars. I like *you*, Emmie. And I don't want anything to get in the way of that."

I couldn't quite believe what he was saying. I heard the words, but it was as though my mind just wasn't computing them correctly. I studied his face and waited for him to laugh and run, but he never did.

"But...why?"

"I don't really know," he admitted. "I just really like you and I think you're stunning, baggage and all. I don't see why we should break up over something so trivial, do you?"

"I-I guess not," I stammered. I should have been happy with his response, but there was a feeling at the back of my mind, telling me it was too good to be true.

"Good!" he clapped his hands loudly and pulled me into a too-tight hug.

I loosely patted his back, suddenly feeling suffocated and breathless.

His hands slowly glided down my back as he slipped his fingertips underneath my t-shirt. I gasped and pulled away, sitting on the other end of the sofa. Benji swore and threw his hands in the air in frustration.

"I just told you I didn't care about your damned scars!" he yelled, the sound coming out more like a growl. I tried not to flinch at his raised voice, telling myself he was entitled to be at least a little bit upset.

I took a deep breath and closed my eyes, pinching my thighs together to get rid of the feeling that everything was spinning out of control and away from me.

"Benji... please."

He rolled his eyes and motioned for me to spit it out. "What?"

"I just... I can't rush this, okay? Nobody has ever been close enough to see my scars before, never mind touch them. I need to go slowly."

Realisation dawned on his face. "Oh. You're a virgin?"

I grimaced and nodded, feeling very small in a very large room.

Beni's expression changed into something softer, and I hoped he understood why things were suddenly such a big deal to me.

"You could have told me, you know," he stated matter-of-factly. "I wouldn't have cared."

It didn't matter what he said, I knew he would have cared. Everyone always said guys were bothered about that sort of thing.

"Look, it's totally fine with me. The scars and the virginity. We'll take it slow, and I won't push you, I promise. Just don't shut me out."

I let out a sigh of relief and fell into his embrace, wishing I felt better than I did about it all. I had expected worse and yet it still…felt wrong.

But before I could think too much of it, his lips found mine and I shivered, kissing him lightly before squirming away from him.

"My mum will be home soon. You should go."

He looked taken aback and a little annoyed as he stood from the plush sofa. "Why can't I meet her?"

I barked out a horrid sounding laugh. "Because she'd kill us both."

"I'm your boyfriend. I'm sure she'd be delighted to meet me." He glared and folded his arms, standing his ground. "Are you ashamed of me or something?"

"Benji, of course not!"

"So why can't I meet her?"

I groaned and grabbed his wrist, trying to pull him to the door.

He pulled away from me and leaned against the fireplace. "I'm waiting."

"You can't meet her because she doesn't approve of me, and I'm her daughter! So, I can't imagine she'll approve of meeting my boyfriend."

I pulled at him again, but he just shook me off like I was an insect annoying him. "You should still want her to meet me, though. Even if she wouldn't approve!"

A low growl escaped my lips as I yanked on his wrist hard. "I do want you to meet her, but I refuse to ambush my own mother! I'm not screwing around here, Benji! Please."

My pleading finally broke through to him, and he reluctantly allowed me to pull him towards the front door, scraping his feet across the hardwood flooring as he trotted along behind me.

I kissed him lightly at the front door and shrieked as he lifted me up off the ground, holding me by the waist.

He was acting like everything was back to normal and I was relieved to have him act so affectionately with me again. Maybe he had meant what he said... I trusted him, and that meant believing him when he told me he didn't care about my scars.

As he dropped me back down, he pretended to wheeze from the weight of me. "Damn girl, I can't do that very often, or I'll need an inhaler!"

It felt like he had stabbed me in the chest, but I laughed at his poor attempt at humour, the response he so clearly craved.

He grinned and placed a quick kiss to my lips again before sauntering off down the street.

Once I had closed the door behind him, I slumped onto the floor and sobbed until my throat was raw.

I knew I was chunky, but I thought I had been losing weight. Whether he had meant it as a joke or not, I couldn't believe he had said that.

I grabbed my shoes from the rack in the hall and decided a trip to the store was necessary. I would lose more weight, no matter what it took.

—

Mum still wasn't back from work by the time I got home, which was a relief. The driveway remained empty, and I wondered how much time I had left. I prayed that she was

115

going to have to work late, leaving me with an empty house to binge on the food I had purchased.

Locking the front door behind me, I padded upstairs to my bedroom. Perching on the edge of the bed, I stared at the wall for a moment, trying to ease the shakiness in my hands. The world was spinning too fast; if I didn't find a way to stay rooted, then I was going to be thrown off balance, left to float about the abyss of self-loathing for eternity.

I dropped my shopping bag on the bed and emptied the contents out on my duvet. Twenty-five pounds later, I had every single snack I had been craving for months. Bingeing on them and then purging my body would make me hate the snacks almost as much as I hated myself. If I wanted to lose weight, hating them so I avoided eating them was my only option.

I had expected to be excited to see it all, for my stomach to growl in anticipation.

Instead, I felt queasy just looking at it.

I supposed that was a good thing; my body was already getting prepared to do what it needed to.

I got up and stood in front of the mirror, looking at my side profile. I ran my hands down my sides as I took a deep breath in, admiring how I would look if I managed to drop a few more pounds. I could already see the difference I had made by missing some meals or vomiting when I had eaten; it had been a painful but effective way to see quick changes and I was so pleased that my clothes had started to hang rather than cling to my repulsive body.

When I exhaled, I monitored the way my belly puffed out, the rolls of fat a stark reminder of just how far I still had left to go.

I glanced over at my bed and tried to mentally prepare myself for what I was about to do.

As I slipped off my shoes and climbed into bed, I spread all of my snacks out in front of me. Packs of crisps, chocolate, and candy littered my bed; it looked like a whole town's Halloween haul.

I took a packet of the crisps and opened them with my trembling hands, almost gagging at the thought as I shoved my first handful of vinegar potato crisps into my mouth.

Remember how disgusting you are.

Fat bitch!

Keep eating, show them how right they are.

Come on, girl. It's the only way you'll lose those extra fat rolls.

My inner demon was on high alert as I stuffed my face with fatty foods, vocalising exactly what I thought of myself and what other people thought of me, too. I tried to ignore the whispers as I ate, telling myself it was necessary to get what I wanted.

I felt myself becoming full very quickly, sharp pains starting to pinch my insides as though my body was physically trying to scream at me to stop.

I closed my eyes and tried to ignore the ache, biting chunks out of the chocolate bar while I thought of the worthwhile impacts it would have on me; the pain was worth everything.

I felt revolting as I continued to eat and eat, pushing the barrier of hunger to greed. Even when I thought I couldn't eat anymore, I crammed more food into my mouth and wiped away the tears. I had to do this. I had to.

Once every single morsel was gone, I congratulated myself.

The first half of my task was over with and all I had to do now was complete the ritual. If I was able to see it through like I had before, I would lose weight. And if I lost the weight, I would feel more like a person rather than a repulsive animal condemned to die ugly and alone.

The food churned in my stomach as I sat on my bed, vomit beginning to rise in my throat without any assistance.

I ran to the bathroom and collapsed onto the tiles in front of the toilet, lifting the lid just in time as I regurgitated everything I had eaten.

The act of being sick itself didn't bother me much; I had grown accustomed to the burning sensation as it clawed at my throat and filled my nostrils, my eyes watering in response. The part that bothered me was afterwards when I would be sitting slumped against the wall, feeling weak and tiny. It was a necessary evil to achieve what I wanted, but it didn't make it any easier to feel horrified by yourself.

I wasn't strong enough to diet—the weight didn't come off quick enough and resulted in me giving up every time.

At least this way was punishment for letting myself become so monstrous.

I lay against the wall and closed my eyes, wondering how easy life must be for people who were born perfect. It would be an amazing thing to just wake up happy and go on about your day, giving no thought or care to what others thought about you.

In another life, perhaps I would be like Penelope or Rosie, and I wouldn't have to skip meals and force myself to be sick in an attempt to pass society's beauty standards.

I wondered what it would be like to just be unapologetically and happy. I couldn't quite recall a time feeling like that.

Hearing keys turn in the front door, my eyes flew open as the click-clack of my mum's heels sounded downstairs. I flushed the toilet and quickly rinsed my face, swaying as I caught myself off balance.

"Emmeline, are you home?" Mum called from the bottom of the staircase, her tone surprisingly light despite the fact that she had been at work all day.

"Yep!" I called back down to her from the bathroom. "I'll be down in ten minutes."

She hummed her response, and I waited until she had gone into the living room before crossing the landing, gripping the banister. I hadn't felt this weak before, but I couldn't complain when I was reaping the rewards. Pain is gain.

I staggered into my bedroom. A mass of wrappers was spread across my duvet and littered on the floor. The sight alone was enough to make bile rise in the back of my throat, self-loathing eating me from the inside out.

I grabbed the carrier bag and deposited the remains into it, shoving the rubbish underneath my bed to be disposed of when my mum next went to work.

I brushed my hair and scrubbed at my face with a cleansing wipe, hoping it made me look less like a zombie. I glanced down at my clothes and saw that sickness had splattered down my t-shirt. With a groan, I swapped an oversized shirt and slid my tee under the bed beside the bag of rubbish, vowing to throw it into the wash once it was safe to do so.

When I got downstairs, Mum was sitting in the living room with a mug of coffee and a magazine. She glanced up as I entered, her lips pursed together.

"Goodness, Emmie. You look dreadful! Are you still ill?"

I was taken aback by her seemingly genuine concern. "I feel a bit better than earlier, but I still don't feel one hundred percent."

She tsked and waved her hand towards the kitchen. "I brought you vegetable broth soup. It's in a container by the microwave. I told Cassidy at work that you weren't feeling great, and she recommended it."

I couldn't stop myself from smiling shyly. "Thank you, Mum"

She didn't respond and went back to reading the magazine in her lap and sipping her coffee.

I was almost completely out of the room when I heard, "Oh, Emmie?"

"Yes?"

She peered up at me, examining my outfit and then went back to reading. "I do hope you studied properly today. I would be terribly disappointed to find out you wasted an opportunity to advance on your subjects."

"I studied all day, Mum. I promise."

She nodded her head, and I made my way into the kitchen, ignoring the way my stomach sank. I wished her concern and motherly interest would last for more than fifteen seconds or revolve around more than grades at school.

The carton of broth was still warm when I got my hands on it. As I lifted the lid, the smell was divine as it filled the air around me. I fished a spoon out of the drawer and took a sip, moaning as my taste buds tingled in reaction to the flavour. It soothed my throat as it travelled down into my body, a comforting warmth blanketing my stomach.

I contemplated eating more. Tt really did taste heavenly, and it seemed to agree with my stomach.

But as I looked at the size of the container, all I could see was the number of calories it would cost me.

After purging myself of everything in my system earlier, it didn't seem right to then eat something.

I sighed and poured the broth down the sink, the plughole gurgling in appreciation. It was really quite depressing to watch it wash away, knowing how delicious it tasted, but I knew it was the right thing to do.

After rinsing the carton out, I disposed of it in the bin and poured myself a mug of herbal tea—apparently, it was good for digestion and metabolism, as well as flushing out the impurities in my system, all of which would be beneficial for me.

I grimaced at the taste, not quite bitter nor sweet, but reasoned that I should keep drinking it anyway.

I propped myself up on one of the bar stools at our kitchen island and sipped away at my tea, finding myself missing Kate. Whenever I was off school, she would always come straight over after her classes with DVDs we liked watching and new pyjamas. We would sit and watch movies together, and we'd both end up falling asleep, leaving my mum to have to call Kate's parents and tell them she was staying overnight.

A small tear escaped as I thought of how strange it was not speaking to her. After my dad died, Kate was the person I felt closest to in the world; losing her was like losing a member of my family. It felt like losing another piece of myself.

That had made the way she spoke about my relationship with Benji even worse. I had been so lost for so many years, fumbling my way through life as a broken shell, but when I was with Benji, it was like I could wrap myself up in him and ignore my pain. He made me happier than I had been in a long time, and I couldn't understand how she couldn't see that.

I sighed and wiped away my tears. I was exhausted despite having slept some of the day, and I needed to rest if I was going to go back to school tomorrow.

I tiptoed back upstairs and crawled into bed. I could still smell the sick on my breath and my teeth were sore, but I didn't have the energy to stand in the bathroom and care for myself.

Instead, I curled up under my duvet like a human burrito and let unconsciousness pull me under.

ELEVEN

I woke up the next day with a pounding headache that made me dizzy whenever I tried to sit up. My joints creaked as I rolled out of bed and I had to practically crawl to the bathroom, my hairs standing to attention as the cold air hit me and threw me off balance. I collapsed onto the side of the bath, trying to gain enough strength to shower.

I pulled on some of my more comfortable, baggy clothes and resigned to look as rubbish as I felt for school.

The smell of eggs and bacon wafted through the house as I made my way downstairs. My mouth watered in anticipation, my stomach grumbling in agreement. But I didn't really want to eat so many calories so early in the morning, but my hunger was slowly winning over my aversion to eating.

I dumped my school bag in the living room alongside a bunch of my folders and eagerly followed my nose into the kitchen.

Mum was standing at the cooker, a bright pink apron tied tightly around her tiny waist. She heard me come in and spun on her heels, almost tripping as her stiletto caught on the groove of one of the tiles.

Her eyes widened before she schooled her face and smiled gently at me. "Good morning, Emmie."

I forced a smile, hoping it didn't look as fake as it was. It was a rarity that my mum would be in the kitchen and actually cooking, but I supposed I couldn't complain.

"Morning, Mum. You okay?"

She turned back to the stove and lifted a pan off, spooning a bunch of spinach and scrambled eggs into a bowl. She brought the bowl over and sat it in the middle of the kitchen island, alongside two plates and cutlery.

"I'm fine," she said, her voice shrill and upbeat. "Tuck in!"

I hesitated and watched her rush around the kitchen as though she were a domestic goddess. My stomach eventually growled, and I gave in, sliding onto one of the stools and scooping eggs onto my plate. After a few seconds, she brought over a plate of crispy grilled bacon and a pitcher of orange juice.

I shoved a forkful into my mouth and groaned involuntarily. "Wow, Mum. This is great!"

She grinned and slid into the seat across from me, spooning some food onto her own plate. "I'm glad you like it. I read on a health forum that starting the day with a healthy breakfast full of protein is a great way to boost metabolism and shed some weight. So, I thought I would get up a little earlier and make us some."

I dropped my fork onto my plate and tried not to glare at her.

Here I was, once again, believing that my mum had suddenly become the type of parent I wanted. Instead, she was just putting on a front in order to have a go at me.

I sighed and pushed my plate away, a bittersweet smile appearing as I regarded my mum.

"What's wrong, Emmeline?" she said as she flicked her blonde locks over her shoulder and touched the edge of her lips to fix any smudged lipstick.

"I'm still not feeling great. I thought I could manage to eat something but apparently not. Thanks anyway, Mum."

She looked me up and down, her long eyelashes fluttering like insect wings. She let out a small exhale and nodded. "Okay, Emmie. Just make sure you ace your practice test today."

I saluted her—knowing it would make her furious—and turned on my heels, escaping from the mad house as quickly as I could.

The walk to school felt weird and lonely without Kate. Normally Benji would wait for me at the corner of my street, but I had forgotten to text him to ask him to meet me. I hoped that he would at least remember to wait outside the school gates, so I wouldn't run the risk of seeing Kate on my own. I couldn't face that.

The streets felt eerily quiet without Kate's loud laughter or terrible singing. When Benji was with me, he would speak the whole way to school, and I wouldn't have a minute to think about the strangeness of not having Kate with me constantly.

But as I walked on my own, everything just felt horribly wrong. I had a dreadful feeling in the pit of my stomach that things were going to get worse before they got better.

Fortunately, seeing Benji's sandy hair and bright blue shirt put my worry to bed.

He pulled me into his arms and crushed his lips onto mine, the breath being ripped out of my lungs. I stood rigidly at first, taken aback by the abruptness, but then I settled into the kiss and melted into his touch.

My cheeks flushed as he pulled away and I gasped for air, watching as Benji grinned at his handiwork. He hung his arm over my shoulder and pulled me tightly to his body.

"Feeling better, girlfriend?"

I shifted under the weight of his arm until I was more comfortable, moving my back to the opposite shoulder. I didn't much like being called *girlfriend* as a pet name—it seemed a little more possessive than I was comfortable with—but I figured I couldn't criticise him just for trying to be a good partner.

"Much better," I said. "Thank you."

Benji pulled me forward and up the steps into Apollo High, glaring at anyone who came too close to us. He walked me to my locker and leaned against the next one, waiting patiently while I deposited my folders and grabbed some of my notebooks. When I looked up, he was staring at me with an intense look in his eye, his lips pursed in concentration.

I closed my locker door and raised my eyebrows at him, chewing the peeling skin on my lips. "What are you staring at?"

He laughed at the question and reached out to stroke my cheek.

"You."

I rolled my eyes and batted his hand away. "Yes, I got that. But I was wondering why?"

He tutted and pulled at one of my curls, rubbing the hair between his fingers. "Can't I admire my girlfriend?"

I sighed and started off down the corridor towards class, knowing we were both in English first period. His footsteps thundered behind me until he caught up, grabbing at my hand.

"You can admire, not stare at me like you're a mad stalker," I growled.

He cackled and I looked around, worried he was bringing too much attention to us. I didn't know what had gotten into him.

"Okay, okay. I'm sorry! I was just thinking about how beautiful you're going to look at this dance. Everyone is going to be so envious of me as I spin you around the dancefloor like you're a ballerina."

I flinched at the mention of dancing but told myself to calm down a bit. He was just picturing our first school dance together, and I was overreacting. How stupid was I?

"I don't particularly like dancing," I said. "But I'm excited to attend with you too. And I'm pretty sure it'll be me that everyone is jealous of, considering I'll be going with you as my date."

I pecked him on the cheek and watched temptation pass over his eyes as he contemplated trying to snog me in the corridor. Just as he was about to tilt his head, I loosened my hand and skipped into class with a giggle.

—

I managed to survive the first three classes before running into Kate.

I was coming out of Political Science in a rush to meet Benji, when I spotted her chatting to a few of the cheerleaders I didn't know too well.

She caught my eye as I walked past, a look of disdain in her gaze. She pursed her lips and shook her head at me before turning back to her new friends, pretending to listen to whatever they were saying. The whole time I was walking away, I could feel her eyes on my back.

Anger flared in me. How could she look at me like *I* was the one who had done something wrong? She had called me *crazy*—the one person who was supposed to understand me, and she had called me insane. Then she basically trash-talked my boyfriend to my face and expected me to be happy about it. Even if she didn't like him, I could have handled that, but it was the way she had said it, like she was expecting me to choose one or the other. I wondered how she felt realising that her unspoken ultimatum had forced my hand in the direction she didn't want.

I wish she had never made me choose. I hated to admit it, but I missed her.

—

By the time the final bell rang, I was exhausted. I thought missing a day of school wouldn't matter, considering I was ahead in all my classes. But I had been so wrong.

Apparently the one day of the year I decided to take off, my teachers had handed out a bunch of study materials and homework. Catching up on everything I had missed was an almost impossible task, but I had scribbled notes and essays until my hand turned blue.

I just wanted to go home, curl up in bed and sleep for a week.

Alas, life had other plans for me, and instead I was to walk Benji into town and help him choose a suit for the dance. I wished it was more of a casual event, but Apollo went all out for occasions, and the Winter Wonderland dances were treated more like charity balls.

Benji met me outside the school gates, patiently waiting as I forced my way through the herd of students exiting the building.

I smiled at him and looped my arm through his, tipping my face up as he placed a gentle kiss on my lips. "Hey, babe."

He barged past a bunch of students and pulled me with him, elbowing anyone who stepped in his way. "Benji, you could've hurt them! We're not in a rush."

Benji grinned and flashed his teeth, a dark twinkle to his icy eyes. "Well, it would teach them not to get in my way."

Scowling, I let out a frustrated sigh, pulling my arm away from him. I hated when he acted rudely, never-mind practically tackling people who happened to step in front of him. I wondered where he got his self-absorbed streak from and why he found it acceptable to treat people in such a manner.

I crossed my arms and quickened my pace so I was walking ahead of him, hoping he would take the hint that I was mad at him for behaving the way he had. I would *never* treat someone like that, and it hurt me to believe that he thought it wasn't a big deal.

"Emmie, come on!" he yelled from behind me as I forged on without him. "I don't see what the issue is!"

Groaning, I spun around to face him. "Are you kidding me? I've already told you before that I hate when you act like that, but you keep doing it. You don't need to be so mean to people!"

I surprised myself by shouting at him; normally, I hated any sort of public confrontations, but he had to be joking if he thought I wouldn't be annoyed by his behaviour.

He reached out to touch my arm and I recoiled, seeing a flicker of anger pass across his face before he composed himself.

"Oh, come off it, Emmie! Stop acting so goddamn perfect all the time. It's so annoying having to live up to your prim and proper expectations."

I gasped at his words and took a step back, almost tripping over the pavement. "It's not about that! I don't act perfect all the time. But you can't go about pushing people and acting like they don't matter."

Benji let out a patronising bark and shook his head at me. His lips curled into a ghastly smile as he spat, "Of course, it's about that! You've been acting higher-than-thou for ages and like I'm so below you just because I don't act the way you want. If you have such a problem with me, why don't you go home and cry about it before you whip out your razor blades!"

I stumbled back from the shock of what he said, his words lashing my face like he had struck me. I dug my nails into the palms of my hands to stop myself from crying as I looked around, hoping nobody had taken any notice of what he had said. A few onlookers from the houses near the school glanced over but quickly went inside, pretending they hadn't heard a thing.

Benji's face contorted as he realised the venomous words he had just yelled for the world to hear. He ran his hands through his messy hair and groaned. "Shit, Emmie. I'm sorry. I didn't mean that!"

It was my turn to bark out a sardonic laugh. "Oh, I think you meant it. I wish I had never told you!"

He stepped towards me, and I flinched as he put his hands on my arms, stopping me from running away. "I promise, I didn't mean it. I can't believe I said that to you. I'll never forgive myself."

I stared at him but kept my lips pressed firmly shut, not trusting myself to speak. My chest physically hurt from the words he had spoken, but I still couldn't bring myself to pull away from him completely.

"Baby, please forgive me," he whispered as tears slipped through his light lashes and down his cheeks. "I love you, Emmie."

I blinked.

Had he just said what I think he had?

Benji pressed his forehead against mine, his lips hovering so close. "God help me, Emmie, but I love you so much. And I'm sorry about what I said. But you need to know I didn't mean it because I would never intentionally hurt someone I loved."

I held my breath and tried to comprehend what he was saying to me. He *loved* me.

His breath was hot against my lips, and I struggled to keep my composure. A few warm tears from his cheeks dripped onto my skin, mixing with the fresh ones falling from my own eyes.

I hated myself as I whispered, "I love you, too," knowing that it was a foolish thing to allow someone to speak to me like he just had. But I did love him, despite everything. And I couldn't lose him too.

Benji smiled and connected our mouths, wiping away the badness with a sweet kiss. I softened at his touch and allowed the taste of him to fill me, consuming my thoughts until his harsh words were pushed to a far corner in my mind.

He trailed his fingers down my cheeks and smoothed across my collarbone, his lips staying firm against my skin.

Minutes must have passed before he pulled away, his eyes large and wild like he was intoxicated.

He held his arm out to me and gestured towards the town. "Shall we?"

I hooked my hand into the crook of his elbow and nodded, a strange feeling lurking at the back of my head as we headed to the tailors to pick him a suit.

Two hours later, Benji had decided on a navy evening suit with a pale blue shirt to match. He looked very dapper, and I stared dreamily at him as he pranced around, admiring himself in the mirror.

"Don't you look handsome!" I exclaimed, clasping my hands together as he buttoned the jacket.

"Thank you, babe." Benji smoothed his hair down and winked at me, full of the confidence I loved. "Have you got a dress yet?"

I grimaced and shook my head, scratching at the inside of my wrist. "Not yet, no."

He hummed and turned around to inspect his reflection again. "Get a pale blue dress. That way you'll match me."

A small laugh escaped my lips. "Babe, no. I can't pull off pale blue with my complexion."

The last time I had worn pale blue was when I got gifted a jumper from Kate, and my mum had delighted in telling me how washed out it made me look. Kate had insisted it looked fine, but I didn't feel comfortable wearing it after that. Now I stuck to dark colours and baggy clothes.

Benji spun around and regarded me with raised brows, a devious look in his eyes. "That's ridiculous. Put your jacket on while I get changed and we'll go dress shopping for you!"

I groaned but did as I was instructed, dragging my feet as Benji pulled me out of the tailors and into the shop which displayed bridesmaid dresses in the window. I pleaded with him to just let me order something online, but he was having none of it.

A tall girl with long flowing locks of chestnut hair greeted us as we entered, her eyes struggling to pull away from Benji long enough to look at me. She smiled flirtatiously at Benji and clasped her hands over her stomach, pushing her breasts out towards him. Benji's eyes grazed over her figure, and I thought about hitting his arm, but the girl spoke and interrupted my thoughts.

"Hi there! My name is Nina. What can I help you with today?"

Benji shook her hand and introduced himself, leering at her like a dog in heat.

I cleared my throat and he glanced at me, taking a moment before dropping her hand.

"I need a dress for our school dance. It's a winter wonderland theme," I stated without so much as a smile, my eyes inviting no friendship.

"Is there a particular style or colour of dress you have in mind?" she asked sweetly, her eyes still on Benji.

Benji smiled and pointed towards a row of dresses towards the back of the shop, the entire row containing various shades of blue. "We'd like to see a pale blue dress, if possible. I would very much like her to match what I'm wearing, Nina."

Nina grinned and motioned for us to follow her. She chatted with Benji while I trailed behind them, not invited to be part of their conversation. She ground to a halt at the row of blue dresses and started to flick through the lighter blues.

She started to pick a handful when I noticed the styles she was picking. "I can't wear those. I need something with sleeves."

She glared at me and hung the dress back up. "Sure. What kind of sleeve?"

I shook my head and pointed to one of the dresses hanging up. "Could I try that? I'd prefer full sleeves and a long skirt, ankle-length if available."

Nina pulled the dress down and told me to follow her to the changing room, showing Benji a chair where he could sit and wait for me to get changed.

Once inside the dressing rooms, Nina hung the dress up and left me to get changed. I turned my back to the mirror and peeled my clothes off, averting my eyes from the marks on my skin.

Despite the colour, the dress was beautiful. It was a floor-length flowing gown with a laced bodice, intricate swirls and beads woven into the gauzy material on the sleeves. It felt expensive and heavy as I held it in my hands, but it was arguably the most amazing dress I had set my eyes on.

I pulled it over my head carefully and let the skirt droop down, falling into place on my hips and dropping to the floor. The material was soft on my skin, and I turned around to view myself in the mirror.

I could hardly believe what I was seeing as I looked at the reflection, seeing myself completely different from the way I normally looked. The dress hugged my chest and my waist without making me look large, while the bodice and sleeves covered any scarred skin.

It was a flattering fit, and I was almost tempted to say I looked pretty.

When I exited the dressing room and made my way out into the store, Benji's eyes popped from his head, and he looked at me dumbfounded.

"Wow, Emmie. You look good!" He beamed from his chair, and I tried not to over analyse his average description of my appearance. I had hoped for a better reaction, but at least he liked it.

I spun around and smiled. "I love it!"

Benji smiled and I watched as Nina walked over to us, putting her hand on Benji's shoulder. "Is everything okay?"

Benji looked up at her and grinned, tapping her hand on his shoulder. "Yes, thank you. She'll take the dress."

Nina fluttered her lashes at him and smiled seductively. "My pleasure."

I picked up the length of the dress and stormed into the dressing room to get changed back into my own clothes, my teeth grinding together as I tore the dress off.

Nina and I glared at each other as I paid for the dress, taking Benji's hand and forcibly yanking him out of the shop.

Once we were outside, Benji laughed and spun me around, pressing me into his hips as his arms slipped around my back and his hands pressed into my bum.

"Were you jealous, baby?" Benji mocked as his fingers dug into my behind.

I smacked his chest and sighed as colour crept onto my face. I wriggled out of his grip and crossed my arms across my chest, cursing him for finding it so funny. "Maybe."

He rolled his eyes and doubled over laughing, wheezing as he gripped his side. He continued to laugh for at least two minutes before he realised how annoyed I was.

"Christ, Emmie," he said, wiping the tears from his eyes. "I was only screwing around."

I scowled. "You were flirting with a random girl. In front of me!"

He stepped towards me and kissed my forehead lightly. "Baby, it was just a bit of fun. It meant nothing. Or did you forget what I told you earlier? I love you. I love you and *only* you."

"I love you too, but you made me look so stupid. My own boyfriend is flirting with someone when I'm standing right next to him!"

Benji flung his arm around my shoulder and chuckled. "Oh, stop being so paranoid. It was just a bit of fun. Come and I'll walk you home."

I grumbled a few more complaints, but he shushed me, and I was too tired to keep arguing. So, I slumped into his shoulder and trotted along beside him, wishing I could escape the dark cloud following me.

TWELVE

Mum's car was in the driveway when I arrived home. The house was in darkness when I entered, the only sound coming from the groans of the boiler. It was pretty weird for my mum to be asleep so early, but I assumed she must have had a hard shift. I didn't want to disturb her, so I tiptoed inside and tried to watch my steps into the hallway.

"Emmie?"

I almost jumped from my skin as a voice whispered from behind me. I spun around and came face-to-face with my mum. She looked bedraggled with smeared makeup and matted hair. I leaned over and clicked the lamp on to illuminate the hallway.

I stifled a giggle as I looked at her crumpled clothes. "You okay, Mum?"

Mum yawned and rubbed her eyes, black mascara coating the back of her hands. "I must have fallen asleep when I got in from work. It was a long day. Did you enjoy shopping?"

I dumped my bags down, hung the dress on the banister, and shifted uncomfortably on my feet. I absolutely did not enjoy shopping, but I wouldn't give her the satisfaction of telling her that. "Yes, it was actually really good. I got a dress for Winter Wonderland!"

I couldn't help but be a little excited about my purchase. It was the most gorgeous and expensive item of clothing I owned, and I hoped I would look okay at the dance. It was hard to look even borderline pretty when all my schoolmates appeared to be fresh out of a modelling academy.

She glanced at the dress bag and a ghost of a smile passed over her lips. "Show me!"

I unzipped the bag and exposed the sky-coloured dress, carefully lifting the bulk of the skirt out to float down.

My mum gasped and clapped her hands together, an excited giggle escaping. "Oh, Emmeline, it's spectacular!"

Tears glistened in my mum's eyes as she took in my dress. Reaching out, she gently stroked the material. She held it in her hands as though it was the most delicate thing she had ever held. It took my breath away to see my mum like that; our relationship had been strained for so long now, to see her genuinely excited was a wondrous sight.

Mum smiled and held the dress up to me, trying to picture what I would look like. I hadn't worn a dress since I was old enough to choose my own outfits, much to her dismay. This would be the first time in years that I was going to look like the daughter she had always wanted.

"I'm excited to wear it, Mum," I admitted, albeit a little sheepishly.

My mum grinned and put the dress back into the bag. "I can see why, darling. You picked very well."

I was taken aback by how pleased she seemed by it. I wondered if I had dressed the way she had wanted me to all my life if our relationship would've been different.

Mum zipped up the bag and sighed, glancing at me sadly. "You'll look very pretty. I do wish that you hadn't cut your beautiful hair, though. Can you imagine how amazing it would have been to have those beautiful blonde locks pinned up? You'd have looked like a princess."

I rolled my eyes. "Well, I'll just need to make do with the hair I have, won't I? I don't regret cutting my hair, Mum."

Mum eyed me, a glare to let me know that was not the response she wanted.

I shrugged, trying my best to ignore how dismayed it made me feel that our bonding moment had passed so quickly.

"Don't take that tone with me, Emmeline. It was a simple statement."

I grabbed my bags and stomped upstairs, not bothering to reply. It was annoying that we couldn't last more than five minutes together without one of us saying something to upset the other. I had prayed all my life to have a normal relationship with my mother, but it hadn't happened. And now we were at the stage where, even if it was unsaid, we were both waiting for me to go to college so we could let the remainder of our relationship disintegrate.

Nothing had been the same after my dad died. I tried to imagine what mum was like before he passed away. It wasn't that she was a horrible person—she was still my mum and I loved her deeply—but she must have been different before if my dad fell in love with her.

I slammed my door shut behind me and threw myself onto the bed, flopping down atop the bundle of blankets and cushions. I hated that life had taken away the one person who had made me feel like the centre of the universe. Losing my dad had left me feeling deserted, isolated from the happiness I was supposed to find as I grew up.

As though he was calling to me, the picture of my dad on the wall beside my bed came into focus. It was my favourite picture of him; he was holding a two-month-old baby, a huge grin the focal point of his face. It always made me laugh to look at—he had grown an eighties-style moustache when mum was pregnant with me, and it looked awful, like one of those stupid stick-on moustaches that people bought from joke stores.

I hugged a cushion close to my chest and sobbed away the pain, asking my dad why he had to leave, and asking whatever higher power might've existed why it had to yank him away from me. It had been the most heart-breaking experience of my life, and I still didn't know how to heal from it.

"I miss you, Dad."

I hoped he was somewhere above, watching down on us and sending healing in whatever ways he could. I didn't know what I believed, but I longed for the day when I would walk into his open arms and never feel another ounce of despair or heartache. That would be the greatest day of my life.

—

Benji wrapped his arms around me as we flopped onto his bed, ready to watch the newest *Avengers* movie on Netflix. I snuggled close to him and laid my head on his chest. I was probably going to fall asleep—comic book stuff really wasn't my thing—but I was happy to try and get through it for him.

His lips brushed against my ear as he whispered, "You comfortable enough, babe?"

"Absolutely," I hummed, my fingertips tracing his hand and wrists.

I could feel him grin as he lowered his face, nuzzling into the crook of my neck. It made me giggle as his hair tickled my skin, his mouth making its way to my collarbone. I closed my eyes and enjoyed the lightness of his touch as he trailed kisses along my skin.

The TV screen lit up as the movie started to play and I elbowed him, pointing at the screen.

"Your movie is starting."

He grinned and brought his head up enough to wink at me. "This is more fun, though."

Shaking my head, I batted at him, but was secretly pleased he found me more interesting than a multi-million-dollar film. I laughed and shifted onto my side as he brought his lips down to my skin again, his hand resting firmly on my hip.

Feeling him on me was weird; I enjoyed the way he made my skin tingle, but I also couldn't shake the fear of letting him near my scars. It didn't matter what he said, I was still apprehensive about what he was going to say when he saw them.

Benji continued to kiss across my tender skin, and I lost almost lost myself.

My hands reached wherever they could, hungry and grabbing for him until I was able to put my lips on his. Kissing Benji was the most exciting thing I had done in my life, and I wanted to bask in the taste of him forever.

I stroked his cheek as I looked into the depth of his icy eyes. I wasn't sure whether I was scared or exhilarated to see the passion behind them, but both options had my pulse quickening, and I pulled him on top of me.

His tongue pushed inside my mouth, his face crushing into mine as he moaned.

I ran my fingertips through his soft mop of curls as my mouth was filled with the sweetened honey taste of him.

My hands travelled down his arms, my nails scraping against the soft flesh of his biceps. He groaned into my open mouth and started to move his kisses lower, sucking on my neck.

I let out a shaky breath and tried to find the words to tell him not to leave a mark, even if it felt good.

"Benji, don't you dare..." I said breathlessly, swatting at his arm as he laughed and did as instructed.

He kissed lightly down my neck and chest, pulling my t-shirt down to kiss my line of cleavage. My breath caught in my throat even though there were no scars there. I tried not to react as his hands made their way down my body, lightly brushing against my breasts before cradling my hips.

His fingers slipped underneath the material and tickled along the waistband of my trousers, closing in on my scars.

I held my breath, going rigid as he started to explore my body. The voice in my head was screaming at me to stop him, telling me I wasn't ready yet. But I also didn't want him to be offended that I didn't want to go further with him when I had told him I was going to work on being ready.

I scrunched my eyes together as he brushed across the first scar. It made me feel nauseous, even though his touch was gentle. I pressed my lips together as tight as I could, wishing myself to relax and enjoy it. Girls my age were already having sex and experiencing more than I was even willing to learn about, and here I was, scared to let my boyfriend even touch my stomach.

Benji pushed my top up further and started to kiss his way down to my belly button. As his lips pressed against my stomach, I gasped and pushed him away from that area.

Benji cursed and sat up, straddling my waist. "What's wrong?"

I flinched and bit on my lower lip, furrowing my brows together. "I'm sorry. I thought I was ready, but I'm not yet. I can't let you see my scars yet."

I watched as his shoulders slumped and he nodded, starting to climb off me with a petted lip and solemn stare.

I reached my hand out to stop him, trying to hold him in place.

"Benji, please don't be mad," I pleaded, hating how pathetic I sounded. I didn't want him to be annoyed, but my mind was in overdrive, and it wouldn't be enjoyable for either of us if I had let him continue.

He sat on the edge of the bed, swinging his legs and hitting his heels off the floor. The silence hung uncomfortably around us, and I wasn't sure what to do to make it better.

The thudding of his feet continued until I rested my hand on his shoulder.

He twitched like he was tempted to shake me off before he shifted around slightly, staring at me.

"Benji, please talk to me."

"I don't really know what to say to you." He scratched at the back of his head before letting out an exasperated sigh. "How are we supposed to have a loving and honest relationship if you can't trust me?"

I frowned and dropped my hands into my lap. "It isn't like that."

He shrugged. "It feels like it to me."

I moved further up the bed so I could rest my back against the headboard, pulling my legs up to my chest. I leaned my chin against my knees and wrapped my arms around my legs, pulling myself into a small ball.

"It's not about trust or love or honesty. It's about how I feel about myself. How can I let you see me when I don't want to see myself? You have to give me time to work through my issues." I pinched my lips together and tried not to cry as I raised my head. "Please understand."

Benji reached out for my hand, entwining our fingers together. "I guess. I'm not going to pretend I understand it all, but I'll give you the time you want."

Relief flooded my system. Understanding and trust was what I needed from him most, and so I was grateful that he was willing to give me the time I needed. "Really?"

He flashed a small smile and squeezed my hand. "Yeah. I mean, I admit that it's difficult for me right now because I obviously want more with you. But I love you, and I'm willing to wait until you're ready."

I lunged forward and threw my arms around his neck, giggling as he fell onto his back on the mattress. He laughed breathlessly and wrapped his arms around my waist, his hands sliding down until they gripped my bottom.

Resting my forehead against Benji's, I lightly brushed my lips across his. I hovered above him until he leaned up for more, pressing harder into him. Whenever we were caught up in an embrace, I was able to pretend that I was normal; I never wanted to part from his lips.

141

Benji's mouth opened slightly, and I pushed my tongue inside, receiving a guttural moan in response. I loved the chill that spread through my body when I was the one to coax a sound from him. Tickling his tongue with mine, my hands cupped his blushed cheeks.

My tongue pushed farther into his mouth, and I escaped the traumatic issues of reality as I lost myself to his touch.

Being with him consumed me and I pressed forward, squealing as my teeth rattled against his. I pulled away, cursing as my mouth throbbed.

Benji groaned and covered his mouth with his hand. "What the hell, Emmie?"

"I'm so sorry, I have no idea what happened. Are you okay?" My eyes widened in alarm as I tasted the blood. Panic clawed its way up my throat, and I could feel my heart pound faster in my chest.

He pulled his palm away from his mouth and I saw that his lip was split, blood smeared across them and onto his cheek.

I made a face and reached out to wipe the blood away, flinching as he pulled away from my touch.

"Apart from the bloody lip, you mean?" Benji sniped, rolling his eyes at me. He pressed the hem of his top against the cut to staunch the bleeding. "I'm fine."

I buried my face into my hands and screeched. "I didn't mean it! I'm so sorry."

Benji sighed and yanked my hands away from my face. He looked angry, but he pulled me into a hug anyway. "I said, I'll be fine."

I nodded against his chest and dug my fingernails into my palms, crescent moons taking form on the soft skin. "Love you."

"Yeah, you too," he mumbled back to me.

My heart tugged in my chest.

I didn't open my mouth to say anything, but he released me from his hug anyway.

"Maybe we should just watch the movie."

I nodded and forced a smile, climbing off the bed. I turned my back to Benji and started to smooth out the duvet, hiding my face as a few tears escaped. Swiping at them roughly, I took a seat at the top of the bed again, resting awkwardly against the wall. Benji flopped down beside me, propping himself against the headboard using his pillows.

I left space between us as much as I could, scared that he wouldn't want to be near me again.

We lay beside each other in a loaded silence for half of the film, Benji practically hanging off the side of the bed so he didn't have to touch me. I was screaming inside and wanted to grab my bag and run, but that would be childish, so I resigned myself to being an adult.

Eventually, Benji reached out and tucked his hand into mine, his eyes never leaving the TV. I smiled inwardly and gripped his hand for dear life. I hated how isolated I felt from the world when he was cold towards me. I never wanted to experience that again and I was determined to do whatever I had to in order to ensure it never did.

—

I was spread out on the fluffy cream rug on the living room floor with textbooks spread around me when mum came in. I stopped chewing on my pencil and sat up, crossing my legs. She perched on the edge of the sofa and attempted to smile, her long teal nails tapping off the leather.

Usually, she didn't disturb me when I was studying which made me assume she wanted something. She also wasn't much of a fidgeter, so I found it bizarre that she was rapping her nails on the couch. Something was on her mind.

I sat with my hands in my lap and stared at her, waiting for her to speak first.

"So, Emmeline, I've been thinking…"

She looked at me with her heavily lined eyes and I resisted the urge to make a joke about that being a rare occasion for her. It was an immature thought, but I sniggered inwardly anyway.

"How are things with you and that boy you've been seeing?"

My jaw dropped and I blinked at her.

We didn't really speak about our personal lives unless it was because she was going to lecture me; but her tone this time was lighter and suggested it was a genuine question.

I tried not to look so surprised as I answered her. "Things are good with Benji. Thank you for asking."

She grinned and clapped her hands together. "Great! Because I would like to invite him over for dinner. I think it's high time I met him, especially if you are going to a dance with him."

I scratched at my shoulder, pushing the nails into the skin as I tried to think of an excuse. The silence hung awkwardly between us while she waited for me to reply.

I sighed, knowing there wasn't any way I would be able to get myself out of it. "That sounds good, Mum. When were you thinking of?"

"How about next week? Your dance is on Friday, correct?" I nodded, reluctantly. "Well, ask him round for Sunday dinner then. I'll cook a roast."

Resisting the urge to groan, I accepted her offer and told her I would ask Benji. He would say yes without hesitation—he had been pestering me to meet my mum for weeks, but I had been worried about it. Benji wasn't posh and proper like Mum would expect, and Mum could be bitter and argumentative. It would be like two different worlds crashing into each other and I was scared to watch my life explode.

THIRTEEN

Sunday came around quicker than I would have liked. Benji had been going on about how excited he was all week, meanwhile I was counting down the hours until it was all over.

I had visions of my mum starting an argument and Benji storming out—I hoped it wasn't a premonition of things to come.

I flicked through all the outfits in my wardrobe, trying to figure out what was best for a meet-the-parent dinner. I didn't see the point in getting dressed up just to sit in my own home to eat, but I also knew that my mum would expect me to dress better than usual. She was a stickler for presentation and always told me that first impressions were everything. And though it wasn't a first impression for me, I assumed she would treat it as one anyway.

A pair of my old, ripped jeans caught my eye from under a pile of clothes on my dresser. They were dark denim and had rose vines embroidered into the seams. My thighs hadn't been able to squeeze into them in months, but I decided to try them again anyway.

I stepped into them and sat on the edge of my bed, expecting to have to lie back flat in order to zip them.

But as I pulled them up, I noticed how loosely they fit around my hips. Where they had once dug into my skin, now there was plenty of room. I'd need a belt to keep them from falling down.

I admired my figure in the mirror, smoothing my hands down the jeans. It had been a year or more since I had last been able to fit into them and I was shocked that they appeared so loose.

When I looked at myself, I could still see the parts of my body where fat clung in rolls. I could see the ruffles underneath my underwear or the red lines under my bra straps telling me that it fit too tight.

The jeans were probably still the nicest trousers I owned though, so I would have to wear them to dinner if I wanted to please my mum.

An oversized, sheer black blouse hung in the back of my closet with a matching vest; I wasn't much of a fashionista, but I assumed they would look okay with the jeans. I completed the look with a pair of slip-on patent black shoes and a red, checkered scarf to match the embroidered roses on my jeans.

I sighed as I walked past the mirror. It had taken me around an hour to choose an outfit, and I still looked like I had just pulled random items of clothing from my wardrobe. The outfit seemed so gorgeous in theory, but on me it was a mismatched mess.

But I didn't have time to change again, and I doubted that any alternative clothing would make me feel more acceptable anyway.

I trotted downstairs and was immediately hit with the smell of a classic Sunday dinner: roasted chicken, rosemary and thyme stuffing, potatoes roasted in goose fat and served with an array of veggies. My mouth watered at the thought of all the delicious food as I entered the kitchen.

Mum stood in front of the stove with a bright pink, kiss-the-chef apron covering her extremely tight-fitting beige bodycon dress. I could see the outline of her underwear through the thin material, and I had to swallow down the impulse to retch.

"Dinner smells lovely, Mum," I stated, startling her. I wasn't too proud to admit it gave me a little bit of glee to watch her jump and almost splatter gravy onto her suede shoes.

"Bloody hell, Emmeline! You almost gave me a heart attack!" She let out an over dramatic sigh and dropped the spoon back into the saucepan, taking it off the heat and sitting it onto the glass panel next to the cooker. "Dinner is almost ready. When will Benji arrive?"

I checked the clock on the wall and tapped my foot nervously as I realised he would be arriving any minute. "He'll be here soon."

Mum hummed as she untied her apron and pulled the clasp from her hair, letting her platinum locks fall down her back and over her shoulders in waves.

It was annoying as hell that she was so gorgeous. How was it fair that my own mother was prettier than me? Puberty had seriously abandoned me.

She looked me up and down as she examined my choice of outfit, her eyes narrowing. "Is that what you plan on wearing?"

Well, that hadn't taken long.

I looked down at myself, pretending not to understand her criticism. "Yes, why? What's wrong with it?"

Mum clicked her tongue and turned back to the countertop, clashing plates as she organised the dishware for our meal. "Nothing, really. I just thought you would have made more of an effort, is all."

I opened my mouth to argue but the doorbell chimed, Benji unintentionally saving me from myself.

Mum shooed me out of the kitchen to answer the door, frantically trying to prep everything to make it look like she cooked feasts like that regularly.

I trudged slowly to the door, knowing that the longer it took me to invite Benji inside, the longer I could avoid the hellish evening that was about to unfold.

My mum was clattering about, dropping dishes and swearing under her breath as I finally reached the door.

Benji greeted me with a huge smile and a large bouquet of daisies. He looked exceptionally handsome with his slicked-back hair and stark white shirt. I regarded him hungrily, wishing I could steal him away for hours of kisses instead of subjecting him to dinner with my mother.

"You look very dapper," I acknowledged as I stood back and welcomed him into my home.

Although he had been here before, it felt different as he stepped past me into the hallway. He walked with his back straighter and a confident smile, making this whole situation seem more official.

He beamed and slipped an arm around my waist, pulling me close as he planted his lips on mine. I melted into the sweet taste of him, allowing all my fears and anxieties to dissipate.

My lips felt cold when he pulled away, still tingling from the feel of them. He winked and stepped back, slowly running his eyes down my body. I shivered from the heat of his gaze and pulled him towards the kitchen, hoping the heat of the house would cover the furious blushing of my cheeks.

Mum had managed to clear the kitchen up some while I had been distracted by Benji and our mini make-out session in the hallway. All of the different food options had been put into dishes and placed onto the dining table. The aroma of the food still hung thick around us, and my stomach grumbled in anticipation.

I placed the flowers into a vase of water and placed them on the countertop as Mum appeared back in the kitchen, a fresh coat of striking pink lipstick applied.

She clasped her hands over her heart and grinned at my boyfriend. "You must be Benji!"

Benji smiled politely and held out his hand. "It's a pleasure to meet you, Olivia."

Mum wrapped her hands around his and widened her eyes as she took him in. "And you, darling. I've heard so little about you."

148

Mum flicked her gaze to me and smirked, a twinkle in her eye from knowing she was going to cause some conflict. Benji also looked at me with furrowed brows and I tried to give him a look which told him to ignore her.

"I'm sorry to hear that." He glared at me but quickly wiped it off his face and grinned at my mum again. "In that case, I'm glad we have this opportunity to get to know each other."

Mum beamed at him and turned on her heels, leading us into the conservatory.

Benji hung behind with me so he could whisper without being heard. "What does she mean she hasn't heard much about me?"

I rolled my eyes. "I've told you before that she likes to cause trouble. She just wants to see how you react and see if we cause a scene at dinner. Ignore her."

His nostrils flared as he smoothed down the front of his shirt, grabbing onto my wrist.

"That better be true," he hissed.

He let go and stalked into the other room, taking his seat at the table as directed by my mum. I took my seat opposite him and hung my head, trying to avoid the piercing hot anger of his stare.

We plated our own food, spooning handfuls from each platter onto our dishes. I was conscious of the fact that I wouldn't be able to run off to the toilet as quickly as I normally would after my meal because I was eating with others. So, instead of heaping on the meat and vegetables, I took a small selection of each item and picked at it absentmindedly as we chatted.

"So, Benji, how are you finding life in Apollo?"

Benji finished chewing on his carrots before answering. "It's definitely been an adjustment for me and my family. However, I'm really enjoying it. And meeting Emmie has been a high point for me, of course."

149

Mum nodded her head approvingly before taking a long gulp of her rosé. "Yes, I'm sure your relationship with my daughter has been interesting. How did you two come to start dating?"

I groaned and picked at the frayed hem of our tablecloth. She was determined to make this evening as embarrassing as possible, I could tell.

"I sat next to her in English class. This wild, strange beauty." Benji smirked, winking at me from across the table. I cringed, embarrassed that he was being flirtatious in front of my own mother. "I was smitten."

Mum smiled at her plate, and I felt goosebumps on my arms as I tried to decipher what she was planning.

"Did you know that Emmeline was once a dancer?" she said at long last.

Benji looked genuinely surprised. "I didn't. That's so cool."

Mum nodded. "She was a ballerina when she was a child. I used to take her to classes down at the community centre and she adored it—"

I scoffed. "I hated it."

Mum pursed her lips and stared pointedly at me with a don't-argue-with-me look that I was all too familiar with. She turned back to Benji and rested her chin on her clasped hands as though she were reminiscing.

"The ballerinas were just stunning. These dainty little things, prancing about the open space as though they could float. I always wanted a dancer for a daughter."

Benji beamed at my mum, sucked into her tale. He didn't take his eyes off of her, and I felt my stomach lurch.

"Ballerinas really are beautiful," he agreed. "They're so flawless and it's incredible to watch."

The more Benji looked into my mother's eyes, the more I felt like I was being punished for something. It was like he was encouraging her because he could see it made me uncomfortable—a way of chastising me for not having told my mum about him sooner.

Did they both really have to make me feel so uneasy in my own home.

Mum let out a soft sigh and wiped a non-existent tear from the corner of her eye. "Alas, Emmie was not built to be a dancer. She was this chubby little thing with two left feet! She flopped all over the place and couldn't keep the beat. I tried to press her to keep working at it—hard work always pays off, I said. But she hounded me until I let her quit."

Benji chuckled and I wanted to crawl under the table and disappear. It was embarrassing enough to have childhood tales shared over dinner, never mind my mum reliving her list of greatest disappointments in life.

"I would have loved to have seen you in your little ballerina costume. It's such a pity you gave it up."

He pouted at me, and I made a face at him.

"Well, too bad," I snapped, glaring at him.

Mum gasped and looked appalled. "Emmeline, don't be so rude!"

Benji chuckled and blew me a kiss. "It's quite alright, Olivia. I love it when she gets sassy."

I waited until my mum looked away before flipping him off. How mortifying it was for him to be like that in front of my mum. I was being petty because I was annoyed at them for discussing my short-lived ballet career, but I huffed anyway. I hated that I seemed to be the brunt of a joke; being at home should have meant I was safe from the humiliation I usually felt out in the world every day.

Mum cleared her throat and turned back to Benji, eager to turn the attention away from me and my supposed rudeness. "How is your schoolwork, Benji?"

I choked on a piece of chicken, affronted by her directness. "Mum, please! You don't need to quiz him."

151

Benji held up his hand to stop me from talking anymore. "Please, Emmie, I can answer for myself."

Mum raised a brow at me over the top of her wine glass but pursed her lips. I willed her to keep quiet and not say anything else.

"My schoolwork is impeccable, Olivia. I never miss a class and I have excellent grades. I'm on target for getting straight A's, and I expect that I'll be ranking at the top of each of my classes."

Benji didn't miss a beat as he rattled off the classes he was taking and his most recent test scores. I hadn't realised that he was quite so intelligent. Truth be told, I found it a little off-putting; I worked extremely hard to get the grades that I did, and yet it seemed to be the easiest thing in the world for him to get A's.

Mum nodded as she listened to him talk, her expression bordering on one of boredom. "And what do your parents do?"

I groaned into my napkin and glowered at my mum. The evening was awkward enough as it was without trying to find out every possible piece of information on him.

Benji, however, seemed eager to keep talking about himself. "Dad is a lawyer for a hotshot firm. He travels quite a bit which is why we've moved so many times. As for mum, she stays home to look after my baby sister. She used to be a lawyer too but gave it up to have kids."

It surprised me how little I actually knew about him. We had never really conversed about his family history; despite the fact I had been extremely open with him about mine. I shifted in my seat, pushing a few peas around the plate as I listened to the back-and-forth between my mum and my boyfriend.

Mum scoffed and I saw Benji clench his fists.

"Your mum must love spending all that time with your sister!" I interjected before my mum could say whatever hurtful thing was on her tongue. "I think it must be awfully rewarding to be a stay-at-home parent."

I watched as Benji slowly uncurled his hands to take a sip of his water.

Mum eyed him carefully, avoiding looking at me completely. She tapped her fingernails on her wine glass, and I knew she was contemplating pushing further.

She let out a bitter laugh. "I couldn't imagine giving up a career like that just to raise children. It seems absurd to me!"

I winced. Benji would not react well to anyone talking badly about his mother. I glanced over at him, praying he would keep his emotions in check. I could understand why he would be angry though; despite my troubled relationship with my mother, I wouldn't let anyone disrespect her.

"Didn't you stay at home to raise Emmie? Surely you understand how important that level of nurturing is."

Mum barked out a laugh and shook her head. "Goodness, no. Emmie's father stayed home with her while I worked. I am not the nurturing type. Quite frankly, I couldn't imagine anything worse."

Benji's face was a picture of confusion and frustration. My head felt like it was about to explode, and I was reminded of the vision I'd had of how the evening was going to play out. I wished I could disappear and not have to worry about what was going to happen. But most of all, I wished that my dad was sitting beside me; he would have been able to make everything better.

"Forgive me if I'm wrong, but wouldn't you have quit work to look after Emmie after your husband passed away?"

My face contorted in a response to his abruptness; his words were like a hard slap, leaving me speechless.

I glanced at my mum who had managed to keep her composure, but I knew that would have hurt her too.

We didn't really speak about dad. It was a horribly lonely way of coping with our grief, but it was the only way we were both able to survive the heartache, and I was okay with that.

I was fuming with Benji. Although my mum had been rude to speak the way she had, it wasn't his place to say something like that. I had explained to him before how much dad's passing had devastated us both, so it's not like he wasn't aware of how tender of a topic it was.

"Benji..." I warned, hoping it would be enough to stop him from crossing any more boundaries. I didn't quite know how to diffuse the tension between us all, and in all honesty, I wanted to just tell him to leave. The sooner he was out of the house, the sooner I could get everything back to normal and calm us all down.

Mum shook her head and rested her elbows on the table. "It's quite alright, Emmeline. He can ask, though he is not entitled to an answer. But on this occasion, I'm more than happy to cater to our guest."

She smiled coldly at Benji, who simply stared blankly back at her.

"No, I did not give up my job when Emmeline's father died. It would not have benefited either of us to have me at home, falling apart and trying to raise a daughter. Emmie attended school, and I had babysitters help when I was unable to leave work. I do not apologise for that because I think it's important for parents to maintain a level of independence away from the household."

I stared at my mum, dumbfounded by her response. Although it still hurt that she hadn't wanted to stay home to look after me, I hadn't quite thought about what her reasons might've been against it. I had assumed that, as she stated so honestly, she was not the nurturing type. But I had never considered that she was trying to protect me from her own grief. I also kind of agreed with her point on parental independence—and it scared me to think that I was agreeing with her on anything!

Benji opened his mouth to speak but closed it again, at a similar loss for words. My mum could be harsh and critical, but she still didn't deserve to have to justify herself in her own home.

Mum rose from her seat, lifting her plate and glass with her. "Thank you for your company this evening. It was nice to meet you, Benji. If you'll excuse me, I have some documents to look over for work tomorrow."

She turned to me once she reached the doorframe, her eyes glistening over with tears. "Emmeline, please do the dishes and lock up once Benji goes home. I'll speak to you tomorrow."

Once mum was away and out of earshot, I rounded on Benji with a blazing fury.

"What the hell was that? Do you think it's okay to use my dead dad for your petty retorts?"

Benji glared and leaned back in his chair, crossing his arms across his chest. "You think it was okay the way she was talking about my mum? And I was supposed to let her say all that without saying anything back?"

I sighed and leaned back in my own chair, rubbing my face. I couldn't tell if I wanted to scream or cry or just run away. If the world ended at that moment, I wouldn't have cared because it would have meant some sort of peace. Eternal silence seemed easier than trying to resolve idiotic arguments.

"No, I don't think what she said was okay. I did warn you about what she's like, but you took her bait anyway." I tapped my foot nervously against the table leg and wished that Benji would leave so I could try and calm myself down. "What's also not okay is the fact that you used the one thing that could hurt my mum *and* me just to make you feel better about what she said. Losing my dad destroyed us both so it's not really acceptable to bring him up when you know nothing about it, is it?"

Benji dropped his macho mask and leaned forward on the table, resting his head in his hands. "I'm sorry, Emmie. I didn't think of it like that. I just wanted to piss her off a bit."

I gritted my teeth and tried not to let it bother me that he had used mine and my mother's grief as a pawn in some pathetic attempt to annoy her. I had to remember that she had goaded him first, but all I could think of was how broken she was after he died. We both were.

Grief could obliterate your whole world in the blink of an eye.

Benji moved from his seat and slid into the empty chair beside me, taking my hands into his. "Emmie, please look at me."

I lifted my head to meet his eyes, my resolve wavering when I looked at him. He did look sorry, and I wondered if perhaps I was overreacting ever so slightly.

He brought my hands to his lips and brushed them lightly over my knuckles. "Please forgive me."

"I forgive you, but I don't know if my mum will. I didn't have high expectations for tonight, but I had at least hoped it would have gone a bit better than *that*."

Benji smiled sadly and leaned his forehead against mine. "It would have been good if it had gone well, honey, but I don't need your mum to like me. All I need is you."

I chuckled lightly. "You sound like a dumb Christmas song."

Soft fingertips traced up my arms, brushing against my neck before caressing my cheek. "I didn't mean to hurt or upset you. You know I love you, right?"

I nodded against his touch and looked into the bright irises of his eyes, my anger disappearing. "I know. I love you too."

His mouth found mine, enveloping my lips in a steamy kiss. He tasted like gravy and bacon as he smothered me in kisses, taking my breath away with every touch. My head felt fuzzy and consumed by him; every thought coming back to him.

I wondered if love was supposed to feel like this; messy and passionate, all-consuming. It was both scary and exhilarating; I never wanted it to end.

Benji ran his fingers through my hair, tugging gently on a few of the curls. "Moving to Apollo and meeting you was the best thing that's ever happened to me."

Something tugged at me, and I found myself at a loss for words. I wasn't sure what it was that was making my stomach flip around, but I smiled anyway, placing a gentle peck on his cheek.

Love was a funny thing.

—

I walked Benji to the bus stop, leaving him with a quick smooch and a promise to text him before I went to bed. It had just turned eight and I was desperate to tidy the house and get some sleep.

The aroma from dinner clung to the walls of the house as I returned home, my stomach churning at the smell. I hadn't heard mum move about since she disappeared upstairs, so I gathered she must have fallen asleep. She had abandoned her plate and her glass of wine on the countertop for me to clean alongside the other dishes.

I entered the conservatory and looked at the dining table, the picture of a disastrous evening. I collected the deserted plates and dumped them beside the sink.

As I looked at the leftover food, I was reminded of how little I had eaten. I had discovered that not eating at all hadn't been helping me lose weight much, but purging was working wonders for me. I contributed that to me being able to fit into my favourite jeans again, and I was eager to keep going, knowing the ends justified the means.

A grumble sounded from my stomach, accompanied by a sharp hunger pain. I eyed the roast potatoes left in the tray and considered my options. I had been too preoccupied to make a trip to the shop for supplies so I would have to make do with what was available to me.

I pulled one of the bar stools over to the stove and took my seat, examining the dishes before me. I picked up one of the roast potatoes and took a bite, making a face as the cold potato hit my tongue. The fluffy texture from earlier was gone and was now firm and lumpy. I shovelled more into my mouth and pulled the slices of chicken. Like the potatoes, the once-tender meat was now dry, but I bit down on as many slices as I could, swallowing quickly so I wouldn't have to chew them.

I hiccupped as I forced more and more down my throat, trying not to gag as bits of broccoli and chicken got caught in my windpipe. My eyes watered as I choked, gulping down a glass of water to clear the food lodged in my throat.

As soon as that was done, I crammed handfuls of carrots into my mouth, telling myself that the dread and discomfort I was feeling was worth it because it would result in me getting a step closer to how I wanted to look.

At least, I hoped it would help me reach my goal.

Handful after handful, I crushed leftovers into my system until the trays and plates were completely empty. My stomach bloated, my jeans digging into the fatty skin. I looked down at myself, my trembling hands prodding my tummy like it was an alien.

How disgusting you truly are, the voice in my head told me. And I couldn't disagree.

I hopped from my stool and emptied the dishes out of the sink. I felt awful thinking that I was about to vomit in the sink, but I couldn't risk using the bathroom in case

Mum heard me. I would clean it out with bleach before I washed the dishes to avoid any bacteria being left.

It shocked me how easy I found it now. The routine had become automatic, and I no longer had to think about the actions I was taking. I was able to do it as easily as I could read and write; it was now nearly an everyday part of my life.

My throat burned and my teeth ached every time, though. It was one of the unfortunate side effects that I had to suffer. Most girls my age wouldn't have to work so hard to be thin and pretty.

I laughed bitterly to myself while I washed up, imagining my life if I were to swap places with Penelope. I could imagine nothing worse than dating Tate, but perhaps being with him was the price she paid for the life she led. I didn't, however, see him groping and grabbing at her without permission like he had with me. I guess I was supposed to feel special about that.

It seemed I had to pay a price whether I was like my peers or not.

Lucky me.

FOURTEEN

When we got into school the next day, everyone was abuzz with excitement for the Winter Wonderland dance. Girls were chatting about what they were going to wear, and boys were discussing how they were going to spike the punch. I rolled my eyes at the idiocy and barged past them, secretly wishing my life was so simple that I could worry about such silly things.

Instead, it seemed like everywhere I turned, I collided with Kate.

I wanted to wrap her in a hug and tell her how much I missed her. But any time I neared her, Benji would squeeze my hand or kiss my cheek, and I would be reminded of why we weren't speaking.

The idea of going to a dance without her was breaking my heart. It felt like the end of an era.

Whenever her eyes caught mine, she would frown, and she would tilt her head as she watched me. Going about life without each other seemed to be an adjustment for us both and I wondered if we would ever find our way back to each other. I hoped so, because I missed my friend and my sister.

Benji was as excited for the dance as our classmates. He seemed giddy as he spoke dreamily about the kind of night we were going to have. According to him, it was going to be incredibly romantic. And the faraway, sweet look on his face made me think he was absolutely correct.

Sometimes, I even dreamt about it. I had never been to a dance with a guy before, so of course I had fantasized about what it would be like; imagining the way he would spin me around on the dancefloor and how we would sway together to the slow songs. I'd pictured the way he would smell as he held me close to him, our cheeks pressed together.

More than once, my cheeks had flushed as I thought about what might happen after the dance.

I had heard stories and watched plenty of movies—sex seemed inevitable. There was a vision in my head of us leaving the dance early, heading back to one of our houses, pausing along the streets for kisses of passion. The house—his or mine, it didn't matter—would be empty and we would make the most of that. But then I would picture him removing my dress and seeing the marks scattered across my skin, which was an unbearable sight.

Maybe he would have prepared himself for the sight, though, and it wouldn't be an issue. I wanted him to love me and my body, even if I didn't love myself.

I pondered my relationship with Benji and considered whether I was ready to take the next step with him.

I felt guilty that I was making him wait so long. I knew he wanted to have sex and he had been trying to understand my issues. It was a big deal for me to ask him to wait. After all, most kids our age were already doing it, so it was weird that we weren't.

It wasn't not like he was expecting us to do anything after the dance—at least, I didn't think he was—but peer pressure was still a huge factor, and I was scared that he was going to get bored of waiting.

My scars were such a complex part of my life and I had to think about them with everything I did. Although Benji had stated that he didn't care, I still feared how he would react. I also worried that I wasn't ready to have sex. I was a virgin, and I didn't know what to do. Benji had had sex before which meant it wasn't a big deal to him like it was for me. He loved me though, and I loved him. I couldn't expect him to wait forever, which meant I was going to have to make my decision before the dance. I didn't want to lose him.

"You okay, baby?" Benji bit gently on my ear, tugging on my earlobe and pulling me from my thoughts.

I nuzzled into his neck, my lips brushing across his skin as I mumbled, "Mhm."

A cool breeze enveloped us as we sat on the benches outside the school grounds, nipping at my cheeks. I rubbed my nose with my mittened hands to try to get some heat back into my body.

As winter quickly approached, Apollo had transformed from the warm colours of autumn to dull and dreary skies. The trees had shed their leaves and the air around us was preparing for the flurries of snow which usually arrived in the late days of November. By Christmas, the whole town would be covered in four feet of snow.

The protective layer of my jacket was doing little to keep the cold from seeping into my bones. I shivered and pulled my scarf up to cover the lower half of my face, inhaling the sweet fragrance of the build-up of my perfume on the material.

"It's so cold."

Benji laughed and took a bite out of his cheese and bacon baguette. "There's barely even a breeze."

I huffed into my scarf and wrapped my arms around my abdomen, hunching over to give myself as much heat as possible. Benji had decided that the weather was absolutely divine and that we should sit outside, but I was seriously regretting agreeing to it.

It was alright for him in his big parka jacket, woolly hat, and walking boots. He was wrapped up for a season which hadn't fully arrived yet. When I had left the house earlier, the sun had been beaming down, and I had foolishly thought that the day would have turned out to be nice. How wrong I was.

"You haven't eaten anything," Benji said as she shoved my Caesar salad towards me.

"I'm not hungry."

Benji scoffed. "It's a bit ungrateful that I bought you lunch and you're not even going to eat it."

I rolled my eyes. It's not like he had to worry about money, so I didn't see what the big deal was. A salad was hardly going to break the bank. But I still felt a twinge of guilt, so I pulled the tub towards me and stuck the fork into the greenery, shovelling some into my mouth and smiling sarcastically at Benji.

"Don't be so bloody childish," he chided.

His agitation made me laugh and I almost choked on my food, my eyes watering.

Benji glared at me, and I straightened my face, dropping all hints of laughter. I wasn't laughing *at* him, at least not really. But I could tell that was exactly what he thought I was doing—mocking him in some way.

I really couldn't face another argument with him after last night, so I focused on eating my salad, trying to tell myself that it was barely any calories, so it would be okay.

Once Benji finished chowing down on his sandwich and I had managed to force half of the salad into my system, Benji relaxed and wrapped his arm around me. I was too cold and tired to pull away from the embrace, so I relaxed into him and stole whatever body heat I could.

"So, what time would you like me to pick you up on Friday?"

I twisted in my seat to look at him. "Pick me up? You don't drive."

A sly grin appeared, and he tapped my nose. "Just answer my question, babe."

"I'm curious about what you're up to!" I laughed. "But you can pick me up at six."

He winked and dropped a chaste kiss on my cheek before rushing off to class, leaving me cold and alone outside. I stared after him and tried to figure out what he was planning. We hadn't really discussed our plans regarding Winter Wonderland, so I was glad that he had at least considered transport because it hadn't even crossed my mind.

I only lasted about two minutes outside before rushing back in and finding comfort in the warmth of the library. The smell of aged books and cinnamon spiced tea floated around the shelves, blanketing over all the visiting students.

Mr. Hubert, the librarian, was hunched over his desk in the middle of the library, lost in the pages of whatever novel he was reading. He looked up through his large, rounded spectacles as I approached the desk. I waved shyly at him, and he smiled in return, his grey moustache covering most of his top lip.

"Hey, Mr. Hubert. How are you?"

The old man stood to greet me, his bones crunching as he moved. He hadn't changed since the last time I had visited the school library—which had been well before last summer, when I was lost and needed somewhere to go when Kate hadn't been around—and still wore a striped vest over grey and khaki corduroys.

I was startled by how pleased I was to see him; I guess I hadn't realised how much I had missed my library visits.

"Emmie, it's great to see you. It's been a long time, dear," he said with a hint of dismay. "I'm doing good, thank you. How are you doing?"

"I've had a hard time, but I think I'm doing okay."

I made my way around the desk and took a seat opposite him, dumping my bag beside me. I helped myself to a mug of the cinnamon tea—I always found it very sweet that most of the library staff had spiced tea and cookies ready for the students during the colder seasons—and I took a long sip.

Mr. Hubert smiled solemnly and nodded. "High school is a tough time. Whoever said that academic years are the best of your life was seriously mistaken."

I found myself laughing which made Mr. Hubert laugh too. "I think you're right, Mr. Hubert."

"It's nice to have you back in the library, Emmie. Me and Mrs. McGovern were worried when you stopped coming. We thought something may have happened."

"I'm pleased you both noticed my absence, but I'm sorry I worried you. I actually..." I blushed at the thought of telling him about Benji. "I met a boy. So, I've been spending my spare time and free periods with him, whenever possible."

Mr. Hubert took a sip of his tea, but the crinkle of his eyes let me know he was trying to hide his smirk. "I see."

I rolled my eyes at him. "Just say whatever you want to say, Mr. Hubert."

"I was just thinking that when a student changes their routine so dramatically, it's usually because they've met someone," he chuckled. "Are you happy, dear?"

I chewed on the ragged edge of my fingernail, wincing as I drew blood.

Was I happy?

I didn't know what happiness really was. I was probably too young to remember my last truly happy experience. But, if I said it enough times, maybe I could convince myself that life was great.

Pulling myself from my thoughts, I tried my best to smile. "I'm very happy, Mr. Hubert."

The librarian chuckled to himself and set his mug down on the desk. "Be sure your special someone treats you well, Emmie. Life can be awfully tough if we're sad all the time."

I already knew how right he was.

I said my goodbyes to the old man and started to traipse around the shelves, admiring all the decorations that had been hung up. Christmas appeared to have come early to Apollo High, and for once I wasn't complaining. Perhaps the forced cheer would push me towards being merry and bright.

Temptation to go and check out the new fictional arrivals was making me jittery, but I knew I needed to utilise my time to study. I headed towards the shelves lined with textbooks for every subject imaginable and searched until I found practice tests for each of my classes. I hated that the dance was before exam season because it seemed like we were getting excited only to be shoved back into reality on Monday.

Nonetheless, I needed to study. I had to ace all my exams.

After I got the books scanned using my student card, I found an empty seat at one of the study tables. I dumped the textbooks onto the table and flopped into the chair. I didn't know what to start with first; with six subjects and six exams, I had endless possibilities.

Chuckling at my own thoughts, I flipped open my Geography textbook and started to plan out my first batch of essays. It felt like my brain was suffocating under the mountain of information I was supposed to retain. It didn't seem possible that anyone could remember all the expected facts and figures that the exam board set out. Didn't they know that teenagers were screwed up and had plenty of drama going on in their lives? There wasn't any more space in my brain.

Dropping my pencil onto the open page, I gave up and let my head rest on the table. My eyes were heavy, and I had to force myself to stay awake. It seemed like I was always tired now; it didn't matter how much sleep I got.

———

Friday rolled in far quicker than I would have liked, and I was left feeling uneasy about the dance. I hated that I wasn't getting ready with Kate, and that I still didn't know what was going to happen with Benji. It was supposed to be a fun night out, but for me it was the most terrifying thing I had done in a long time, and I was not prepared.

Friday's classes passed by in a blur as the school hummed with anticipation. I avoided the crowds and talk of the dance as much as possible as I felt my anxiety soar beyond control. By the time the final bell rang, and the school was filled with the cheers of students, I had an uncontrollable shake in my right hand, and my left wrist was stinging from the tiny pierces my nails had caused.

Benji waited for me outside the classroom, pulling me into him the moment I was within reach.

He wrapped his arms around my waist and brought his face down to mine, his eyes alight with glee. "Are you excited, baby?"

I was too nervous to feel excited, but I didn't want to ruin his buzz. "Of course, I am!"

My overenthusiastic reaction seemed to be the answer he wanted, and he beamed at me before pulling me alongside him. I tried to relax my nerves as he walked me home, listening to him chat about how he couldn't wait to see me in my dress. I hoped that I looked as good in it as he wanted me to.

Once we reached my house, he pressed me against the door, his arms outstretched at either side of my head. A sly smirk made its way onto his face as he lowered his mouth to mine, his oxygen becoming mine. My fingertips traced across his jaw, keeping him in place. I let a small moan escape my lips and get lost somewhere in our kiss.

His body was pressed tight against mine, his ribs pressing into my stomach.

I wrapped my arms around his shoulders and smiled as he crushed against me, lost in his touch. My nerves dissipated as I focused on him and only him. The harsh blue of his eyes watched me and made me weak at the knees. I wished he would kiss me with such passion all the time. When he made me feel like I was the only person in the world, I couldn't think about anything other than him. My worries and fears disappeared, and I was left feeling like everything was right in the world.

Benji was first to break the kiss, groaning as he did so. He let his face hover over mine and his breath on my skin made my lips tingle. It felt like my whole body was beginning to flush, awakened by the feelings that Benji was stirring inside me.

I looked into his eyes and marvelled, thinking how lucky I was to have him. He could have easily chosen one of the other students who had been swooning over him at Apollo. Instead, he had sat next to me and changed my life.

"I can't wait to see you in your suit tonight," I whispered. "You're going to look like a dream."

"Like your dream I hope?" Benji countered.

"Well, you better not be in anyone else's dreams!"

"I can't help it if I'm irresistible, baby."

Benji chuckled and winked at me as he pulled away and started to walk from my door. I stared after him, feeling lonely even though I knew we were going to be together again in a mere two hours.

I leaned back and let the door support me as I watched him until he turned the corner of my street. It was only then that I realised how little time I had to get ready.

"Is that you, Emmeline?" Mum called as I made my way inside, dumping my back on the bottom stair.

I looked in the living room thinking she was sitting watching TV after work, but I couldn't see her. "Yes, Mum. It's me."

"I'm upstairs, darling! Come up here, please."

I trudged up the stairs and found her in her bedroom, perched on the bench in front of her vanity table. She was wearing pink jogging bottoms and a baggy sweatshirt, which surprised me. I hadn't seen my mum in casual clothes like that in years. Her hair was wrapped up in a floppy bun on top of her head and her face was bare, not a hint of makeup in sight.

I stared at her with my mouth hanging open, at a loss for words.

"Emmeline, it's rude to stare. What is it?"

"I... Um, are you okay, Mum?" I stammered, unsure how to phrase my question without causing offence.

Mum snorted and turned around to me; a false smile plastered on her face. "I'm fine. Now, are you ready for your dance this evening?"

I was taken aback by her apparently genuine interest.

Was I ready? Probably not.

"I think so. I'm just about to go and get ready. I am a little nervous though," I admitted.

Mum nodded and turned to rummage in her jewelery box.

I stood patiently, wondering if it was her way of dismissing me or if I was supposed to wait.

After a minute of plenty of mumbling and curses, she produced a long pendant. I gasped and covered my mouth as I took in all of its beauty. It was a silver teardrop adorned with the deepest sapphire stone, surrounded by tiny white diamonds. It was the most stunning piece of jewellery I had ever laid my eyes on.

"Wow, Mum! That's gorgeous."

Mum jumped from her chair and came over to me, her eyes glazed over with tears. She held her hands out, the necklace laid across her palms.

"Yes, it is. Your father bought me it for our first anniversary together and I treasured it so much. I figured you would like to borrow it for tonight since it matches your dress."

Tears pricked my eyes as she placed the necklace in my hands. It was even more beautiful close up, so many little delicate details in the metalwork. I was speechless that she would consider letting me wear it; perhaps there was a part of our lost mother-daughter relationship that we could still salvage.

"I'd love that, Mum. Thank you!"

She smiled and cupped my cheek gently. "I'm sure it would have made him very happy. Now go and get ready or you'll be late!"

Mum rounded and went back to sitting at her dressing table, patting her face with a cleansing wipe. It occurred to me that when Benji had mentioned Dad at our dinner and consequently dug up some old wounds, that it might have affected Mum more than I had first thought.

I wiped away my own tears and staggered into my room, clutching the necklace tight in my hands. I sat on the edge of bed and let myself sob, looking at the picture of Dad on the wall.

"Thank you," I whispered to him, feeling that he had somehow played a part in Mum allowing me to wear the necklace.

When I finally got myself together, I jumped in the shower and made sure that my entire body had been scrubbed to the inch of my life. My skin was gleaming, and my hair was a mass of wet curls by the time I exited, the scars on my body looking angrier than usual. I sighed and hoped they would calm down by the time I finished getting ready.

The first thing I had to do was try and style my hair. I pulled out my hair dryer and straighteners and got to work on ironing out the curls.

I searched my bedroom for the hairpiece I knew I had, before finding it hidden underneath my bed. It was a silver hairband with tiny dahlias placed across it strategically. I slid it behind my ears and looked at myself in the mirror.

I looked like a different person.

Next on my to-do list was a light layer of makeup. I wasn't much of a makeup person—mostly because I always ended up looking like a clown by the time I was finished—

but I figured the special occasion meant I should try and look pretty for once.

I searched my cupboard and found my bag of makeup buried beneath a bunch of cardigans and scarves.

I dumped the products out and tried to remember what to do first. In the end, I attempted to replicate the smoky eye look on my eyeshadow palette and topped it off with an imperfect winged eyeliner. A dusty pink lip completed the look.

As I applied a clear coat of gloss and puckered, I gazed at my reflection in the mirror and was almost pleased with how I looked. I wouldn't be on the same level as most of the other girls my age, but I felt prettier than usual.

My dress was hanging up in a bag at the back of my wardrobe and I unzipped it, lifting it out gently. I laid it flat across the bed and stood back, admiring my purchase.

Oh no, I thought, as I remembered I hadn't looked at underwear. What if I didn't have anything to match? If anything with Beni did happen, I wanted to at least have an underwear set that complemented each other.

I started to raid my drawers, throwing clothes across my bedroom floor until I finally found a matching black set. It was a gift from my mum for my birthday last year. I had opened it with a scowl, and she took offence; she'd thought it had been a good present because it was something she would have liked. But the lace and lack of material had made me frown, not to mention the gaudy silver embellishment.

I was cringing internally at the thought of actually wearing something so revealing, but it was the only matching underwear I had, so I didn't have a choice.

I slipped the lacy material on, feeling strange at the caress of it on my skin. Admittedly, it was more pleasant than I thought it would be. I clipped the bra at my back and adjusted my breasts in the cups, surprised that it fit perfectly. I walked over to the mirror and admired how it flattered my shape, enhancing my curves.

But as I spun around, the sight of my scars took me aback. For a second, I almost forgot I was screwed up.

My phone alarm beeped to let me know how little time I had left, and I let out a sigh. I was going to have to pretend that my scars didn't exist if I was ever going to leave the house.

I walked over to the bed and picked up my dress. It was time to do this.

—

By the time I had wriggled into my dress and fastened my heels, there was a loud knocking on the door. I swore and grabbed my clutch, trying to figure out if I had forgotten anything. Mum would hate having to do small talk with Benji—she had told me very bluntly that she did *not* like him and did not approve of my relationship. But I was practically an adult now and I could do as I pleased, she said.

I glanced back at my bedroom door before leaving and saw the photo of my dad on the wall. It felt like the smile on his face was more vibrant than usual and I grinned, blowing him a kiss. I held onto the beautiful pendant hanging around my neck and thanked him for sending me love from wherever he was.

My heels clicked against the laminate flooring as I walked across the landing, alerting my mother and Benji to my arrival. Both of them stood together at the bottom of the stairs to watch me walk down. My heart melted at the sight of Benji; he looked so dapper in his suit, his hair slicked back, and a single white rose in his buttonhole.

Mum clasped her hands under her chin and looked at me with a love I hadn't seen for a long time. "Emmeline, darling, you look gorgeous."

I reached the bottom of the stairs and took Benji's outstretched hand. He went to kiss me, and I shook my head, telling him not to mess up my makeup. It was hard enough to do the first time without having to try and replicate it. He rolled his eyes and the corner of his mouth tilted up into a smirk.

"I can't believe how different you look!" he exclaimed, spinning me around on the spot so he could see the full effect of my dress. "Absolutely beautiful."

My cheeks flushed, and I hoped my foundation was thick enough to cover any colour. "Don't you look handsome, too!"

Benji fidgeted with the collar of his shirt and winked at me.

Mum stepped forward and smiled. She shifted from foot to foot, and I wondered what she was going to do before she awkwardly tried to hug. I looked at Benji over her shoulder who just shrugged at me.

I couldn't remember the last time I had hugged my mother and I didn't particularly want to waste the opportunity. I wrapped my arms around her waist and enjoyed the moment, however random it was.

"If your father was here, he'd tell you how beautiful you are." She took a step back and smiled at me again, moving a bit of hair out of my eyes. "Have a good night, Emmeline."

"Thank you, Mum."

She nodded and patted my shoulder. "Curfew is off for tonight. Just be careful."

"Let's go, babe," Benji said as he pulled me along.

I gripped tight onto his arm as we walked, trying not to fall and break a bone. I was not used to walking in heels and I was terrified that I was going to trip.

When we stepped out of my front door, I almost cried when I saw what awaited us: parked at the end of our driveway was a huge black limo.

I turned to Benji and saw he was grinning from ear to ear. "You did this?"

He laughed and helped me walk across the driveway, opening the door for me to step into the limo.

I crawled inside, sliding along the seats into the centre. I had never been inside a limo before, but it was the most magnificent feeling. Tiny strings of lights were hung from the ceiling, illuminating the interior. A black partition separated us from the driver and there were buckets of iced drinks in between the blocks of seats.

I was star-struck by how amazing it was. Most of all, I couldn't believe my boyfriend had organised it.

"Benji, this is amazing!"

"I told you I'd pick you up, baby." He climbed in beside me, instantly taking my hand to interlock our fingers. "I wanted to surprise you."

"Best surprise ever. I can't believe you did this for me, Benji."

I leaned forward and placed a kiss on his cheek, laughing at the mark left behind by my lipstick.

I took a tissue from my clutch and wiped the smudge away.

"Fancy a drink?" Benji said as he reached for the open bottle of champagne beside him, wiggling his eyebrows at me.

I grimaced and shook my head. "I don't really drink."

He took a swig straight from the bottle and held it out to me. "Let go a little, Emmie. Everyone drinks at dances."

He shook the bottle, and I could hear it fizzing inside. I really didn't like drinking, but I did want to have the same experience as everyone else in regard to the dance.

I hesitated only a moment before accepting the bottle from him and taking a swig. I scowled and contorted my face as the bitter bubbles hit my tongue. Swallowing the liquid was like drinking poison, but I took another drink anyway. Wasn't drinking what normal teenagers did?

It was only a ten-minute drive to the school, and I was secretly disappointed that the journey had been so short because I wouldn't get to enjoy the experience of being in a limo longer.

I tapped my foot on the floor, taking another drink from the nearly empty bottle of champagne as Benji encouraged me to drink up before we arrived at the school.

As though sensing what I was thinking, Benji gently squeezed my hand. "I've booked it to wait to drive us home."

I let out an excited squeal and hugged him tight. "Benji, that's amazing! Thank you!"

The limo pulled up outside Apollo High and the chauffeur got out to open the door for us. Benji stepped out first and held his hand out for me to grip as I found my footing.

I staggered a little as the air hit me and I suddenly felt the impact of the champagne coursing through my veins. My dress draped down around my ankles, tickling the tops of my feet. I was grateful to have picked a dress that successfully covered up every inch of my skin, leaving me to feel confident enough to attend a dance in a dress for the first time.

As we got closer to the entry doors of the school, I could hear the thumping of music and cheering of students echoing through the building. Students gathered around the entry, some staggering inside, while others remained outside chatting to each other.

I looped my arm through Benji's elbow and took a deep breath before heading inside.

Although the corridors had been decorated for the past few weeks, more banners and streamers were draped from the ceiling now. The lights were dimmed so that the luminous arrows painted on the walls could direct us where to go.

My stomach did backflips as we reached the doors to the massive gymnasium which was doubling as the dance hall for the night.

Benji turned to me with a cheeky grin. "You ready for this, gorgeous?"

I laughed through gritted teeth and let out an unsteady breath. "Nope, but let's do it anyway!"

"That's what I love to hear," he said with a wink, throwing the door open.

I gasped as I looked around at the gym that I had visited so many times before. The student council had outdone themselves this year. The walls were lined with fairy lights and glittery snowflakes. Hanging from the ceiling were hundreds of globe lights and shining streamers, connecting in the centre where a huge faux-diamond chandelier lit up.

There were tables and chairs at the back, lined with party food and punch. Some of the teachers lingered about, but most were preoccupied with dancing to the upbeat music being played by the hired DJ on the built-up stage. The whole dance floor looked like a mosh pit as students jumped around to the music.

I stood at the door and watched as my peers chatted and danced, smiles and cheers everywhere I looked. The girls were all as perfect as I had expected them to be in their designer dresses, professional makeup, and hair as high as Amy Winehouse's.

I felt out of place in my too-plain dress and cheap makeup, but when Benji looked at me, I realised I didn't much care. I was here to have fun with my boyfriend, and I was determined to do that.

We descended into the hall and onto the dancefloor, getting swept up into the festive spirit. Benji wrapped his arms around my waist and spun me around, keeping a tight grip on me so I didn't trip over the length of my dress. I felt like I was going round in slow motion, the watching, the dancing and laughing taking place around me. The lights shone bright and blinded me as I twirled.

I threw my head back and laughed. It was a freeing moment to be dancing in the arms of my boyfriend, for once not caring about what others thought about me.

I wanted to enjoy the night as much as I could.

I wanted to feel free.

FIFTEEN

Astounding me completely, I found myself having more fun than I would ever have expected. The champagne made me giggle uncontrollably as I let loose, prancing about the dancefloor in Benji's arms like I didn't have a care in the world. The décor made me feel like I really was in a wonderland—although perhaps that was due to the alcohol consumption, too—and I thought to myself about how magical it all seemed.

I didn't know how long we had been dancing before my feet started to get sore.

I pressed my mouth to Benji's ear so he could hear me over the booming music. "I need to sit down!"

He nodded into my cheek and pulled me across the gymnasium until we reached the tables at the back of the hall. I slumped into the seat he pulled out for me and pulled off my heels.

"Ouch, those hurt when you wear them for too long. My feet are going to be wrecked tomorrow."

Benji chuckled and slid into the seat beside me, threading his fingers through mine. "I'm having such a great evening. This is the most fun we've ever had, Emmie."

I looked at him dreamily and tried to place a kiss on his lips, almost missing his face completely. He laughed and tucked a finger under my chin, pressing his lips to mine so I didn't have to try.

"Want some punch?"

I smiled gratefully at him. "Yes, please."

He jumped from his seat and left me sitting alone while he waited in the long queue for our drinks. I leaned back against my chair and observed the night unfolding around me. I spotted Tate and Penelope grinding together on the dancefloor and I wanted to vomit at the vulgar sight. The chaperones walked over to them, and I assumed it was to tell them to cool it off a bit, but they continued on as soon as the teacher walked away.

I peeled my eyes away before I could be scarred for life, and instead watched some of the younger students jumping around together. The huge grins and reckless dance moves made me smile. I couldn't remember ever being that happy or carefree, but I was glad they got to experience it. It was sad that we got tarnished by the reality of life as we grew up; I hoped they never lost those grins or that joyful innocence.

As I watched my fellow students dance, I became acutely aware of how different I was from everyone else. Even tonight, when I had tried so hard to blend in, I still managed to stand out. My hair was short and my makeup a rushed job, my dress cheap, and my heels from a high street store. The comparisons were endless, and I sensed that it would always be the same, no matter how hard I tried to change things.

I pulled my sleeves down further, trying to cover my hands with the material as far as it would go. I felt exposed all of a sudden, alone and facing the crowd. It didn't matter that my dress covered all my areas of issue, it wasn't enough. I felt like a fake, a child playing dress-up. I didn't belong and it was stupid to pretend I did.

My insecurities were ruining the one night I had to finally feel liberated, and I hated it.

My pulse quickened as the negative thoughts started to swirl about in my head. I bit down on my lip and tried not to cry, knowing it would ruin my makeup and I would end up looking like a panda—the last thing I needed was another reason to be mocked.

I was hanging on by a thread when the click-clack of stilettos sounded behind me.

I swivelled in my chair and came face to face with my former best friend.

"Kate," I greeted coldly.

She was a picture in a beautiful floor-length halter neck gown. It hugged tightly to her body, and the ruby colour complimented her warm, ivory skin tone perfectly. She was wearing a silver wig, tied into a bundle of curls at the back of her head. Braided through the front was a hairpiece similar to mine, and I was reminded of how similar we were, which made it hurt all the more that we were no longer friends.

Kate sighed and perched on the seat Benji had been in.

I glanced over at the drinks table and saw he was almost at the front of the queue. I prayed that he would be quick so I could have my support network. I couldn't face another minute without having him to rely on.

"It's good to see you, Emmie. You look amazing."

I chewed on my lip and tried to think of something to say. I wanted to tell her how much I loved and missed her, but it had been too long, and she didn't approve of my relationship. Everything had gotten so complicated so quickly.

Kate put her hand on my upper arm and twisted me around to look at her. "Emmie, come on. Please just speak to me."

The pleading tone of her voice broke my resolve, and I shook my head sadly at her. "I don't know what to say, Kate. A lot has happened."

"I know that. But I hate not speaking to you. Surely, we can fix this?"

Tears brimmed at the edges of her eyes, and I begged silently that she wouldn't cry. I hated seeing her upset. It always broke me. I had vowed never to let anyone make her cry, and here I was doing it myself.

"I hate not speaking to you too," I admitted sheepishly.

It was true. The past few months without her had been so difficult. I had needed her so many times; to talk to my best friend about my relationship dramas or whenever my mum was extra snippy.

She smiled and I watched as her eyes lit up, the sparkling lights reflected in them. "That solves it then! We absolutely need to fix this."

"Fix what?" came a familiar voice.

Benji smiled down at me before his eyes flickered to Kate, a harshness behind his stare.

"Excuse me, we're having a private conversation," Kate snapped.

I looked between the two of them and felt the tension accumulating around me. It was horrible to see the anger emanating from both of them, and I felt smaller than ever. Both turned to look at me, expecting me to defend one of them. I wasn't sure what to do or say, but I didn't have much of a choice.

I stood up and turned to Kate. "This is our problem, you know. Benji is my boyfriend and I'm not just going to cut him off for you. Benji can stay—this involves him, too."

She huffed and stood up, pushing her chair back. "Well, maybe you should reconsider that. He's not good for you. You think you were lonely before? You have nobody now!"

"She has me." Benji stepped behind me and wrapped his hands around my waist, clasping his hands on my stomach.

Kate flipped him off, her eyes ablaze as she spun on her heels and stormed off, exiting the hall.

I rested my head back against Benji's shoulder, letting my frustration wash away. Exhaustion was beginning to creep up on me, but I was adamant that I wasn't going to let anything ruin our night.

Benji nuzzled into the back of my neck, humming contently. "I'm so proud of you for standing up for us. I love you."

I was puzzled as to why he was proud of me for that because I felt absolutely rotten. It didn't seem right that I was saying goodbye to my childhood best friend, but she was the one making me choose. And I had to believe that I had made the right choice.

"I love you too," I mumbled back to him.

I collapsed back onto my chair and slumped onto the table.

Benji slid a cup across the table to me with a smile. "Drink something, baby. You'll be dehydrated from the heat and all the dancing."

It looked like a fruit punch, so I took a large gulp. Something didn't taste right in it though. I assumed the students I had overheard earlier in the week speaking about spiking it had been successful. I wasn't sure what was in it, but it burned the back of my throat and sent warmth through my limbs.

It was probably the alcohol talking, but I felt *happy*.

I must have been pulling a face because Benji chuckled as he watched me drink the rest of my cup. I didn't like the taste much, but I was thirsty and there wasn't anything else to drink. It made me feel more carefree, and I needed it to help me relax. There would be no way I would make Benji happy if I was an uptight grump all evening.

"Want to dance again?" he asked, wiggling his eyebrows at me.

I beamed at him and took his hand. "Let's go!"

I pulled him onto the dancefloor just as a slow song began to play. I wrapped my arms around his neck and pulled him into me, looking into his eyes. He stepped closer, and I inhaled the scent of his aftershave, my senses tingling.

… sweet sunshine, you are my love… my life… kiss me sweet and tender … never leave my side…

The sweet love song that was playing was the most beautiful of melodies, filled with passion and tenderness. It

182

was the song I would want to most represent the love story of my life, and I hoped that it was with Benji.

His eyes found mine and the edges of his crinkled as he beamed down at me.

I searched his gaze for the love I wanted to see reflected. I wanted to be sure that I was going to make the right decision after the dance because the more he danced with me and I felt him pressed against me, the more I found myself wanting to be with him in the same way he did. My barriers were breaking down the more I lost my inhibitions, and it was a glorious feeling.

There was a feeling at the back of my mind telling me I should be more concerned about being drunk, but I didn't quite care enough to listen to it.

Benji lowered his hands slowly, his fingers smoothing over the dress covering my backside.

I giggled into his shirt and feathered the hair at the back of his head. "Benji?"

"Mhm?"

The sound of his voice in my ear made me melt against him. "Want to get out of here?"

Benji picked me up and kissed me hard, his mouth crushing mine. "I want nothing more."

—

The limo ride back to Benji's house was filled with nervous anticipation. I was straddling his lap, our faces pressed close. My lips explored every inch of his face until we pulled up to the house. I untangled myself from him and shifted my dress back into position before we shimmied out of the car.

Benji placed my hand into the crook of his elbow and led me up the driveway. He fumbled in his pockets at the door trying to find his keys, barely managing to unlock the door.

I was surprised as we entered the house, and it was in complete darkness, despite it only being about ten o'clock.

"My parents took Anya away for the weekend," Benji explained as he brushed past me to switch a lamp on. "They wanted some family bonding time or something."

I blew Benji a kiss and started my ascent to his bedroom, beckoning for him to follow. I deliberately didn't turn the light on—a subconscious part of my brain still sober enough to remind me of the ugliness of my body—but Benji hit the light switch as he came in behind me.

His bedroom was in complete disarray; clothes strewn across the floor, books and stationary cluttering the bed. It was like an obstacle course as I kicked off my shoes and tried to find my way to the bed without falling. Benji pulled the throw and the items off the bed, letting them clatter to the floor.

I sat on the edge of the bed and chewed on my lip. I could feel the nervousness starting to seep back into me, and I was no longer as forthright as I had been in the limo.

Benji pulled his suit jacket off and sat beside me, placing a hand on my thigh.

"You looked so beautiful tonight."

I chuckled and rested my hand on top of his, my thumb circling the soft skin on the back of his hand. "You looked rather dashing yourself."

He lifted his hand and slowly reached out to sweep some of my curls away from my eyes. He held his hand beside my cheek, staring at me intensely. "I love that you're mine."

Benji lowered his face to mine, his lips hovering in front of mine. I held my breath as our lips met and he pressed forward, pushing his tongue into my mouth. I could taste the bitterness of champagne on his tongue as our mouths merged.

His hands brushed against my shoulders, pushing me onto my back, and I obliged. He came with me, propped on his elbow, his lips never leaving mine.

I was in his bed. I was probably going to have sex.

My mind raced as a thousand thoughts ran around, a list of worries and fears bombarding me with doubt. What if I wasn't good at it? What if he wasn't good at it? Did he know what he was doing? Would I?

I played the scenarios out in my head and tried to think of the best solutions for each problem I imagined. But there was one question that I couldn't find an answer for, no matter how deeply I searched for it.

What if I wasn't ready to have sex?

"Breathe, baby. You're okay," he whispered to me in a low, sultry voice.

I took a deep breath and looked into his bright eyes, hoping I could find some reassurance there. My fingers found their way into his blonde, slicked back locks. I tousled them and smiled as his hair became the messy mass of curls I was used to. There was comfort in the familiar, I guessed.

Benji trailed his lips down my neck, placing delicate kisses across my collarbone. I closed my eyes and told myself to relax and enjoy the feeling. My body was still on high alert from the extra steamy make-out session in the limo, and I tried to tell myself to get back to that point again. Having sex was a normal thing, so why couldn't I just relax and enjoy it?

Benji pushed himself up and pulled his shirt over his head, revealing his torso. He was surprisingly toned despite never going to the gym. I sucked in a breath as I examined every inch of his exposed chest. I reached out to him tentatively, lightly feeling the smooth skin leading to his stomach.

"Like what you see?" he said with a wink, climbing over me so his legs were at either side of my hips.

185

My body was betrayed my mind as something stirred inside me. I wanted to press my lips to his chiselled chest and feel the beating of his heart against my mouth.

Benji pushed his hands under me, and I felt my dress unzip, the material being pulled away from me.

I felt the urge to reach out and grab Benji's arms to stop him from pulling it any further, but I didn't quite have the nerve to do it. Our relationship had been building up to this moment and if I stopped him, it would mean I was nothing but a tease.

He pried the dress from my shoulder and slipped it down, tugging it from under my legs. It fell to the floor on top of a pile of clothing and I pondered that I often felt as easily discarded as that.

I felt too bare as his eyes worked their way up my body, taking in every imperfection and mark. His hungry smile faltered as he saw the words carved into my skin.

"Jesus, what the fuck did you do to yourself?"

This was a mistake. I should've never let him see me. I wriggled uncomfortably and closed my eyes, folded my arms across myself.

Why couldn't he have just left the lights off?

His soft hands curled around my wrists, peeling my arms away from my chest. "Look at me."

I opened my eyes slowly, biting on my lip. He climbed on top of me again, his weight resting on his shins as he hovered over my hips. He gazed down at me, licking his lips.

"I've waited so long for this," he groaned.

His fingers blazed a hot trail as they brushed over the lace of my bra, pulling the cups down to expose my breasts. He let out a low moan, bringing his lips down to my chest. His mouth circled my nipple, sucking on the tender skin, his tongue working hard to send shivers down my spine.

I imagined it should have felt like pure ecstasy, but it was strange, his teeth digging in too much, his breathing too heavy on me.

I held my breath and tried to avoid making a sound as he derived pleasure from his own actions, a low growl emanating from his lips. I couldn't deny him what he had been denied so long—my only option was to let him take what he needed. It was a sacrifice I had to make. Whenever he glanced up at me, expecting a reaction, I hummed to feign pleasure. The sooner he got what he wanted, the sooner it would be over.

I just wanted it to be over.

His tongue made its way downward, stopping just before my scars. His face twitched and he brought himself back up to meet me, a chaste kiss placed upon my lips.

He climbed off me and unbuttoned his trousers, pulling his boxer shorts down with them. My attention lingered between his legs. This was happening. I felt nauseous, wishing I hadn't ever encouraged this.

Benji winked and kneeled at the bottom of the bed between my legs. He ripped a condom open with his teeth and slipped it over his length.

My breath hitched as he reached up, his fingers brushing my inner thighs. and pulling the delicate fabric of my underwear down my legs. He nudged my legs open with his knee and crawled back onto the bed; his body pressed against mine.

He placed a hand on either side of my head and propped himself up, bringing his lips down my neck where he explored with his tongue. He started to move against me, his length rubbing against my thigh. He was engrossed by what he was doing, his face never leaving the crook of my neck.

But I wasn't enjoying myself. I stared up at the ceiling and wondered why. Wasn't this supposed to be the fun part of being in a relationship? Was I really so abnormal that I couldn't even enjoy sex?

Benji bit on the small of my shoulder before thrusting himself into m. The action was so unexpected, the pain so sudden, it caught me off guard and I shrieked.

Benji mistook it for a sound of pleasure and started moving faster. He grabbed my wrists, pinning them above my head.

"You feel so good, baby," he panted into my ear.

I gritted my teeth and dug my fingers into the duvet as he pounded. The skin between my thighs burned, the hair on his legs aggravating my skin. hated the warmth of his breath beating down on my neck, hated the sounds coming from his throat.

"Benji," I said as I tried to pull my wrists free. "Benji, I can't do this. I need you to stop. *Please.*"

He let go of my wrists only to grab my breasts, squeezing them too tightly, his nails digging into my tender skin. My mind flashed back to Tate and the way he had grabbed me—it felt the *same* and I had to swallow down the bile that rose to my throat.

Benji paid no attention to the squirming of my body and lack of any sign of satisfaction; he was focused entirely on his own fulfilment.

As he moved against me, his grunts low and breathless in my ear, I knew how much of a mistake I was making. I wasn't ready to have sex, but now it was too late. He was already ripping away at my virtue; the last part of myself that I could keep safe from the tarnish of anyone else was now lost to me and I would never be able to get it back.

"Benji, please stop," I sobbed, my voice breaking.

I wanted to shove him off from me and run. I wanted to never see or speak to him again. He had taken something from me, and I would never be the same.

I wanted to hate him. I wanted it to be his fault. I was in pain, and he was causing it.

But I was letting him do it. I wasn't stopping him.

If I was going to hate anyone, I would hate myself.

Benji let out a loud moan, his body going limp on top of me.

Before I could make sense of what had happened, he pulled out of me roughly and rolled over, lying beside me on top of the duvet.

I felt a surge of sickness well inside me again, but I swallowed it, trying not to let the vomit rise in my throat.\I was worthless. Weak. Now every part of me was disgusting, from the inside out.

He fumbled for my hand, uncurling my fingers from the duvet to link our fingers. "That was so good. Did you enjoy yourself?"

"Mhmm," I whispered.

I sat up in bed, trying not to press my thighs together, knowing it would sting. I fumbled around and tried to find my underwear. Tears pricked at my eyes as I clipped my bra back on and pulled my dress over my head.

Benji put his hand on my arm. "Where are you going?"

"Home," I croaked, my voice shaking.

"What? Why?" His grip tightened on my arm as he pulled me around. "You're leaving so quickly?"

I yanked my arm free and stood up, letting the skirt of my dress fall into place, covering up what had just happened. I took comfort in having material to cover my body again, to be able to hide from the world.

"I need to get home. Mum will worry if I'm out much longer."

"I heard your mum say you could come home anytime." Benji hopped up from the bed and pulled his boxers on, standing in front of me. I couldn't hide my face from him, and I wiped the tears away. He rolled his eyes, crossing his arms. "Why are you crying?"

"It's nothing."

He laughed bitterly and shook his head at me. "You shouldn't be the one crying."

I screwed my face up. "What's that supposed to mean?"

He laughed again. "Well, that was literally the worst lay I've ever had. So, it should be me crying, not you."

I stifled a sob and tried to push past him, but he grabbed onto my arm, his fingers digging into my wrist.

"You're hurting me!"

He glared down at me, his eyes empty of the love and compassion they normally held. "That's awfully rude of you to just fuck me and then go. You haven't even apologised for giving me the worst sex in my life. You just lay there, lifeless, while I was trying to give you an amazing experience."

I squirmed, trying to wrestle myself free. "Let me go. Please!"

My eyes stung as my mascara smeared down my face, mixing with my tears. He snarled at me but let me go, pushing me slightly as he did so. I stumbled backwards, twisting on my ankle. I tripped back, falling on top of a pile of books. Screaming, I held my back where it had hit off the corner of a hardback. Benji stood above me, just watching it play out before him.

Quickly, I grabbed my heels and clutch bag from the floor and pushed myself up. I turned my back on Benji, sobbing as I hobbled out of his room and stumbled down the stairs. He followed me out, an uncomfortable presence watching me as I moved. I ran as fast as I could, wincing as my ankle continued to give way beneath me.

Once I was out of his street and away from his gaze, I collapsed against the wall of a building, weeping into the sleeve of my dress.

SIXTEEN

By the time I got home, I was a broken and beaten mess. The soles of my feet were cut from walking without shoes. My body was numb—I couldn't tell if it was from the cold winter wind, or if it was from heartbreak.

The front door to the house was unlocked and all the lights on, and for once I was glad my mum was home. I found her sprawled on the couch in the living room watching a Christmas movie, a bowl of salted popcorn in her lap.

She glanced up when I came in. "Emmie!"

She threw her blanket and popcorn to the floor when she saw me. I fell to my knees in front of her and she dropped down with me. She wrapped her arms around me and clutched me close, rocking me back and forth as I sobbed into her chest.

She spoke softly to me, smoothing down my hair as she held me. "What happened, Emmeline?"

I opened my mouth to speak but no words came out.

How could I explain to her that I had betrayed myself? I had trusted someone I thought I loved, and I had been left devastated in return. I was heartbroken and in pain. Worst of all, I had nobody to blame for it but myself.

I shook my head and she nodded, humming softly to me until my sobs eased. I felt dirty and nauseous as she held me in her arms; I wanted to get clean but perhaps for the first time in my life, I was finding comfort in my mother, and I didn't want to give that up.

Mum cupped my face in her hands and wiped away my tears, searching my eyes for some hint of what happened. "Did someone do this to you? Do I need to call someone?"

191

My blood chilled at the idea of anyone else knowing about what happened, so I emphatically shook my head, my eyes pleading. "No. Please, no. I just need some rest."

She pursed her lips, contemplating whether to pacify me or take action despite my request. "Very well, Emmeline. But I would like for you to tell me what happened, at some point." I nodded and hugged her tight. "Go and get yourself cleaned up. Do you need help?"

"No, thank you. I can manage."

I stood slowly to try and regain my balance, groaning slightly as my feet touched the carpet. My body ached and I wanted to crawl into my bed and never leave it again.

As I reached the doorframe, I clung to the wall and turned back to my mum. She was watching after me with careful consideration and I found myself saying words I hadn't said out loud for the longest time.

"I love you, Mum."

Her eyes widened as my words hit her. She looked almost as surprised to hear them as I was to say them. She stuttered a reply, taken aback by my sudden burst of emotion towards her. "I love you too, Emmeline."

I climbed the stairs almost on my knees, trying to prevent having to walk on my battered and bloody feet.

I crawled into the bathroom and started to run the hot water, filling the bath with salts and essential oils. A sweet aroma filled the air and flooded my nostrils. It appeared to be too strong a smell for my stomach to handle, bile rising in my throat and burning my mouth. I leaned over the toilet bowl and vomited the entire contents of my stomach, the alcohol in my system making it feel like acid.

Once the bath was full and piping hot, I tore the dress from my body. It felt good to hear the material rip apart, falling to the floor with a thump. I pulled off my underwear and shoved them into the small waste basket underneath the sink, eager to get rid of the memory of tonight but knowing it wouldn't be so easy.

I looked down at my body and felt disgusted at myself. My thighs were raw, chaffed from the harsh movements. Stepping into the bath, I winced as the water scolded my skin. Despite the extreme heat, I lowered myself into the water and gritted my teeth to prevent myself from squealing—I'd endured far worse tonight already. It wasn't hot enough to cause serious burns to my body, but it did allow me some measure of punishment, letting me teach myself a lesson for my foolish decisions.

The salts worked their way into the open wounds on my legs, cleaning out only a little of the dirt I wanted to wash away. There was a new body scrub in packaging on the bathroom cabinet and I ripped it open to expose the rough loofah. I dipped it into the bath water before scrubbing at my body. I scoured my body with the loofah, scraping it into my skin as much as possible.

I didn't realise I was crying until my tears splashed down, causing ripples in the water. I let out a scream and listened as the aching in my voice echoed around me, chilling my bones.

Whenever I closed my eyes, I saw Benji's bedroom ceiling, felt his rough hands grabbing at me, felt him pounding into me. Fingerprints were visible across my breasts and wrists, physical marks for the turmoil in my brain. I was reminded of Tate's brutality and the similar marks he had left on me. I would never have entertained the thought of them being alike in any way. I cursed myself for being so unbelievably wrong.

I held my breath and slipped under the surface, bubbly water clinging to my hair and flooding over my face. I closed my eyes again and stared at the blackness behind my lids, wondering if that was what death felt like. The silence which would have once seemed eerie was now a welcome comfort.

Was the end more peaceful than the torment of my life?

A muffled knocking broke my trance. "Emmie?"

I leaped from the bath, gasping for air. I quickly grabbed the towel and wrapped it around myself, wiping my face.

I opened the door to find my mother holding a mug of my favourite tea: honey and cinnamon. I took it from her hands and took a grateful sip of the hot beverage.

"Are you okay?"

I did my best to smile. "I'm fine, Mum."

She nodded and pursed her lips. "It's just... You've been in the bath for a while. I just thought I should check on you."

I took a long gulp of my tea and awkwardly reached out to pat her arm. "I'm okay, Mum. I just wanted to make sure I was clean. I'm going to go to bed now."

She opened her mouth, but I brushed past her and made my way into my bedroom, shutting the door behind me with a click. I slipped my robe off and shoved on some of my baggy pyjamas, slipping my feet into a pair of extra fluffy socks.

As I clambered into bed and wrapped the thick layers of bedding around my shoulders, I became overly aware of how fragile I felt. I propped my pillows up against the headboard and leaned my head against the wall. I looked up at the lightshade on my ceiling, and I realised I didn't think I would ever be able to lay down and sleep again. This one decision had ruined so many things.

I was broken and I would never be able to feel anything else.

Numbness was once again my closest friend.

—

The next day dragged with an unbearable amount of silence for me to contemplate the things wrong in my life. If I let myself have the freedom to think about anything for even a second, my mind would immediately go to the single most horrid experience of my life, and I would be left feeling even more distraught than before. It left me in an awful and lonely state of shock to think that losing a parent was no longer the most traumatic thing to happen to me.

The chat with my mother thankfully never occurred as she was rushed into work. I wondered if it would have been better if I had spoken to her about what happened; would it have made me feel better? I had the suspicion it would have been worse.

Monday crashed into me like a bulldozer. I considered skipping school and avoiding Benji and his onslaught of calls for as long as possible—maybe my mum would forgive the one day of truancy after seeing me in such a mess—but my upcoming exams were enough to convince me otherwise.

I picked out the baggiest clothes I owned and dressed quickly, avoiding looking at myself. I had an old stretched-out beanie hat at the back of my drawers, so I pulled it out and shoved it over my head, covering up the matted mess of greasy curls which was starting to resemble a bird's nest.

I walked as slowly to school as possible, dragging my feet along the ground. I arrived with five minutes to spare and resigned myself to being in hell for every one of those minutes. The grounds around the school were almost empty, everyone already making their way inside, crowding the hallways before they made their way to class.

The chatter in the corridors stopped abruptly as I entered through the doors, all of the students turning their eyes to me. I took a step forward, wondering if perhaps it was what I was wearing, but their stares followed me as I continued to walk in. The people behind me began to whisper and I wondered what had been said now to make me once again the talk of the school. I didn't believe that I had made a fool of myself during the dance—everyone would have been too inebriated to notice if I had anyway—and the events afterwards were a private hell that would haunt only me and Benji for the rest of our lives.

195

I bit down hard on my lips as I walked through the hallways, finding it bizarre the way the students moved out of my way to let me have free passage. I ignored the way my body still ached, my feet throbbing as I disturbed the wounds which had only just started to heal and headed towards my locker.

People around me sniggered and whispered behind my back, which was something I had become accustomed to, but it felt different today. Instead of the usual taunting, an uneasiness crept over my skin as though I was missing out on a private joke.

I curled my fingertips into the palm of my hands and felt the familiar touch of my nails finding their marks, keeping me grounded as I tried to ignore being the amusement of my peers for yet another day. I could survive the day and run home as fast I could, being enveloped by the comfort that only my bed could bring.

Clusters of students surrounded my locker, parting like the Red Sea as I walked towards it.

Laughter echoed around me as they anticipated my reaction to the graffiti on the door. It didn't register at first what the doodles carved into the red paint were; the jagged lines just looked like scrapes from a car key.

It wasn't until I was standing directly before the locker that I saw what it really was: imitations of my scars.

The words *ugly* and *freak* were etched into my door.

My lip quivered as I stared at the markings, knowing that only one person had been close enough to see the scars to be able to mimic them. Underneath the words was *freak* carved into the paintwork in a scrawl that I recognised from seeing during homework dates after school.

My stomach knotted as I imagined Benji taking time to paint such a vile picture; I could see the bitterness in his eyes as his lips curled viciously. How had things changed so dramatically? I couldn't believe that my life had gotten worse; I thought I had already hit an all-time low.

I turned around, my vision blurry, seeing the judgemental looks in everyone's eyes as they examined my reaction to what I had just seen. Surely, they didn't know about my scars. They would probably just make assumptions, but nobody could know for sure...could they?

"Emmie!" A familiar voice yelled from down the hall.

I spun around and tried to recognise the figure among the crowds as she made her way to me.

Kate grabbed me by the wrist and pulled me forward, pushing some of the younger students out of her way. She dragged me along the corridors until we reached one of the girls' bathrooms, yanking me inside and standing guard behind the door.

"What in the actual fuck, Emmie?" Kate threw her arms up angrily and I wrapped my arms around myself, feeling a wave of nausea that I was accustomed to.

I shifted weight from one foot to the other, telling myself to breathe. "What?"

"Show me your arms."

I dipped my head and sighed. "No."

Kate groaned and rubbed at her cheeks. "You know that Benji is going about the whole school telling people that you've sliced yourself to pieces, right? Tell me he's wrong."

My insides clenched together, knotting up in an attempt to stop me from vomiting where I stood. No wonder everyone was laughing and talking about me behind my back. They had been told the one thing in my life that I had kept private from everyone. Trusting Benji had been a mistake, and I should have known that from the beginning.

"He's lying," I managed to croak out, my voice barely a whisper.

Kate shook her head and looked at me through her layers of thick painted eyelashes. "I know you, which means I can see it when you lie to me. Out of all the messed-up things you've done recently, I can't believe you would abuse yourself like that."

I couldn't bear to see the frustration in her eyes as she stared at me, her lips pursed tightly together to stop her from saying things she'd later regret. I felt like I was suffocating; a bird locked in a wooden cage, no way of escaping from the prison it was trapped in. I felt like I would never be free again.

My body throbbed with pain, and I couldn't decipher whether I was still hurting from the rough sex with Benji, or if it was a physical reaction to the storm happening around me. It didn't really matter—as long as I was confined to the walls of Apollo High, I wouldn't feel better.

I barged past Kate, shoving her slightly so I could pull open the door. She opened her mouth to protest but I shot her a glare that welcomed no retorts.

The hallways were still busy with students waiting on the bell to sound as I exited the bathroom. I hung my head and tried to make my way outside as quickly as I could, telling myself to shut out the sniggering and demands to see my wrists.

If Benji wanted to humiliate me further, he had succeeded tenfold. I just didn't understand what he could possibly be getting out of destroying my life; I had nothing left. No one.

I was alone.

The cold air wrapped around me, enveloping me in a cool embrace as I ran home. My sides ached from the exercise and my lungs burned as I panted, desperate to make it home before I saw anyone else. I wouldn't be able to keep it together much longer and so I had to get home as fast as I could.

I breathed a sigh of relief when I got home and saw that Mum was still at work.

The house seemed eerily quiet, and I wondered if it was because of how I was feeling, or if I just hadn't realised how empty it had become after my dad died. Life had started to lose its beauty after that.

I made my way upstairs and flopped on top of my duvet. Even my bedroom felt different as I glanced around at the four walls that had previously provided me protection from everything that hurt me; now they were just structures confining me to a life I no longer wanted.

My hands twitched as my gaze fell upon my bedside table. Despite the drawer being closed, I could see my kit as clearly as though it were in front of me. Thoughts swirled around in my head, whispering to me like demons bargaining for a soul. I licked my lips, my mouth dry as I pondered what I was going to do.

I climbed out of bed and took my kit out, laying it all out in front of me in the same order as usual. The sun shone through my bedroom window, rays stretching across my room and catching on the silver surface of my razor blade. I looked down at the glinting piece of metal; I could barely take my eyes off it, as though it had called to me and had found a way to grip onto my soul. The room around me faded away and all I was left with was the kit before me, and my pain.

I closed my eyes and tried to block it out, attempting to think back to a time before my world had been consumed by darkness. But I couldn't think of a single moment, my happiest memories now replaced by the bitter void in my heart. Going on family trips; my dad making his infamous French toast; learning to ride bikes with Kate—all of them had soured. Sadness had slowly crept into every orifice of my mind until everything was shades of grey, tainted by despair.

My body ached as I tried to block out the horrors in my mind, remembering each time I felt someone's hands on my skin, grabbing it greedily as though they owned me.

Though the bruises and suffering I had endured by the hands of others was nothing compared to the inner turmoil they had left me with.

I thought I knew what loneliness was, but I couldn't have prepared for the way true isolation made me feel. I was nothing but an empty shell of a person, bitterness and sorrow the only things left coursing through my veins.

Blinking, I allowed myself to look down again. The blade called to me as it had before, the coldness of the metal a welcome touch to my fingertips as I picked it up and examined the sharp edge. My skin tingled in anticipation, sensing what was coming, and I tried not to frown at how screwed up I had made my body.

Everyone knew about the cuts and scars now, and I wouldn't be able to hide it anymore. There was something so wrong with me and I just wanted it all to go away.

I was never going to be normal, so what was the point?

I took a deep breath, slowly exhaling until I had nothing left. I only had one option and it was going to be the most difficult thing I ever had to do, but I didn't have a choice. I had to end it and let everyone get on with their lives. Suicide was my only way out.

Putting everything back into the pouch except for the razor, I propped myself up with my pillows. If I was going ahead with my plan, I wanted to make myself comfortable. It would be the last time I would ever be in my home, in the safe space of my bedroom.

I glanced around my bedroom for a final time, smiling as the picture of my dad caught my eye. He smiled back at me, the warmth in his eyes making me want to cry, but I wouldn't because I was going to be strong. Life had no guarantees, but something in my gut told me I was going to see that smile of his and fall into his loving arms again soon.

Perhaps what I was planning was selfish, but seeing my father again was worth everything awful anyone had ever said about me.

I closed my eyes, taking a few moments to focus on my breathing before I brought the razor to my wrist. I hissed through my teeth as the blade opened the skin. The heat of my blood trickled down my arm and I bit down on my lip. I struggled to switch the razor into my other hand to make an identical cut down my other wrist.

When I was finished, I dropped the blade onto the bed and slumped back against the soft cushioning of my pillows. Pain hummed through me, pulsing in my veins; I found it bizarre that my body felt more alert as I was letting my blood pour from me, than it did normally.

I didn't know if I believed in God—why would He or She ever let such horrible things happen in the world if they were an all-powerful being capable of changing them—but I truly hoped there was an afterlife. It mattered to me more than anything that I would be able to reunite with my father again and be welcomed into a better existence than the one I was leaving.

My eyes became heavy as my blood soaked into my duvet, leaving a crimson stain that would never be able to be removed. After a while, the pain that I felt started to disappear and a strange calmness washed over me. I took a final glance at the picture on the wall and smiled before letting the abyss envelop me.

I'll see you soon, Dad.

SEVENTEEN

Light shone through my curtains, waking me out of my sleep. I glanced to the photo of my dad like I did every morning, furrowing my brows to see it missing. Had I brushed past it and knocked it over without realising?

A male voice was singing Paradise City out of tune, and I rolled my eyes. Surely, Mum hadn't left the radio on again? She was so bad at leaving it on while she went off to get dressed for work.

I sat up with a groan and stretched my arms above my head, but something tickled my back.

My first thought was that there was a spider and I panicked. I reached around, praying that I wouldn't touch a hairy eight-legged creature, and almost gasped in surprise as my hair fell halfway down my back. I scooped a few strands over my shoulder, blinking at the blonde hair.

Hadn't I chopped this all off and dyed it brown months ago?

I threw my duvet off my legs and stood up. I glanced down at the white nightgown I was wearing and smirked. What had I been thinking when I picked this out?

The house seemed bright as I left my bedroom, a warm white emanating from all of the windows. It was nice to see such a bright light despite the time of the year—normally Apollo remained dull throughout the entirety of the winter months.

Making way into the kitchen, I rounded the corner prepared to turn off the radio but stopped dead in my tracks.

Standing at the counter with a you're-the-best mug was my father.

My mouth gaped as I stared at him, watching as his fingers tap against his mug in rhythm with his singing.

"Dad?"

My voice was barely a whisper. I didn't dare believe that he was really with me.

He stopped singing and looked up at me, his eyes crinkling as a smile spread across his face. "Emmie-bear!"

I blinked rapidly in a poor attempt to stop the tears from falling. I hiccupped and ran into his arms, burying my face against his chest.

He chuckled and wrapped his arms tight around me, holding me close. He still smelled like a mix between cedar and coffee, and I inhaled, wishing I could bottle the scent and savour it forever.

He pressed his lips to the top of my head. "Let's sit down, petal."

Reluctantly, I unwrapped my arms from around his waist and took a seat at the kitchen island.

I wiped the tears from my eyes and laughed as I spotted the wet patch on his t-shirt. "I ruined your top."

He looked down and smirked before sitting beside me. "Worth it for one of your hugs."

I smiled and placed my hands on the countertop. I glanced down absentmindedly, noticing large scars on the inside of my wrists. I couldn't quite remember what had happened, but it looked sore.

I traced over the mark on my right wrist tenderly, my fingertips brushing lightly on the scar. As I touched the skin, my body ignited with my memories that flooded back through me.

I looked up at my father, my lip quivering as I remembered what I had done.

"I did this to myself?"

Taking my hands into his, he squeezed softly. "I'm afraid so, petal."

I let out a strangled sob. "Oh God, what have I done, Daddy?"

"Hush, now. It's okay," he told me. "You had your reasons."

My stomach dropped. My dad knew what had happened—what I had done. I looked up, my sight blurry from the onslaught of tears. "You know?"

"Sweet girl, did you think I would ever leave your side? I am so sorry you've been through everything you have. You deserve better than the life you've been given."

I didn't know what hurt more: knowing what I had done to myself or knowing that my dad had watched me do it. Despite myself, I couldn't help but feel relieved. I had achieved what I had set out to do. I no longer had to suffer.

As though he could sense what I was thinking, my dad shook his head and patted my arm. "This isn't the end for you, you know."

I furrowed my brows and looked at him. Surely, I was dead if I was with him? There was no going back.

"What do you mean?"

Dad reached out and tucked a curl behind my ear, his eyes home to a thousand different emotions. "You can go back, petal."

I shook my head in disbelief, pulling away from his hand. "Don't be ridiculous."

To my surprise, he let out a chuckle as he ran a hand through his dark hair. "Oh, how I've missed you, Emmie."

"I've missed you too, Dad. That's why I'm not going back. I'm staying here. With you."

"That doesn't mean that you belong here. You need to go back, petal." His voice was cautious as he spoke, and I could see his heart break just as much as mine.

I shook my head fervently. "No, I want to stay with you. There's nothing left for me there."

He smiled ruefully. "Emmie, there is so much left for you to do. I want nothing more than to be with you again, but you don't belong here. Not yet. You still have a lot of living to do, and there's a whole other life waiting for you when you return."

"No."

"Stubborn as always, I see," he chuckled. "But this isn't up for discussion. I won't let you throw your life away."

"What life?" I threw my hands up in frustration. "I have no friends, Mum hates me, and my boyfriend... I've never been more alone so why would I want to go back to that?"

"Because I'm telling you that it won't always be that way, Emmie. You won't always feel hurt and alone. There's so much love in you, and I know that there's an amazing future waiting there for you. But you need to live to see it."

Tears rolled down my cheeks as I fumbled for his hands, squeezing them as tight as I could for fear that he would let go and leave me again.

"Please don't make me go."

A tear fell from his own eyes, and he brought my hands to his lips, placing a chaste kiss on the back of my hand. "If there was any other way, I would have you with me in a heartbeat. But this is how it has to be."

Letting go of me, he stood and made for the door, his scent lingering in the air where he had sat. I sobbed, choking down the urge to scream, watching as he turned around at the door.

"Just remember something, Emmie. There aren't enough stars in the sky that could amount to your worth. Don't ever let anyone tell you that you don't matter, because you are all that matters. I love you, petal."

I closed my eyes, willing him to stay. I prayed to whoever was out there—to whoever had led me here and let me see him again—just to let me stay with the only person who had ever made me feel protected and safe.

When no reply came and the doorway stood empty, a scream ripped from my throat until I had nothing left.

205

I couldn't do it again. I couldn't be alone.

I sank to the floor, letting the tears fall and wash away the pain of losing my father for the second time.

When the light started to fade and the abyss whispered to me again, I welcomed whatever reprieve it offered. I didn't notice when the world cut to black, and I was pulled back into the life I had tried to escape.

EIGHTEEN

Beep.
Beep.
Beep.

The noise of a monitor beeping awoke me from a slumber. I let out a breathless groan, waves of pain rushing through my veins as I moved. My eyes were heavy, and I struggled to open them, the lids stuck together with slick layers of sweat.

I reached out, expecting to find my phone next to me with the alarm buzzing, but instead my hand hit a bar instead.

Finally peeling my eyes open, I gasped at the sight of my bandaged wrists. I felt as though someone smacked me in the face as it hit me what had happened, visions of my bloody duvet and the musky smell of my father in my nose. It took me a moment to fully comprehend what had happened, and a further moment to realise that silent tears dripped onto my hospital gown.

My body throbbed from head to toes, but I managed to push myself up into a sitting position, thankful for the tight bandages on my wrists as I felt the wounds threaten to open. I glanced around the room, sickened by the smell of acidic sanitizer. My eyes burned with the smell of bleach, the odour tickling the back of my throat.

The room was too bright, the walls the brightest white, and the bed sheet covering me a shade of ivory. Machines were plugged in beside my bed, one hooked up through an intravenous drip and feeding into the crook of my arm. Something was clamped around, monitoring my heart rate, but most machines looked far too complicated for me to fathom what they were for. They beeped continually and

207

after a while, I found myself drifting back into the unconscious, lulled by the same noise which had disturbed my earlier sleep.

—

When I next awoke, I found a nurse pressing the keys on one of the machines. Her lips were pressed in a thin line as she concentrated, which made her look far older than I would have estimated her to be. Her honey-coloured hair was swept up into a tight ponytail, and she wore a thin layer of mascara to highlight the amber hue of her eyes.

She startled when she noticed I was awake. "Sorry, doll. I didn't know you were up. How are you feeling?"

She had a thick accent—Polish, if I wasn't mistaken—and I couldn't help but return the smile she had flashed me, even if it made my cheeks hurt. "Like death."

Apparently, my joke was insensitive because the corners of her mouth dropped, and she patted my hand. "It'll get better soon, doll. The pain doesn't last forever."

I caught sight of the nametag on her tunic. "Thank you, Lena."

"You're welcome. Are you feeling up to a visitor? Your mother is outside."

"Not really," I groaned. Shame ate at my insides. Not only had my suicide attempt failed, but now I had to face my mum when it was the last thing I needed. "But send her in. I guess I should face her sooner or later."

Lena nodded and patted my hand again before leaving the room. I could hear her speaking to someone outside. A moment later, my mother walked in. She wore a pair of tight black jeans and a flowered red blouse, complete with red lipstick and a curled ponytail. She clicked into the room, her hair swishing as she walked.

"Emmeline, darling," she whispered as she perched on the edge of the seat beside my bed.

Despite her layers of foundation and powder, I found that she looked rather pale in comparison to usual. She blew a heavy breath and finally brought her eyes to meet mine. I couldn't quite decipher the look on her face; it was like a mix between disappointment and grief—both tugged at my heart in ways I hadn't expected, and I couldn't help but feel a little ashamed.

"How do you feel?"

I attempted to shrug but a sharp pain shot through my arm, and I hissed through clenched teeth. "Tired. Sore."

Mum nodded. "I can imagine with the amount of blood you lost. The doctor said you were very lucky."

I raised my eyebrows but didn't say anything. What could I say? There were no words to make any of this better.

She locked her fingers together and placed her hands in her lap. "The doctor wants to send you to a facility. A special mental health facility, that is. I told him he was being overdramatic."

My head snapped up. "Are you serious right now?"

She furrowed her brows and looked at me puzzled. "I don't know what you mean."

"Mum, I've been starving myself for months and then tried to kill myself. You seriously think a *doctor* is being overdramatic by thinking I should get some professional help?"

"Emmeline, you've clearly been struggling, and this was your way of letting everyone know. If you wanted my attention, you have it. We can get you weekly therapy sessions—you'll get over it soon."

"You can't be for real." I clenched my fists in anger.

How was she so blind?

"Mum, I've been more than struggling. I wanted to *die*. I can't just get over that because you want me to. That feeling doesn't just go away."

I took a breath to calm myself. Without realising, I had raised my voice and she was looking at me with fury in her gaze. She was embarrassed—she was always embarrassed—but I couldn't take it anymore. What was her problem?

"This is going to alter your life tremendously, Emmeline. Everyone will already be talking about what your tried to do—missing school will only make matters worse. Surely it would be better if you come home, and we get you help there?"

It was difficult to tell if she was genuinely concerned about how this would impact my life, or if she was trying to save face. Either way, it infuriated me. I didn't want everything to be swept under the rug like it was nothing.

"My life has been screwed up for a long time, Mum," I said solemnly, trying to let go of my anger. "If this facility can help me, then I think I should go. There's no way of me getting better if I'm at home. I think I need to get away from everything if I want to heal."

Mum stood up, throwing her bag over her shoulder. "If you want to go to the facility, then you can go. I won't stop you."

Without saying anything else, she stalked from the room and left me lying on my hospital bed alone.

I could feel the tears threatening to fall as I stared at the empty doorway, wondering what it would be like if it was my dad who had walked in instead. Such thoughts weren't helpful to my frame of mind, but I couldn't help myself.

"Hello again, Emmeline," Lena greeted me with a warm smile.

I forced a smile in return as she entered the room, standing at the foot of the bed to watch me. "Would you mind calling me Emmie? Nobody apart from Mum calls me by my full name."

Lena nodded and winked at me, her dark lashes fluttering. "Of course, doll. Emmie it is. Now, did your mother talk to you about the facility? Doctor Roscoe would like to send you there tomorrow if your vitals are okay. He thinks the sooner we get you into treatment, the more beneficial it will be for you."

I didn't bother to sugar-coat my response. "She says I don't need to go, but I can if I want to. So yes, please tell the doctor that I'll go. Even if it just means that I won't need to stay in that damn house for a while."

Lena's smile turned sad, but she merely nodded. "Okay. I'll let him know, Emmie."

It wasn't until she left the room and left me to my own thoughts that I realised just how lonely I felt. I prayed that the dreams I had experienced had some hint of truth to them and that, as my father had told me, I would be okay.

At that moment, though, I didn't know if I would ever be okay again.

—

It took two more days before Doctor Roscoe cleared me for transfer to the mental health facility. He was a kind man with striking green eyes and a greying goatee. He reminded me more of a biker than a doctor, something which I shared with him—it made him laugh.

The thing I liked most during our check-ups was that he never once looked at me with pity. I cherished that.

I surprised myself when it was time to leave, and I discovered that I was nervous to go. I was eager to leave the stark whiteness of the hospital, but apprehension drowned me as I imagined walking into the same thing in another location. Thankfully, they had told my mother that she didn't need to attend. They emailed her the paperwork and she signed the forms, never once coming back to visit me.

A taxi was arranged by the hospital to pick me up and drop me off at the mental health centre a few towns over. I had never heard of it, but Lena had explained that it was new, a measure to combat the rising numbers in mental health cases apparently. It was only thirty minutes before we pulled up outside a large sandstone building and the driver announced that we had arrived.

It was probably one of the most beautiful places I had ever seen. The building was surrounded by trees, flower patches and benches lining the grassy areas.

He parked the car and grabbed the bag of clothes that my mother had dropped off for me, and then we headed up the front steps and into the building.

The inside was just as beautiful as it was outside. The floor in the foyer was made of gorgeous grey marble and the walls were painted olive green. I was surprised at the colour scheme, it made me feel far more welcome than the plain white of the décor of the hospital.

A large black desk was situated in the middle of the foyer, ornate white and gold stairs spiralling up at each side. A young man sat behind the desk; his copper hair slicked back behind his ears.

I made my way up to the desk and he looked up, a cheery smile lighting up his freckled face.

"Hi there! I'm Freddy. How can I help you today?"

I couldn't help but smile back at him, his whitened teeth glinting at me. He must have noticed the bags that the driver had deposited in front of the desk, but I appreciated him treating me like I was anyone else coming in.

I shifted uncomfortably on my feet, still sore and battered from the night of the dance, determined not to let my smile falter. I could be strong.

"Hello. My name's Emmeline Beaumont, and I'm supposed to be checking in."

Freddy beamed and jumped from his chair, walking around the large desk to greet me face-to-face.

"Of course. I've been expecting you, Emmeline!" He smiled at the driver and motioned for him to leave. "Let me take you through and introduce you to Paula and Mark."

I raised my brow at him. "Paula and Mark?"

"They're the leaders who will be your go-to people during your stay."

He started up the spiral staircase and I lifted my case to trudge after him. He glanced back at me over his shoulder. "You can leave that there. I'll get someone else to bring them up to your room."

During my stay. He made it sound like I was on a weekend retreat.

If only.

I followed him up the winding stairs and almost ran into his back as he stopped abruptly on the first floor, keying in a code to a door on our right. Like a gentleman, he held it open for me and bowed slightly to make me laugh before he led me through the corridor.

We were locked in? My anxiety spiked at the thought of not being able to go where I wanted. I knew I needed to be here if I wanted to get better, but it didn't take that initial feeling of apprehension.

The building reminded me of an old hotel with long corridors and lots of doors, but where there used to be walls, transparent panes of plexiglass allowed the light to shine brightly into what I guessed were productivity areas for the patients. We passed by a large room which was filled with art supplies and paintings covering the walls. A few teenagers stood behind easels, lost in their work as they left loose brushstrokes on their canvases.

"So, this is our activity and living areas. Each room is usually set up for what it's used for. We have the art room as you saw, a music room, an IT suite," Freddy explained as we walked, pointing out all of the rooms that we passed. He stopped outside a dimly lit room and pushed open the door. "This is my personal favourite: our reading nook."

213

He stepped inside and I followed, my feet sinking into the plush maroon carpet. A luxurious looking corner sofa was placed into the room, almost blending in entirely with the carpet. Shelves and small bookcases lined the walls, hundreds of different coloured spines whispering to be read. A television was sitting on a large black unit across from the sofa but from the small layer of dust gathering around the remote controls, I guessed people didn't use it too often.

"It's beautiful," I whispered to Freddy.

He hummed his approval and guided me out of the room.

The rest of his tour was lost to me as I struggled to get the reading nook out of my head. Something about it seemed so private and safe and I wondered how soon it would be before I would be able to curl up with one of the intriguing books that had caught my eye.

Everything so overwhelming; touring this whole new space that was going to become my home for a while, with people I didn't know. What if they were as cruel as all the others in Apollo? What if this was just an enclosed space where I would be ridiculed like before?

Freddy stopped outside a door labelled OFFICE: STAFF ONLY and knocked gently.

A plump, middle-aged woman with curly black hair and a pierced eyebrow greeted us. She looked from Freddy to me and beamed, her purple lipstick making it almost impossible not to stare at her mouth.

"Is this the lovely Emmeline?" She shoved Freddy out the way with a chuckle and guided me into the office.

I glanced back at Freddy who offered me a sheepish wave before he turned on his heels and took off.

The office was as grand as the rest of the building; high ceilings, plush chairs tucked neatly behind large oak desks, and stacks of neatly organised files lined any available space on top of the storage cupboard.

214

The woman motioned to a padded black leather chair with a fluffy white cushion. I perched on the edge, wrapping my arms around my waist as I looked around the room. Pictures of children of all ages smiled out from the frames on the wall, the woman and a man of similar age stood proudly in almost every photo—Paula and Mark, I presumed.

"I'm Paula," the woman confirmed as she lowered herself into the chair behind the desk. She leaned forward on her elbows, grinning at me. "It's a pleasure to meet you, Emmeline."

"Emmie, please."

"Emmie, I like that." Paula nodded and typed something into the computer, her nails tapping rapidly against the keys. "So, welcome! We are so happy to have you here. Normally we'd try to have both me and Mark greet you, but he's in a meeting with one of the other guests, so you're stuck with just me."

I smiled and shrugged, trying to show that it wasn't a big deal. If I could find my voice, I would tell her that I was happy to just be in a place where someone was willing to speak to me and look at me like I wasn't completely crazy.

Though we hadn't interacted much yet, I liked Paula already.

"This might be a weird situation for you—there's always an adjustment period, but I want you to know you can come and find me or Mark if you ever need anything. This is a safe space for you, and you're free to treat it as your home."

She glanced at me to check if I was listening, and I nodded.

"There're a few rules. Firstly, you attend at least one private session of counselling each week—we can increase it if you or the doctor feels like it will be beneficial. You must also attend one group session each week. We require everyone to eat meals together, until the last person

215

finishes. In this establishment, we are here to teach each other about community and respect.

"And last but not least, this is a Co-Ed building and youth are encouraged to socialize. However, please don't have any guys—or girls, for that matter—in your room unless your door is fully open and one of the leaders is aware that the person is in there with you. Does all that sound okay?"

I blinked a few times and tried to process how she had managed to get through all that in one breath.

All things considered, I didn't find the rules to be so bad.

"That sounds fine."

Paula beamed and signed a form in the folder opened on her desk. "Okay. Now I see in your file that there's a history of self-harm and a recent suicide attempt. Because of our protocols to keep everyone safe, even from themselves, we're going to be watching quite closely for the first few weeks you're here, to make sure you're managing okay."

I didn't relish the fact that I would be being monitored constantly, despite knowing logically that it was what needed to happen. All I could think about was that I wouldn't have any quiet, peaceful time on my own. There was no way to prove to them that I wasn't going to try and kill myself again.

Maybe I needed to prove it to myself too.

Paula tucked all the paperwork back into the brown folder and stood, walking around the desk. "Shall I show you to your room?"

I stood with her, ignoring the way my stomach twisted into knots. This was a new beginning, even if it was nerve-wracking. "I'd like that."

NINETEEN

My bedroom was on the second floor and was situated on the right-hand side of another winding hallway. A number twelve marked the door with brass plates.

Paula explained that the guys and girls were split into separate floors, and everyone had to be in their rooms by nine in the evening, but we were free to mingle and make use of the facilities as soon as breakfast was over.

"We'll have dinner around five tonight, and then you'll get to meet everyone. I'm sure you want to get settled in, but you know where to find me if you want to talk before then," she told me before leaving me to unpack my clothes.

The room was larger than I expected, with a double bed and vanity set taking up most of the space. There was a wardrobe, and shelving painted a pale grey to match the walls.

After I had neatly unpacked the few items I had with me, placing them carefully into the shelves and hangers I allotted them to, I took a seat on the edge of the bed and looked around the room.

I didn't feel any less awkward here than I did at home, and something about that felt wrong to me.

A clock ticked along on the wall beside my window, the pink hands telling me it was just after three. What was I supposed to do for two hours until I was able to meet everyone else? It wasn't like I could go to school or anything.

I decided to change into a pair of leggings and a loose knit jumper that hung down, just above my knee. It felt nice to be in something that was comfortable and familiar when so much else was changing.

Walking through the hallways and peering into the rooms with open doors, it was clear that there were girls from as young as ten living in the facility, if the walls covered in posters and diamante butterflies were anything to go by. I felt like I was prying, peeking into the private lives of people I hadn't even met yet, so I quickly continued on my way until I found the library room again.

I turned the handle gently and peered inside to make sure nobody was in there before I entered.

The room was still dimly lit from my earlier tour with Freddy, so I flicked the switch on the wall, illuminating the plush carpet and colourful books.

I couldn't quite figure out what drew me to this room in particular—I enjoyed reading, but it wasn't something I spent every spare moment doing—but something pulled me, my stomach only settling once I finally walked inside.

I brushed my fingertips across the books, enjoying the way the spines felt against my skin. It had been a long time since I appreciated the smell of the ink on pages, anticipation pulsing as I discovered the worlds I could lose myself in.

I picked a book at random, a battered black hardcover with a missing dust jacket and took a seat on the sofa, sinking into the comfort of the cushions.

I flicked to the first page without reading the title, determined to let the mystery unfold without anything to give me hints, and I found myself captivated by a tale of lost loves and college overachievers. Under normal circumstances, it would not have been something that would have kept me engaged, and I would most certainly not have chosen it. However, something about the use of intricate phrasing and beautiful imagery made me hold my breath as I flipped from page to page, not wanting the story to end.

"I've read that one."

I jumped as a feminine voice broke me from my trance.

A girl, only a year or two younger, stood in the doorway, leaning against the frame as she flipped through a magazine. Her hair was cut into a short bob, the front strands tucking under her chin and framing her delicate features and big doe eyes.

I tried not to stare as I noticed the way her bones protruded and how loosely her dress fit against her pale ivory skin.

"Not my usual genre but it was good, nonetheless." She looked up and smiled—a bright, full smile that made her eyes twinkle even from across the room. "Sorry, I didn't mean to give you a fright. I was just curious to meet the new girl."

I couldn't help but beam back at her, hoping it reflected my genuine happiness to see her. "Ah, everyone always wants to meet the newbie, right?"

She stepped into the room, her yellow sundress swishing around her knees.

"Absolutely." She held her hand out and I shook it, smirking at the politeness and formality of it. "Hannah."

"Emmie."

"It's awesome to meet you, Emmie. Welcome to Pinewood Grove—we're all mad here."

She screwed her eyes together and I chuckled, appreciating the laughter and familiar *Alice in Wonderland* quote.

"I would like to say I'm sure that's not true, but if other people are here for similar reasons as me, I fear it might be."

Hannah let out a girlish giggle and flopped down beside me on the sofa. "What're you in for? If you don't mind me asking, that is. I get that some people don't like to talk about it."

I tugged at my sleeves and chewed on my lip, wondering if I had the level of courage to say it all out loud. Especially to a stranger. But I had shared my dark secret with someone

219

I trusted before and look at where that had got me. Maybe it would be easier to admit it to someone I didn't know.

I took a deep breath and stared at the wall in front of me so I couldn't see the pity in her eyes. "Started with self-harm and then progressed into mild bulimia until I eventually tried to kill myself a few days ago." Admitting that out loud was more of a relief than I ever thought it would be. Putting a name on my issues made it more real, something tangible that I could do my best to fix.

Hannah drew in a breath, the sound hissing through her teeth. "Jesus, that'll certainly land you in a mental facility."

"That's for sure." I let out a dry laugh. "What about you?"

She smiled and gestured at her tiny torso. "Didn't much like eating and those damn bitches at school made sure that my issues got worse. Skinny was never skinny enough. Pretty was never pretty enough. I wasn't the right height or weight or had the right personality. And it all led me here."

Anorexia, then.

I looked at the skinny kid next to me and wondered how difficult it must have been for her. My life had always been hard, but I hated to see other people experiencing even a fraction of what I did. She was so beautiful and seemed genuinely kind; how was it fair the people in the world told her she was anything other than perfect the way she was?

"I'm sorry that happened to you, Hannah."

She waved her hand. "It's fine. Shit happens and we have to move on with our lives."

Her eyes flicked back to the magazine she was reading. It was opened on an article about some pop star cheating on his movie star girlfriend. I couldn't help but roll my eyes.

I was about to ask her how long she had been at the facility when a little bell chimed in the corner of the room. It took me a few seconds to locate where the sound was coming from before Hannah pointed it out to me.

220

"The bells signal mealtimes. It's not like a tannoid or anything, but there's one in every room so that we can always hear."

I nodded and closed my book, sliding it back onto the shelf where I had taken it from. I would need to come back to it later to find out what happened at the end.

Hannah jumped up from her seat and sauntered out the door, looking over her shoulder when she didn't hear me following. "Come on, friend! It's awkward walking in when everyone is already sitting down, especially if it's your first day."

I smiled and flicked off the light as I trailed after Hannah, anxiety gnawing at my insides as I realised I was about to meet a whole bunch of people at once. I didn't do well meeting new people under normal circumstances, never mind meeting a bunch of them who all knew I was crazy.

The dining room was very much like the room a large family would have; the walls a warm beige, a large wooden table with high-back chairs and a white tablecloth flung over the top to prevent any damage to the surface if fighting broke out. It was so strange that an unfamiliar place with unfamiliar people reminded me more of a home than my real one had in years.

If that wasn't messed up, I didn't know what was.

Hannah took a seat at the furthest away side of the table, sitting proudly as though she had claimed it as her own. I stood awkwardly, not quite knowing where to sit.

At that moment, Paula walked in with a pile of plates and a huge grin on her face.

"Emmie, love! Glad to see you got here alright. Take a seat wherever you want—everyone will be here soon."

Biting the inside of my cheek, I made my way around the table and slipped into the chair beside Hannah. I didn't know anyone else yet so I figured sitting beside the one sort-of friend I had would be a good idea.

Apparently, Hannah thought so too, if the wink she gave me was any indicator.

While Hannah set the table, plopping plates down in front of every chair, other teenagers began to saunter in and fill up the empty seats. Some glanced over at me before returning their gaze to the ground. Some smiled. Some straight up applauded at the sight of a new arrival.

Once all the seats were filled—except one which I assumed was reserved for Mark, whom I still had yet to meet—Paula began bringing in dishes of roast potatoes, vegetables, roast chicken, grilled portabella mushroom and spaghetti squash.

My mouth gaped as I stared at all the food being placed in front of us. I didn't think I had ever seen so much food in one place before.

Hannah elbowed me to catch my attention. "We have loads of options so that those of us with food issues have at least something that we can eat without being sick. Sometimes we even help prep or cook dinner too. Helps us get a handle on dealing with our own food again."

I nodded my understanding but couldn't formulate words, my mouth watering at the idea of having something to eat that wasn't the stale cardboard stuff they gave me in hospital. Perhaps my body could be tricked into thinking it didn't need to vomit the deliciousness up.

Time would tell.

Paula took her seat at one end of the table while everyone chatted among themselves. Hannah explained that Mark was often late because he was usually the one who stayed in contact with the hospitals and families, which meant lots of hours and phone calls. She said that Paula would probably make a joke about it, but it's what made the facility seem more like a family—not even the people here were perfect.

That made me smile.

As if summoned by his name, Mark came jogging in and slipped into his chair, apologising breathlessly for being late. He looked around the table before his eyes caught mine.

"You must be Emmel—"

"Emmie," Paula interrupted, winking at me.

"Emmie," Mark repeated, offering a smile. He looked almost exactly the same as he was in the photos in the office, the only difference being some extra grey hairs peppered in his stubble. "It's a pleasure to meet you. Has everyone introduced themselves?"

Paula shook her head. "We were waiting on you."

"Well, don't let me interrupt. Everyone go around the table and introduce yourselves to our new friend, Emmie. Then we can feast!"

As I looked around the table at the strangers I would be staying with, I noticed one clear thing: their eyes lit up around the bubbly personalities of Mark and Paula.

A voice that sounded an awful lot like my father's whispered in the back of my head that I was going to settle in just fine.

There were ten of us sitting at the table, including myself. As instructed, everyone went around the room and introduced themselves: Becca, Jane, Kylie, Robbie, Adam, Rhian, Luke, Hannah and Anya. Everyone attempted to smile, welcoming someone they knew nothing about.

I appreciated the hospitality, hoping they would come to like me on their own terms when they got to know me.

Dinner passed by in a blur, and I devoured everything on my plate, my stomach swelling in protest. I regretted it almost immediately, the familiar sickness rising as I cleared my plate away. I was determined, however, not to begin my attempt at wellness by forcing my fingers down my throat. I could survive a day, even if my mind was telling me otherwise.

"Emmie?" Mark called out to me from the dining room after almost everyone else had vacated.

Hannah mouthed that she'd wait outside for me as I chewed on my lip.

I approached Mark hesitantly, anxiety swelling inside me even though I knew logically that there was nothing wrong. After so many months of constantly being on edge, I just couldn't shake the feeling that I had already said or done something to get me in trouble.

Mark folded the tablecloth and set it neatly on top of a cabinet in the corner. When he turned to me, he wore a warm smile that made him look significantly younger. His eyes were soft as he glanced at me, though he didn't look with pity the way everyone else had been.

"I just wanted to see how you were settling in. The first few meals can be hard. Coming to a new place, meeting new people, it can be overwhelming."

My limbs relaxed and I blew out a sigh of relief. He was just checking on me, no issue.

"It's a lot, but I'm doing okay, I think."

"You think?"

I shrugged. "It's been an adjustment and I'm just trying to come to terms with everything. But I really am grateful to be here; to get the help I need. The help I *want*."

Mark nodded, eyeing me suspiciously. "Well, if it's okay with you, I'm going to schedule your first therapy session for tomorrow. I would really like you to get into a routine here and get you settled. I think speaking to the therapist could help with that. What do you think?"

It felt weird to be given options about my future; nobody had really taken the time to check if I was okay with whatever was happening.

"That's okay with me."

Mark beamed and clapped his hands together. "Great! I'll get you all set then. Paula or Freddy will come and get

224

you tomorrow to take you to the appointment. It's very nice to have you here, Emmie."

When I left the dining room, Hannah was leaning on the wall across the way, arms folded over her chest as she examined her nails in boredom. Her eyes lit up when she saw me, jumping up and linking her arm through mine.

"How'd it go?" she motioned back towards Mark.

I shrugged. "Wasn't a big deal. He asked if I wanted to go to therapy."

Hannah looked up at me expectantly. "You said yeah, right?"

"I didn't think no was really an option. But yeah, I agreed to go to a session tomorrow."

"Good! It seems scary but I swear it's fine. I really love Doc."

My mouth twitched as I tried not to laugh. "You guys really call him Doc? Like from *Back to the Future*?"

Hannah rolled her eyes and snorted. "Yes, we really call her Doc. She finds it funny and it just kind of stuck, I guess."

"Well, I'm excited to meet the infamous Doc."

TWENTY

I wiped my palms against my jeans, hoping to rid myself of the sweat that was accumulating there. My foot tapped nervously against the floor as I waited outside the office door, hoping that therapist had suddenly had an emergency and couldn't fit me in.

The idea of sitting in a room, discussing everything wrong with my life made me feel claustrophobic. I just hoped that Hannah was right; perhaps talking to Doc really would help rid me of the darkness I felt digging its claws in me.

"Emmie?" A voice called to me from behind the door, which was now slightly ajar.

My throat constricted as I made my way inside the room. Sitting behind a glass desk was a young woman, early thirties if I were to hazard a guess. Her raven hair was swept into a messy bun on top of her head, a pair of striking cat-eye style glasses framing her ochre irises.

With high cheekbones and plump lips painted plum, Doc was probably the most striking woman I had ever seen.

She smiled at me, revealing a set of startling white teeth against the dark colour of her lips, and motioned for me to take a seat on the brown leather sofa in the centre of the room. "Please, take a seat and make yourself comfortable Emmie."

I did as I was instructed and sat in the middle of the sofa, placing my hands into my lap so I wasn't tempted to fidget. Doc grabbed a folder and a notepad from her desk before taking a seat in the matching leather chair directly across the coffee table from me.

226

She tucked her right leg over her other knee and rested the notepad on her thigh. Linking her fingers together, she smiled brightly.

It was easy to understand why everyone seemed to like her so much.

"Hey there, Emmie. As I'm sure you've been told, I'm the resident psychologist and trained counsellor on staff at Pinewood Grove. Everyone calls me Doc, so please feel free to call me that too. Doctor Minniver always seemed like too much of a mouthful," she laughed. It was light and joyful, and I hoped that I would hear that laugh more throughout my stay.

"Doc it is."

The woman grinned and settled back into her chair. "So, how are you?"

I barked out a laugh, assuming that was a ridiculous question because clearly, I wasn't doing too hot if I was in a mental health facility after trying to kill myself, but apparently Doc didn't find it as amusing I did. Instead, she quirked her eyebrow at me and pursed her lips, refusing to speak until I answered.

"I've been better," I admitted, although a laugh was still tickling the back of my throat.

Doc nodded and scribbled something in her notepad which made my skin itch. What was she writing? Patient deflects serious questions using humour?

Noticing my apprehension to her notes, she explained, "I take notes during the sessions so that I can keep track and circle back to any subjects that need further discussion."

I nodded, though I still didn't like the fact that I was unaware of *what* she was writing.

"What would you like to discuss today?"

My brows furrowed. "I get to choose?"

Doc smiled. "Emmie, these sessions are for your benefit, first and foremost. I am here to help you with whatever has been impacting your life and affecting your mental health.

227

We can discuss movies, books, weather—everything or nothing. Whatever you feel will help you most in this moment. I'd like to use this as a chance to get to know you, so that I can help you as best as I can."

I squirmed and bit down on my lip. I didn't know what was going to help me. I didn't even know how to comprehend what was going on in my own head.

"I don't know how to talk about it. Everything happened so quickly, and I feel like my mind is just mush."

"When you say *everything happened so quickly*, what do you mean?"

I took a deep breath and let it out slowly, unclenching my hands which had curled in my lap. "My life is going to hell. I mean, I guess it technically didn't happen quickly because I think I've been messed up for a long time. But it just feels like over the past few months, everything has spiralled out of my control, and I ended up here."

I glanced down at my bandaged wrists and winced. How had I let everything get so bad? I hated myself for thinking it, but I wished I hadn't woken up in that hospital bed. Then I wouldn't have to think about any of this ever again. I wanted to get better, but it seemed like such a big task, and I didn't know it was possible.

"Tell me whatever you're thinking," Doc said softly.

The way she spoke, I wanted to unburden myself and tell her everything. Something told me she would understand.

"If I hadn't acted so differently growing up, been so lost in myself, then maybe people would have liked me."

Doc scribbled something else down and then set her notebook aside, leaning forward with her elbows resting on her knees. "Emmie, has anyone ever told you the definition of unique?" I shook my head. "Unique means being unlike anything else in the world. It is being so special because there will never be anything else like that. Humans are fascinating creatures, but perhaps the most amazing part of our species is the fact that every one of us is unique."

I couldn't help but scoff. "You clearly haven't been in my high school. Being unique is practically a death wish."

"I was in high school once, and I can guarantee it hasn't changed as much as you think. People group together because they think it will make their lives easier if they can blend in. What they don't understand is that being unique is probably one of the most incredible things in the world because nobody will ever be like you."

"That's the issue; I don't want to be unique. I'm already lonely. Why can't I find someone like me? Isn't that what you're supposed to do? Find people like you and spend your life with them because they understand you."

"What would the world look like for you if you weren't unique?"

"I don't really know," I admitted. "I would be look like all the girls I went to school with. I'd fit in and wouldn't be a complete social pariah."

"But would you be happy?"

"Is anyone ever really happy?"

Doc smiled encouragingly. "Yes, they are. You can be happy, too, Emmie. It will take some time and hard work, but it's possible."

Shrugging, I ran my fingers through my hair. Maybe I had misplaced my faith in her; she obviously didn't understand. She didn't get what it was like to feel so closed off from everyone. Kate was the only person who had even come close to understanding me, but even she didn't fully get me.

"Happiness won't be found in wishing you were someone else, however. I think we can delve further into your experiences which lead you to wish you were less unique."

I sighed and shook my head. "I don't want to do that right now."

"I want you to do something over the next few days until our next session. You can consider it homework, if you like. I want you to come up with a list of your good qualities. It can take you as long as you want, but perhaps it will help you to begin realising that your differences make you a better, brighter and far more interesting person."

"I can try," I mumbled.

I didn't know how I was supposed to come up with a list of my good qualities when I could barely look at myself in a mirror without wanting to smash it. But I would try.

If it led to healing, I would try anything.

—

Group therapy was easier for me to manage than my one-on-one session with Doc. Everyone sat in a circle and listened to each other talk about whatever they needed to get out. Thankfully, it wasn't a requirement to share with the group, so I was able to slump in my chair and get to know the people I was living with.

My appointment with Doc the following week was surprisingly better than the first. I had expected her to ask me to give her the list I was supposed to write—a list that so far consisted of only two qualities, empathy and compassion—but instead, she told me that it was a personal thing, and I didn't need to share with her if I wasn't comfortable. I suspected she was going to make me do regular homework for her and that, at some point, I would have to start sharing. I wasn't looking forward to that day.

"If you aren't going to share with me," she had explained, "then we need to at least focus on some techniques for when you feel like you're spiralling."

I heaved a sigh but nodded in agreement. "Fine."

"What does it feel like when you're starting to become anxious?"

"Like everything is spinning out of control and there's nothing I can do. It's like everything keeps hitting me until I feel all the pressure and just collapse."

Doc smiled. "See, you can share!" I glared at her which earned a snicker. "Okay, for when you feel like this, try focusing on your breathing more than anything. It's what's going to ground you and help keep you steady."

We worked on breathing techniques for well over an hour—apparently, she had lengthened our appointment and had forgotten to tell me—until I was itching to get out of her office which suddenly seemed very small. Doc, happy with me making at least a little progress told me we could finish the session there but made me promise that we would revisit it at some point.

Yay for me.

Hannah had taken to hanging out with me the majority of the day after I was finished with therapy, and I was extremely grateful to have a friend in a foreign place. Her singsong laughter and optimism were something I had grown to rely on. Without fail, she made me smile and I felt like I could get through anything when I had her support. I knew she had a wall up, everyone at Pinewood Grove knew how to wear a mask, but I hoped that she would trust me enough to let me support her one day if she ever needed it.

Family wasn't allowed to visit guests of the facility for the first three weeks. Paula said that they wanted everyone to have time to settle. So, while I wasn't allowed guests, I had grown to hate the days when Hannah's mother and brother visited, and she would have to leave me. I would mope about the facility, hiding out with a book in my favourite room, while Hannah went to the movies or out for dinner with her family. As much as I was enjoying my time away from home, I started to feel like a cooped-up chicken when I was stuck in the same monotonous routine.

Mark called me into the office when my three weeks of mother-free time expired.

Flopping down into the seat opposite his desk, I offered a strained smile. "Hey, Mark."

He grinned. "Emmie-B! How we doing?"

I groaned and rolled my eyes at him, the corners of my mouth threatening to break into a smirk. He knew I hated the nickname, but it also made me happy that he cared enough to give me one. "Not bad, Marky-Mark."

He chuckled heartily and pretended to scowl. "Good one, kid, good one. Now, you know that the three-week probation period is up, and you can have family visits again, right?"

I nodded. "Yup."

"Obviously we've been keeping in contact with your Mum and giving her updates, but I wanted to check to see if you wanted me to invite her for a visit?"

I froze in my seat, shifting under his gaze. Was I allowed to say absolutely not? Had he spoken to Doc and been told that speaking to my Mum would send me into a spiral that I knew I wouldn't come back from. I had been working so hard. I hadn't vomited or hurt myself—the urges had been there, but I was starting to manage. The whole time I had been in Pinewood Grove, I had managed, and I didn't want to mess with that.

"No. I don't want to see her," I whispered.

I wasn't sure if he had heard me but when I dared to look up, he nodded, his smile never faltering. "That's completely fine, Emmie."

I sat up straighter in my chair, surprised that I was allowed to make that call. "Really?"

Mark let out a soft chuckle. "Yes, of course. We're here to help you and if seeing your mother would hinder your progress, then you absolutely don't have to do it. At least for the moment"

I beamed at him, my face lighting up with a newfound happiness. It felt good to be in charge of decisions regarding my own life.

When I got back to my bedroom, Hannah was sprawled across my bed reading a magazine. Her small frame was covered entirely by a black jumpsuit, a long piece of golden ribbon tied around her tiny waist as a belt. Her eyes flicked up as I entered the room, and she flashed me a smile.

"Where have you been?" she asked.

I rolled my eyes and flopped down onto the bed beside her, grabbing the magazine from her hands as I looked over the article she was reading. Some actress had started dating after divorcing her A-list actor husband. I shot Hannah a look—how was this newsworthy?

Hannah huffed and nudged me with her shoulder. "So?"

I groaned. "You're relentless. Mark was asking if I wanted my mum to visit. I said no."

Hannah nodded her understanding, her lips pursed together. For all the messed-up things that had led us to Pinewood Grove, I was happy that it at least meant there was someone who understood that part of my brain. Hannah had told me that it took her almost two months before she allowed her family to visit, and that even then, she had only allowed her brother at first. I hadn't met him yet, but they were extremely close, and I liked that Hannah had someone she could rely on.

"What are you going to do today?"

I kicked my boots off and wiggled my toes. "Paint my nails? Maybe watch a movie."

Hannah jumped into a sitting position, grinning like a Cheshire cat.

My eyes narrowed at her. "What?"

"I have a great idea!" she yelled as she gripped my arms to pull me up. "You can come out with me and Remy today!"

My eyes widened as I shook my head fervently. I was not going to hijack her day and be the awkward addition to an already-planned outing. Staying at Pinewood was all the excitement I could handle.

"Hannah, no! I'm fine, honestly."

She tutted and pouted her bottom lip. "Oh, please, Emmie? Come with us. It'll be loads of fun. We're going to go to the beach."

My eyebrows shot up as I laughed at her plans. "Han, it's freezing outside. You can't go to the beach in December!"

Hannah rolled her eyes and swatted at the air in my direction. "You can go to the beach any time of the year. December is just as nice as July as long as you wrap up."

Sighing, I shoved my boots back on and looked through my drawers for a cosy jumper. "Fine. But I need to ask Mark if I'm allowed first!"

A high-pitch squeal from the blonde on my bed made me flinch, but I laughed anyway. It was hard to say no when she made puppy-dog-eyes to get her own way.

"Be ready in an hour if he says yes!" she called as she ran excitedly from the room.

I hoped Remy wouldn't mind a stranger imposing on his day out with his little sister.

TWENTY-ONE

Mark had told me that leaving Pinewood so soon after arrival wasn't usually permitted. But, after a lot of begging from Hannah, he had agreed that Remy had been around enough to be deemed trustworthy, proving that we weren't out the entire day. A couple hours was our limit, and we had to make sure we signed out.

I could manage that.

It turned out that Hannah really did love going to the beach. By the time an hour had passed, and had I made my way downstairs to meet her. She was practically jumping in anticipation. She wore chunky black trainers and a long waterproof coat over her jumpsuit, her neck covered with a scarf the same colour as her ribbon-belt. I smiled at her as she yanked a bright orange pom-pom hat over her head, making her look absolutely tiny for her age.

She looked me up and down as I approached her, appraising my outfit choice. I had pulled on a thick grey jumper over my shirt, tucked my jeans into my boots, and added a pink rain jacket for extra measure.

"You look good," Hannah said approvingly.

"As do you, goldilocks," I teased back, loving the way she scrunched her nose up in disgust every time I called her that.

She grabbed my hand and pulled me out the door and down the stairs, taking two at a time which made me fear for my life. I hissed at her to slow down but she only giggled.

Freddy was sitting behind his desk as usual, gulping coffee from a stainless-steel travel mug. He waved at us as we jumped from the last stair, swallowing down his last mouthful of caffeine. "Hey guys!"

"Hiya, Freddy," we both said in unison. He held out the clipboard for us and we signed out, dating and marking the time.

Hannah tugged me towards the front door.

"Have fun, girls!" he yelled, barely audible as the door slammed behind me.

A large Kia Sportage sat idly in the long driveway. The driver's side door opened, and a pair of long legs attached to probably the most gorgeous young man I had ever seen stepped out.

Remy was nothing like I had imagined he would be. Where Hannah was small and blonde, Remy was over six feet tall and had a gorgeous head of mousy-brown curls which hung messily around his ears.

I tried not to make it too obvious that I was admiring him as I stared, my eyes running over every part of him.

He stepped forward and stones crunched under his boots as he wrapped Hannah in a tight hug. He kissed the top of her head gently and smiled into her hair. My heart melted.

"Hey, squirt," he greeted her cheerily.

Hannah smacked his stomach, which looked dreamily toned through the tight white t-shirt he had on and let out a laugh. "Don't be a twat, Remy."

He grabbed at his stomach and feigned pain from her smack which only made her laugh more. It took him a few seconds before he realised I was standing behind Hannah.

I felt chills as his fierce green eyes met mine. He stared for a minute, neither one of us willing to tear our eyes away, before he blinked and brought himself back into the moment. I let out a small sigh as his lips formed into an earth-shattering smile, bright and inviting.

"You must be Emmie," he stated. His voice was low and melodic, a soft song to my ears.

I opened my mouth, but my throat felt super dry, and I had to cough. I cringed internally at myself before saying, "You must be Remy."

Thankfully, Hannah's brother seemed unphased by my awkwardness and instead gestured towards the car. "Awesome to meet you. Shall we get going?"

Hannah didn't need to be told twice and flung herself into the passenger seat. I made a beeline for the door to the backseats, but Remy beat me to it, holding it open for me like a gentleman. I looked up at him and he smiled again, which made my stomach flutter.

Get a grip, Emmeline, I chided myself, though it did nothing to wipe the smile from my face.

Hannah fiddled with the radio stations until she found a song playing that she liked and turned the volume up, blasting it as she scream-sang along. Remy glanced at me through the interior mirror and rolled his eyes, but it wasn't long until we were all singing along.

The drive to the beach was pleasant enough and I was grateful to be outside. Remy had his window cracked open and I relished how nice it was to breathe in the fresh, icy air. The closer we got to the sea, the more the smell of salt-water and seaweed wafted into the car. Hannah groaned, saying it smelled horrible, but I secretly liked it. It reminded me of family trips to the coast as a child when life had been simpler.

Whenever both my parents could get the weekends off from work, we would pack up the car and head to the ocean. It didn't matter what the weather was, we always spent the entire weekend splashing in the water and eating chips drenched in vinegar. Even my mum had been happy back then, a smile on her face whenever she caught dad looking at her.

I missed those days.

Remy carefully pulled into a parking spot and turned off the ignition, a hearty laugh shaking the car as Hannah bolted, running into the sand with her arms open wide. I cringed as I imagined sand filling the tiny crevices of her trainers, but I said nothing and exited the car.

Remy grabbed a bag from the boot and jogged to catch up with me as we followed Hannah's path. "So, how're things, Emmie?"

I glanced at Remy from the corner of my eye. He shoved his arms into a fitted black coat and flung the bag over his shoulder. Scratching at the small growth on his chin, he smiled again.

"I'm not exactly at the best point in my life." I couldn't stifle the sarcastic giggle that came out of me. "But I'm doing okay, all things considered."

Remy chuckled, a deep rumble that sent shivers down my spine. "Hey, at least you're laughing, right? Life gets boring if you don't laugh instead of cry."

Grinning, I nodded in agreement. "That's pretty accurate."

"Hurry the hell up!" Hannah called as she waded through the sand, kicking it up into the breeze. I scrunched my face, imagining it sweeping into her eyes, but she seemed unfazed and continued to spin.

Wrapping my arms around my midsection, I forged onwards until I caught up with Hannah, leaving Remy to trail behind.

I felt somewhat awkward being on a day out from Pinewood. I couldn't tell if it was just being outside of the centre for the first time in weeks, or whether it was being around a stranger—even one as insanely hot as Remy. That in itself was another issue causing me far more anxiety than I wanted to admit; after everything with Benji, men were the last thing I wanted to occupy my mind.

Besides, Remy was my friend's brother. Initiating anything—not that I was in the headspace to do so—would cross so many boundaries.

Shaking myself from my thoughts, I took Hannah's hands in mine and spun around with her, letting my head fall back as the wind whipped around us, nipping at our cheeks. I was breathless by the time she let go of me, the cold air burning the back of my throat.

"Don't you just love the fresh, sea air?" Hannah asked, taking in a large demonstrative breath.

Remy rubbed his hands together and cupped them in front of his mouth, letting out a groan as he blew into them. "In thirty-degree heat during summer, absolutely. In the freezing temps of December, I'd have to go with no."

Hannah rolled her eyes at her brother and pulled to a halt in front of him, smacking him on the arm. "Too bad. You picked the last thing we did, today it was my turn."

Remy groaned again but flung an arm around her, pulling her into his waist for a hug. I had never yearned for a sibling because I had always had Kate, but seeing Remy and Hannah together made me wonder what it would've been like if I had a brother. Would he have protected me fiercely and without hesitation, the way I knew Remy would for Han?

I faced the sea and closed my eyes, letting the sound of crashing waves fill my senses. Thinking about Kate made my heart ache. I hated the way I had cut her out of my life, especially for someone who had ended up breaking the last pieces I had left of my resolve and sanity. I couldn't blame Benji for everything—I had shut Kate out from parts of my life for a long time before he had ever turned up—but keeping so much a secret from her made me feel rotten. My blood curdled as I imagined someone telling her what I had done. If her expression in the school bathroom when she had confronted me about my self-harm had been anything to go by, she would have felt almost as broken as me.

I hated myself for doing that to her.

I hated myself for a lot of things.

Trying one of the control methods Doc had told me to use—*for when the negative thoughts threaten to break the surface*, she had said—I exhaled until my chest burned, feeling like all the air in my lungs had been successfully let

239

out. With that long and steady breath, I let out all the thoughts swirling around my brain, casting aside the negativity that was my prior downfall.

Opening my eyes, I smiled and watched the waves roll in. Contentment washed over me, and I made a note to tell Doc that I had actually paid attention to something she had taught me, and it had actually helped

"You okay?"

Hannah pressed a bony hand on my shoulder, squeezing gently. Her expression was soft and full of compassion. It made it easier knowing that she understood; even when she didn't, she was still able to sense what I needed.

My smile didn't falter as I nodded, placing my hand over hers. "I'm great."

It surprised me to know that I wasn't lying. For the first time in months, my answer to that question had been genuine and positive.

Maybe I could do this.

"Good, because I wanna paddle!" she squealed as she kicked off her shoes and sprinted towards the water.

My eyes widened in horror as she shrieked when her toes dipped into the icy water. I would have turned and sprinted back to the heat of the car, but apparently Hannah loved adrenaline. She yanked her trouser legs up around her knees and sprinted into the waves, her cheerful laughter carrying in the wind.

I flopped down onto the sand and let the grains slip through my fingers. I brought my knees to my chest and wrapped my arms around my legs for extra protection against the wind and watched Hannah delight in creating her own fun.

"She's been so much happier since she met you," a voice said from behind me.

I had almost forgotten that Remy was with us. He was pretty quiet, and I wondered to myself if he felt as awkward as I did.

He plopped down beside me, sending a swirl of sand into the air around us. He turned to me with a smile, one I couldn't help but return. I had never met anyone who smiled as much as he did.

"So have I," I replied softly. "She's an amazing person and I'm lucky to call her a friend." Remy chuckled and I furrowed my brows at him. "Why is that funny?"

He shook his head. "I'm not laughing at you. It's just weird because Han said almost the exact same thing to me the other day. I think you both are lucky."

My cheeks flushed and I turned away again, gazing back out to the ocean. It seemed weird to be thankful for the events that had forced me to Pinewood Grove, but in a twisted way, I was. I wished I could have found help and met Hannah through different circumstances, but things happened for a reason and fate clearly had other plans for me.

"How are you liking Pinewood?"

It was my time to chuckle this time. "Somehow I like it better than both the hospital and my own home."

Remy smirked. "Hell, I think Pinewood is better than my home too. It's the coolest damn place."

He was right. Mark and Paula had gone to so much effort to create the perfect environment for people who were struggling, and I felt safe there. I didn't need to worry about my mother watching my every move or having to go to school and face the stares and whispers of my peers. Instead, I could be myself and focus on what I needed to do to get better, as difficult as that seemed to be.

"Have you and Hannah always been close?"

Remy grinned as Hannah waved over at us. "Yeah, always. I think it made it easier because I'm older, so I would do everything possible to protect her. When I first noticed what she'd been doing to herself—man, it broke my soul apart. I would do anything to save her from whatever haunts her mind."

241

His voice trembled and I couldn't bring myself to look at him. It pained me to know how deeply it hurt him to see Hannah that way. I couldn't imagine my mother being pained by what I had done.

"It's nice that she has you to rely on," I finally managed to croak out.

He let out a strangled laugh and I glanced at him, noticing the way a few stray tears slipped down his cheeks. He rubbed them away and I pretended not to notice. "Not that it's much help to her. She always ends up back at Pinewood and I can't seem to stop it from happening."

Without overthinking it, I reached out and covered his hand with mine, squeezing it gently. "You're doing your best, and I can guarantee she loves and appreciates you for that. From the way she talks about you, you're her biggest support and her best friend."

Remy sniffled and squeezed my hand back.

I blinked, forgetting that I was still holding it, and pulled my hand away. I didn't want him to think that I was coming onto him. Not that I would even be on his radar if I was.

God, why was I even thinking about that? My mind was screwed up enough without adding anything else to the mix.

"Thank you for saying that" he said, blinking away the tears that remained. "What about you?"

"What about me?"

Remy rolled his eyes. "Do you have someone to rely on? Someone to support you?"

I snorted. "That would be a hard no. I had a best friend, Kate. But I fucked that up. I let so much get between us."

Remy nudged my arm with his shoulder. "It's never too late to fix things. If you were such good friends, I guarantee she'll have been worried about you and will want to repair your relationship just as much as you."

"You really think so?"

He puffed his chest out and flexed, winking at me. "Trust me, I'm an intelligent old dude."

"*Old?* You're like twenty."

"Twenty-one actually," he corrected with a smirk.

I bit down my laughter and placed a hand over my heart, trying to act sincere. "My mistake."

Remy jumped up and dusted himself down, wiping the sand from his butt. Once he was done, he reached down and offered me his hand. "You're forgiven, new girl. Now what do you say we round up Han and go get something to eat? I'm freezing my ass off."

I smirked and tried not to blush at the mention of his behind. Gripping his hand, I allowed him to pull me up, ignoring the way my skin tingled at the contact. "Sounds good to me."

TWENTY-TWO

Remy drove us to a diner in the middle of town and my stomach betrayed me with an almighty grumble. Neither Remy nor Hannah heard—or if they had, they had chosen not to mention it.

My palms were clammy as we slid into a booth, and it hit me that I would need to eat in front of a stranger.

At least at the facility, Mark and Paula were always with us to make sure we were eating and monitoring us afterwards. Panic seeped into my pores, thinking that I had the choice of whether I wanted to eat. I could say no. The all-too-familiar sensation of wanting to skip the meal or eat until my stomach felt like it would burst burned inside of me.

Hannah reached out across the table and squeezed my hand. "You okay?"

I forced a tight smile and nodded, ignoring the way Remy watched me from over the top of his menu, pretending he wasn't looking.

"I'm fine."

I opened up the laminated menu in front of me and glanced over the options. I was too anxious to eat something heavy; I couldn't stomach a full meal. But the idea of eating a tasteless salad made me want to cry. I hated the way everything seemed like such a difficult decision when it came to food.

It didn't help that beside every option was the calorie count. Written in bold, I could see exactly what would be entering my body. I had enough experience to know how many calories contributed to weight gain, what I could afford to eat to keep my figure slim, or what would fatten up my hips.

Pinching the skin of my lower lip between my teeth, I shut the menu and let out a deep breath.

One.

Two.

Three.

You can do this, Emmie. Weight does not define you. You are more than a number.

"You know what you want?" A waitress appeared at our booth while I was deliberating. Her voice was gruff and scratchy, as though she had been smoking forty cigarettes a day for the past forty years.

Remy, without hesitation, beamed and closed his own menu. "I certainly hope so. I'm famished!"

That earned a smile from the waitress, who pulled out her notepad from her apron. "What can I get you, doll?"

"I'll take a bacon cheeseburger with fries and extra gherkins, please."

The forty-year-smoker scribbled in her notebook and Remy winked at me while her attention was caught elsewhere. He clearly knew the effect he had on people. That was interesting to know, though it reminded me of how Benji had flirted with a waitress or two, thinking it made him appear charming.

She glanced up at Hannah, her cheery exterior dropping now that she wasn't speaking directly to Remy. "You?"

"I'll take a tomato salad."

Remy turned to her, his voice dropping low. "I thought you were going to try to get something more…substantial?"

Hannah rolled her eyes and ripped at the napkin in front of her. "I'm not that hungry."

"Han, please," Remy pleaded, taking the napkin out of her hands before she shredded it into confetti. "That was the deal. On days out, you gotta try and eat something that isn't just rabbit food."

Hannah glanced up at me for only a second, not able to hold my gaze long.

I wanted to rescue her.

"While Hannah decides—" I addressed the waitress— "I'll take a bowl of spinach and feta cheese fettuccine."

The woman grunted in response and scribbled my order down. Remy whispered to Hannah and my heart ached for them both. He was being a good big brother and wanted to help her, but I also understood how difficult it was for her. It wasn't something we could just switch off in our brains. And being pressured to do so, only made it worse.

It made my heart break to think that she had been fighting this battle for years already.

Hannah let out a sigh and looked up. "I'll have the ragu, please."

The waitress nodded and shuffled off with a huff. I was almost tempted to laugh. We clearly weren't all as charming as Remy Austen.

Remy hugged Hannah, "Thank you."

She elbowed him in the stomach, but her mouth tugged into a smile.

I fidgeted in my seat, settling my hands in my lap. I could do this socialising thing; Hannah was my friend and Remy seemed really nice. There was nothing for me to worry about.

"Hannah tells me you attend college," I said to Remy. "What're you studying?"

Leaning back against the booth seat, his shoulders visibly relaxed. "Teaching. Apparently, I'm a glutton for punishment and can't seem to leave the education system."

I snorted which resulted in everyone laughing. "I would imagine that would be difficult, yes."

"Difficult? It's hell on earth. But let me tell you a secret," he leaned across the table conspiratorially. "I actually really love it."

Hannah tutted at his dramatics, but I loved it. He should love teaching if that's what he wanted to do. What was the point in studying for something for years if you didn't like doing it?

I, on the other hand, had no idea what I was going to do. Exam season was upon us, and I was missing everything. I doubted I'd even be allowed back into school to do the mock-ups later in the year.

"What about you? Any plans?"

Hannah beamed and professed to Remy, "Emmie should be a writer! She's very good at English and loves books."

Scoffing, I waved a hand passively. "How can you know I'm good at English?"

Hannah raised her eyebrow at me smugly. "You speak properly enough."

"Well, if that's all I need to become the next big thing, I think I shall do rather well, don't you?" My voice dripped in sarcasm.

"Is that something you'd want to do?" Remy asked.

I shrugged. "I honestly don't have a clue. I've missed some of my exams already."

Remy sighed and pulled his phone from his pockets, rather rudely signalling the end of our conversation. Hannah was oblivious and started to chat absentmindedly about the movie she wanted us to watch after Remy dropped us off. I heard something about witches and blood oaths, but my mind was elsewhere.

I smiled at the right times and nodded, offering passing responses whenever she spoke directly, but I couldn't help but watch her brother instead.

Stooped over, he typed into his phone and stared intently at whatever was on the screen. From this angle, I could see the way his eyelashes curled and almost touched his brows when he blinked or looked up.

He exchanged a quick glance with me, one corner of his mouth tugging upward, but his attention swiftly went back to his reading. I was curious as to what had captured his attention so much that he had stopped spending time with his sister, even though I knew this time meant so much to them both.

When forty-year-smoker came back to us with a pitcher of ice water and three sparkling glasses, Remy finally put his phone down and thanked her. She winked and quickly rushed away, leaving me and Hannah to giggle among ourselves.

"What?" Remy looked between us, brows raised, which made us laugh harder.

Hannah snorted, barely able to get the words out in between her hysterical giggling. "I didn't think that she was your type."

Remy looked at her incredulously and shook his head. "You're ridiculous."

I cackled and a smirk appeared on his face, his mask finally dropping. He glanced over at me again, licking his bottom lip. "And she's not, you know. She's definitely not my type."

My cheeks flushed under his gaze, and I wanted to look away, but I couldn't tear my eyes away. He watched me and my stomach flipped a hundred times over. The green in his eyes seemed brighter under the fluorescent lights, hypnotising me as I stared right back.

Hannah coughed and I startled, peeling my eyes away from her brother.

He's your friend's brother, Emmie. Get a grip.

"Well, your new girlfriend better hurry up with our food because we need to be back soon."

As though summoning her, the waitress returned with a stacked tray of food in the crook of her arm. She practically dumped mine and Hannah's down in front of us but took extra care setting Remy's down before him.

"Enjoy, doll," she rasped to him before running off.

When Remy saw me trying to suppress a grin, he rolled his eyes and shoved a crispy French fry into his mouth, gasping when he realised how hot it was. I didn't bother to stifle my laugh.

Hannah looked down at her bowl of pasta, her brows furrowed in thought as she forked a pasta shell and hovered it before her mouth. I could see the tears in her eyes as she quickly chewed and swallowed, knowing her brother was watching her. I reached out across the table and squeezed her hand, just as she had done for me, and tried to get her to see my support.

Smiling, she took another bite, and I felt my chest swell with pride. It was difficult for people with eating disorders to eat a meal anyway, never-mind doing it in public where it felt like all the eyes in the place were on me.

As I stared down at my own plate, I felt a similar sinking feeling in my stomach. What did you do when the thing you needed to survive was the very thing you felt was like poison to you?

I glanced over at Remy's plate, the juicy burger and mountain of chips making my mouth water. I could have ordered what he had—I would have loved every mouthful—but I wasn't sure I was ready to eat something like that yet. When I looked at it, all I could see was the hundreds of calories which would expand my waistline and fatten my cheeks. After all my hard work, I didn't want that to happen.

You are worthy no matter what you weigh, I heard Doc's voice whisper to me.

I sighed and scooped some of the pasta into my mouth, almost moaning as the rich tomato sauce touched my tongue and set my tastebuds alight. Barely chewing, I forced more into my mouth, savouring the taste explosion.

It took me a minute to fully register what I was doing, how quickly I was falling into old patterns. I needed to be smarter. Especially in front of company. Instead, I took a long gulp of water in between mouthfuls, balancing what I ate and ensuring that I didn't demolish the entire meal in two seconds. If I finished too quickly, I knew I wouldn't be able to refrain from running to the bathroom.

Remy glanced at Hannah quickly from the corner of his eye, making sure she was still eating. Adopting almost the exact same system as myself, she made sure she was drinking plenty at the same time as eating. Doc had called it a 'preventative measure' to our disorders; we needed to keep our body hydrated if we weren't giving it enough food. If we made sure to drink in between eating, it would ensure that we were giving our bodies a fair balance of nutrition and hydration.

When Remy lifted the burger to his lips and took a huge bite, I couldn't resist staring. I didn't know whether I was jealous of the grease dripping down his chin, or if I was just caught up in his beauty—either way, I was most definitely staring and he knew, which was confirmed when he looked up and licked the oil from his lips in a slow, sultry motion.

I coughed and forced my eyes away from him as he laughed, trying to enjoy another delicious mouthful despite feeling his eyes still on me. Surely there was something wrong with me for letting him occupy my brain like that. I truly hoped I wasn't being as transparent as I felt, otherwise Hannah would never want me to spend time with her again.

"So, Emmie…" Remy spoke up as he swallowed down the food in his mouth. "I was doing some research."

I raised my eyebrow and smirked. "Well, you are studying to be a teacher. I kind of assumed research was part of that."

"Smartass." He laughed and threw a chip at me across the table. "I mean, like five minutes ago when I was pretending both of you didn't exist so I could focus on my phone."

Hannah rolled her eyes and held her fork up to her brother as a pointer. "Pray tell, dear brother, what have you been researching?"

"Well, dearest little sister of mine, Emmie here said that she was sad about missing her exams. I was researching to see if she'd be able to do make-up exams at any point."

I dropped my fork, and my jaw. "Really? What did you find?"

"I don't know how long you'll be at Pinewood, but I'm assuming you'll want time to revise first. So, between June and August, there's like eight weeks where you can choose your catch-up exams and for which subjects. If you manage to do them on time and you get passing grades, I think you could probably get into an October or January start for college or something. Even university."

I stared at him completely dumbfounded. "That was one hell of a research trip." I looked between them. Hannah was beaming. "You really think that could work?"

Remy shrugged. "I mean, I don't see why not. You were already studying, I presume. It's not like all of that would have gone away. It just means you've been delayed a bit. I think you can do whatever you set your mind to. Just believe in yourself, Em."

TWENTY-THREE

I spoke to Doc at my next appointment to see if she thought thinking about school after Pinewood was a good idea. Thankfully, she understood how hard I had worked for my grades and said that as long as I wasn't putting pressure on myself, it was something I could definitely consider.

I was happy that therapy sessions with her were going well. After my month's anniversary at the facility, Doc had advised that we start tackling some of my deeper issues, like the loss of my father. I wasn't too happy about it and told her so, but she insisted I wouldn't feel better if I didn't talk about it.

"Why do you think you skirt around the subject without actually going into detail on how you feel?"

It was the first session I had actually agreed to talk about it, but I think I underestimated how hard I found it to speak about losing him.

"Because it hurts."

"But how will you ever get it to stop hurting if you avoid healing?"

I stared up at her and pressed my lips together. She was right, of course. I had to process it at some point. But I had lasted this long.

Sort of.

"Emmie, tell me what it was like for you when you found out your dad had passed."

I tugged at the hem of my shirt and tried to remember that day. I had shut it out for so long that everything was fuzzy, memories of memories.

"It was like the air around me was so dense that I couldn't breathe. I kept picturing him, how he always smiled and hugged me when I was sad, and I couldn't imagine him not being there to do that."

Doc nodded, scribbling in her notepad. "Continue please."

I sighed and closed my eyes. Picturing that day had always been a nightmare. Seeing the horror and heartbreak on my mother's face. Knowing that she was alone to look after me. I wondered if it had been my fault, if I had somehow caused it in one of my tantrums when I screamed that I wished they would disappear.

"My mother was a wreck. She barely slept. Barely ate. She just sat in her bedroom crying her eyes out. Kate would visit and her parents helped as much as they could, but nothing could fill that void. Mum grieved on her own and it meant I did too."

Doc stopped writing and met my eyes. "Do you think that is perhaps why you harbour so many emotions, particularly negative ones, when it comes to your mum? Could you resent her for not supporting you?"

I scoffed and let my shirt fall from my hands, leaning back on the sofa. "Of course, I resent her! I was a child and instead of wiping my tears and telling me it would be okay; she chose to sit on her own and scream about how she hated her life! I thought she would end up killing herself because she was so fucking miserable."

A strangled sob broke free from my throat, and I covered my face with my hands, drowning in tears like I had back then. I grabbed a tissue from the box on Doc's table, wiping my tears angrily.

"It's okay, Emmie. You can let it out."

I shook my head. "I don't want to. I don't want to be hurt like that again."

Doc nodded. "I understand, dear. How do you feel letting that out after keeping it inside so long?"

I blew out a shaky breath and ran my fingers through the curls on top of my head. "Relieved? It feels weird to talk

253

about it after burying it for so many years, but also quite comforting to talk to someone about it. But I'm scared of delving further into it. I don't want to face the pain."

"We can take it one step at a time, don't worry."

When she moved back to her own chair and set the notepad back into her lap, I decided maybe I could let some of it out. If I stopped holding it all in, my heart wouldn't hurt all the time.

I wiped the tears from my cheeks and picked at a ragged bit of nail on my thumb.

"My dad...he was everything. My relationship with my mother was never great, so I always relied on him to make me feel better. Losing that, the only person who could make my world stop spinning, it was the single hardest thing I ever had to go through." I stopped fidgeting and looked up at Doc, surprised that her eyes didn't gloss over with pity the way everyone else normally did. "School got really hard after that. It's like I forgot how to be a person, how to socialise and function. After a while, it was just me and Kate facing the world together."

"Are you and Kate still friends?"

I winced despite myself and shook my head. "Not anymore."

"What happened?"

"Benji, my ex-boyfriend, twisted my head a bit. I thought Kate was against me, so I closed her off."

Doc hummed and I ignored the way she frantically paraphrased onto her paper. Was she writing about how much of a rubbish friend I was? Or would she want to talk about Benji? My chest tightened at the thought.

"Hey, Emmie?"

"Mhm?"

Doc set her pen down and beamed. "I'm proud of you. I know that was really difficult for you to say, but you handled it amazingly. Remember, you are worthy of love and acceptance, even when you are hurting. Benji was an unkind, harmful presence in your life and isolated you from your friends; it's okay to feel the pain from that and to be unsure going forward. But it's important that you keep trying to work through the trauma and live your life to the fullest, because you deserve a good life, Emmie."

My eyes burned with tears I didn't know were waiting to fall. It felt so bizarre to hear someone congratulate me on just talking about my messed-up head, but it made my body hum with gratitude for her.

"Thank you," I managed to mumble, my voice still croaky from crying.

Doc offered me a soft smile. "Why don't we finish the session there today? It's been a tough one for you. Go and enjoy the rest of your day. I'll see you again at your next appointment in two days, and we can explore this topic again if you like."

After thanking Doc again and leaving her office, I made my way to the art room and decided that throwing some paint across a canvas could be a different kind of therapy. I wasn't sure where Hannah was since she always gave me a bit of time to process after an appointment with Doc, but I knew she would probably be going out with Remy anyway.

I didn't realise how much time they actually spent together until Remy came onto my radar. Their bond was so precious, and I longed for someone to care about me like that. Whenever he wasn't at school, Remy would visit and bring Hannah a new magazine to read or her favourite sweet treat in an attempt to get her to eat—it usually worked and, if it didn't, Remy's sad eyes were enough to make her try.

He always offered a crooked smile or small wave whenever he saw me, making me all flustered when I had absolutely no right to be. I had shut people out of my life for so long that it appeared I had no idea how to be around them, especially ones with killer looks like Remy.

Sometimes he would just hang around Pinewood and listen to Hannah ramble for ages. Those were my favourite visits because whenever I walked past them, I could see the way Hannah brightened around him. It made me even happier whenever her mother could visit around her work schedule, her hugs making Hannah's eyes light up in a way I had never noticed.

It was so strange to see functional families. Kate's family was nice and all, but her parents argued, and her dad worked too much. Despite their issues, I still always felt jealous that Kate had a family that seemed more normal than mine. She had both her parents, at the least.

It was hard not to imagine another life when you saw the Austen's together.

The art room was empty when I set up an easel and gathered paints. I was never very good at drawing, but expressionist paintings. I could ace those.

I perched on the edge of my stool and dipped the paintbrush into the blob of Prussian blue acrylic paint. I let the brush flow freely across the canvas and watched as the brushstrokes formed into something before my eyes. When the colours started bleeding together and creating an image of loss and redemption, I couldn't stop. Maybe nobody else would ever be able to see it, but I was telling my story in my own way.

Losing yourself in painting felt different compared to anything else. It was hard to understand but, in my head, it felt like a blanket of security wrapping around my emotions as I poured my soul out onto the canvas.

"That's really beautiful."

I jumped and fell off the edge of my stool as a male voice came from the doorway, breaking my concentration. Fumbling to pick up the paintbrushes I had dropped onto the floor, it took me a minute to realise I recognised the low, deep voice.

Remy smirked at me from the entrance of the art room, his arms crossed over his chest as he watched me flounder. I yelped and turned my back on him as I set the brushes back on the easel shelf, wishing I had closed the door.

"You gave me a fright, you big idiot!" I cried at him, scowling as he threw his head back and laughed.

"I wasn't expecting to be yelled at for complimenting your artwork."

I huffed at him and folded my arms across my own chest, mocking his stance. "Well, maybe you shouldn't be spying on people when they don't know you're there."

This made him laugh again, and he stepped into the room, walking over to inspect my painting. I wanted to grab it and throw it into the trash so he couldn't look at it. I made to take it off the easel, but he batted my hand away with a smirk.

"Let me admire it, please." He sounded so sincere that instead of telling him no, I simply nodded and stood back.

Remy tilted his head as he looked over it, his hand tracing the air in the shapes of the brush strokes. A small breath escaped from his lips as he smiled, his eyes crinkling. "It really is beautiful, you know."

My cheeks flushed with colour, and I avoided looking at him as he stepped back, turning to face me. I didn't ever allow someone to see any of my artwork; it seemed too personal. Allowing him to study it made me feel exposed, all of my scars on display. I hated it.

Remy reached out and put his hand on my arm, a gentle touch to force me to look at him. I wasn't expecting it and pulled my arm back in response, the unwarranted contact reminding me of something I would sooner forget.

Remy's face flashed with hurt, but he quickly wiped it away and held his hands up in surrender. "I'm so sorry! I didn't mean to freak you out."

I noticed the hoarseness in his voice, and it pained me to know he didn't understand. But it wasn't something I wanted to talk about yet.

I shook my head and searched his eyes as I spoke, hoping he could see the truth in my words. "It's okay, really. I'm just not good with being touched without being told first. I didn't mean to pull back like that."

Remy's expression turned softer as he nodded. "I don't know what happened, but I'm sorry that someone made you scared to be touched."

His voice was so soft and filled with such genuine emotion that it made my eyes water. He was such a gentle soul, and it made me sad that I hadn't met someone like Remy before I allowed myself to be manipulated by Benji.

"It is what it is, I guess." Deciding the conversation had gone far deeper than I was used to, I shrugged and offered a nonchalant smile. "Anyway, what are you doing down here? Where's Hannah?"

Remy looked like he wanted to say more but decided against it. "She's with our mum. Hannah mentioned you had a session with Doc and when I didn't see you around, I wanted to make sure you were okay."

He tucked his hands into the pockets of his jeans, shifting on his feet as though he were suddenly uncomfortable.

I ignored the flutter in my stomach as I smiled at him, this one genuine. "Thank you. It was tough but I'm okay. I just needed some time," I said as I gestured to my painting.

He ran his fingers through his curls which made the sleeve of his t-shirt twist, revealing the hint of a tattoo. I must have been staring because when I finally drew my eyes away, he was watching me with a smirk. I thought he would call me out, but he winked and headed towards the door instead.

"Are you leaving?" I scolded myself for sounding so transparent in my wish for him to stay. Hannah and Remy being around made it easier for me to breathe somehow and I hated when they had to leave.

He spun around and leaned against the doorframe, tapping his fingers against the varnished panel as he watched me. "I need to go study. I was going to come again this weekend though. Hannah wants to go to the cinema, and I thought maybe you'd wanna come?"

I bit my lip. "I wouldn't want to impose. You both spend enough time with me whenever you're here. It's a shame for me to take so much family time away from you."

Remy chuckled and rolled his eyes at me. "Em, I wouldn't have invited you if I thought you'd be imposing. Besides, you're Hannah's friend and you coming along makes her happy. I'll always be happy to see her enjoying herself, and she seems to really have fun with you."

"Um, okay then. I guess I could come. Thank you for inviting me."

Remy's eyes sparkled as he beamed at me, making him look like a child on Christmas morning. He smacked his hand off the door as he turned to leave. "Awesome. I'll see you Saturday, Emmeline."

Hearing him say my full name was oddly attractive. It felt like he was unintentionally rewriting the bad memories of having my mum say it with such disdain. I wanted him to say my name forever.

He swaggered off—genuinely *swaggered*, as though he knew exactly how cool he was—and I shook my head. Something about the Austen siblings made it impossibly hard to say no to anything they asked.

TWENTY-FOUR

I was woken on Saturday morning by a very excited Hannah as she shook me out of sleep. "Excuse me, we have plans today! Get your lazy butt out of bed!"

I groaned and swatted at her, but she yanked my covers away. I shot up as I remembered that I was wearing a tank top and shorts, my scars on full display for her to see, but she barely even glanced at them as she flopped down onto the bed beside me.

"Jesus, Hannah! Can't you wake me up like a normal person? Or at least bring me a cup of tea?"

I scowled at her, but she laughed and flipped me off. "You are not a morning person. Go and shower because Remy is picking us up in like an hour and I am not being late for my movie. Do you have any idea how hard it is to convince that damn brother of mine to go to a cinema?"

I furrowed my brows at her. "Wait, really? Why?"

Hannah rolled her eyes and flicked her hair out of her eyes. "Haven't you noticed how much he fidgets? The boy can barely sit still for ten minutes, never mind two hours."

I still didn't quite understand. "Why did he agree this time then?"

She just shrugged, "Who knows? I'm just glad he said yes. So, *please* go and get dressed!"

Hannah left me to pick out an outfit while she got herself ready. I hadn't been out in public much since I arrived at Pinewood and I could feel the anxiety building in my chest, ready to explode as a full-blown panic attack. I hated the idea of being around people and I cursed myself for saying yes.

I didn't have many nice clothes with me, but I managed to find a pair of faded grey denim jeans and a long-sleeve black chiffon blouse. I couldn't wear my comfort cardigan, so I decided on my charcoal cape jacket and matching boots.

"Damn, you look hot!" Hannah preened approvingly as she sauntered into my room.

She had chosen a knee length knitted jumper dress and thick red tights. I loved her style but what I loved more than anything was that I could see her starting to fill her clothes again, her bones less noticeable against her sallow skin.

"You're looking pretty good yourself, you know."

Hannah's face lit up and she curtsied before winking at me deviously. "Oh, I know."

She really was a little minx. I loved it.

I fluffed at my hair. My blonde roots were coming in thick and fast, contrasting against the dyed curls. I had grown accustomed to the brown locks, and I missed the way they looked when I first got it done.

As though sensing my anxious frustration, Hannah came over and styled it using her fingers. I couldn't do much about the colour, but I trusted her to make it look far less messy than I was capable of.

"Let's go," she said as she slipped her hand into mine and guided me out of my bedroom. I would much rather have buried myself in my duvet and watched movies from the comfort of Pinewood Grove, but it appeared there was no way for me to back out.

Remy was parked in his usual spot outside when we came outside, but we both bundled into the car before he could get out to help. He peered over his shoulder at me as I sat in the back, grinning from ear to ear.

"Howdy!"

I snorted and waved, "'Sup, cowboy."

My eyes widened as I realised how weird I had made that sound, but Remy threw his head back and laughed in response, my nerves melting away at the sound.

261

"Good one, Em. Are you ready to go?" He was asking, gaze zeroed in on me.

My cheeks flamed which was becoming a regular occurrence when he was around. I didn't know how to feel about that.

Hannah huffed from her seat in front of me. "We've been ready all morning. Can you just start driving already or are you going to continue to flirt with my friend for the next half hour and make us miss our movie?"

I choked on the saliva in my mouth. I tried to steady my breath to make it clear that we were *not* flirting, but Remy winked at me and put the car into gear, flipping his sister off in the process.

"I'm sure we can find some little boy squirt for you to flirt with, sister dear."

"Bite me," Hannah snapped back in response, but there was a lightness to her voice that made me realise she wasn't actually mad.

Not that we were flirting.

I slumped into my chair and tried to disappear as we drove to the cinema, my skin still flushed with unexpected embarrassment. By the time we arrived at, I feared that my body was going to burst the first time someone looked at me. My anxiety was so high that my head was pounding with thousands of thoughts.

Hannah bounced eagerly from the car, and I slipped out before Remy could get my door for me; I didn't want anything to make us seem any more friendly than we were for fear that it would upset Hannah. She may have been joking before, but I didn't want to cross that line.

Remy looked at me with raised eyebrows but thankfully didn't say anything.

Why did everything feel really awkward all of a sudden?

I rolled my eyes at myself. Stop overthinking, Emmeline.

Kids ran by and into the large blue building in front of us. Built up with huge glass windows and automatic sliding doors, the cinema was certainly eye-catching.

Hannah beamed and linked her arm through mine, pulling me through the doors. Remy trotted along behind us, smiling when I glanced at him over my shoulder. He looked delicious in a chequered shirt and low-slung jeans. I absolutely should not have been admiring him, but anyone with eyes on their head would have to appreciate how good he looked.

The inside of the cinema house was packed with people, chatter and laughter sounding from every direction. The sweet smell of popcorn and chocolate filled the air and wafted around me, my mouth watering in response. It had been a while since I had been to the movies, let alone near the type of food that made me so hungry my stomach hurt.

I glanced at Hannah and saw the way she was eyeing the queues at the food court, similar thoughts likely swirling around in her mind.

"So, ladies," Remy said as he caught up to us. "What sweet treats are we having?"

My stomach grumbled traitorously, and I chewed on my lip, considering my options. Doc was eager for me to try and make decisions regarding food again; I couldn't be scared to be independent, she said. But the thought of eating what I wanted produced more negative thoughts than I would have liked.

As I imagined eating some delicious nachos or the bittersweet taste of sweet and salty popcorn, it made me aware of the way my body was starting to fill my clothes again. While I knew in my heart that it was a good thing, my head was telling me that it had been too long since I found the comfort I found when I shut myself off and emptied the contents of my stomach.

I shuddered and wrapped my arms around my waist. I had worked so hard. I wanted to be able to do this. I just had to make the first step and try.

"I think I'll have nachos with cheese and salsa," I announced, mostly to myself.

Remy regarded me, the corner of his mouth twitching as though he wanted to smile. If I didn't know any better, I would think he was proud of my decision.

"Done." He clapped his hands together and turned to Hannah. "What about you, squirt?"

She stared up at the neon menus above the counter. "I want toffee popcorn and the biggest banana milkshake they have."

Remy chuckled and looked at us approvingly. "Good choices, I must admit. I, myself, think I'll get a hotdog and maybe I can steal some of Emmie's nachos," he declared with a wink before going to the counter to order.

My mouth gaped after him.

I turned to Hannah and tried not to show how curious I was as I asked her, "Does he always act like that?"

"Super flirty?" I nodded which earned a slight smirk as she shook her head. "Afraid not. Guess he must fancy you, my friend."

I scoffed, but Hannah's expression remained neutral and completely serious.

"You're totally joking, right?"

Hannah patted my arm. "Not in the slightest. Remy can date whoever he wants, and I'll always be happy if he is. If he was to date my best friend, who I *knew* was cool and could make him happy... I certainly wouldn't have an issue."

When Remy waved us over to help him carry the food to our seats, I couldn't help but blush furiously any time our eyes met. What did it mean if he did fancy me, as Hannah so bluntly put it? It was so weird to think of my friend's brother that way. Even still, there was no denying the way he made the world around me seem calm when I knew it was actually chaos.

It turned out that Remy had booked our seats prior to arrival and had chosen to pay for the premier section. With more leg room, reclining chairs, and individual tables to sit our snacks on, I felt like royalty. Hannah slid into her seat and patted the seat beside her. I wasn't even sure what movie we were about to watch, something with witches if I remembered correctly, but I found myself excited as I flopped into my seat.

I glanced at Hannah who made sure she was looking at the screen in front of us, even though it wasn't showing the credits. When I glanced over at Remy, he stole a nacho from my plastic tray and blew me a kiss before I could protest. He was a scoundrel in every sense; I rather liked it.

I relaxed in my chair and tried to ignore the way goosebumps covered my arms, especially every time Remy shifted in his seat. Hannah was so right when she said he couldn't sit still for more than five minutes; even after the movie had started, he twisted around or tapped his foot incessantly.

"Can you chill out and just watch the screen?" I whispered.

"I am *trying*," he replied, though it made no difference and he continued to move.

I made an effort to keep my eyes on the screen and try to keep up with the battle of covens that was taking place. If I was being honest, my excitement started to vanish the longer the movie went on. The main character was insufferable, and her voice was grating on my nerves. Combining that with Remy tapping his fingers off my armrest, I was about ready to explode. I felt guilty for being annoyed – after all, I understood being uncomfortable in a social situation. It was obviously his way of coping with whatever uneasy thoughts was running through his mind.

265

When I glanced at Hannah, she seemed genuinely happy as she watched the drama unfold, her hand dipping into her popcorn every few minutes as she rammed handfuls into her mouth.

If I had to suffer through simple nuisances to see her happy, I would do it with a smile on my face.

The nachos Remy had bought me sat untouched on my table, despite the salty tortilla chips making my mouth water. I couldn't decide which option was more damaging to my progress: eating them and risking the possibility of wanting to make myself sick or leaving them untouched and falling back into the pattern of not wanting to eat anything at all.

I decided on the first option and prayed that I was strong enough to fight the demons lurking. I loaded it up with the gooey cheese sauce and thick tomato salsa, my taste buds tingling as I groaned in appreciation of the savoury treat soon to hit my grumbling stomach.

I counted to ten before taking another one and repeating the process. Perhaps if I left myself enough time in between, I wouldn't feel like such a disgusting monster for eating them.

Remy stretched his legs, accidentally knocking my knee as he put his recliner down. He mumbled an apology, and I nodded my acceptance, feeling sad for him; he really wasn't comfortable here.

I loaded another nacho and nudged his elbow, holding it out to him. He looked surprised but took it from me, his fingers brushing against mine for a beat longer than necessary as he tried not to drop any of the toppings onto my clothes. I watched as he shovelled the full crisp into his mouth, crunching down on it like it was the most delicious thing he had ever tasted. As soon as he was finished, he grinned wolfishly and helped himself to another.

I ended up sharing the whole tray with him, resulting in him sitting happily for a few consecutive minutes and me feeling far better about consuming something so unhealthy.

Hannah jumped at something happening on the screen, and I giggled as her popcorn spilled onto the seat. She swore and glared at me, though a playful smile tugged on her lips.

I stifled a yawn and rubbed at my cheeks, trying to keep myself awake. Normally I was engrossed during movies, but this one was not keeping my attention and I was slowly becoming as fidgety as Remy.

"I'm going to the bathroom," I whispered to Hannah who nodded without taking her eyes off the screen.

As I tried to manoeuvre around the seats without getting in anyone's way, I was suddenly very thankful that Remy had paid for the more luxurious seats otherwise I would have basically been crawling over his lap.

I let out a sigh of relief as I entered the hallway, grateful for the coolness of the air and the lack of people loitering around. I thought about going to the bathroom and washing my face, but I knew that I would be tempted to rid myself of the nachos if I did.

Instead, I walked through the cinema foyer until I was outside, the air nipping at my cheeks and sweeping the exhaustion from my body.

The sky had turned a murky shade of blue, the clouds rolling in making everything darker. I supposed it would start raining before we were even finished with our movie, and I was grateful that I had worn clothes that would be warm and comforting if the weather did shift.

I leaned against the wall farthest from the windows, taking comfort in the quiet and peacefulness now that I was alone. I hadn't anticipated feeling so anxious, though I guess I shouldn't have been surprised given my deteriorated mental state.

Resting my head against the cold stone and closing my eyes, I could breathe without the fear of someone watching.

"Are you okay?"

I jumped when a voice disrupted my silence, smacking my head off the wall in the process. Remy came over and perched against the wall beside me, looking far cooler as he crossed his arms and looked at me with those big, beautiful eyes.

"Yeah, I'm good."

He turned so he was facing me, his breath hot on my cheek as he closed whatever distance was between us. He reached out slowly, his hand skimming my fingertips.

Remy was handsome and kind and having him touch me so gently sent goosebumps across my arms. Butterflies fluttered around my stomach at his proximity.

When I didn't object or pull away from the contact, he saw the permission I was giving him and locked our hands together.

"Are you really good, though?" he asked. "I got worried when you rushed off. I didn't know if you were going to..."

"Stick my fingers down my throat?"

Remy winced at my bluntness, and I reprimanded myself for being so cavalier about my situation.

I squeezed his hand. "Sorry. I didn't mean to say it like that."

He shook his head, his thumb stroking the back of my hand and sending shivers up my arm. Was it supposed to feel so electric to do something as mundane as holding hands?

"You don't need to apologise. But if we're being honest? Yes, that's what I was worried about. I thought you might need a friend."

I peeled my eyes away from his gaze, looking out towards the busy car park. I didn't know where I found the gall to ask, but I finally whispered, "And is that what you are? My friend?"

268

He didn't say anything, and for a beat I thought I had said something wrong. His hand remained in mine, but the silence suddenly seemed deafening. I willed him to say something, anything.

When I looked up at him, his eyes were still on me, his eyes so intense that it made my heartbeat quicken. His gaze travelled the length of my body, lingering on my lips before he returned his eyes to mine, his Adam's apple bobbing as he swallowed.

I wanted to speak, to ask him why he wasn't answering me, but my voice was lost to me.

Finally, he answered, "At the very least, yes."

The sound of his voice thudded in my ears, a huskiness that made my heart leap from my chest every time, no matter what he was saying.

But this time, I knew what I wanted him to say. Consequences be damned.

"And at the most?"

My own voice was a whisper, barely audible, even to myself.

But he was so close to me, our breath mingling together, and he swallowed again, licking his lips.

"At the most, I want to tell you how insanely beautiful you are. And then I want to pull you close to me while I wrap my arms around you and kiss you until I forget my own name, and you sure as hell forget yours."

It was my turn to swallow, my throat suddenly dry and constricting. I turned my hand in his, threading our fingers together as I looked at the golden flecks in his eyes. "I think you should do what you want."

His lips formed a mischievous smirk as he took a step forward, our chests pressed together. His mouth hovered just in front of mine, the heat of his body flooding into me and making me feel like every inch of me was on fire.

"I think I can manage that," he said in a voice that made me feel weak.

269

With the hand that was free, he slipped it around my waist and held me into him. I could feel his muscular frame pressing into my stomach and I had a flicker of fear as I imagined my stomach pressing against him. I expected him to pull away, declare his flirtations as nothing more than temporary insanity, but he did neither.

"Emmie?"

"Mhm?" I mumbled into his lips, unable to pull myself away.

"You are the most stunning person I have ever seen," he whispered to me before capturing my mouth with his again.

This kiss was different; it was everything he had said, an unspoken promise. There was a hunger to it that I had never experienced before, a hunger that I didn't know could exist.

I craved him as his tongue skimmed my lips, pushing into my mouth as I parted my lips for him.

It seemed wrong to want him as much as I did. I barely knew him, not to mention I was friends with his sister. It screamed forbidden, stupid, and totally reckless. But he made my pulse quicken and my heart pound in my chest.

All I could think about was how different it was to kiss him. With Benji, it had always been rushed and never quite satisfying, serving a purpose to him and only him.

Remy seemed to want only to please me as his tongue explored my mouth, making a moan escape my tender lips. After everything that had happened with Benji, I knew getting caught up in my feelings for someone else so soon would be an irresponsible thing to do, but it was futile to try and pull away.

I wanted Remy as much as he wanted me. Although I still couldn't figure out why he would be interested in a fucked-up chick like me, I wanted to find out.

TWENTY-FIVE

I was lost for breath by the time Remy broke us apart, though he kept his arm around my waist. I couldn't help but grin, touching my fingertips to my lips, now plump and red.

"Wow," I finally managed to croak out after my breathing had slowed some.

Remy closed his eyes, resting his forehead against mine, his breath tickling my sensitive lips. "You taste really good."

I laughed and enjoyed the way it felt to have his arm around me. I felt safe and protected. It wasn't fair to keep making comparisons to Benji, but how could I not when this already felt so different? Our relationship had ended so disastrously, it had broken me apart. I *wanted* to feel safe when I was with the people I cared for.

"What? Nobody ever told you that you tasted good before?" he asked incredulously, shaking his head.

I stiffened against him, remembering all the things that Benji had told me. Somehow, I couldn't remember any of the nice things or whether he had told me something like that; it had all just been erased by that one night.

Sensing the change in me, Remy took a step back, cupping my cheeks in his hands. "Hey, what's wrong?"

I shook my head. Would he be like Benji and throw me away when he saw my damage in all its glory? I didn't want to believe he could be like that—he understood some of my issues already, at least in part, because Hannah had been through the same. But he would have to see the way I had brutalised myself and I couldn't be sure he could handle that.

I broke myself free of his hold, hoping that my mind would be clearer if I wasn't so close to him. He made me feel intoxicated when I was near him, and if I wanted to think straight, I couldn't have his hand in mine or his arm around my waist.

"Emmie, talk to me," Remy pleaded. "What's wrong?"

"This was a mistake," I gestured between us. "This shouldn't have happened. I'm sorry. I just can't. We just kissed while your sister, my best friend, is in there waiting on us. God, she's going to hate me."

His face fell and I watched as he went through a series of emotions, his eyes mirroring the hurt I felt in my soul. He reached out for my hand, but I pulled away, knowing I wouldn't be able to be strong if he touched me.

If I wanted to be better, I would have to do it on my own. Relying on people meant getting hurt, and I would have nothing left in me if I had to go through something like that again. I had gotten so caught up in the moment, of feeling wanted and beautiful, that I hadn't thought rationally.

"Emmie, you're scaring me. I'm sorry if I was too forward. I'll tell Hannah what happened and make sure she knows that I initiated it. It's okay if you don't want that to happen again. I just need to know you're alright."

My heart ached as I looked at him, seeing the gentleness I associated with him. Even when he thought I was rejecting him, he cared about making sure I was okay. I wanted to fall in love with someone like Remy one day, but I couldn't do that before my heart had healed from its last break.

"I'm okay," I announced, straightening my back as I tried to appear strong. "I just don't know if I'm ready for something romantic right now. Besides, we should get back inside."

He nodded and I headed back into the cinema, hoping that the feeling in my chest would disappear.

—

Hannah never mentioned the fifteen minutes I had disappeared, or the fact that her brother had followed me. She did smirk at me every so often though, which only made me feel more guilty. I stayed away from Remy as much as possible after our cinema outing. Whenever he would visit, I made excuses to leave or tried to schedule appointments with Doc if I knew in advance when he was coming. When I had no way of escaping, Remy was every bit as sweet as he had been before, although he pretended like nothing had happened. And somehow that was even worse.

My moping, however, did alert Doc to something going on. After a few weeks of wallowing in self-pity with a broken heart and enough bad memories to drown me, she requested that I attend a last-minute appointment that hadn't been on my schedule.

I took my regular seat on her sofa and kicked off my shoes, curling my legs under me. Doc sat across from me, but her notepad was nowhere in sight as she leaned on her elbows, resting them on the ripped knees of her jeans—I truly loved the woman's style.

"I'm worried about you," she stated matter-of-factly.

I waved a hand in the air and scoffed. "I'm fine."

"If you were so fine, you would have opened up to me more during our sessions the last couple of weeks. You were making a lot of progress before, and now I can barely get you to talk. And your leaders have told me that they've noticed your lack of interest with food, which we both know is not a good sign."

I chewed on a ragged piece of skin on my lower lip, trying to resist the urge to dig my nails into my palms. I hadn't yet reverted back to my old habits, but I would be lying if I said it hadn't becoming increasingly more difficult to fight the urges.

"It really is nothing to worry about."

273

Doc scoffed. "Why don't you let me worry about that. Tell me what's bothering you. Please."

I huffed and crossed my arms over my chest, immediately uncrossing them as I realised how petulant it seemed.

"Okay, fine. I have a huge crush on Remy, and we kissed a couple of weeks ago. It was great until I realised how royally screwed up in the head I am. I pictured him seeing my scars and reacting the way Benji did, and I couldn't bear it, so I told him it was a mistake."

Doc hummed and sat back in her chair, crossing her legs. "This would be Remy Austen, Hannah's older brother?"

I nodded. "Yup, that's him."

Doc studied me, her lips pressed into a thin line. I could see her trying to figure out the best way to say what she was thinking, but I never dreamed that the next words would come out of her mouth.

"We haven't spoken about what happened with Benji yet. You are more comfortable with skirting around it. I wonder, if perhaps, it was something you would like to discuss now?"

I shivered and scrunched my eyes closed. I didn't want to tell her that every day since Remy kissed me, I had been reminded of the way Benji had acted. I could feel him pressed against me when my head was too foggy to really comprehend it, the way his breath was suffocating as he towered over me.

"What do you want to know?"

"Tell me about that night. I will be here with you, every step, and I promise you are safe."

I nodded and closed my eyes.

I started from him picking me up for the dance and goosebumps covered my skin. If I thought of it as a story, a tale to be told rather than cruel memories that I feared would never leave me, I could get through it. I could tell

274

her everything and finally be free of the prison my mind was keeping me in.

Doc listened intently, nodding her encouragement whenever my voice caught in my throat. By the time I was done, finishing with the moment I woke up in the hospital, I noticed the way her eyes were glazed over with tears. She was more composed than I—my tears had started falling long before I was even aware of them, and my eyes now burned from the way I had rubbed them angrily.

"Thank you for telling me, Emmie. I know that was not easy to share."

I sniffled and nodded, not trusting myself to say anything else.

"There's a lot of trauma from that relationship that we need to work on, but since the reason I brought you here was because of your sadness over Remy, I would like to discuss him. Would that be okay?"

I nodded again. I felt like one of those bobbleheads that people put on their dashboards of their car, thinking it was funny when in actuality they looked ridiculous.

"Why would you think Remy would react the same way as Benji? Has he given you reason to think that?"

I paused. Had he?

"No, not really. He's always been kind to me, and I feel safe when he's around."

"Everyone has scars, Emmie. People process life differently, but nobody goes through their years unscathed. Our scars, both physical and emotional, make us who we are. I should think that if Remy is as kind-hearted as his sister, then you shouldn't fear opening yourself up to him. It takes strength to let someone in after you've been hurt, but you are so much stronger than you realise."

"I don't know if that's true."

After I had stopped crying into my hands, Doc told me we could finish our session there, as long as I promised to cut myself some slack. She advised me to talk to Remy and

275

let him know how I was feeling, assuring me that I'd feel much better by doing so.

I walked back to my room with an uneasy feeling in the pit of my stomach. Doc was a smart woman, but I didn't know if this specific piece of advice was right. Allowing Remy to be a part of my life meant bringing him into my chaos, showing him the dark parts of my mind, and that felt like a very selfish thing to do.

I passed by Hannah's room, expecting it to be empty since she was out for lunch with Remy, but I heard voices coming from behind the open door.

Hannah's short blonde bob was the first thing I saw as she took a seat on her bed, crossing her arms over her chest as she frowned at her brother in concern.

Remy stepped into my eyeline as he took a seat beside her, his ruffles of chestnut curls messier than usual. He buried his head in his hands and I felt my heart break a little, seeing him upset.

Hannah reached her hand out and rubbed his shoulder, a sad smile spread on her lips. "Remy..."

He shook his head and stood up, staring out of the window. He gripped the window ledge, and I watched his muscles flex under the tight fit of his t-shirt.

"Please, just leave it, Han," he pleaded with his little sister, his voice gentle but inviting no room for debate.

Hannah, ever the stubborn teen, took no notice of him. "Why are you doing this to yourself? Why put yourself through all this worry and pain?"

Remy scoffed and turned to face her, tears in his eyes. He wiped a hand across his cheeks, and I felt myself well up at the sight. "You know why."

Hannah shook her head at him and offered him a simple nod. "I do know. But you can't save her, you know. She's damaged in the same way I am, Remy. Why can't you learn from that?"

276

A strangled sob escaped from his lips, and I bit my mine.

They were talking about *me*.

"I don't want to save her." Remy stated, with a matter-of-fact tone that caught Hannah off guard, judging from the horror on her face.

"Then why are you doing this to yourself? She's my best friend, and you know I love her, but I don't want to see you get hurt. I've already watched you fall apart over me. You both are acting so goddamn stubborn, constantly moping, and I can't take it."

He looked up at the door and I managed to dodge out of the way just before he saw me, my heart racing at the thought of being caught eavesdropping over such a private conversation.

Despite knowing I should give them privacy, I still couldn't bring myself to walk away. I wanted to hear what he had to say.

"I don't want to save her," Remy repeated softly. "I know that she's going to save herself. She's so strong, Han. I know she's going to go on to live this beautiful, amazing life. She's going to find the strength to live, and I want to be by her side when she does. I just need to get her to talk to me again, so I can tell her that."

My breathing slowed and I stared at the small sliver of him that I could see, feeling my walls breaking down just at the thought of him feeling the same way I felt about him. Tears slipped down my cheeks as I imagined living a life with Remy by my side, seeing a strength in me that I couldn't see myself.

I smiled and put my hands to my lips to stop myself from squealing. I wanted to barge into the room and tell him I had heard everything and that I wanted that life with him too.

But reality dawned on me, and I remembered the extent of my damage. I couldn't burden him with more than he already had. He had devoted his life to trying to help Hannah get better; it wasn't fair for him to spend the rest of his life worrying about me as well.

As much as I wanted Remy and the hope he offered, I refused to be responsible for absorbing the light he had left in his life.

If I truly cared about him, I couldn't let him do it to himself.

I would have to reinforce the walls that he had been working so hard to tear down.

—

It was easier than I thought to shut Remy out after I heard him talking to Hannah. It broke my heart every time she told me he was coming, but I made my excuses and shut myself away.

Being an amazing friend, she never pried, though I knew she desperately wanted to talk to me about it. I imagined that it must have been difficult for her to watch her brother so upset. It wasn't my intention to hurt him; I wanted to save him, but I couldn't tell her that.

It made it even easier to avoid Remy when I found out Hannah was being discharged from Pinewood Grove.

The news of her departure hit me so hard that I felt as though I had been punched in the gut. I sat on the edge of her bed, trying my best not to cry. It was good news, after all.

"I am happy for you, I promise," I sniffled.

Hannah laughed and sat beside me, her own eyes glossy with tears. "I know that, silly. I'm just as sad to be leaving, trust me."

I pulled her into a tight hug. "What am I going to do without you?"

She tutted and kissed my cheek. "You're going to be the badass lady I know you to be and get yourself out of here too. I know you're struggling, but you are so capable. Take what you learn here and apply it to the outside world. It's hard, but you can have the life you want. This time, I'm determined to do that too. I'm not coming back here."

Her face was set in fierce determination like I had never seen, and I thought to myself that if anyone could succeed in life, it was Hannah Austen. This sixteen-year-old had so much potential, and I was so lucky to have met her. Any strength I had was from her teaching me to be strong.

"I'm going to miss you so much," I told her, wiping away a few of her stray tears.

"We're going to see each other all the time. Just think of it as an incentive for you getting out too. We can hang out whenever we want. Although, I will be back in the wonderful hellscape called school."

I snorted my laughter and shook my head in disbelief. "That sounds like a really awesome plan."

True to her word, Hannah contacted me every day after she left. It felt so lonely without her at Pinewood, but I held onto the fact that it was completely amazing that she had worked so hard that she found her way out. She fought against the darkness, and the light was finally starting to surround her again.

When I thought about it too much, I started to cry as I pictured how amazing it was going to be to see her succeed.

I increased my sessions with Doc after Hannah left, determined to take her advice and find a way to get better. I wondered what my mum was thinking, if she was sad over why I hadn't been letting her visit or not. Mark never passed along any messages from her though, so I assumed she was happy to not have to worry about me.

Doc smiled kindly when I plopped down onto the sofa in her office, crossing my legs underneath me.

"Good afternoon, Emmie."

"Afternoon, Doc. How are you today?"

279

"I'm doing very well. Thank you for asking. How about you?"

I sighed and closed my eyes, resting my head against the back of the sofa. "Honestly?"

"Complete truth, please."

"Today isn't a good day. I'm struggling."

It felt quite good to admit that out loud. While it was a minuscule change, I was starting to see the way my sessions with Doc were helping me. Before my arrival at Pinewood Grove, I would have hurt myself and buried whatever emotions I was battling so far down that they festered inside me. But now I was admitting how hard I was finding things, I had been the one to request more appointments with Doc—I was a little proud of myself for that.

"Thank you for telling me that. Would you like to discuss why you feel like you're struggling?"

"Not really," I said with a smirk. "But I can't keep things buried forever, right?"

Doc gave me a knowing smile when I opened my eyes. "Nice to see you taking things on board, Emmie."

"I woke up this morning with this horrible wave of anxiety washing over me. All I wanted to do was talk to Hannah about it, and then I remembered that she's not here right now." My fingertips tapped against my palms as I tried to keep my breath steady and my emotions in check. "And then I started to feel really claustrophobic in my own skin. And I am fully aware of how ridiculous that sounds, but it's the only way to describe it."

"I don't think that's ridiculous at all. It's quite common for people with anxiety to feel that way at times."

I was grateful for Doc's reassurance, even if I didn't completely believe her.

"When I used to get like this, before Pinewood, I would...I would hurt myself. So, it's been a little difficult for me to try and not do that."

280

Doc got up from her chair and went to her desk, rifling about in one of her drawers until she pulled out a pencil case. "I want you to try something, Emmie."

I eyed her nervously as she sat beside me, pulling a red marker from the case.

"What's that for?"

"This is a technique I think may help you when you're feeling overwhelmed like this or have the urge to harm yourself. It works like this: when you get the compulsion to hurt yourself, you take the marker, and you draw a red line on your skin instead."

She pursed her lips together in a tight line and uncapped the marker, rolling up her sleeve to demonstrate. As she drew a line across the inside of her wrist, I had flashbacks of doing something similar with my own razor blades.

"It works by giving yourself control over the damaging, compulsive thoughts," she explained. "Where you may have hurt yourself before, you are now choosing a much healthier and less permanent way to mark your body. Would you like to try it?"

Doc held the pen out to me, and I took it with shaky fingers. I had started to become more comfortable wearing sleeveless tops, if only around the facility, which meant I had easy access to the already scarred skin on my arms.

"Go ahead, Emmie. I'm right here."

The certainty in her voice made me want to try it. It would definitely be less painful than the usual way I marked my skin.

I lowered the pen to my inner wrist, the bristles tickling my skin as I drew a jagged line.

I blew out a breath of relief as I looked at the ink on my skin. My eyes watered as I imagined how much pain I could have saved myself if I had met Doc and learned this technique a lot sooner.

Doc leaned back and regarded my composure. "How did that feel?"

"Amazing. Like I just learned how to ground myself without destroying my body in the process," I whispered as a few stray tears slipped down my cheeks.

Doc smiled at me proudly, her own eyes surprisingly glossy. "You have no idea how proud I am of you. That was a huge step, and I think it may be very useful for you in the future."

She sat with me until my tears dried.

"Keep the pen on you at all times. And remember something: even if you get nervous about doing it in public, just tell yourself, *it's how I am learning to survive*, because that is what you're doing, Emmie. You're teaching yourself all over again how to live, and there is absolutely no shame in that."

TWENTY-SIX

"Emmie?" Paula peeked her head into my room, beaming at me from the doorway. "Can I come in, darlin'?"

"Yes, of course!" I motioned for her to step inside.

It's not like I was busy. Ever since Hannah returned home, I either spent my days reading books or getting my feelings out in the art room. This was the first time in days that I had decided just to stay in my room.

Paula sat at the edge of my bed, careful not to disturb the sketchbook I had open. I was working on a charcoal drawing, though I had no idea what it was supposed to be yet.

"I know you've decided not to see your mum until you go home, which is totally fine of course. But there's a young lady at reception who says she really wants to see you."

My brows furrowed as I tried to imagine who it could be. "Who is it?"

Paula smirked and patted my shoulder. "I think it's a friend from school. Kate, I believe."

"Can you send her out to the gardens? I want some fresh air."

"You got it." She waved over her shoulder and headed off to get my visitor.

I stood in front of the mirror in my room and stared at myself. My hair had grown slightly over the past few months, and I eagerly awaited getting it cut again. I rather missed the short pixie cut, the curls twisting around my ears and tickling my eyes. I had gotten used to the way it shaped my face and the change had thrown me a little, making me re-evaluate how I looked at myself.

It surprised me that when I looked at my reflection, I didn't immediately want to throw something at the mirror and watch it splinter into hundreds of shards before me. While that would have been my first reaction before, I now simply regarded myself with slight discomfort. I was slowly starting to understand that my issues did not really have to do with how I looked, and instead they were more about how I viewed myself. I was trying to learn how to deal with the opinion I had of myself and change my outlook—it wasn't an easy process, but I was doing my best.

I brushed my hair out, frowning at the sandy roots running through the brunette dye. I thought I most looked forward to getting my hair transformed again once I finally got out of the facility. It would be nice to get pampered and take comfort in the quick burst of confidence it gave me.

I picked a thick knitted cardigan from the wardrobe and pulled it on, snuggling into the cosiness it gave me. I glanced at myself in the mirror again and smiled, watching as the reflection mimicked my action. Sometimes it felt as though I was living my life as a reflection of other people in the world, mimicking their actions in order to survive. Perhaps I should bring that thought up in therapy.

With a sigh, I made my way to the sitting area outside and took a seat on the bench next to the flower patches. I enjoyed watching the bees visit them, climbing inside to take the pollen from the petals. There was something very soothing about taking time to sit and watch the scenery, despite how boring it might have seemed.

"Emmie?" a quiet voice spoke, and I whipped my head around, my mouth falling open in surprise.

My former best friend stood at the door with her wild eyes brimming with tears. She was wearing a violet wig, styled into a side braid and adorned with butterfly clasps. Her face was bare, no trace of makeup in sight, but she still radiated beauty.

"Hello, Kate."

At the sound of my voice, she burst into tears. She buried her face in her hands and I felt the world stop around us. No matter what had happened, I couldn't bear to see her upset.

I jumped from my seat and made my way to her, wrapping her up in a tight hug. "Shush, it's okay."

She sobbed into my arms, gasping for breath. I continued to hold her until she managed to pull herself together, her voice barely a whisper. "I'm so sorry, Emmie. I can't tell you how sorry I am."

I pulled her over to the bench and sat her down before she started crying again. I offered a small smile, unsure that anything I could say would actually make her feel better.

"You don't have anything to apologise for. None of this is your fault."

She shook her head, strands of her purple hair blowing in the slight breeze. "You're my best friend. I should have noticed. I let it all happen and I did nothing—"

I took her hand in mine and squeezed gently. "I hid it from everyone, including you. I hid it for so long that nobody would have been able to see the signs, and that's okay. You can't blame yourself when I wouldn't have let you help."

She nodded through the tears, and I pulled her into a hug again.

I hadn't realised how much I had missed speaking to her, hugging her. I felt like a missing piece of my soul had been returned to me, my sister finally returned to the family.

"Can you talk about it?" Kate asked, a sheepishness to her voice.

I smirked and rolled my eyes. "You don't need to be scared to ask me about it. Yes, I'm fine to tell you what happened. But are you sure you want to know?"

"Of course, I want to know. I want you to tell me everything and anything you feel comfortable talking about."

I took a deep breath and started the long tale of how I ended up in a mental health rehabilitation centre with bandaged wrists and a messed-up head.

When I started to explain the way Benji had manipulated many of the situations leading up to my suicide attempt, Kate's face hardened. She swore loudly, and I hushed her with a smile, pleased to know she hadn't lost any of her ferocity while we hadn't been speaking.

"After we...after the incident, he turned really cold and cruel. I was crying and that made him mad, so he started telling me names and telling me how screwed up I was because of my scars. I felt broken and just assumed we would break up or make up the next day, but when I got to school, he had told everyone about my scars. And well, I assume you can figure out the rest from there."

Kate wiped the tears from her cheeks and looked at me sadly. "I'm sorry that happened to you. And I am sorry that you couldn't talk to me about it—and don't tell me not to apologise because I will anyway."

I nodded and patted her hand. "It's really good to see you, Kate. And I owe you an apology for letting myself be manipulated like that. I should never have chosen him over you."

"Oh, please." She waved her hand dismissing the apology. "You don't need to apologise for any of it. Let's just promise to always have each other's backs, okay? I want you to be able to tell me anything."

I grinned and she elbowed me playfully. "Noted. What about you, though? How have you been?"

Kate sighed and threw her hands into the air dramatically. "Well, I've been okay besides the fact that I haven't been able to text you constantly. Do you have any idea how many times I've watched reruns of Gilmore Girls? It's an embarrassing amount, Emmie, I tell ya."

She burst into laughter, and I joined in, pulling my friend into a hug. I had missed her so much and the sound of her laugh was comforting. I would appreciate her coming to see me and allowing me the opportunity to fix our friendship forever.

"So, you've been having tons of time off and I've been slaving away at school. What have you been up to in this retreat of yours?"

Trust Kate to think that I was off on some adventure. I had nothing of note to tell her.

Well, apart from one thing.

"I had a friend I met here. Her name's Hannah, and she really helped me survive in this place while I was working on sorting my head out."

Kate threw her arm over my shoulder, pulling me in for yet another hug. "Well, I can't wait to meet this Hannah, and thank her for looking after my amazing bestie."

"She really is the sweetest. I think you'll love her," I said, unable to wipe the grin off my face. I couldn't help telling her more. "She also has a big brother called Remy, and he's the nicest person in the world."

Kate's face lit up at the sound of me mentioning Remy. "A guy, eh? Tell me all about him."

And so I did.

I told her about how insanely good looking he was— nobody in the world deserved to look that hot and dishevelled. I told her all about the way he had invited me to hang with him and Hannah, making me laugh and smile even on my bad days. I explained to her how he made the air around me seem lighter, made everything hurt a little less, and how I missed him, a lot.

It was nice to talk about him with someone other than Doc.

287

"Remy sounds like the most perfect, imperfect dude. When can I meet him?"

I shifted uncomfortably next to my friend. "I messed up. We kissed and—"

"I'm sorry... You kissed?" She cocked her head. "Why wasn't this the first thing you told me!"

I rolled my eyes at her. "Chill out. I didn't tell you because I freaked out and told him it was a huge mistake. I don't want him to have to live his life worrying about me *and* his little sister. Do you know how cruel it would be to expect that of him?"

Kate harrumphed and crossed her arms. "Have you ever thought that it's cruel *not* to give him the chance? If he's as amazing and as lovely as you've described, I think you owe him that. He should be allowed to make up his own mind, Emmie."

I managed to get her to change the topic after another ten minutes of being lectured on free will, but I was grateful for her advice. I wasn't going to change my mind, Remy deserved better than me, but I loved having her back in my life for support.

—

When Hannah's next visit rolled around, I was excited to fill her in about my reconciliation with Kate. I was eager to bundle her into a tight hug and find out all about her schoolwork and how she was getting on. After living with her every day, weekly visits just weren't enough. I missed my little, sassy blonde sidekick.

When her drop-dead-gorgeous brother walked in beside her that Friday, I almost turned and sprinted in the other direction.

Instead, I sat and offered up as much of a smile as I could manage, despite the way my heart was having palpitations at seeing Remy for the first time in months.

"Emmie!" Hannah screeched as she dove forward and enveloped me in a tight bear hug.

"Hey, pretty gal," I answered, happy that the smile on my face was now far more genuine.

Remy sat in the seat opposite me, his smile tight as he nodded. "Hey, Em."

I sat up straighter in my chair, shifting uncomfortably. I hated the way I wanted to cry just hearing him say hello to me. Immediately, I felt my pulse quicken and my cheeks flush. I had missed that beautiful boy.

"It's nice to see you, Remy."

The corner of his mouth tugged and, knowing him, he was fighting off a smug smirk. "How're things?"

I couldn't decide whether his nonchalance was endearing or really damn annoying. I wanted to tell him everything still sucked—because truthfully it did. For the most part, at least. But when I opened my mouth to speak, I didn't have the words. Because he made me fluster and fumble just to say something stupid.

I leaned over to Hannah, placing a quick kiss on her forehead. "I'll be back in a minute, Han."

I left the table and made a beeline for the door, hearing Remy mutter to his sister, "I told you she'd be mad."

Once I made my way back to my room, I walked over to the window and stared out at the flower gardens. My mind was buzzing as thoughts swirled around and threatened to drown me.

Why was he here, now? When I was just getting used to doing things on my own?

I hated that just thinking of him made me infinitely happier. It was so unbelievably stupid to let myself get so attached to someone, I knew how much it could break a person when it went wrong, but something about Remy made me want to challenge the world rather than hide from it. And it terrified and excited me. I just didn't want to have to pick up the pieces of my heart again. Once had been enough, and I wasn't even over that yet.

Someone knocked on my door and opened it slightly before I could respond.

Remy checked to see if I was inside, before pushing the door open further, leaning against the doorframe as he watched me.

I stood at the bottom of my bed and wrapped my arms around myself, watching him curiously. He stepped inside and leaned against the doorframe, crossing his arms as he looked at me.

"Remy, you can't be here."

He looked at me with mild amusement, a mischievous glint in his eyes. The edge of his mouth twitched up. "Don't you know, I'm a rulebreaker, baby."

I rolled my eyes and snorted, losing all hope of remaining stern while he was this close to me, with no one else around. "That was beyond cringe."

He smiled fully as I laughed at his lame joke, clearly pleased that I had let my wall break so quickly. I regained my composure and did my best to wipe the smile from my face. "I'm serious, Remy."

He let out a frustrated sigh and ran his hand over the stubble appearing on his chin. It was such a subtle, mundane movement, but it made me want to run to him and place my lips on his anyway.

The tattoo on his inner bicep peeked out from under his t-shirt, his sister's name a reminder of why nothing could happen between us.

I pulled my eyes away from him and stared at the floor, trying to keep my composure.

"The facility has rules in place," I said. "You know that. We can't do *this*." I waved my hand around, gesturing between us, hoping it would be enough to get him to abandon whatever impulse he was acting on.

"Emmie—"

I held up my hand and shook my head, cutting him off from saying anything else. Tears threatened to spill as he said my name, breaking my heart into a thousand pieces. "You know we can't break the rules. What if they send me home?"

"We both know they aren't going to do that," he said as he stepped towards me. His hands brushed my arms lightly, sending shivers down my body. "Tell me what's really going on. Please, Emmie."

I didn't want to tell him.

I didn't want him to know the fear that I felt in the deepest parts of my soul that I wouldn't be enough.

I was damaged beyond measure, carrying more baggage than a single person ever should have. He didn't deserve to deal with any more than what life had already thrown his way. I wouldn't do that to someone I cared about. I couldn't.

I looked up, determined to stand my ground and force him to leave.

But as I looked into his gemstone green eyes, my resolve melted away, and I knew I couldn't keep lying to him. Maybe Kate had been right. Maybe he did deserve to make this choice for himself.

"I'm broken," I whispered, turning away to hide the tears that had begun to cascade down my cheeks.

Saying the words out loud was like a hard slap across my cheek, snapping me back to reality. Maybe it was good he saw me like this. Nobody, not even an amazing person like Remy, would want someone so broken.

He took a step towards me, his gentle hands gripping my arm and turning me back around to face him.

Lifting his hand to my cheek, his thumb slowly wiped away the tears.

I closed my eyes against his touch, wishing I could live there forever.

"We're all broken in some way, Emmie. Life is messy and painful, but it can be so beautiful too," he said. His voice was soft and quiet as though he knew he could melt away all the walls I had built to protect myself.

He took my hands in his, his fingers reaching around to my wrists. I hitched a breath as his fingertips grazed lightly along the reddened, grizzly lines, his gaze never leaving mine.

"Your scars don't make you any less beautiful, Emmie."

He was the only person I had ever allowed to touch my scars and the tenderness he used brought tears to my eyes. Trusting someone was difficult after Benji, but Remy treated my boundaries with respect. Even now, I could see the question in his eyes as he silently asked to hold my hand. I nodded slightly and a soft smile spread across his lips as he linked our fingers together, an unspoken promise being made.

"Your scars may come from a place of darkness, but they're the reason you shine brighter than anyone else I've ever met."

I opened my mouth and tried to respond, but I didn't have the words. I couldn't fathom how he had touched my scars without flinching. I could barely look at the permanent reminders of what I had done.

And yet, here he was, this beautiful human being, telling me my scars were not something to fear.

"You are not weak for needing help or having gone through horrific times."

"Remy—" I started, my smile faltering as I realised how much it was going to hurt for me to tell him that nothing had changed.

As though he could sense what I was about to say, he shook his head and groaned at me. He ran a hand through his messy hair before cupping my face in his hands once more.

"You know what? No. Listen to me," his voice broke as tears glistened in his eyes. He looked at me with those beautiful big eyes that made my heart beat ten times faster. "If you don't want to be with me because you don't feel the same, then I understand, and I won't push you any further. But if you're scared or think you're doing me a favour, then I am telling you, I can handle it."

A tear slipped down his cheek and I wiped it away with my thumb. He closed his eyes and rested his cheek in my hand, gulping down more tears.

"I'm scared," I whispered.

"I'm a big boy, Emmie. You can't make decisions for other people because you think it's best for them. I am telling you that you're not alone, and I want to be with you. I want to explore whatever this is between us because it feels pretty damn magical to me. Now you have to decide if that's something you want, too."

I rubbed my face in my hands and tried to form words. I could see the heartbreak in his eyes, pleading for me to say something. My head was pounding as thoughts swirled around. I was terrified but I wanted nothing more than to fall into his arms, knowing how safe I would feel in his embrace.

He took a step back as he waited for my response. That small act of making sure he wasn't invading my personal space or crossing boundaries was enough for me to make my decision.

I trusted him.

"I do want to be with you. It was never a question of how I felt about you," I whispered, pulling him close and linking my shaking fingers with his. "There's so much about me that feels heavy and messed up. I didn't want to ruin your life by pulling you down with me. But I think I was wrong—I'm doing my best to get better and heal and pushing away the people I care about most won't be beneficial. I care about you, Remy."

It felt as though a weight had been lifted from my shoulders as I said it, relief washing over me.

A relieved smile spread across his face, and he let his tears fall, resting his forehead against mine. I let out a slow breath, my tears mixing with his.

I lifted my face up until our lips met. As though reading my mind, Remy wrapped his strong arms around me, pressing me against his body as he deepened the kiss.

I rested my head against his chest, smiling as I felt his heart beating fast against my cheek. I closed my eyes and took comfort in being in his arms.

"Are you okay?" Remy mumbled into my hair, tightening his embrace.

"I'm okay," I whispered into his chest, nuzzling my face into his t-shirt as I inhaled his scent. A mixture of sweet and spicy, an intoxicating blend which filled my nostrils and made my mouth water.

I pondered over my words and found the ghost of a smile on my lips. I wasn't okay yet; recovery was going to be a very long road for me, and I couldn't avoid that. But being in Remy's arms, I was hopeful. I wanted nothing more than to be okay, to be better. A sense of calmness hung in the air around us, and for the first time in a long time, I believed that perhaps everything would work out. I allowed myself a brief moment of peace, lighting a spark of optimism inside me.

—

The piece of paper in front of me was offensively blank. I had been staring at for over an hour, wishing the words would just magically appear. Doc had given me homework again, though this time it was a little more difficult than self-retrospection.

Writing a letter to your mum will be cathartic, Emmie. Even if you don't send it, Doc had said confidently. I wasn't so sure.

I had so much to say to her, but the words were escaping me. I had always found talking to her to be a task in itself, and a letter was no different.

Be brave, Emmie. I could do this.

Dear Mum,

I've started this letter so many times and ended up throwing them straight into the bin. You see, I don't want to hurt you by telling my truth, even if it will help me heal. Isn't it funny how I'm worried about how you'll cope with my feelings when you're the adult and I'm the child?

It makes me sad that you got pregnant with me because I know I ruined the life you wanted. I think I've always been aware that I messed up your future, no matter how happy Dad was about having me. And even though it wasn't my choice, I'm sorry. I'm sorry that you became a parent before you were ready; I'm sorry that I wasn't the perfect little girl you wanted; and I'm sorry you had to do it on your own all these years.

But as sorry as I am, I also recognise that I shouldn't have to feel sorry. I've spent my life so far constantly feeling less than because I knew you didn't want me. I think you love me because I'm your daughter, but I don't think you like me very much. It shouldn't be like this, Mum. I shouldn't always have to try and prove myself, to be perfect just so I feel an ounce of love from you.

You lost your husband, the person who loved you unconditionally and showed you what it was to be happy. I can't imagine how hard that was for you. I remember how broken you were afterwards. But I lost my dad. I should have still had a parent, someone to help me through the grief, but you shut yourself off and let me shut off too. I miss him so much. Losing him broke my heart in ways I can't even describe, and you're the only person who can understand that pain. I hope one day we get to the stage where we can talk about him. Don't you want to share stories of the person we both loved most?

What I did to myself... it was a cry for help, Mum. And I'm getting help here. Doc, my therapist, has helped me understand a lot about myself and I really enjoy working with her. I think I want to continue therapy – I know I certainly need to – once I leave Pinewood. Would you ever consider joining me for a session? I know that is a truly big ask, but I want a relationship with you, Mum. I've spent so many years wishing to escape Apollo, but I want something different now. All I truly want from life is to be happy, and I won't be happy if we don't repair whatever rift is between us.

Doc says my progress so far has been really good. If I continue to take her advice and focus on healing, I should be able to lead Pinewood within a couple months. I'm a little scared to leave here and be back in the real world. But I think I'm strong enough and that I can do it. You're really strong, Mum, so maybe you could help teach me how to be like that too?

I wasn't sure whether I was going to send this or not, but I think I will. If you don't reply, I'll understand. But I hope you do get back to me.

Please know I love you. Despite everything, you'll always be my mum and that means something to me.

All my love,
Emmeline

Emmeline,

I miss your dad too. I don't know how to deal with all of this, or your mental health, but I will try.

I don't hate you. You're my daughter and that means something to me, too.

Therapy is not something I'm overly comfortable with,
but I do suppose one session can't hurt. Please ask Doc if
something can be arranged.
    Love,
    Your Mother

TWENTY-SEVEN

Two Months Later

I stretched out my legs and tucked my feet into the warmth of my duvet. I smiled as Remy shifted beside me, turning onto his side so he could look at me.

"You okay, beautiful? I'm sorry, I didn't mean to fall asleep."

His eyes still drooped sleepily, and he wiped at them with the back of his hands, stifling a yawn. I found a smile appearing on my face as my heart leapt just at the sight of him next to me. It still felt surreal to have him laying on my bed next to me, calling him mine. There was a flutter in my chest every time he crossed my mind, and it was the best feeling in the world.

"I'm good." I leaned over and placed a soft kiss on his cheek, basking in the tingle on my lips as they touched his skin. "You look tired, so I just let you sleep. Besides, you looked so peaceful, I couldn't wake you."

He grinned lazily at me, his hand reaching over to hold mine. I linked my fingers with his, bringing our hands up to my lips.

"What are you working on?" he nodded his head towards the browser page I had open on my laptop.

Ever since I had been released from the Pinewood, I had been trying to find ways of not hating my body or the marks I had created. It was a difficult task to love something that looked so gnarly, but I was trying my best.

"I'm thinking about getting a tattoo to try and make me appreciate my skin a bit more."

I tilted the laptop screen towards him so he could see what I was doing, pleased when he nodded his appreciation. "Those are some pretty cool designs."

I shrugged and continued to scroll through the endless images. It wasn't that I didn't like any of the designs. Some were beautiful and I would have loved to have them on my body. But they wouldn't cover the scars and it would ruin the beauty of the design if I just placed them randomly.

I sighed, and Remy lifted my arm to his mouth, kissing along the jagged scar. I closed my eyes at his touch, surprised that I didn't find myself wanting to pull away from him.

"You're beautiful. With or without scars or tattoos, you are the most beautiful person I have ever met," he whispered as he dotted kisses from my wrist to my elbow. "You take my breath away."

"Remy..."

I loved how he tried to make me look at myself the same way he did, but sometimes it was a reminder of how much I disliked the image of my own body.

Remy glanced up at me and smirked, tracing his fingertips across my skin so lightly that it tickled, and I had to suppress a giggle. "Don't *Remy* me, Emmie. We've already discussed that I will tell you how amazing you are every day until I die. And then I might even haunt you just to keep reminding you."

I shook my head and laughed at him, wondering how he always managed to distract me from my dark thoughts.

I tapped my chin in mock consideration. "You would make a pretty hot ghost."

Remy's deep laughter vibrated through my bones, satisfying chills washing over me. His hands glided carefully up my arms until his hands reached my face, cupping my cheeks so he could look into my eyes.

The golden glint to his honey-brown eyes always made me melt into him. The way he looked at me was extraordinary; I felt like the centre of the universe. I hoped he knew that he was the centre of mine, too.

His crooked smile as he ran his eyes over me was the most precious thing and was easily one of my favourite things about him. Whenever he flashed that smile, I was as good as gone. I still wasn't sure what I had done to deserve such an incredible person in my life, but I definitely wasn't going to question it.

"I don't deserve you," he mumbled quietly.

I scoffed and placed a soft kiss on his lips. "You deserve better than me. But deserving doesn't matter; feeling does. And I feel plenty for you, Remy Austen."

I hadn't expected to get choked up, but my voice caught in my throat. I desperately wanted to tell him that I loved him, truly and deeply, but I didn't want to rush things or scare him off, even if it was how I felt.

The look I received in return made me feel like maybe he was thinking the same thing, and I knew that neither of us needed to say it; we loved each other.

I loved that his eyes glossed over with a layer of tears as he pulled my face towards his.

I always thought people were being dramatic when they said kissing the right person felt like fireworks going off, but they were right. Kissing Remy was like the stars were exploding around us, our own cosmic display of affection.

I wrapped my arms around his neck and pulled him onto me as I fell back against my pillows. Remy tucked his hands under me, his fingers gripping the small of my back. I caressed the back on his neck with my fingertips, taking pleasure in the way he shivered. Being so close to him made me feel intoxicated, the most terrific high of my life. Every time his lips left mine, I felt bereft and breathless, like I never quite got enough of him.

He pulled off me slightly, a sexy smile slowly tugging at his lips. "You really are irresistible, you know."

I groaned and smacked his arm playfully, wishing he didn't have the willpower to resist at all.

We had agreed to take things slowly—he hadn't wanted to push me after everything that had happened with Benji, which I appreciated immensely. But it didn't mean that I didn't want to quicken the pace sometimes. I found him just as irresistible as he found me.

He tutted at me and rolled off, so he was laying at my side again. "Go back to your research, my love."

I pulled the laptop back up to my chest and continued to look through the google search. Remy flicked through channels on the TV before deciding on reruns of an old sitcom. His laughter broke the silence, and the sound made me relax. I always felt more at peace when he was around.

He picked up his sketch pad from the foot of the bed and began to doodle some of the characters as he watched. It was mesmerising to see him be able to bring things to life just using paper and a pen and I wished I had his talent.

I wasn't quite aware of when he switched from drawing on the paper to my arm, but it was a welcome surprise. He traced the tip of his marker up and around my arm, winding its way around the scars.

It wasn't the first time he had doodled on my skin; it was a fun habit of his to just start drawing these masterpieces on whatever part of my body was exposed. I didn't mind really because everything he drew turned out so breath-taking.

I let him continue to draw as I flicked through wrist tattoos, wishing something would make me gasp or cry. I imagined that if something really spoke to me, I would have an outward reaction and would know that it was the one. But everything seemed too cliché or too perfect to suit me.

"Done!" Remy announced, grinning from ear to ear. He must have created something spectacular if he was this proud over it.

I glanced down at my arm and felt like my heart was going to burst. In a mere ten minutes, Remy had drawn the most intricate and stunning flower vine crawling up my arm. I bit on my lip to stop myself from crying as I looked from the drawing to Remy.

"Oh my god, baby! I'm sorry," Remy said quickly, the nervousness apparent in his voice. I can go and get a cloth to clean it if you don't like it."

The panicked look in his eyes made me feel awful for being at such a loss for words.

"No, Remy. I love it!" I finally forced out, watching as relief passed across his face.

I looked down at my arm again and didn't resist when a few tears began to drip from my eyelashes. For the first time, probably ever, I could see something beautiful about my body. Even though it was just ink on my skin, somehow it made the scars seem not so bad. The way the vines wrapped around them somehow enhanced them in a weirdly captivating way, as though they were necessary to complete the drawing.

His smile in response was like the sun lighting up the entire world; bright, captivating and making my eyes water just to behold it.

I pulled him into the tightest embrace I could muster, holding him so close to me I was sure he could feel my heartbeat.

When I eventually let him go, he placed a soft kiss on my forehead. "I told you before and I will tell you again: every part of you is beautiful in its own way. It doesn't matter how it came about, whether through happiness or terrible sadness, it's a part of you as much as everything else. Embrace the reminder you have of how strong you are because you're still here, fighting."

I didn't have the words to communicate how deeply what he said had touched my soul. It was a hard truth to accept, but he was right: my scars were part of me, and they weren't going away any time soon. I would have to get over their presence on my body at some point. And, whether I liked it or not, I had inflicted them upon myself. I couldn't spend the rest of my life hating myself, or I would remain in that dark, depressive place forever if I did.

I closed the screen on my laptop and slipped under the covers, snuggling into Remy. He wrapped his arms around me as I rested my head on his chest. I closed my eyes and smiled as my head moved on his chest, rising and falling in time with his breathing.

He switched the TV off and lay back against the pillows to get comfortable, placing a kiss to the top of my head.

I stifled a yawn and rubbed my cheek onto his t-shirt. Remy chuckled lightly, running his fingers through my hair knowing it would help me to fall asleep.

"I don't want to go to sleep," I moaned, immediately reminding myself of a petulant child.

Remy tutted and cuddled me tighter. "I'll still be here when you wake up, love. I promise."

I wanted to argue more, but I was exhausted. I found that I had the best sleep when Remy was around, especially if I was in his arms.

As he held me to his body, I allowed myself to relax. My mind slowly let go of all of the anxious thoughts that had been swirling around, and instead focused on the idea of sleeping in Remy's arms for the rest of my life. It was a comforting thought that I clung to whenever I needed to calm myself down.

I began to drift to sleep, finally being lulled over by the soft beat of Remy's heart. That, as it turns out, was my favourite sound in the world.

—

When I woke the next morning, I was pleasantly surprised that Remy had indeed stayed with me. He lay beside me in my bed, his hair splayed out on the pillow underneath him. I watched him with appreciation, wondering if he knew how handsome he was. Sometimes I felt like I didn't appreciate him enough for all he did for me.

"Can you stop staring at me like we're in *Twilight*?"

I giggled as he squinted at me through one eye, groaning as he sat up. I admired the way his tee had crawled up during his sleep, exposing some of the sun-kissed complexion underneath.

"Good morning, you handsome man." I leaned over and placed a firm kiss on his lips, smirking as he pulled me on top of him and passionately kissed me back. It was a struggle to pull away from him, feeling bare without his lips on mine. "My mum is going to kill me for letting you stay over without asking her first."

Remy smirked and rolled his eyes. "Oh my God, she's going to absolutely freak," he mimicked.

I smacked him in the chest, and he feigned injury. "I'm serious!"

He shook his head and kissed me lightly before quietly crawling out of bed.

"I know, I'm sorry. I just didn't want to wake you when you were finally getting some sleep. Do you think I can sneak out without waking her?"

I checked the time on my phone and saw that we had roughly half an hour before she would be getting up for work. "If we're super quiet, yeah."

He nodded and pulled his sweatshirt over his head, running his hands through his messy hair as though it would tame it. I climbed out of bed and took his hand, pulling him across the landing.

I paused outside my mother's room and peeked inside, pleased to see she was still fast asleep in the middle of her silk sheets. I pulled her door over as much as possible without clicking it closed and motioned for Remy to follow me again.

I gasped as one of the floorboards creaked under his boots, loud enough that I would be surprised if it hadn't woken my mother.

I yanked him down the stairs as fast—and as quietly—as I could, practically shoving him out the front door.

He stood on the front step and winked at me, blowing me a kiss. I melted into the doorframe and wished he wasn't leaving me.

"I'll see you later, love."

I whimpered and waved him off. "Text me when you get home!"

Waiting until he was out of sight before stepping back inside and locking the front door. I was pleased that he always remembered to park a block or two away to keep out of sight of my mum. I sighed in relief and practically crawled back upstairs, wondering how I had managed to sneak him out without being caught.

I jumped back into bed and laughed into my pillows.

That was kind of exciting.

—

I was pleasantly surprised when I got a text that afternoon telling me to meet Remy in town because he had a surprise for me. I brushed my hair and tried to style it using gel, knowing it was a pointless effort because the short curls would stray wherever they wanted.

I had chosen a pair of skinny khaki-coloured jeans and matched it with a loose button-down black blouse. It had three-quarter sleeves and was a present from Remy to try and encourage me to love myself; I had almost cried the first time I tried it on and saw skin exposed.

But as I put it on today, it felt really great to let my arms breathe for the first time in this town in years. I figured it would be okay to wear it, considering my jacket would cover it when I was outside anyway.

Nobody would know, but it was my own personal victory.

As I walked through the town, I was startled by how much I loved seeing people milling around the streets. I had never noticed before how comforting it was to see people laughing and shopping together, embracing their lives.

The shift in season from spring to summer had brought with it the increase of pollen—according to my runny eyes and blocked nose whenever I was outside—and the burning heat of summer sun. I longed to be in a place to expose my arms to the world and embrace the idea of tanning, instead of looking sickly-white all year long. Perhaps, in time I would get there.

"Emmie?"

I froze at the sound of that voice, one that haunted my nightmares. Turning around, I came face to face with Benji. He stood with his hands in the pockets of his jeans, a bright green hoodie on in place of a colourful shirt. I used to find his quirky style cute, but the sight of it now assaulted my eyes – though I couldn't be sure that wasn't just the sight of him in general.

"I was hoping to run into you at some point," he said after a minute, obviously mistaking my shock as permission to keep talking. "I owe you an apology for what happened. I shouldn't have told everyone about your scars."

My fingers curled as I clenched my fists at my side. The audacity of this pathetic excuse for a boy, thinking he had earned the right to talk to me after everything that happened. Why did the male species always think they could do what they wanted?

"*That's* what you think you have to apologise for? Benji, I don't want your apologies or anything else. All I want is to never see your face or hear your voice ever again."

His smirk dropped and I saw the mask drop with it. Gone was his playful expression, the coldness seeping back in. "That's just rude. I'm trying to make amends here. We had a good run, and I'm sorry that you don't seem to be over it yet."

I couldn't help the bitter laugh that escaped my lips. "Benji, I'm not sad that we aren't together. I'm *fuming* that you think you can talk to me after you *abused* me! I don't need apologies or amends to be made – I need for you to crawl back into whatever hole of hell you were born in and never step foot near me again."

Spinning on my heels, I started to walk away from him, determined not to let him have the last word. But Benji never understood the word no, or any variation of it. Following me, he reached out and yanked my arm to turn me around.

"You absolute bitch! Do you have any idea what an accusation like that could do to me? You could ruin my whole life out of spite!"

Spittle landed on my cheeks as he spewed his viciousness at me, his grip on my arm tight enough that my skin would bruise if he didn't let me go soon. I wasn't the same person who had met Benji and fell for his lies, and I wasn't going to let him leave me with anymore marks.

Slamming my heel onto his foot, I pulled my arm free and shoved Benji as hard as I could. He stumbled back, cursing as he tripped and fell onto his ass.

"Don't you EVER TOUCH ME AGAIN! If you ever come near me again, I swear I will ruin you. I'll tell *everyone* what you did to me. I'm stronger than you think I am, and I'm not scared of you anymore. Rot in hell, Benji."

Feeling my body trembling – whether from anger or adrenaline, I didn't know – I left him on the ground and rushed away. I was surprised by myself and the fact that I hadn't broken at the sight of seeing him again. I had worked so hard to move on from what he had done to me, and I wouldn't let him destroy that.

Remy had told me to meet him outside the town college as he was in class during the afternoon. I would tell him what happened, but not until later. He had told me to meet him outside of his college because he had a surprise for me, and I didn't want Benji to ruin another second of my life.

I took a deep breath and tried to compose myself; I would process what had just happened later. But for now, I was going to spend time with my boyfriend who treated me like I was the most important person on the planet. My happiness was dependent on nobody but myself, and I would never let anyone take that from me again.

I was a survivor and survivors didn't give up.

—

True to his word, Remy met me outside the college a mere five minutes after I arrived. His face lit up as he saw me, his huge grin making his honey eyes glisten in the sunlight. I felt as though I would melt under the intensity of his gaze every time he looked at me with those eyes, knowing they made my insides turn to goo.

He picked me up by the waist and spun me around as I giggled, slowly bringing me down to meet his lips without ever setting me back onto the pavement.

I wrapped my legs around his waist, my fingertips trailing across his stubble as I basked in the sweet taste of his kiss.

"Good afternoon, my beautiful girl," he grumbled into my mouth. If he hadn't been holding me, I may have swooned at the sound of his voice.

"Mmm, good afternoon, my love." I winked at him as he finally let my feet touch the ground, exchanging my hips for my hand as we started to weave through the car park to his sleek gun-metal grey Kia Sportage.

His car was a large, beautiful vehicle and I was insanely jealous. Remy promised that if I worked towards getting

308

my license then he would let me drive it, providing I was careful. It was the most precious thing he owned, and I knew how much he took care of it, and the idea of actually being in the driver's seat of the car was terrifying.

"So, what's my surprise?" I asked as I jumped into the passenger seat and clicked my seatbelt into place.

Remy closed my door for me and climbed into the driver's side, chuckling to himself. "Why would I tell you? Then it wouldn't be a surprise."

I moaned and rolled my eyes but was secretly pleased. It meant a lot to me that he was going to put in so much effort for me. I had chosen every birthday and Christmas present I had ever received from my mum since the year my dad died. Surprises were rare in my life. Kate, Hannah and I were saving to have a girl's weekend trip when we had time, but it wasn't a surprise since I was helping to plan it.

Remy winked at me as we pulled out of the car park, linking his fingers through mine in my lap.

I beamed at him, blowing him a kiss which made him blush.

"How was class?" I asked, genuinely interested in his answer.

Whenever we spoke to each other about our days, it made me think of my childhood. My parents would come home from work and chat about their days, taking great pride in the enjoyment they got from it. I never understood how they could care about such boring topics. Then I met Remy, and I completely understood, because it didn't matter what he was telling me, it sounded like the most interesting thing in the world, and I loved every second of it.

He smiled without taking his eyes off the road, and I knew it was meant for me. "It was pretty boring if I'm honest. We were going through one of the grading systems again and if I didn't need to know it to pass, I swear my brain would have completely shut off."

309

I laughed and the sound made him smile even more. "How was your day, sweetheart? Did I manage to get out before your mum caught us?"

"Only just! I can't believe we slept for so long. But other than that, my day was okay. I just spent it studying for my final exam on Tuesday. I can't wait to see my results in a month. If I don't pass after all this hard work, I'm going to be fuming."

Remy brought my hand up to his lips and kissed my knuckles softly. "You know that no matter what, you should be proud of yourself, right? You've worked really hard to catch up with everyone else and there are always other options if you don't do great. However—and I mean this sincerely, and not just because I'm your boyfriend—I have every faith that you will have aced them."

I loved how much faith he had in me. The most amazing part about being with Remy was that he had seen me at my lowest point and still chose to support me. It made everything he said to me so much more truthful because he looked at me in a way no one else did and it was magical.

I reached over and switched the radio on, pleasantly surprised when an old Abba song came on. Remy let out an exaggerated groan as I turned the volume up, blasting the music through the open windows. I attempted to sing along—I sounded like a cat being strangled, but what was the point in singing if you couldn't have fun, no matter how bad you were.

Within minutes, Remy had joined in. He had a surprisingly good singing voice, his deep baritone perfectly accompanying my screech to create something that didn't sound completely awful.

I tried to work out where we were going as Remy drove through some of the neighbouring towns. As we entered Remy's hometown of Orion, just a few miles past Apollo, I assumed we would be going to visit his parents. Then he

310

drove past the turn to his street with a cheeky grin, and I pondered where else there was that he would be taking me.

I leaned over in my seat and placed a delicate kiss on the small of his neck, knowing it would drive him crazy. "Can't you tell me where we're going?"

"Dirty tactics, Miss Beaumont!" Remy shook his head and barked out a laugh, his thumb circling the back of my hand. "But no, we're nearly there so you'll just have to wait."

I blew out a frustrated sigh and sat back in my seat, resting my head against the window as the trees blurred. Remy laughed beside me, basking in how agitated I was the longer it took to reach our destination.

After what seemed like three hours, but was probably only thirty minutes, we pulled into a car park behind a bunch of shops. The parking bays were extremely crowded, despite it being late afternoon and it took almost ten minutes to find a spot, cramming between two cars parked far too close to the lines.

Remy switched the engine off and unbuckled his seatbelt, turning to me like a giddy twelve-year-old. "Are you ready?"

I eyed him suspiciously, but failed to keep a smile off my face, seeing how enthusiastic he was. "I'm as ready as I'll ever be."

He clapped his hands together and jumped from the car, coming around to open my door like the perfect gentleman he was. I slipped out of my seat and tucked my arm in his as he led me through the alleyway into Orion town centre.

Although I had been to Remy's a few times since we started dating, we spent most of our time in Apollo. It was easier for him to visit me since he had his own car, and we liked going to the beach at the edge of town.

I was surprised to see that most of the stores were built into the front of antique-looking buildings. Above the majority of the shops were flats and homes, while the shops themselves were modernised with large glass storefronts and vibrant signs hanging out front.

I looked around me in awe, bewildered at how bewitching the town seemed. It was a far cry from the outdated and dilapidated buildings in the Apollo shopping sector.

My phone buzzed in my pocket, and I smiled when I saw it was a text message in my group chat with Kate and Hannah.

Hannah: We on 4 movies 2moro?

Kate: Sounds good 2 me. Can't wait to eat my body weight in nachos

Me: Def stealing nachos from u. Cinema nachos are elite

Hannah: lol

"Everything okay?"

I grinned up from my phone, sliding it back into my pocket. "Just arranging movie plans with the girls. Sorry, babe; it's girls only."

Placing a hand over his chest, Remy faked a gasp. "How ever will I survive without watching yet *another* chick flick with you three?"

I smacked him on the arm as I laughed, shaking my head. "You love a rom com more than any of us, so don't even lie."

Remy rolled his eyes but squeezed my hand gently, before pulling me past the hustle and bustle of shoppers.

We rounded a corner into another alleyway, but this one was different from the other: where the first had been dark and dingy, this alley was lit with strings of fairy lights and neon shop signs.

I gasped as I looked up, the lights above resembling fireflies.

"It's beautiful, isn't it?" Remy whispered to me, a glow in his eyes that matched mine. "Come on, it's just down here."

312

We walked a few more feet until Remy skidded to a halt outside a tattoo parlour. The words, *Tatted Out!* were displayed on a flashing neon sign above the door. The shop window was covered in hundreds of tattoo designs just waiting to be selected, and I felt my heart beat faster in my chest.

I turned to Remy with tears in my eyes. "Remy..."

He wrapped his arms around my waist and pulled me into his hips, his lips finding mine. I let my body relax into his touch, my tastebuds set alight by the taste of tongue on mine. His hands were firm and stable on my waist, holding me to him.

When he pulled away, his mouth still hovering just above my lips, I had to blink myself back into reality. It was fantastic and strange that the world just disappeared around us whenever we got lost in each other.

"This is the place where I've gotten every one of my tattoos, so I made some arrangements to get you in. I hope you like it?" He looked nervous as he glanced from me to the shop.

I jumped gleefully and wrapped my arms around his neck. "Of course, I like it, you fool! This is the most thoughtful thing anyone has ever done for me."

I rushed through the door of the shop, giggling as the bell tinkled to announce our arrival.

A lanky young man sat behind a desk in the front of the shop. He had spiky black hair and tattoos covering every inch of his skin; it looked so cool that I found myself staring at him.

Remy had to nudge me with an amused look on his face as he walked up to the desk and greeted the man. They clapped their hands together and pulled one another into a bro-hug over the top of the desk.

"Remy! It's so good to see you, man." The young man smacked Remy's back and grinned at me over his shoulder. "Who's this?"

I stepped forward as Remy slung his arm over my shoulder, looking down at me with pride. "This is my absolutely incredible girl, Emmie. Emmie, this is Darragh. Darragh grew up with me and then opened this badass shop with his parent's money."

I reached out and shook Darragh's hand.

He beamed at me with pearly white teeth, winking at Remy. "She's well out of your league, brother."

Remy punched his shoulder playfully, but a low chuckle rumbled from his lips. "You're not wrong, friend. Anyway, I booked an appointment for Emmie. Who's working today?"

Darragh checked the open ledger in front of him and tapped what I assumed was our appointment scrawled inside. "Andy and Cara-Anne are with clients, so it looks like me and Zoey are the available ones."

Remy leaned down and whispered in my ear, "Darragh is a train wreck, love. You better go with Zoey."

Darragh glared at him but motioned for me to go through the back to a door with Zoey's name decorated on it. Remy blew me a kiss as I walked down the hall away from him, leaving him to joke around with Darragh.

A middle-aged woman with bright red hair was seated on a stool in the corner of the room as I entered, her feet tucked up on the tattoo chair as she browsed her phone.

I cleared my throat and she jumped, sending her stool flying into the cupboard.

I stifled a giggle. "I'm Emmie. Darragh told me to come through?"

She grinned at me through her painted black lips, her teeth dazzling against the stark contrast. "Yes, of course! I'm Zoey."

She held out her gloved hand to me which I gratefully shook, pleased to see she was so friendly. She gestured for me to take a seat as she binned her gloves and washed her hands in a thick sanitiser.

She smiled at me, the corners of her eyes crinkling and making her winged liner crease. I felt myself staring at her eyes, wondering if there was a way to make mine look like hers.

I shook myself, my therapist's voice ringing in my head to tell me that I didn't have to make comparisons against everyone I thought was pretty. It was a hard habit to break, but slowly, in time, I would break free of it.

"So, what is it you want done, honey?"

I pulled at the sleeves of my jacket and told myself to be brave. With my scars exposed to Zoey, I expected her to gasp and look away in horror. But instead, she looked at me caringly and smiled.

"I'd like these covered."

The scars from my suicide attempt stood raised against my skin, more prominent than the other lines across my arms. I had never expected to live, of course, so I hadn't considered how my arms would look if I failed. I would never be able to hide what I had done, but I could at least make them look less vulgar.

Zoey pressed her hands gently into mine and turned her hands over, exposing her own tattooed wrists. "I have similar scars, hon. Let's see what we can do for you."

Zoey's scars were now faint marks under the ink covering her arms, butterflies escaping from their cocoons hiding most of it. I appreciated her sharing it with me so openly, and I wondered if one day I would feel free enough to simply show someone my scars without a second thought.

I hoped so.

I pulled my phone out and opened up my gallery, flicking through images until I found the one I wanted. I grinned as I turned the phone to Zoey. "Do you think you could do this?"

—

315

I winced as Zoey wiped away the blood spots on my skin, revealing the tattoos beneath. I gasped as I saw the complete image, beautiful and bold against the paleness of my skin.

"Do you like them?" Zoey asked while she prepared the salve to cool my skin.

"Like them? Zoey, you are an artist! I love them!" I let the tears stream down my cheeks despite knowing how ridiculous I looked.

I held my arms out in front of me and admired the detailed picture on my wrists. When I had shown Zoey a picture of the flower vines Remy had drawn before, I was apprehensive that she would be able to match the beauty he had created. It amazed me how perfectly she had matched the design to the photo, every small detail the same as what Remy had doodled onto my skin.

I cried happily over how perfect they were. Remy had brought me so much joy and happiness out of so much tragedy, and this was just another thing I could add to the list. Without knowing it, he had created the one thing I needed to feel a little bit of the strength everyone kept telling me I had.

Once Zoey had applied ointment to my tattoos and covered them up with plastic wrap, I hugged her as tightly as I could. "I can't thank you enough."

The woman chuckled into my shoulder and hugged me back. "Thank me by living your best life, Emmie. Everyone deserves a chance at happiness, even if we don't think we do."

She led me back out into the waiting area where Remy and Darragh were deep in conversation about some video game they liked playing.

Remy looked up from his seat as I approached them, a huge grin appearing as he saw my cellophaned arms. "You okay, gorgeous?"

When he looked at me like that, so happy and bright, I couldn't help but smile. He was a beacon of light, forever pulling me away from my own personal darkness.

I pecked his cheek and took a seat beside him. "I'm perfect."

Darragh glanced at my arms, and I had the impulse to put on my jacket and run for the hills. But as I caught sight of my tattoos peeking through the wraps, I tried to remind myself that there was a reason I had just gotten tattoos. I had to learn not to fear my scars or people's reactions to them.

Darragh beamed at me and wiggled his brows comically. "So, what did you get? We've been dying to find out what design you picked."

Remy looked at me expectantly. I tutted and shook my finger at him as I showed Darragh the images Zoey had taken of my tattoos. He whistled and hooted, making Remy punch him in the arm. Darragh just laughed and punched him back, clearly over the moon to have one up on his friend.

Remy pouted. "Why can't I see?"

I scoffed and kissed his forehead. "Because I want it to be a surprise for you to see them all healed up."

He huffed but pulled me into him anyway, wrapping his arms around me. "Well, I can't wait."

"How much do I owe you, Darragh?"

The young man shook his head. "Your man here has already taken care of it for you."

My mouth gaped open.

"Surely not!" I barged Remy with my hip. "You didn't?"

He shrugged and rubbed his hand across my waist.

I wanted to be mad at him for wasting his money on me, but it was such a kind-hearted thing to do that I couldn't actually be annoyed.

"Remy, you shouldn't have done that," I reasoned. "That's such an expensive gift!"

He brushed it off and gave me one of his sexy smirks. "I should be able to treat my girlfriend whenever I please. Besides, it's selfish really. I wanted to be the one responsible for helping you see yourself as beautiful."

My heart melted at that moment. If only he knew how responsible he was—and soon he would. I felt a flurry of excitement as I pictured his reaction when I showed him my tattoos. He would be so pleased to find out that I had used one of his own drawings as my inspiration.

I hoped he would realise one day that he didn't need to buy things to treat me; being part of his world was the biggest treat I could ever ask for.

I had wanted to be normal for so long, but Remy had made me realise that normality wasn't real; everyone had quirks they needed to embrace. And I was learning to embrace mine.

TWENTY-EIGHT

We went for dinner in a cute little restaurant that Remy liked. It felt amazing to be out with him and not want to hide in the shadows. People glanced at my wrapped-up arms with mild curiosity, and I basked in the feeling that they were more interested in what the tattoos were, rather than what they were hiding.

When we got back to my house, I was pleasantly surprised that my mum still wasn't home. It meant that Remy could come in and relax without the fear of my mum quizzing him on my mental state. She did that a lot now, and while I appreciated the concern, I found it to be a bit too late. But I supposed it was something we would have to work on when we went to the family therapy sessions Doc had assigned as part of my release conditions.

Remy followed me upstairs and flopped down onto the bed, yawning loudly as he ran his hands through his hair.

"Tired, babe?"

He smiled and blew me a kiss. "Exhausted, but I'll be fine."

I grinned and walked over to him, slotting myself in between his legs.

He let out a soft moan against my lips as I kissed him, wrapping his arms around my waist so I was pressed against him. It was hard not to completely forget myself when I was in his arms, lost to the world and myself. Remy could make me feel like all that existed in the world was me and him, a partnership I was eternally grateful for.

When his hands slipped down and into my back pockets, gripping my ass, I let out a chuckle and pulled my lips away. He groaned half-heartedly and pressed a light kiss to my neck.

319

I pressed my hands to his chest, happy to admire his chiselled pecks while I held myself off from devouring his mouth with mine. "I thought maybe you'd want to see the tattoos."

His eyes lit up and he removed his hands from my back, resting them on my waist. "I'd love to."

I stepped back and held my arms out to him, gesturing for him to start unwrapping my wrists. He took extra care to be gentle and I loved how happy it made him when I allowed him access to the parts of me that I hated most. Although, after Zoey's extraordinary work, I didn't think I'd hate those specific scars much anymore.

As he finished unwrapping, I watched as he drew in a breath and held it. His gorgeous eyes flashed brighter than usual as he teared up, looking from me to my wrists. I couldn't help but beam at him, knowing he had created something spectacular to make me love myself.

"Did you—Are those...are those the designs I drew on your wrists before?" His voice was a whisper, but I could hear the emotion steeped in it, threatening to break alongside the flood of tears he was barely keeping at bay.

"Yes," I whispered back, cupping his face in my hands. "You took my breath away when you created something so beautiful on top of something I felt was the ugliest part of me. You gave me part of myself back, even though I didn't think that would be possible."

That was his breaking point. Within seconds, we were both emotional messes as we wiped each other's tears away.

When he wrapped his arms around me again, I felt him hold on just a little bit tighter. I never wanted him to let me go.

I stared down at my wrists with a newfound love, a part of myself I could appreciate without hesitation. They were now the perfect reminder of where I had come from, and the future that lay ahead of me.

—

"Emmie?" Remy's voice crackled from my phone, husky and deep.

My body shivered in response. "Yeah?"

"I need to see you."

I pulled the phone away from my ear to check the time and smirked. It was already after midnight, but somehow it was exhilarating that I was in his thoughts so late at night.

"It's late," I whispered.

Remy groaned. "Please. I need to see you."

The urgency in his voice made my skin tingle and my heart pound. I didn't know what was so urgent, but I wouldn't ever deny him.

"Okay."

I didn't need to be able to see him to know he was smiling smugly. "I'll pick you up. Meet me out front."

The call disconnected and I chewed on my lip. What was I supposed to wear? I glanced down at the shorts and tank top I was wearing to bed and shook my head. It definitely wouldn't do.

I searched my drawers furiously for something that was clean and semi-pretty. Eventually I settled on a pair of navy jeans which hugged my hips, something Remy had commented on enjoying more than once, and paired them with a black camisole, pulling on a knitted cardigan in case it was cold.

By the time I was ready, I assumed Remy would already be waiting outside. Tiptoeing barefoot past my mother's bedroom, I took the stairs two at a time and pulled on a pair of boots once I had reached the bottom.

The front door groaned as I closed it behind me and I prayed that it wouldn't wake my mum, but when I caught sight of Remy leaning against his car, I found I didn't much care.

His muscled arms were protected by the tightness of his leather jacket, stretching the material as he crossed his arms over his chest.

A slow grin crawled onto his face, and he held his arms out to me. I ran to him.

He enveloped me in a hug, and I pressed my cheek tight against his chest, breathing in his scent. It didn't matter how often I saw him; it was never enough. I would never have enough of being with him, breathing his air, and feeling the heat of his skin on mine.

Pressing his lips to my forehead, his trimmed beard tickled my skin, and I breathed a sigh of relief. It was a welcome feeling, his lips on my body, his arms around my waist.

"Let's go, baby," he said as he slipped his hand into mine and opened the door for me.

We drove in comfortable silence, the music on the radio a low hum to keep us from speaking. Every time I looked up, Remy glanced over at me with a look I couldn't decipher. He smirked slightly, placing his hand on my thigh where he rubbed his thumb in circles absentmindedly.

I didn't know where we were going, but excitement was coursing through my veins.

I was surprised when we pulled up at the beach. The streetlamps lit up the promenade, though the sand and sea were blanketed in the night's darkness. I looked up at Remy who only smiled and bounced from his seat, running around to open my door.

Extending his hand to me, he pulled me out of my seat and guided me down to the sand. I grumbled about getting sand in my boots, but he only laughed and pulled me ahead.

I was thankful that the summer was upon us because even in the middle of the night, it was warm enough that I didn't need a jacket.

I looked out and tried to make out where the waves broke against the shoreline, but I could only see a reflection of moonlight on the ocean's horizon. I would once have feared the bleakness of such darkness, but Remy had taught me that darkness led to light.

Instead of focusing on what I couldn't see, I looked at the things the moon illuminated: the small fishing boat way out in the distance, the tiny house almost a mile away.

It was beautiful.

He always let me enjoy my own thoughts, never prying until I wanted to share. I admired him for that because I had no patience; I wanted him to tell me everything going on in that beautiful head of his at every minute.

I smiled at him, reaching out to entwine our fingers. Remy moved to stand behind me, wrapping his arms around my waist. He placed gentle kisses along the side of my neck.

Eventually, I let curiosity pull me from my thoughts. Twisting around in his arms, I reached up and linked my fingers behind his neck.

"So, why are we at the beach at almost one in the morning?"

Remy licked his lips and locked eyes with me, his irises the brightest and most stunning shade of green, even in the dead of night. He took a step back, letting his arms fall to the curve of my hips, his eyes running over every inch of my body.

"I couldn't stop thinking about you," he said slowly.

I smirked. "I never stop thinking about you."

He rolled his eyes at me and ran his fingers through the curls on his head. He was nervous.

"Remy?"

He took a step closer again, closing the gap between us. "I really couldn't stop thinking about you. You have consumed every thought, and when I'm not with you it's like I don't even know how to function."

I placed my hand gently on his cheek, caressing the soft skin.

"I tried to write you a letter. Did you know that?"

I grinned. "A letter?"

He chuckled and nodded, his lips so close to mine that I could tilt my head and we would touch. But standing like this, together, was intimate in a way I had never felt.

"Yup, a full-on letter professing how I feel about you. There's about ten crumpled pieces of paper littering my bedroom floor right now."

I opened my mouth to say something, but he shook his head, running his thumb across my lips.

"I couldn't wait any longer. I hope you already know how I feel, but I can't just assume that. I even wrote you a text and then deleted it. And then wrote it again. I was so scared that maybe my lack of words, of actually saying it, made you blind to it. I don't want to wait around anymore."

"Know what?" I asked quietly, my voice betraying my nerves. Remy was never this tense and it spiked my anxiety to see him like this, unsure and nervous.

Remy held his breath before exhaling, cupping my face in his hands. His palms were warm against my cheeks. "That I am completely in love with you. That every breath I take is for you. Every smile on my face is because of you. Every thought in my head is of you. I am so utterly in love with you that I can think of little else."

My breath caught in my throat as our eyes connected. He loved me.

I wanted to speak but my words were lost, my brain unable to think of anything but the words he had just spoken to me. The gentleness in which he said them. The ferocity and meaning behind them.

Remy Austen just told me he loved me.

"You don't have to say anything back to me. This is in no way an attempt to pressure you. But I couldn't sit up another night without you knowing the way you have infiltrated my mind and completely bewitched me."

A single tear slipped from my eye before I crashed my lips against his, pulling him towards me until there was no space between us. His hands feathered through my hair, gripping me as he moaned. The sound made my body tremble with desire, and I had to pull away, leaving us both panting.

"Remy?"

Remy's flushed cheeks puffed out as he grinned. "Yeah, baby?"

I closed my eyes for a second, willing myself to have the strength, before I grabbed him by the shirt and brought him close to me again. "I am entirely and completely in love with you too."

His sigh of relief was music to my ears. His hands slipped around my waist again and we pressed against each other, thinking only of each other. When his lips found mine again, there was a new intensity and passion. I craved him in a way I never knew possible, and I knew that I would love him with every fibre of my being until the end of time. It didn't matter that we hadn't said it before; this love between us had been there from the beginning.

Wait, from the beginning?

"Remy?" I whispered against his lips, not willing myself to pull away anymore. "Why are we at the beach?"

His lips pressed into a smile against my skin, his hands slipping into the back pockets of my jeans as he held me to him. "The first time we ever met, we came here with Hannah. And we sat next to each other on the sand and watched the water. You were oblivious, but I was staring at you the whole time. I was in love with you from the moment we met, even if I didn't know it. I couldn't imagine how such a beautiful, strong person had been subjected to so much pain. I wanted to take it all away for you. But then I learned something else."

Tears escaped and cascaded down my cheeks, soaking Remy's skin in the process. "What did you learn?"

"That you didn't need to be saved. You just needed someone to tell you that *it's okay to save yourself.*"

AUTHOR NOTE

Mental health awareness is a topic very close to my heart and Ugly Words is a direct result of that. It is my wish that there is more conversation around mental health so that we can help people understand that there will always be someone to talk to.

In preparation for writing Ugly Words, I spent time investigating and talking to people who had/have suffered similarly to Emmeline. I wanted her story to be as authentic and relatable as possible, and I hope I managed to do that justice.

I want to thank all the people who spoke with me and shared their stories. While it was heartbreaking to hear how you suffered, I'm so truly grateful to know that you continued to fight and that you survived. Thank you for sharing your stories with me, for letting me hear such a personal part of your life, and for helping me shape Emmeline's character before I started writing. I hope that I did you justice too, and that I honoured your stories in the way you hoped.

While I am not going to share their names as a mark of respect and privacy, I want it to be known that these people are survivors and the reason that I saw this book until the end, even when it was difficult.

Thank you.

ACKNOWLEDGMENTS

First and foremost, I want to thank my amazing street team for everything they did to help me in the run up to publishing Ugly Words. Y'all rock!

To my ARC readers, thank you for your feedback and your reviews – I appreciate you so much.

The platypi, my crazy fam across the seas. Eri, Chani, Jesa, Cass, Dee, Dani and Tiff – I don't have enough words to thank you all. I wrote this book during the first few months I met you all and your support from then until now has been everything. Thanks for never letting me give up on writing or throw out the entire manuscript. Author besties for life!

To Cam, who was the first ever sounding board for Ugly Words. I had a title and an idea, but you helped me turn it into a plot. I would never have written the book without you. Thank you for always encouraging me to write – even when it was really bad short stories and fanfiction that I had you reading every other day.

Eliza, who has supported me since the moment we met. Your tough love, humour and kindness spurs me on and ensures I never give up. Your friendship is treasured, and you know that this book is published because of you (and your constant DMs demanding a physical copy). I love you and baby S.

Gabbie, I love you. My bestie, my soul sister, my hype woman – thank you! Thank you for inspiring me and always being by my side to offer advice or support or anything I need. Facetiming with you and crying over our WIPs will always be my favourite thing. You're my sunshine person.

To my family, for always believing that I would be an author and cheering me on. I did it!

Annie, my lil sunflower. Thank you for always being a happy, bright presence in my life and supporting whatever I do.

Jesa – Thank you for taking time out of your *crazy* busy schedule to help me edit

To Ashley R. King – An inspiration to me as an author and a friend. We clicked as soon as we first started talking and I'm so grateful to be friends with you. You're so insanely talented and I'm always so honoured that you love and enjoy my work. Thank you for being one of my beta readers and biggest fans. You're the best"

Kristen Granata – A favourite author, my favourite mental health warrior, and a treasured friend. Thank you for always cheering me on and believing in me. Your books helped me to keep writing and I hope you know how much your friendship means to me.

Sasha Peyton Smith, Jordan Gray, Shelby Mahurin, Debbie Cromack, Jessica S. Taylor – Such kind, supporting and encouraging people. Thank you for your books, your advice and your kind words. Y'all are what makes the author world such a fun and exciting place to be, and I can't thank you enough for being inspirations in my life.

To Kathleen Glasgow who wrote a book called *Girl in Pieces* that impacted me so greatly during my early teenage years. Your book taught me so much and has remained with me for the years since. *Girl in Pieces* was a massive reason I wanted to write a book like Ugly Words, because I wanted to impact and help someone the way your book helped me. I will forever recommend *Girl in Pieces* and I will always hold it in a special place in my heart.

Kayleigh – You're an angel and I'm really glad I met you. Emmie would love you because you're the coolest and unapologetically you – never let anyone change you.

To my bitch babies, because I can't not tell everyone how much I love you guys and how much you mean to me. Thanks for dealing with all my breakdowns, for hyping me up every single day, and for never letting me quit (no matter how many good reasons I come up with!).

Domino, the best cover designer a girl could ask for. You took my vision and created the perfect duo of covers for Ugly Words and I'm still not over them. Thank you for finding the beauty in my book. But more than that, thank you for being the most amazing friend. You inspire me, you're there for me, and you let me know I'm never alone. I love you so much and being your friend is an honour. And also, I have to shoutout Gabe, my hype-man! You're the best and I'm thankful for you. Y'all are family and I love you both.

And to Eri, who has already been mentioned but deserves to be mentioned again. My bestie and the most wonderful PA in the world. Thank you for making this process so much easier and enjoyable. I truly would not have been able to publish without you by my side. I also wouldn't be able to function daily without you.

Lastly, to you, the reader – Thank you for picking up my book. I hope you enjoyed Emmeline's story and know that there is always hope. I love you and I will always be a safe person for you to talk to if you need someone to reach out to.

About The Author

Colby Bettley is an author from Scotland, so if you aren't reading this in an accent, you're doing it wrong. She splits her time between her editing company (Novel and Noted), writing, and also writing but under a different name (shhh!). When she's not writing or editing books, she's taking photos of them for her Instagram @colby_bettley.

She also loves to talk to readers so don't hesitate to reach out and say hello!

You can find all her social media and relevant links at: https://www.authorcolbybettley.com

Also by Colby Bettley
Christmas at the Grotto

—

Available on Amazon!

Book Blurb:

Leita and Rhett are polar opposites.

Leita loves Christmas. Seeing everyone come together to celebrate the holidays is her favourite thing in the world.

Rhett despises festivities. He hates the way everyone pretends like their lives don't suck the other eleven months of the year.

Out of desperation, Rhett takes a job at the local Santa's Grotto, and whether by fate or by chance, he meets his new colleague, the very festive Leita.

But what happens when opposites are forced together at Christmas?

Printed in Great Britain
by Amazon

18187899R00190